THE LUNATIC FRINGE

A NOVEL WHEREIN:
Theodore Roosevelt
Meets the Pink Angel

William L. DeAndrea

M. Evans and Company, Inc.
New York

Library of Congress Cataloging in Publication Data

DeAndrea, William L
  The lunatic fringe

  I. Title.
PZ4.D2836Lu [PS3554.E174] 813'.54 80-15065
ISBN 0-87131-325-1

M. Evans and Company, Inc.
216 East 49 Street
New York, New York 10017

Design by Robert Bull

Manufactured in the United States of America

9 8 7 6 5 4 3 2 1

To Celina, and to dreams

Author's Note

This is a work of historical fiction. A strenuous effort has been made to recreate an authentic background for the story, but in some cases, as far as actual facts of history or geography are concerned, I have taken more liberties than the Founding Fathers. I ask only that the reader keep in mind that at least some of the inaccuracies he is sure to find are intentional.

Finally, there are some people who must be thanked: Carol Brener for the use of her splendid library; Brian Ault for getting me to Maine, and Nancy and Mike Harrington for putting me up while I was there; and all the anonymous but unfailingly helpful people at the public information department at Consolidated Edison, the New York Public Library, the Port Chester (New York) Public Library, and the New York Historical Society.

FRIDAY
the twenty-first
of August, 1896

I.

They had discussed the matter before; the publisher had thought it settled, and was perturbed at having to go over it again.

Still, despite the provocation to anger, the conversation was civil. William Randolph Hearst was always civil; even his Publisher's edicts tended to begin, "If you don't mind . . ." One was not, however, to get the idea one was at liberty to decline.

Hearst regarded the man on the other side of his desk. "Won't you reconsider, Mr. Crandall?" he asked. Despite his position, Hearst was by at least a decade the younger man. He was thirty-three but seemed younger still. He was tall and fair, with large, blue eyes that showed a lot of white, and he had a very high voice.

Evan Crandall had always been irritated by that voice, and

it pleased him to know this was the last time he would have to hear it. "I have considered the matter quite thoroughly. I have done considering it, Mr. Hearst." Crandall called his employer "Mr. Hearst," but he thought of him as "Willie" and coldly loathed him. Loathed him not over anything to do with the newspaper business, but over Art.

Hearst bought Art, but not the work of anyone still alive. And Evan Crandall was an artist. He wore his goatee and pointed moustache as a badge of his European training. It made him look like an inkstained Napoleon III.

Hearst knew how Crandall felt about him—that was why he dealt with the man personally instead of passing him along to an underling. Crandall's vanity needed careful handling, and Hearst needed Crandall, especially now.

Hearst had no intention of letting the man thwart him. Few people had ever been able to stand between William Randolph Hearst and something he wanted.

Hearst's father had been unlettered and crude, but he'd found enough gold in the rush of '49 to make him attractive to a cultured, but poor, beauty half his age.

Willie was an only child, and his mother had used her husband's money to spoil the boy from scalp to sole. On his first trip to Paris, he asked her to buy him the Louvre. It was one of the few things he ever wanted that he didn't get, but by now, he had begun a collection that would one day rival it, in size if not in quality.

He had always done as he pleased. Before he was invited to leave Harvard, he had kept both a mistress and a pet alligator. He still had the mistress. His current desire was to make his New York *Journal* the most powerful newspaper in America, and himself the most powerful man.

"I'm very sorry, Crandall," he said, "but you have signed a legal contract, and the *Journal* intends to hold you to it."

Crandall snorted; Hearst begged his pardon. "That is my final word. I will appreciate it if you will inform Pulitzer of that."

Crandall snorted again, more loudly. He knew he was being rude, and he enjoyed it immensely. "Pulitzer has nothing to do with this. I no longer require this position, it is as simple as that."

Hearst wasn't the kind to snort in return, but he would have felt justified in doing so. There was a newspaper circulation war in progress, the like of which New York (or any other city) had never seen. Outside in Printing House Square, around the feet of the statue of Ben Franklin, flowed a torrent of money for anyone who could help make the public part with its daily penny. Crandall acted as if Hearst weren't aware of that. As though he hadn't, in fact, been the one who'd started that very flood.

Young Mr. Hearst had come to New York a year ago, and immediately declared war on Pulitzer and his New York *World*. Hearst prepared for the battle by changing the San Francisco *Examiner* from a wheezing voice for his father's political ambitions to the best known and best selling newspaper in the West.

He'd done it by using Pulitzer's own formula—low price, mass appeal, and crusades for popular causes. It was generally conceded there was nothing a Hearst reporter wouldn't do to get a story.

And Hearst would have the best reporters. Cost didn't matter. To Hearst, money was as accessible as air. If Pulitzer had the best people when Hearst came to New York, he wouldn't have them long.

There were constant bidding skirmishes that might see a reporter's salary soar to twice or three times what it had been just a few hours before. Until now, Hearst had won most of these skirmishes. But Pulitzer had arrived in this country a penniless immigrant from his native Hungary, and each dollar had a meaning for him it could never have for Hearst. Still, he could spend if it meant keeping some upstart from ruining his business. He was nearing fifty and losing his eyesight (some said he was already totally blind), but he wasn't so blind that people could rob him and expect to get away with it.

So reporters and editors lined their pockets with gold notes just by marching back and forth across the Square.

Cartoonists were getting their share, too. Richard Outcault, the creator of the sarcastic little imp known as the Yellow Kid, had enabled Pulitzer to sell copies of the Sunday *World* to people whom only the most generous could describe as literate. Hearst had gone after Outcault (and the Kid) and had gotten them.

In retaliation, Pulitzer had snatched E. Noon from the editorial page of the *Journal*.

Evan Crandall was E. Noon. It was his particular hell to be

an artist forced to earn his bread with pen and ink rather than brush and oils. It only made things worse that he had to work for a man who spent thousands of dollars annually on works by dead Italians and Frenchmen. As a protest against the injustice of it all, he adopted as his signature the words "no one" spelled backward.

E. Noon was the most effective editorial cartoonist since Thomas Nast. He might have been fully as great as Nast, but he had no convictions and no opinions other than a love of Beauty for its own sake and a deep contempt for everything else. It was the contempt that powered his pen; some said he compounded his ink of one part vitriol, one part venom, and one part blood from his previous victims. He could make a newborn babe look depraved, and he had a genius for grafting the heads of public figures on the bodies of the more loathsome of the lower animals. And since he hated everyone equally, he gladly followed the policy of whatever paper he was working for at the moment. It was his opinion that anyone he might attack undoubtedly deserved it.

He was, all in all, a powerful tool in the shaping of public opinion, and Hearst wasn't about to lose control of him. He'd called Crandall to his office, and offered to double Pulitzer's offer, without even asking how much it had been. The money didn't matter. To avoid future inconvenience to the *Journal*, though, Hearst had had Crandall sign a contract binding E. Noon to the paper until 1950—a date so far into the future as to be synonymous with Eternity.

And that had been that. Or so Hearst had thought. Apparently, Pulitzer didn't agree.

"How much has he offered you now?" Hearst demanded. Politely, of course.

Crandall's beard wiggled wtih impatience, something he'd never allowed to happen in Hearst's presence before. He'd had to subdue pride in the interest of his wallet. Never again.

"As I have already told you, I have neither seen nor spoken to anyone from the *World* in weeks."

Hearst wondered if this might be a practical joke. For all his reserve, Hearst was inordinately fond of practical jokes. Crandall, though, struck him as the last man in New York who would play one. The tall young publisher leaned over his desk and narrowed his eyes, examining the cartoonist for signs of drunkenness. It was standard policy at both Hearst's newspapers that a drunken man might be forgiven anything.

But Crandall wasn't drunk. Hearst was intrigued. "Who is it, then? Who is trying to take you away from me? May I ask? Reid at the *Tribune?* Dana? Ochs?"

Crandall sniffed. "You have my resignation. I bid you good day."

"It was Hanna, wasn't it? Hanna and the Republicans."

Crandall gave him the ghost of a smile, as though he laughed at a private joke.

So *that's* it, Hearst thought. He felt positively elated. He had them worried, and the campaign wasn't half over yet.

The Presidential race of 1896 was scarcely two months old, but there had been enough acrimony in those two months to make even Horatio Alger give up on human nature. It was Mr. William Jennings Bryan of Nebraska and Free Silver versus Governor William McKinley of Ohio and Sound Money. There were no other issues, and there was no middle ground.

Every paper in the East, including Pulitzer's traditionally Democratic *World*, backed the Republican McKinley. Every paper, that is, but the *Journal*. Hearst was four-square behind the "Boy Orator of the Platte."

Not that Hearst had any great love for Bryan or his program. Hearst felt the free coinage of silver to be a foolish, Utopian cure-all that could accomplish nothing but the erosion of the American dollar. He had worked against Bryan's nomination at the Chicago convention, but after the thirty-six-year-old Bryan had mesmerized the convention with the thunder of his already famous "Cross of Gold" speech, there was to be no stopping him.

So be it, Hearst decided. If he couldn't stop him, he would help him. If Bryan were to be elected (an end the *Journal* was striving mightily to bring about), Hearst alone would have the new President's gratitude. Hearst alone, of all the powerful Democratic publishers in the East, would have kept faith. Pulitzer and all the others would have their influence drastically reduced, and it would be hard to think of a more powerful man in the United States of America than William Randolph Hearst.

But McKinley's backers were playing to win, too. It was no secret that it was Marcus Alonzo Hanna who had raised the million-dollar "war chest" and that he called all the moves in the McKinley campaign.

That very Friday afternoon, "E. Noon" had done a wicked drawing of Hanna as a puppeteer working McKinley's strings; the editorial writers continued to make much of the fact that the first use to which the "war chest" had been put was to pay off a large debt McKinley had assumed.

And now, Hearst was convinced, he had them worried, in spite of Bryan's poor showing last week at Madison Square Garden.

This was the time to hit them again, and harder. "I'm afraid I can't accept your resignation, Crandall." He tried to sound deferential, but he knew one thing for certain: E. Noon had a lot of cartooning to do before the election was past.

Crandall sneered. "You have no choice. I'm leaving."

"Not if you plan to eat," the publisher told him. "I'm sorry to have to say this, but if you leave this building without submitting tomorrow's panel, you'll never work in the newspaper business again."

Crandall lifted his pointed beard and spoke with supreme haughtiness. "At this particular moment, you could have said nothing more agreeable. I have no intention of ever debasing myself and my God-given talent by working for this or any other newspaper. Thank God I shall not have to. Newspapers. Bah!"

"And what, pray tell, do you plan to do?"

"What Nature intended me to do, Mr. Hearst. Now I must go; I'm wasting daylight."

He spun on his heel and left.

Hearst watched him go. He had been defeated. By a cartoonist. It was disconcerting. He drummed his fingers on his desk top while he decided what he intended to do about it.

II.

Franklyn and Libstein left New York on the 5:45 train for Philadelphia. A contingent of policemen (sprinkled with a few Pinkertons) was there to see them off.

In any city, the departure of Franklyn and Libstein was an

Event. Franklyn and Libstein were Anarchists. No one knew their first names, few ever even learned which was which. No one bothered, any more than anyone would bother to draw distinctions between Meshach, Shadrach and Abednego. For the record, Franklyn was the squat, bushily bearded one who looked like everyone's conception of what an anarchist should be, and Libstein was the one who looked like a prosperous family doctor.

"Wave to our friends," Franklyn urged his companion.

"They aren't our friends," Libstein replied. Franklyn often complained that Libstein had no sense of humor. "Besides," Libstein went on, "there's no need to antagonize them."

Franklyn laughed and waved anyway. He had no fear of the police. He and his friend had been arrested a few times, but never in this country.

The reason was simple: they broke no laws. They came to town, spoke to rallies about Universal Brotherhood and the Rise of the Working Man, but only in the most general terms. And the police knew it.

But the police also knew that Franklyn and Libstein had left Belgrade three weeks before a bomb went off in the town square; Paris three *days* before the assassination of the *juge d'instruction*; and Boston eleven days before the attempt on the life of the Governor, to name but a few of what Franklyn referred to as "unfortunate co-incidences."

Libstein wiggled in his seat. "I hope the operation goes well."

Franklyn raked his bush of a beard with stubby fingers. "We've planned as well as we could. Baxter will do the job."

"He failed in Boston."

"Inadequate preparation. We should have used a loyal worker from Boston instead of interrupting Baxter's work here in New York."

Libstein was still skeptical. "Mmm," he said. "How long before the plan goes into effect?"

"Little more than a week. Relax. Look who's come to see us off." He pointed out the window.

The train had started to move, so Libstein had to crane his neck around to see. "Ah," he said. "The President of the Police Commission himself."

Franklyn grinned. "Are you sure you don't want to wave to Mr. Roosevelt?"

"No thank you." He turned his attention to a book of essays by Engels as the train gathered speed.

And out on the platform, dreading what might be in store, Mr. Theodore Roosevelt was almost sorry to see them go.

SATURDAY
the twenty-second
of August, 1896

I.

Young Officer Muldoon nearly had to carry the old tippler the last block and a half, but he got him safely to his building.

"You're a nice boy, Dennis," Mr. Harvey said dreamily, with a puff of breath that could curdle milk.

"So that's why you've been molestin' the lamplighter, eh?" Muldoon said. He was a strapping lad, over six feet tall and handsome with it, with sandy hair curling out from under his helmet, and a robust handlebar moustache—made two shades darker from the wax. "Tryin' to get his job are you? Fixin' to light the lamps just by breathin' on the jet. What are you goin' to do when the electricity comes to the neighborhood the way they have it on Broadway?"

Muldoon drew his billy, for emphasis. He knew from experience that shaking a finger at the old man wasn't enough—he couldn't focus well enough to see it.

"Now mind this, Mr. Harvey," the officer warned. "Until the electricity *does* get around to this beat, I want you lettin' the lamplighters be." He put the billy away and smiled. "This isn't the blasted Dark Ages, you know."

Mr. Harvey wobbled and laughed; at least he said, "Ha, ha." But Harvey's face was never happy. He was a little, lonely old widower who drank because he missed his wife. Muldoon felt sorry for the poor soul. Lord knew there were better reasons to drink.

Not that Harvey couldn't have used a wife, if only to choose his clothes for him. This evening, he was wearing a jacket of a large houndstooth check in colors that were almost yellow and almost brown. It made Muldoon wonder if the hound shouldn't have gone to see a dentist.

The old man started to collapse. He was just a little bit of a man, but when he got all loose like that, he was harder to carry than two hogsheads of pilsener. Muldoon had to call the landlady for help.

"Ahh," she said, looking wistfully at the patient. "It's a pity he let his wife's death get him down so. Not that I'm saying he shouldn't miss her, but—"

Mrs. Sturdevant was a respectable widow lady, a blonde woman with an ample, motherly form and a kind word for everyone. Usually more than one kind word. It was Muldoon's opinion that she had the single most tireless jaws between the Hudson and East rivers.

The only way to get a word in was to interrupt. "You'll be gettin' him upstairs, then?"

"What? Oh, of course, Dennis. Now where was I? Oh, yes. When Mr. Sturdevant was alive, he told me, 'Esther, if I die first'— of course I never thought he would, Dennis—"

"I'd appreciate it," Muldoon said, "if you wouldn't be callin' me Dennis while I'm wearin' me uniform."

Mrs. Sturdevant looked at him with reproach. "Dennis, you know I never see you when you're *not* wearing your uniform." She leaned across Mr. Harvey to give Muldoon a sly nudge in the ribs. "And you cut a fine figure in it, too. I'll bet you're a devil with the little girls."

Muldoon reddened. Something about him seemed to make

folks all too ready to presume on his dignity as an Officer of the Law. The fact that Mrs. Sturdevant's surmise had been largely true just made matters worse.

It was best to change the subject. "Try to keep Mr. Harvey from leavin' the buildin' tomorrow, ma'am. It's me day off, and the relief might not be as understandin' of the poor man's affliction as I am if he should happen to be caught by one of the raidin' parties."

Muldoon was happy whenever he got a Sunday off. It gave him a chance to spend some time with his sisters, and it spared him the ordeal of closing saloons. Ever since Roosevelt had been named President of the Police Commission last year, things had been done completely by the book, and no liquor on Sunday was definitely in the book. The controversy over strict enforcement had kept the city in an uproar for over a year now, and Muldoon was tired of it. He took his work seriously, and when duty demanded it, he could close an ale shop with the best of them, but it pained his soul to stop men from having a good time.

"I'll take care of him," Mrs. Sturdevant promised. She bent over, grasped Mr. Harvey under the arms, and lifted him with no effort at all. The little man murmured something.

Mrs. Sturdevant looked grim. "This may be a bad night; sometimes he sees ghosts. Well, I'm baking bread tonight, so I'll hear him yell if he does. Goodnight, Dennis."

Officer Muldoon fluttered his moustache with a sigh of resignation. "Goodnight, Mrs. Sturdevant," he said. He turned and walked down the stoop.

For all it was a hot, sticky night, and his helmet was starting to feel heavy on his head, and the high collar of his stiff wool tunic was chafing his neck, Muldoon felt good as he walked his beat through the friendly, lower- middle-class neighborhood. He lived in a similar one a few blocks to the south and east. He felt at home in both.

Unlike those in some places a man with just one year's experience might be assigned, the citizens here were respectable enough to be easy to tell from the hoodlums. Muldoon's duty consisted mostly of preventing loitering and hooky-playing, and keeping an eye on the shops that fronted the street on the ground floor of some of the buildings.

Muldoon was a contented man. He still counted as holy that day fourteen years ago when Ma and Pa and the five little Muldoons (including ten-year-old Dennis Patrick Francis-Xavier Muldoon, second oldest) had landed in America. They'd been processed at Castle Garden, a converted fort at the southern tip of Manhattan Island. Of course, immigrants came in by way of the new center on Ellis Island nowadays, but Muldoon thought that was a shame. You'd think a nation of immigrants like this one would have more of a sense of tradition.

Muldoon had loved America ever since that first day, when they'd turned him loose to discover it. That was how he thought of it. Though he'd never been west of Newark, Muldoon had the heart of an explorer. The idea of a whole big America stretching endlessly to the west was exciting enough, let alone the fact that it was filled up with Red Indians and snow-capped mountains and buffalo. Muldoon had never actually *seen* any of these things (he'd had to work overtime the last time Buffalo Bill's show had been in town) but he was still young. He'd get to them. In the meantime, New York was enough.

In fact (though if his mother had lived to know he felt this way she'd have whaled the living bejesus out of him), Muldoon didn't care if he ever saw Ireland again. Sometimes he thought he hadn't been paying attention while he was living there. He didn't remember the Auld Sod as a little bit of God's own heaven dropped into a grateful sea, or anything close to that. To him, Ireland had been peat bogs, and no shoes in winter, and a thatched roof that leaked, and not enough to eat. Worst of all had been the mind-numbing boredom and frustration of trying to get a crop from land that wasn't interested.

America (or New York—to Muldoon the terms were practically synonymous) was a wonderland of unimaginable excitement. Gaslight, and now, this new-fangled electric stuff. Bicycles. Nickelodeons. Telephones. Good Lord, *telephones*. Be heard in Boston—all the way to Chicago now—without yelling. In Ireland, you couldn't even get that far away from someone, let alone talk to him once you did. His sister Brigid, next oldest to him, had an important job as an Operator for Mr. Bell's telephone company.

And the people. Every boat, it seemed, brought a new sort of people, with strange names and exotic ways to them. Muldoon's previous beat had been by the docks, and one thing he'd decided was that God didn't make any people but he'd sprinkle some beautiful girls among them. And he'd put that theory to a stiffer test than just watching folks get off boats.

He'd even kept some company with a Chinese girl, and enjoyed it, too, until her father had come at him with a big sharp thing when he found out Muldoon had taken Blue Jade to Coney Island. Come to find out, Chinamen were very particular about who got to see their daughters' feet. New York was very educational.

Muldoon had learned to read since he'd arrived in New York, and the years he'd struggled on to graduate high school had made him very good at it, if he said so himself. He read as many newspapers as he could lay his hands on, and he was addicted to Ned Buntline's stories about the adventures of Buffalo Bill.

If this hadn't been Saturday, with the stores all closed since noon, Muldoon would have liked to step into Listerdale's Literary Emporium down near the end of the block and borrow a tale of the Wild West. He could do with a little excitement.

It was fully night now. There was a sliver of moon, but all the light worth anything came from the flames of the street lamps. Muldoon made the adjustment from looking to listening automatically, locking into the sounds of the city on Saturday night—horses' hooves, saloon singing, couples talking low to each other as they walked out.

Muldoon was twirling his nightstick and whistling while he walked. That was one advantage of night duty—it gave him something to do with his hands. The daystick was a short truncheon totally useless for twirling, or anything else to Muldoon's way of thinking. If you *had* to biff somebody, you had to biff him just as hard in the daytime as in the night. You might as well have the proper tool for it.

Two doors from the corner, Muldoon heard a clicking noise from inside Listerdale's. It was a quiet sound, drowned out momentarily by an Italian woman calling for her child to come home so she could whip him. It didn't sound like much of an inducement. When the yelling stopped, Muldoon still heard the clicking.

It was beyond him why anyone would want to rob Listerdale,

unless it was someone very much behind in his reading. The Emporium had only been open a few weeks, and the steps to the oak-and-glass door were in no danger of being worn out by the feet of eager customers.

Still, Muldoon thought, go figure a criminal. The matter was simple. He had his duty. There never had been a burglary on his beat since he'd come there, and he wasn't going to let the buggers get into the habit.

Muldoon drew his revolver, then ran through the alley to the back of the building. He stopped to light his dark-lantern, then edged along the wall to Listerdale's back entrance.

The door wasn't locked. Muldoon inched it open, wincing with every creak it made. He entered, ducking so his helmet wouldn't knock the top of the door jamb. He heard the rustling noise again. It seemed to stop short, as though whoever had been making it had become aware of Muldoon's presence.

Muldoon held the lantern as far to his left as he could, and pointed it where he guessed the noise had come from. He slid back the lens cover with his thumb.

"Stop in the name of the Law!" Muldoon barked. It was the first time he'd had a chance to say that, and he felt a bit of pleasure at the note of command he heard in his voice.

The beam of light, meanwhile, had illuminated the left side of a man. The figure, or half figure, actually, had its arm raised high, holding a walking stick as if for striking. Behind him Muldoon could see the open safe, with just a few dollars and a piece of yellow paper visible inside it.

Muldoon moved the lantern to reveal the surprised and somewhat desperate face of Hiram Listerdale.

Muldoon was surprised, too. He let fly a Gaelic oath his father used to use, of which Muldoon only suspected the meaning. He let out all his pent-up breath in one gust of impatience. "And what are you doin' battin' around in the dark like a burglar in your own blasted establishment?" he demanded.

Listerdale let his own breath go. "Officer Muldoon?"

"Who'd you be expectin' to come bustin' in in the name of the Law? Nick Carter?"

Listerdale started to laugh. For all he looked like a parson, Listerdale was as fond of a good laugh as any man Muldoon knew. Sometimes, he'd find his laugh in things Muldoon could see no humor at all in, but this time the policeman laughed right along with him. "I heard the clickin'," Muldoon said. "I knew someone was at the safe."

"Well," Listerdale said at last, "I'd better sit down and catch my breath. I thought *you* were some thief out to rob *me*."

"You're just lucky I didn't come in shootin'," Muldoon told him.

"So are you. If you'd shot me, you'd have to walk all the way to Fifth Avenue for your Wild West Tales." Listerdale rose and closed the safe, then struck a match to light the gas.

Hiram Listerdale was in his late thirties, but he looked to be forty-five or more. He was a man of good height, but he was sparely built, with a schoolmaster's stoop to his posture. In fact, he'd told Muldoon he'd been a schoolmaster before a small windfall had enabled him to move to the city and open the Emporium. Listerdale's brow was very smooth and high. It made him look intellectual (which he was) but it also added to the illusion of greater age. He wore a set of lush, brown side-whiskers, which tended to make his narrow face look pinched when he wasn't smiling.

"Well," Muldoon asked after a while, "What *were* you doin' here at this time of night?"

"What do you expect of me, Muldoon? I'm just a poor merchant, after all. I sell books. Nothing to steal here but the Truth, and I don't believe thieves are particularly interested in that commodity."

"Never mind what I expected," Muldoon said. "Instead of raggin' me, you should be draftin' a note to the Police Board, thankin' them for the Force's bein' ever vigilant, even if the public insist on runnin' around in the dark like a pack of damn fools."

Listerdale's smile became apologetic. "You're right, Muldoon. The explanation is simple. I usually devote Saturday after closing to straightening out the shop—wash the floor and so forth—but today, for the first time, business during the week preceding was so brisk—"

"Congratulations," Muldoon said, sincerely.

Listerdale had a twinkle in his eye. "Thank you. I believe

I will find unexpected benefits in this venture. At any rate, in the case of this establishment, at least, prosperity leads to disarray, and I was busy setting things in order until just a few minutes ago. I had turned out the light, and was preparing to go to my rooms upstairs, when I remembered I had neglected to take pocket money for myself. Since there was sufficient light from the street lamps to find my way across the shop and to open the safe, I spared myself the trouble of lighting the gas again."

Muldoon nodded. "Makes sense." He rose. "Ah, well, I'm glad it's just a misunderstandin' then."

The officer was looking carefully at Listerdale's shelves and tables. He saw the day's best sellers, among them *Coin's Financial School*, which had had a revival due to the election, and a novel called *The Red Badge of Courage*, by someone named Stephen Crane. Muldoon had read part of it. He thought it was a shame to waste such a good Western title on a mere war story.

"A misunderstanding," the bookseller echoed. "And I appreciate your zeal, Muldoon, truly—"

Listerdale sold magazines and fine stationery as well as books. Muldoon looked over the racks, and his face lit up. "I—ah—can't help noticin' you've still got the August *Lippincott's Magazine*." The issue featured "The Great K&A Robbery," a story of a daring train hold-up out West.

"Yes, that's the last copy."

"Well . . . Would I be puttin' you out if I were to sort of borrow it? Sometimes," Muldoon went on, warming to his subject, "in between episodes of riskin' life and limb on behalf of an indifferent public, you might say, there are lonely, dreary, periods of waitin' that try even the most hardened—"

"Please, Muldoon, you'll break my heart." Listerdale chuckled. "Take it, by all means. And I see now how the variety stage has sadly maligned our men in blue. Your interests, Muldoon, seem to embrace more than the occasional apple from the Italian's push-cart."

"That's true," Muldoon agreed. "And then, there's no returnin' a borrowed apple, either. But speakin' of the variety stage, did you get to see the kinetoscope?"

"The what?"

"A movin' picture. Mr. Edison invented it. I was assigned

to traffic back in April when Koster and Bials was showin' one. Took a peek inside. You'd think some Bolshevik had gone flingin' a bomb in the place. Had a kinetoscope of a locomotive steamin' straight at you."

"Amazing."

"It was a daisy. That thing hasn't got much of a future, if you're askin' me—too unsettlin'. Even though I knew it was some kind of a trick, when I saw that train roarin' at me, I ducked for me life. And you should have heard the women screamin' . . ."

Just then, they did hear a woman screaming, a series of shrieks from out in the street that would have frightened a banshee.

"Help! Murder! Police!"

Muldoon called a hurried thanks to Listerdale for the magazine, dashed to the front of the store, and plunged into the street.

II.

It was Mrs. Sturdevant who was doing the yelling. The normally placid landlady was standing in front of her tenement with her hands cupped around her mouth, like a man in a crowded saloon calling for another beer.

Muldoon ran up to her. She grabbed him by the sleeve, and started to drag him into the building.

This was a bad night for Muldoon's dignity. He pulled his arm free. "I'm comin', ain't I? What's goin' on?"

Mrs. Sturdevant was so wrought up she had to stop and grab his sleeve again before she could tell him. "It's Mr. Harvey!" she blurted, near tears. "The poor soul has done himself in." She shook her head, and the tears came loose and rolled down her cheeks. "That's what happens when a body lives all alone!"

"Now, don't go blubberin' at me!" Muldoon commanded. "Where is he?"

"In his room, where I left him before. I—*sniff*—I went back upstairs to see if the poor little man was all right, and I smelled gas something awful."

Her tone fell to a hush. "This is the anniversary of the day his wife died, you know, and now he's blown out the gas. And he's locked his door, as well."

Muldoon pushed past her, and raced up the stairs to Mr. Harvey's room on the second floor. The air was heavy with coal-gas, and the door wouldn't budge.

"Bring me the pass-key!" Muldoon yelled to the landladly, who was puffing up the stairs.

"There hasn't been a pass-key since eighty-eight," she told him. "I lost it in the blizzard. Never had call to get another one."

Muldoon sighed, then coughed as he drew in a lungful of gas. It was too bad, but Mrs. Sturdevant was going to be out the cost of a new door. He backed across the hallway, then rushed forward, throwing a meaty shoulder against the door to Harvey's flat. This building had been put together by someone who knew what he was about; Muldoon might as well have thrown a snowball. After three more attempts, his shoulder was numb, but the door was finally showing signs of wear. Twice more, and it burst inward, sending Muldoon staggering into the room.

About a half second later, Mr. Harvey wobbled in from the bedroom, dressed in his nightshirt, waving an empty whiskey bottle and swearing no damn ghost was going to get him.

Muldoon took the bottle away and swore under his breath, while Mrs. Sturdevant came forward to try to calm the old soak down. The only gas in the room was what was now leaking in from the hall. Muldoon checked the wall jet—it was closed tight.

The patrolman went back into the hall. The smell was as strong as ever. It was so pervasive, Muldoon found it difficult to tell where it was coming from. He wasn't a blasted bloodhound, after all.

He deduced the answer. Muldoon knew his beat. This building had three flats to a floor, and Muldoon knew that the couple who rented the one fronting the street were away to a cottage in Brooklyn for the summer. The answer, therefore, was probably a simple gas leak, unless the new fellow, Randall, or Crandall or whatever his name was, was trying to do himself in. He'd knock on the fellow's door and make sure, then go tell Mrs. Sturdevant she should call in the gas company next time, instead of distracting a public servant with her damned overheated, melodramatic, female imagination.

But neither knocking nor shouting could raise an answer from the fellow's apartment. Muldoon rattled the doorknob and found it locked. That made two locked doors. Muldoon wondered what New York was coming to, if neighbors didn't feel they could trust each other anymore.

As much as he wanted to, he couldn't let it go by. He smashed his sore shoulder against this new door. He was getting the hang of it—the door gave on only the third try.

Muldoon took a whiff of the air inside, gasped, and called across the hall for Mrs. Sturdevant. This was the place, all right. He could hear the hiss of escaping gas, and the smell was nauseous.

For one crazy moment, Muldoon wanted to light his lantern so he could see his way to the window, to open it, and get some fresh air into the room. He actually had a lucifer in his hand before he realized that would be a particularly messy (not to say embarrassing) way of committing suicide.

He made his way in the dark, stumbling once or twice. He opened the broad window at the other end of the room, and thrust out his head. The view wasn't much—the fire escape, the backs of the other buildings on the block, and the alley below—but the air was delicious. He drew in all of it his lungs could hold, then plunged back to the center of the room.

Muldoon had never been in this particular flat before, but it seemed to be a mirror image of Mr. Harvey's place across the hall. Keeping that in mind, and following the hissing, he was able to find the gas jet without too much blundering around.

By the time he'd twisted the valve shut, his eyes were adjusted to the darkness. This time, he walked confidently to the window, refilled his lungs, then surveyed the place.

Crandall was sitting tall and straight in a wingback chair. In the half darkness, the only way Muldoon could tell he was dead was by the way his head was thrown back over the rim of carved wood that projected above the upholstery.

No one could have slept with those walnut knobs digging into his neck, but Crandall certainly looked as though he were doing it. He was immaculate in a flowered smoking jacket, with a silk scarf around his neck. Not a hair in his continental beard was out of place.

Muldoon nibbled at his own moustache while he checked for

a pulse. He wasn't very good at doing that—he kept feeling his own instead of the patient's. He bellowed for Mrs. Sturdevant again, then dragged Crandall to the open window.

He lay the man chest down across the broad sill, and began artificial respiration by pushing vigorously on his back, the way he'd seen lifeguards do it at Coney Island.

Mrs. Sturdevant joined him. She wasn't enthusiastic about the idea, but she held a corner of her apron over her mouth and nose, and walked to Muldoon. Now that she had Mr. Harvey safely back in bed, her maternal instincts took a back seat to her curiosity.

"Mr. Crandall?" she asked. Muldoon nodded. The landlady shook her head. "Now why would a young man want to do something like that?" To Mrs. Sturdevant, anyone fifty or under was young.

"Don't be worryin' me about that now, woman," Muldoon scolded, in rhythm with his efforts. "I can't stop doin' this, so you must go for help. I don't suppose you'd be havin' a telephone?"

"I'm not," she said coldly, "Mrs. John Pierpont Morgan."

"Just askin'. Here." Muldoon let up pressure just long enough to hand her his whistle and nightstick. "Put the whistle in your mouth and toot while you're poundin' the sidewalk with the billy. That'll bring every cop within ten blocks runnin'. Now *go!*"

The landlady looked dubious, but she put the whistle between her lips, took a firm grip on the nightstick, and dashed away.

It was only a few seconds before Muldoon heard her start to raise her ruckus. Help would be here soon.

As the gas dissipated and the smell of it diminished, Muldoon was able to notice the odor of something else that made him realize that whatever help did come would be too late for Mr. Crandall. He'd soiled himself. They only did that at the moment they gave up the ghost, so Muldoon knew for certain that it was hopeless.

Muldoon gave up the life-saving as a bad job, happy to leave off touching the dead man. He sniffed the air again, and decided it would be safe to have some light. He made the flame from the wall jet as bright as possible, and began to search the room for a suicide note.

The first thing he noticed was the bright red color of the dead man's face, the same color his Uncle Liam used to turn when he was in his cups and spoiling for a fight. The gas had done it for Crandall, though; and there'd be no more fighting for him.

Muldoon suppressed a shudder. Not only was getting gassed a terrible way to die, but to sit in a chair and just wait for it to happen . . . It gave him chills to think about it.

Aside from the chair the body had occupied, the only other furniture in the room was a plain, straight-backed, armless wooden chair and a big, handsome rolltop desk. Muldoon picked the desk as the most likely place to find the note. He resigned himself to having to bust that open, too, but got a pleasant surprise when he found it unlocked.

Little wonder. It was nearly as bare as the room. It did contain one thing of value—a Kodak, one of the new kind, where the owner could remove the film and send it to Rochester to be developed, instead of having to mail the whole camera. Aside from that, Muldoon found only a pencil, a pen, a bottle of black ink, and a crumpled piece of good-quality paper that bore a none-too-flattering portrait of Mayor Strong. The drawing looked familiar to Muldoon. He puzzled over it for a few seconds, then recognized it as part of a cartoon the *Journal* had run a few days ago. For some reason, the patrolman decided, Crandall had been trying to copy the style of E. Noon.

Muldoon decided to move his search for the note into the bedroom; there was certainly nothing to be found here.

The bedroom was as opulent as the sitting room had been bare, and the second most opulent thing about it was the huge four-poster bed with the red silk coverlet. The first most opulent thing was the woman who lay on it.

III.

She was jaybird naked, and as beautiful as anything Muldoon had ever seen. The sight of her took his breath away far more thoroughly than the gas ever could.

He had, in fact, a double portion of her beauty, because by a corner of the bed, just where the light from the open door could strike it, stood an artist's easel holding a painting, beautiful though unfinished, of this same woman, equally naked.

Muldoon looked back at the real woman, and offered a wordless prayer that she not be dead. The prayer was immediately answered by a muffled groan and a writhing. The thwarted movement of a beautifully tapered leg led him to observe that she had been cruelly bound hand and foot, to the four bedposts, and blindfolded and gagged with scarves.

Some subtle instinct Muldoon didn't even bother to notice told him it was rude to wear his helmet in the presence of a lady, especially a naked one, and he doffed it as he entered the room. Before doing anything else, he drew the curtains on the bedroom window to afford the poor girl *some* modesty, then lit the gas.

Muldoon was frankly at a loss. It wasn't the first time, by any means, that he'd seen a female clad only in what God gave her to wear, but all the other times, it had been with the lady's consent, if not her eager cooperation. This, though in the line of duty, was going to be a bit too much like taking an indecent liberty for Muldoon to feel comfortable about it.

Still, duty was duty. He had to get her out of this—the unfortunate thing was probably suffering tortures untold. "Don't . . . ah . . . don't worry, ma'am. I'll be havin' you out of there in . . . ah . . . a jiffy."

He started with the blindfold and gag—they were safe enough. The face he revealed was fully as lovely as the form it went with. The girl's shiny black hair made a widow's peak, which in turn made a Valentine's Day greeting of her whole face. She had large, clear brown eyes that looked at him with mute appeal, while her wide red mouth shaped words to reinforce the message.

"Oh, Officer," she breathed. "Bless you, bless you. You are sent from God to rescue me. Please untie me, quickly!"

It was an intimidating prospect. She had been tied, spread-eagle, with a single length of rope, which crossed her ivory skin many times, and was knotted in the vicinity of some her most appealing curves.

Muldoon felt sweat start to form on his forehead.

"Please hurry," the girl pleaded. "I am in such discomfort, and you are so strong and kind. I entreat you to end my suffering." She closed her eyes and bit her lip before saying, "Nothing can remove the scars of my humiliation." The lip quivered.

To hell wth it, Muldoon thought. "Thank God I'm wearin' me gloves," he said, and began to work on the rope. Besides, she was far too delicate to be gawked at like a hootchy-cootchy dancer by the boys on the squad.

That she was painfully shy was obvious; she wouldn't even tell Mudoon her name. Muldoon, remembering the easel, thought she might be a professional model, and asked her that.

"Not usually," she replied, then turned her head to the pillow, as if in shame.

"Well," Muldoon said, "maybe you'll be talkin' more easily when I've got you free, mmm?" He tried what he thought would be an encouraging chuckle, but his voice sounded strange. It was getting hard for him to keep his mind off where his hands were. He'd undone the knots in all the decent places first—the only one's left were in places only a doctor or a husband was entitled to touch. In spite of his situation, he couldn't help but feel he was taking advantage of the girl, yet he also felt a nagging, sinful regret that as soon as the last knot was gone, he would have to leave off taking advantage. Nobody'd prepared him for anything like this when he'd joined the Force.

To make matters worse, she was a Catholic girl. A gold cross on a fine gold chain nestled in the cleft of her bosom. Muldoon tried to concentrtae on that—the cross, not the bosom—but it was difficult to do when it seemed that every time he'd try to take hold of the rope, his hand found some soft, springy part of the girl instead.

It was hell, never mind that certain evil parts of Muldoon's mind were acting as if they were enjoying themselves.

The last knot was the hardest. In order to get leverage on a particularly stubborn bit of rope, Muldoon had to lean far over the bed in a way that had him staring, at close range, at a birthmark on the inside of her (he couldn't help noticing) perfectly firm right thigh. The mark itself was fascinating, almost hypnotic. It was a "T" shape, bright pink and about an inch long, with wedge-shaped arms and a circle on top centered over the upright. It reminded Muldoon of an angel, complete with wings and nimbus.

With an effort that almost hurt, Muldoon brought his mind back to his work. He freed the last knot, and fairly leapt away from the bed. Judging from his breath, he might have run six times around the block, or gone fifteen with the great John L.

The Angel Woman might have been a bit stiff from her ordeal, but she didn't show it. She was talking again, blessing Muldoon in her sweet voice. She got up, rushed to him, embraced him, and began to cry on his strong blue shoulder. She was just tall enough to reach it. Her hair hung straight and glossy to her waist.

It must be reported, in fairness to Muldoon, that he wanted to push her away; indeed, he tried, but in the very act, his hands were brought back to places they'd just left. He pulled them away as though he'd been burnt. This was no longer the line of duty.

"Oh, Officer," the woman pleaded. "You must take me away from this place before another minute passes!"

"Ah . . . I'm afraid I can't be doin' that, ma'am. Sorry," he added feebly. Having nothing better to do with his hand, he scratched his head. "Wouldn't you rather be lettin' go of me? The wool they use in these uniforms is mighty itchy."

She held him, if that were possible, all the more tightly, putting her hand *inside* his tunic, as though she wanted to touch his heart physically as well as with her words.

"Oh, please, *please*, take me away! Surely . . ." she tilted her head back and looked deeply into his eyes. "Surely you must know a place where an unfortunate girl can hide her shame from the world in safety. Don't leave me here where the murderer may return and butcher me!"

Muldoon was surprised. It had looked like an open-and-shut, if somewhat perverted suicide to him. "Murder?"

The Pink Angel shuddered against him and cried the harder. "I—I can't speak of it. Oh, is there no man who is not cruel?"

Muldoon's heart bled, but the boy was born to be a policeman. "How do you know it was murder?" he asked.

She would give him no answer.

"Look at me," he commanded. Tear-filled brown eyes opened to him. "You say it's murder, do you? Well, if that's the truth of it, the only way to be sure of bein' safe is to catch the murderer, isn't that so?" And in spite of himself, he enfolded her in his arms, and gave her back gentle pats of reassurance.

"Well?" he asked.

"Yes," the girl said, sniffing back a further tear. "I heard it, while I was bound and helpless in here. I know it was murder!"

Suddenly, she dissolved into near hysteria. "Now take me away from here, or I shall die!"

Muldoon didn't want her going all to pieces, both for the girl's own sake, and for the sake of the detectives who would be questioning her later.

"There, there, me darlin'," he told her, allowing himself one final pat. "You won't have to be stayin' here much longer, I promise. I'll leave you to . . . ah . . . get dressed while I see what's delayin' me reinforcements."

"Thank you, thank you, and thank God for sending you to me in my time of trial." She took his hand, and covered it with kisses, something Muldoon found profoundly embarrassing.

He went back through the sitting room to the hall. Mrs. Sturdevant was still pounding determinedly on the sidewalk with the nightstick, but her blasts on the whistle were getting a mite breathy.

All the neighbors, who should have been home in their beds, to Muldoon's way of thinking, were trying to get her to stop the racket. All but the children—they were offering to help blow the whistle.

Muldoon was about to go outside and break up the show, but before he could, heard a familiar voice calling from the far end of the block. "Don't worry, Mother, help is on the way!"

Well, well, Muldoon thought. The captain himself—there was no mistaking the church-organ tones of Captain Ozias Herkimer, the commander of Muldoon's precinct. In quality of voice, and in ability to say things that *sounded* just beautiful, whether you could understand them or not, Muldoon ranked the captain second only to William Jennings Bryan himself, whom Muldoon had heard speak at the Madison Square Garden a week ago Wednesday.

Muldoon wondered what had brought the captain out, but it didn't matter as long as someone was coming to help. He climbed back up to Crandall's flat to reassure his witness.

"I'm back, miss," he called, as heartily as he felt was proper in the presence of gruesome death. "Are you ready to be leavin' here yet?" It was almost as if Muldoon were calling to take her out walking.

There was no answer from the bedroom. He tried the door; it

was locked. He put his ear to it; there was no sound from within, no movement, no rustling of petticoats, no anything.

Muldoon called on all three of his name-saints to preserve him as a feeling of dread washed over him. Had the murderer somehow returned? Had the poor girl been unable after all to withstand the shame of her predicament and chosen the final way out?

For the third time that evening, Muldoon broke down a door. His shoulder fairly throbbed with pain, but he gave that no thought. There might still be time.

The door gave way. The bedroom was empty. Muldoon stood a moment, stupefied, then rushed to the open window. Out there and down the fire escape was the only place she could have gone.

And so she had. Sticking his head out the window, Muldoon saw the young woman, wrapped only in a sheet, hurrying down the ladder to the alley below. Her small, bare feet made no sound on the rungs. She was descending toward a light-colored rectangle. Muldoon turned momentarily, and saw the easel now stood empty. She'd taken the painting and dropped it before her—not wanting to leave behind any evidence of her degradation, Muldoon thought.

"Hey!" Muldoon shouted. "Hey, stop! Are you daft?"

She paused for a moment, and looked at him almost wistfully. Then she went the rest of the way down the ladder, picking up the painting, and the length of rope she'd been bound with, when she reached the bottom.

Muldoon was hampered by his great size, but he managed to clamber out onto the fire escape. Before he could start down, though, the young woman paused again, this time raising her arm.

She's wavin' me goodbye, for the love of Pete, Muldoon thought. She *is* daft.

Then there was the roar of a gunshot, and the whine of a bullet ricocheting off the brick wall above his head. Muldoon went sprawling on the metal slats.

He would never have fired at a woman, of course, but Muldoon's instinctive response to being shot at was to reach to his holster.

It was empty. She'd shot at him with his own gun. Feeling the biggest fool God ever made, Muldoon risked sticking his head out over the edge of the landing. He had to have one more look at this creature if he died for it.

She was still there. Her anxious look changed to a smile when she saw him; a sad smile, but a smile nevertheless. She raised her other arm, brought it to her mouth, blew Muldoon a kiss, then disappeared around the corner of the building.

IV.

"You," Captain Herkimer told Muldoon a half hour later, "are the biggest fool God ever made!"

Herkimer looked more like a sea captain than a police captain, with his weatherbeaten face and grizzled, half-circle beard. Right now, he resembled a sea captain in the act of putting down a mutiny. The veins stood out on his neck and broad forehead. He sought to dominate Muldoon, not by leaning over and yelling down at him—he lacked the height for that—but by leaning forward and yelling at the bottom of the patrolman's chin. Muldoon was vaguely afraid the captain would leap up and bite him on the throat.

"If you expect me to believe that . . . that *tale* of yours," he went on, "you're even a bigger fool than that!"

It hadn't been a good night for the captain. He and most of the boys had been busy on a raid on a bawdy house a few blocks away (just in time for the Sunday editions), and who had been hauled in but the captain's wife's brother? That was the last time *he* led a raid, at least until there was a change in administrations. In his good old days, when he'd had a nice juicy slice of the Tenderloin, brother-dear would have been no problem. Hell's bells, the whole bawdy house would have been no problem.

Not any more, though, damn all do-gooders. There had been too many witnesses around to let brother-dear go, so he'd been booked with the rest. When the alarm had come from Mrs. Sturdevant, Herkimer had been glad to take a few of the boys and go, just as an excuse to delay the inevitable reckoning with his wife.

He left Muldoon for a moment, and walked in a small circle around the sitting room, mumbling to himself. In the process, he very nearly stepped on the corpse. The Police Surgeon looked up at him, but said nothing.

The end of the trip had him beard to moustache with Muldoon again. The patrolman noticed that the captain was no longer yelling, but somehow that failed to make him feel any better.

"'Why do you still have your shield, Muldoon?" the captain asked.

"Beg pardon, sir?"

"Why did you bother to keep possession of your shield? You gave away your whistle and your truncheon. You abandoned your helmet, didn't even hang it up, just left it on the floor for me to trip on when I tried to keep you from escaping out the window."

"Captain, I swear—"

"Quiet! God alone knows what's become of your revolver. So I wondered why you didn't get rid of the tin. Not to say you mightn't yet, eh?"

Muldoon could feel himself turning red. He clenched his right hand, while the left covered the shiny metal rectangle on his heart as though to protect it. He mumbled something.

"I can't hear you, *Officer* Muldoon," the captain said. "Speak up."

"*The woman took me flamin' gun!*" Muldoon snapped.

"*There was no woman!*" the captain roared in return.

Over the captain's shoulder, Muldoon could see a round-eyed Mrs. Sturdevant peering around the frame of the open door. Some of her tenants stood behind her. Muldoon wanted to die. It was bad enough to be yelled at, without the public's making a free entertainment of it.

Herkimer spotted the landlady and waved her into the room.

"Now then, Mother," he said, "you were here when this officer found the body, were you not?"

"I was." She looked at Muldoon and nodded at him. "And I saw him trying to save poor Mr. Crandall's life. I think instead of bedeviling the poor boy, you should be out looking for that little hussy that stole his gun. That's what *I* would do."

The captain smiled a deadly smile. "Would you now? Isn't that nice? Well, it so happens, Mother, we *have* been looking for her. Had men asking questions all over the neighborhood. But nobody saw or heard her, any more than you did."

Though the captain's voice remained calm, even sweet, a curious thing was happening to his face. A tide of red was climbing it from the neck up, like a thermometer, or a burning fuse. Muldoon recognized it, even through his own anger. When the red reached the top, the captain was going to explode.

It wasn't quite time yet—his voice was still sweet as he said, "That is the way of it, isn't it, Mother? You didn't actually see or hear this unclad woman, now did you?"

Herkimer didn't know it, but he was making a fiercer and fiercer enemy of Mrs. Sturdevant every time he called her "Mother." The landlady set her jaw. "If Dennis says she was here, then she was here."

Muldoon winced.

The Captain exploded. "That's not all *Dennis* says, Mother! *Dennis* implies some things about you, too!"

"I don't know what you're talking about," she said, but she wore a dubious look.

"Well, Mother, *Dennis* says she ran off wrapped in a sheet. That would mean she'd left her clothes behind her, wouldn't it? Yes! *But there are no woman's clothes in this flat!* I have a higher regard for the character of your establishment, Mother, than to believe Muldoon's implication that you rent apartments to single gentlemen who keep naked women the way some people keep canary-birds!"

Mrs. Sturdevant gasped in horror. "How *dare* you . . ."

Herkimer ignored her. Muldoon suffered in silence.

"Dennis says there was a painting of the woman, but she took it with her. Really, now. Dennis *also* says that she ran around the corner of the building. You know your building, Mother—the only place she could have gone from there was back to the street, where, you'll recall, a crowd had gathered to watch you make a spectacle of yourself."

That was enough for Mrs. Sturdevant. She opened her mouth, decided words would be inadequate, clamped it shut, then gave the captain a resounding slap on the face with a right arm made strong by years of floor-scrubbing and bread-kneading. She stamped angrily from the room, slamming the door behind her.

The captain was rubbing his face, and scowling at Muldoon, who was having the battle of his life, trying to keep the smile he felt in his soul from appearing on his face.

"No one saw a naked woman on the street, *Dennis*," the captain said. Muldoon was beginning to hate the sound of his own name. "We knocked on doors. No one in any of the other buildings took her in, and believe me, Muldoon, people would remember if they'd taken in a naked woman carrying a pistol and an oil painting!"

Muldoon decided that either he or the world had gone mad. He had no great love for his superior, but he knew him to be a shrewd, and—when he wanted to be—thorough investigator. The captain seemed to have covered every possibility.

Still, he had to say it. "I saw her, Captain, that's all there is to it." It was more of a vote of confidence in his own sanity than a gesture of defiance.

"I won't stand for these lies, Muldoon."

Muldoon started to shake. No one had ever before called Dennis Patrick Francis-Xavier Muldoon a liar without suffering for it. Muldoon said not a word; his jaw mucles no longer existed, only the ones that swung his fists, and he was controlling them. But just barely.

Herkimer took the silence for an admission. He assumed a fatherly air. "Now look, Muldoon. This is a suicide. You've seen dozens of them. Word is, the man recently lost his job. Naturally, he'd be blue. The surgeon says he died from the coal-gas. There isn't a mark on him, just a bruise on the back of his neck that was undoubtedly caused by his head's lolling over the back of that chair.

"Now, you say this woman, this beautiful, naked woman, whom nobody can find, told you it was murder, stole your revolver, and fled into oblivion.

"You know what I say? I say losing his gun is something that can get a young patrolman in a lot of trouble, and a bright young man would know that. Even the most honest of young men might be tempted to sort of call on his imagination to account for the loss. Doesn't that sound logical to you, Muldoon?"

Muldoon chewed on his moustache, ruining its beautiful symmetry.

"Of course," the captain went on, "the patrolman might not realize that his little flight of fancy could change a nice, simple closed case into a messy, unsolved murder that would reflect badly on the whole precinct."

So *that* was it, Muldoon thought grimly. Ambition had reared its head. It was no secret that the Police Board was to meet soon to decide which of the city's police captains was to be promoted to inspector. Herkimer evidently wanted to be among them.

"No one would want to make trouble for the precinct, now, would he, Muldoon?" The captain was beaming at him with a smile that could charm the gold from a leprechaun's teeth.

It was an easy way out of his predicament, and Muldoon was tempted, but virtue and honesty had been instilled in him by means of numerous clouts on the head, and just the thought of telling a lie, for insufficient reason, seemed to raise lumps on his noggin once again.

"There *was* a woman, Captain," he said quietly, almost resignedly. "She was dark-haired, and young, and beautiful. She was naked as a newborn babe. She had a gold cross around her neck, and a pink angel on her . . . limb. She was tied to the bed; I untied her, and she fell to blessin' me. Stealin' me pistol while she was doin' it, mind. The instant I turned me back, she wrapped a sheet around her, stole a paintin' of herself, and beat it down the fire escape. When I called on her to stop, she fired at me with me own gun. The she bl—" Muldoon decided to leave out the kiss "—then she ran away.

"And that's all I can say about the matter. Sir."

"Oh, it is, is it?" Herkimer said between strong-looking dentures. "Well, I can say a good deal more than that." He sniffed the air. "There's the smell of liquor on your uniform, Officer."

Muldoon had expected that particular accusation a good deal earlier, and was ready for it. "Yes, sir. I'll wager that every patrolman who's ever walked a beat with a saloon on it of a Saturday night has finished off the tour smellin' of liquor. It'd be impossible to avoid—if a man was doin' his duty."

The captain looked at him with utter contempt. "That's as may be. We shall discuss this further in my office, tomorrow at noon. Until then, you may consider yourself off duty, as of this moment."

"But it can't be later than nine o'clock," Muldoon protested. "I'm on me beat till midnight!"

Herkimer pulled an ornate gold watch from his pocket and snapped it open. Muldoon saw a portrait daguerrotype that had been pasted in back, of a stern, light-eyed woman, who was probably Herkimer's rich wife.

"It is ten minutes past the hour," Herkimer said. "I shall tell the paymaster to adjust your wages for the time you miss."

"But Captain!"

"You may *go*, Muldoon. Must I have you thrown into the street?"

Muldoon was burning. That would have been the ultimate humiliation, to be pitched out by his brother officers. He'd kill Herkimer if he stayed in the room another minute, so he gathered up his helmet, his whistle and his nightstick (which Mrs. Sturdevant had returned) and fled. But not before he'd taken a silent oath that *somebody*, he wasn't sure who, was going to regret making this happen to him.

V.

Muldoon would have liked to think it over a little longer, but he didn't have enough time. He had to decide now.

On the one hand, if it really had been a murder he'd stumbled into, every second lost would take that poor girl deeper and deeper into danger. On the other hand, one did not lightly break the chain of command of the Police Department of the City of New York, no matter how insulting a superior had happened to be.

Mr. Theodore Roosevelt, President of the Police Board, wasn't a good man to have for an enemy. And he had a lot on his mind these days, what with that string of Mansion Burglaries and all. Muldoon was happy his beat wasn't in one of the rich precincts —the boys there had been hearing some harsh words. Some had even had to give up the tin.

Muldoon didn't want that to happen to him—it had been too long in the getting for him to look on the possibility of losing his shield with anything short of pure horror.

It wasn't that Muldoon had any objection to Mr. Roosevelt's hewing to the straight line of the rules. To the young man's mind, that was the main point in the Commissioner's favor; it was what had made it possible for Muldoon to join the Force in the first place.

Prior to 1895, if you wanted to be a cop, someone with pull had to do you a favor—which you could be a lifetime paying back. But Roosevelt, as Mayor Strong's Police Commissioner, had held out for impartial competitive examinations like the ones he'd instituted when he was Civil Service Commissioner in Washington, D.C.

But he brooked no nonsense. One night, on one of his periodic street-prowling expeditions (the newspapers sometimes referred to him as Haroun-al-Roosevelt), the Commissioner spotted Officer Blinky Meyers taking a harmless beer near the back window of a convenient saloon, shouted at him, chased him, ran him down, put him under arrest, and threw him from the Force. Muldoon wondered what a man like that would do to a cop who'd lost his gun. Hang him? Shoot him and have him stuffed? Roosevelt was always getting written up about his big-game hunting out West.

For a cop who stood by his duty, though, Roosevelt would go the limit. At least that's what Ed Bourke had told Muldoon, and he ought to know. Bourke broke up the party at "King" Calahan's place one Sunday afternoon. Calahan was New York's foremost gentleman-crook, and he sicced every mug, grafter, shyster, and tame judge in the city on Bourke. Roosevelt not only kept his man healthy and working, but by God, he'd made Calahan keep the Sabbath and like it.

Bourke, naturally, had been astounded. "Dennis," he'd told Muldoon over a (perfectly permissible) off-duty beer, "this Roosevelt is something I never thought I'd live to see—a rich man as likes an honest cop."

That was the problem in a sentence. Could Muldoon make the Commissioner believe he was honest? If he could, things would be jake. Or at least a lot more jake than they seemed at the moment. But if he couldn't make the Commissioner accept his story, Roosevelt would surely have Muldoon's hide for shoe-leather.

Muldoon sighed over his indecision, looked up, and discovered to his surprise that the question had become irrelevant. His feet had decided for him, bringing him, without his knowledge, to the door of the Manhattan New Christian Fellowship.

That name was a surprise, too, but Muldoon checked the chipped gilt number on the door with the one on the scrap of paper in his hand, and they matched.

Wonderful, he thought, he'd have to interrupt the Commissioner while he was singing his psalms, or whatever Dutchman Protestants would do of a Saturday night.

A feeling of calm fatality came over the young officer. He took off his helmet and gloves, the way any God-fearing man would do on entering a church, and pushed open the carved-wood-and-glass door.

He found himself not in a vestibule, as he had imagined, but in something very like a hotel lobby, complete with a desk clerk wearing a green eyeshade. He was somewhat younger and more wholesome looking than most desk clerks of Muldoon's experience, true, but he said the same words every last mother's son of them used as a greeting: "Yes, Officer? Nothing wrong, I hope."

"Ah, no," Muldoon said, then cleared his throat to push that little lie away. "That is, I want to see Mr. Theodore Roosevelt, and someone at Headquarters down on Mulberry Street told me this is the address where I'd be findin' him. It's probably some sort of mistake, I'm sure, and . . ."

"No, there's no mistake," the clerk told him. "Is it a police matter?"

Muldoon tilted his head to think about it. "You might say so," he said at last. "I'll be wantin' to talk to him, and I'm a policeman, after all." For the moment, anyway, he thought.

"Very well," the clerk said. "He's in the assembly room. Follow me."

"Now . . ." Muldoon was very embarrassed. "There's no need to hurry, mind. I can wait. I don't want to be breakin' up his prayer meetin'."

The clerk laughed. "Prayer meeting? Oh, no, sir. Mr. Theodore Roosevelt is content to leave the prayers to me and the rest of the professional prayer-makers." He laughed again. "Prayer meeting," he sighed. "No, Mr. Roosevelt is holding a meeting, right enough, but I don't think he's leading the boys in prayer."

By now thoroughly bewildered, Muldoon followed meekly as the man showed him through a swinging door, up a flight of stairs, and down a long hallway. He was only halfway up them when he started hearing the noise, and the closer he came to the assembly room, the louder it was. Whatever was going on, it was too noisy and too happy to be any kind of prayer meeting Muldoon had ever heard of any white people having.

The noise was coming from about thirty boys, evenly divided into two groups. The fair ones with the freckles were easy to recognize as Irish—practically any of them might have been Muldoon ten years ago. The swarthy young fellows were Southern Europeans of some sort, Italians, probably. Scrapes, bruises, and black eyes were distributed more or less uniformly among them. Muldoon guessed, rightly, that there had been a discussion over who had wandered onto whose territory.

That, however, had been forgotten. The boys were looking from their benches at a one-man melodrama, and responding accordingly.

The cast of this melodrama was Mr. Theodore Roosevelt. At this moment, he was a roaring grizzly bear. He did not especially resemble a grizzly bear; to Muldoon's mind, there was more of the walrus to him, with that squint, the large white teeth, and the drooping brush of a moustache the editorial cartoonists had so much fun with.

"GrrraaAARRrrr," said the President of the Police Board of the City of New York. The boys laughed nervously; some of the younger ones gasped.

The grizzly bear made a swipe with his paw. He was a bit small for a grizzly—five foot eight, reared up on his hind legs the way he was, but he was an imposing figure just the same. He weighed about a hundred fifty pounds, practically all of it compact muscle. He was a vigorous thirty-eight years of age, which is old indeed for a grizzly bear, but practically infancy for a politician.

"And there I was," the Commissioner said, leaving the grizzly looming in the boys' (and Muldoon's) imagination. "My horse was dead, I was lame with a twisted ankle, and the beast was set to make a meal of me." The Commissioner's voice was high, but he lent it force and urgency by emitting it in the clipped barks of an agitated terrier.

"I grasped the handle of my bowie knife—I'd lost my gun, you see . . ." Now the Commissioner leaned back across the speaker's rostrum, depicting himself, the hapless frontiersman awaiting death. Again, he created his illusion despite the drawbacks of setting and costume. The dingy little meeting room had windows that offered a splendid view of the tenement neighborhood, but it was unlike the Great Plains as anything Muldoon could imagine. And no cowboy who ever lived could have gotten away with the outfit the Commissioner had on.

Mr. Roosevelt was known as a bit of a dandy, but Muldoon had never suspected just how dandy. Right now, the Commissioner was wearing a fine grey silk suit, with the jacket unbuttoned to reveal a shirt nearly as pink as the missing girl's birthmark. Instead of a vest, Roosevelt had a white sash of tasseled silk wound around his middle. The only thing plain about his wardrobe was his spectacles, two wire-frame ovals of glass that did nothing to conceal the energy in his eyes.

"I reached for my knife," the Commissioner said, groping blindly across the top of the rostrum until his fingers found a lead pencil. "I knew I'd have only one chance, so I waited, the bear's breath rank in my face, for the proper moment."

The boys were silent, caught up in the suspense. "Then, at the last possible second, when I could fairly count the bear's teeth, I *struck!*" The pencil was swept violently upward.

There was a collective gasp.

"With all my strength, and with a prayer to guide my arm, I used my knife. The blade pierced the grizzly's throat, and killed him in the instant. I barely had time to roll out of the way, before the beast would have fallen on my body and crushed me!"

The Commissioner rolled off the rostrum and finished by facing his audience. He accepted their enthuiastic applause with a wide, toothy grin.

There was no doubt he enjoyed it, but after a few seconds he held up a hand to stop the applause. "Boys! Harumph. I mean gentlemen!"

Just like a vaudeville turn, Muldoon thought. The boys were spinning their heads around, trying to catch sight of a gentleman.

"Gentlemen!" the Commissioner said again, this time gaining the crowd's attention. "Now, I didn't tell you this story just to boast.

"You may hear it, and envy me my adventure. Adventure it was, but it was also terrifying. I thought I had seen my last second as a living man. That is not an uncommon feeling, in the wilderness.

"But the city of New York is not a wilderness! Any citizen of this city is entitled to go anywhere within the city he chooses, so long as he behaves himself, and that will be the case for as long a time as I am given anything to say about it. If you harass persons wandering into your neighborhoods, or if you go into a neighborhood with the idea of causing trouble, from this night on, it will go hard with you. This is your only warning.

"Secondly, the very *idea* of 'Irish' neighborhoods, of 'Italian' neighborhoods, or 'Jew' neighborhoods, or 'German' neighborhoods is un-American! We must all cherish our heritages, but we must give our only loyalty to America. I say now, and will continue to say, there is no room in this country for 'hyphenated' Americans!

"There are times of trouble ahead. Many of you are newsboys, are you not? Wasn't the fight I broke up this evening about who would sell newspapers where? Well read them, the truthful ones at any rate. Spain is acting like a hungry grizzly bear, set to devour the helpless people of Cuba and the Philippine Islands. And there are the filthy jackals of Anarchy, who belong to no country, who want to destroy the nations of the world, this one included.

"We must be ready to face them. We must stand together. You may take my word for it that when that bear was set to devour me, I would have welcomed the aid of a comrade, no matter where his parents had been born.

"This is not to say we must be soft. A man must know how to fight, or he is no man at all. But we—all of us now, *Americans* —must not fight among ourselves!"

Muldoon wanted to cheer. The boys took it quietly, thoughtfully. They knew that if they happened to be spotted in the wrong neighborhood at the wrong time, their heads were still likely to be cracked open.

But Muldoon mused, if each kid in the room could manage to avoid or prevent just *one fight* in the coming week, it would be like a holiday for cops all over the city.

There is, however, always the skeptic. The scoffer in this crowd was a red-headed Irish—Muldoon made that *formerly* Irish—lad who was just about ready for long pants. Doubtless he was the leader of his gang. He turned to the boy next to him and said, not quietly, "Ahhhh, what's a four-eyes like him know about fightin'?"

VI.

Muldoon saw red. He grabbed the loudmouth by the scruff of his grimy neck and lifted him off the bench. "You want to be havin' a little respect for your betters, whelp. If you had the wit God gave a lamp post, you'd be on your knees thankin' Mr. Roosevelt for not runnin' in the lot of you."

The boy's mouth and eyes were open wide. His head was still filled with grizzly bears, and Muldoon suited the part pretty well.

"P—put me down," the boy stammered. Muldoon looked at the Commissioner, who was trying, without much success, to hide a grin behind his moustache.

"By all means, Officer," he said. "Put the boy down."

Muldoon was reluctant. "I ought to box his ears for him, at least, sir," he said. "It'll do him good."

"Perhaps, but he has offered me a challenge, and I prefer to accept it than to punish him. I will show him what a 'four-eyes' like me knows about fighting."

The Commissioner started to doff his coat. Muldoon felt the boy tremble under his hand. Roosevelt removed his gold cuff-links, and rolled up his sleeves to reveal forearms bronzed by the sun and knotted with muscles.

"Now," he said.

"This is—is *loony*," the red-headed boy said. "I ain't gonna fight *him!*"

The Commissioner folded his arms. "Afraid, eh?"

The word was as good as the first blow. To be branded yellow was the worst thing that could befall a boy. It was to be hated, held in contempt. He was like a carrier of plague to his former comrades, except that they might hold some pity for the carrier of plague.

"Well?" Roosevelt demanded. He took a hissing breath through clenched teeth.

The boy looked at the Commissioner's arms again. He had to raise his hand to his chin to stop it from trembling in order to speak, but he said, "I—I ain't afraid," and began rolling up his ragged sleeves.

The Commissioner threw back his head, held his stomach, and laughed in a series of high pitched explosions of mirth. He ruffled the boy's hair, and gave him a firm clap on the shoulder. "What's your name, son?" he asked.

The boy was too stunned with relief to do anything but answer. "Brian O'Leary."

"Brian O'Leary, *sir*," Muldoon corrected.

"*Sir*," the boy echoed.

"Where do you live?" the Commissioner asked.

"Avenoo C, at Eleventh Street. Sir."

Mackerelville. Muldoon knew it well—he'd grown up there.

"Well, Mr. O'Leary," Roosevelt said, "I'd be dee-*lighted* to shake your hand."

Numbly, Brian put his hand in the Commissioner's. "Oh, come," Roosevelt scolded gently, "a boy with your spirit and grit should have a grip firmer than that. That's better; much better. Now, you take your seat, Brian, and the officer and I will show you what a four-eyes knows about fighting."

He looked at Muldoon, who wore a quizzical expression. "If duty permits," the Commissioner added. "Have we time? Is it another of the Mansion Burglaries?"

"No, sir."

"Is it something that can wait a few minutes?"

Muldoon was still deciding when Roosevelt said, "No? Bully. Now, off with that tunic. That's it, hurry."

Muldoon was cursed, that's all there was to it. You could hardly ask for a man's help after you've beaten him up, even if he ordered you to do it. He was more than half a foot taller than the Commissioner, and a good fifty pounds heavier. He thought of pointing these things out to Mr. Roosevelt, but before he could say anything, he was astonished to hear the man himself calling the attention of the audience to that very contrast. The boys responded with a collective "Oooh."

"I would not ordinarily do this, of course, but simply for

demonstration, I shall not remove my spectacles." He turned to Muldoon, who by this time had removed his tunic, however reluctantly.

"All set, Officer . . . ?"

"Muldoon, sir. Dennis P. F.-X. Muldoon."

The Commissioner beamed and extended his hand. "Dee-lighted. I am Theodore Roosevelt," he said, exactly as though he believed Muldoon needed to be told. "Shaking hands with you would be a breach of decorum, but since we might as opponents instead of as officer and superior, I believe it will be permissible."

Muldoon took the hand. He had hesitated because he thought he was being tested.

"Shall we begin?" Roosevelt suggested.

Muldoon could only shrug and put up his dukes. He resolved to go easy on the fellow. That resolution was shaken scant seconds later when the Commissioner ducked under Muldoon's guard and planted a short left jab squarely on the patrolman's nose. The boys cheered.

Muldoon's reaction was automatic. While he was still counting the stars dancing in front of his eyes, his right fist shot out and sank into Roosevelt's stomach.

"Fine punch!" Muldoon heard him croak, over a roar of disapproval that was led by young Master O'Leary.

The match continued for some minutes, but no further damage of a serious nature was done. Once Muldoon discovered that Mr. Roosevelt was by no means a pudding, he became a much more wary fighter.

They ended it by mutual consent (disappointing the boys, who wanted to see blood, preferably Muldoon's), and broke decorum once more by shaking hands. Muldoon got back into his uniform while the Commissioner addressed the boys.

"So you see, I trust, that the wearing of spectacles in no way makes a man less manly. I count the day I first received my spectacles as one of the great events in my life. I may now and forever be a 'four-eyes'—a term, by the way, I expect none of you to use, or allow to be used in your presence, to taunt someone; it is mean spirited and unworthy of a man—but before, I was so short sighted as to be almost a 'no-eyes' which is far worse." He adjusted his spectacles while the boys laughed.

"Now, all of you, go home. I fear I have kept you out far too late." There were sounds of disappointment. "However," the Commissioner went on, "if any of you ever feels the need to speak to me, my office is in Police Headquarters on Mulberry Street. I shall be delighted to see you. So long," he added, "as you walk in and are not hauled in by Officer Muldoon or one of his brother officers."

The boys agreed happily, and scurried out, shooed along by the desk clerk, who had been standing in the doorway the whole time.

The clerk was troubled. He approached the Commissioner and said, "Mr. Roosevelt, I was pleased when you happened upon these ruffians and broke up their fighting, and I made no objection to your use of the assembly room to lecture them, but this exhibition of—of *pugilism*—"

"Ha!" said Roosevelt happily, shooting a pink cuff as punctuation. "Bully idea! Glad I thought of it, Reverend. In fact, I think it will be a fine idea to make a regular thing of it."

"A regular—" The rest of the Reverend's sentence was swallowed up in a horrified gasp.

"Oh, I won't box a policeman every Saturday night, that would be silly."

The Reverend showed a degree of relief.

"It would serve no purpose," Roosevelt went on. "To really help the boys, we must give them lessons!"

Now even Muldoon was shocked. "Beggin' your pardon, sir, but you ain't aimin' to teach them little hellions how to fight, are you?"

"Ha! That is exactly what I purpose to do. Let them prove their mettle in a ring, with gloves, or bare fists, instead of in the streets with whiskey bottles and cobble rocks. This should be done in every neighborhood in this city!"

He turned to the minister. "I know just the man for you."

"For *me?*" the clergyman squeaked.

"Yes, indeed. Fellow who used to help me keep in trim when I was in the Assembly in Albany. He has just recently left prison and is looking for honest work. He is doing a small chore for me at present, but he will call you in two or three days."

"Prison?"

"Burglary. But Roscoe has paid his debt, Reverend." The Commissioner was suddenly grave. "And he has reformed, or I am no judge of character. It is our Christian duty—"

"But that's just my point," the clergyman protested. "Do you honestly believe it proper to offer instruction in fist-fighting at the New Christian Fellowship?"

"I have never seen anything un-Christian in healthful recreation and exercise. Conversely, I have never thought it particularly desirable for young Christian men to face the world with pale skins and shoulders that slope like champagne bottles."

That convinced the Reverend. Either that, Muldoon thought, or he had simply decided that arguing in the face of one of Mr. Theodore Roosevelt's enthusiasms was like trying to tie a knot in a nightstick. In any case, the clergyman mumbled something about expecting the Commissioner's man to call, and withdrew to his desk.

Roosevelt took in air through his strong white teeth. "And now, Officer Muldoon, I shall rub my stomach, and you shall rub your nose, if you wish, now that no one is watching us." Both men laughed.

Muldoon gently touched his nose. It was bright red, too, he'd wager. It was a good thing Captain Herkimer wasn't here to smell him now.

Muldoon stopped laughing. "Mr. Roosevelt, sir . . ."

"Yes, Muldoon?"

Muldoon told him his story, leaving nothing out from the time he brought Mr. Harvey home—to the current moment. Roosevelt listened without comment, but he'd stroke his moustache, and once or twice, his eyes popped open from their habitual squint, and he'd blow out a breath that would flutter the black ribbon of his spectacles.

". . . So there it is, sir. I don't know if I'm doin' right to be here or not. I'll leave it this way: If I haven't lost me mind —and I'm first to be admittin' the story *sounds* daft—then there's a killer and a naked woman runnin' around this city. Runnin' around *my* beat."

"Hmph," Roosevelt said. "You say Captain Herkimer said you'd been drinking. There *is* the smell about you, you know."

Muldoon tightened his lips. "It's the spillin's of drunks, period. You can smell me blasted breath, if you like."

To his surprise, the Commissioner took him up on it. "Ha!" he said. "No beer. And more important, no cloves or anything else that might disguise the smell of beer." Roosevelt slapped his hands together, as though dusting that part of the problem off them. "Your breath proves you an honest man, Muldoon, so far as your tunic is concerned, at least. The rest, I must say, is the rummest story I ever heard in my life."

Muldoon's heart sank. "Yes, sir," he said sadly.

The Commissioner was mumbling to himself, and took no notice of Muldoon's despondency. "Herkimer" and "blasted crook Byrnes" were among things he whispered. Muldoon had to wonder what Byrnes had to do with anything—he'd been pried away from the Force (but not from his grafted fortune) back in '94.

"I guess I'll have to take whatever's coming to me," Muldoon said but didn't exactly mean.

"Well," Roosevelt said, "rum story or not, all my men will be dealt with squarely. You will come with me immediately, Muldoon, to the scene of the alleged crime."

"You're comin' personally? Now?"

"Naturally. What good is a promise of square dealing if the words are not turned into action?" He motioned for Muldoon to start moving. "Besides, your record speaks in your favor."

"My record?"

Roosevelt's laugh reminded Muldoon of someone triple-tonguing a cornet. "I fought for those competitive examinations, Muldoon. You may wager I shall keep a close eye on those who score the highest grades. I have kept track of your progress, from the waterfront, and now to your current beat. I am pleased to find crime is significantly reduced there."

Muldoon felt the best he had all day. He'd heard of Mr. Roosevelt's prodigious memory, but it never occurred to him that he was important enough in the workings of the Department to have come to the attention of the Police Board, let alone be filed in the mind of the President.

"Thank you, sir," he said. "I do me best. I don't allow the mugs and grifters to go crowdin' the decent citizens off the street.

I don't go in swingin' me billy, mind, but I make sure they know I've got it tucked in me belt. You might say I walk softly, but I carry a big stick."

Muldoon was surprised at the Commissioner's reaction; you might have thought he'd said something clever. Roosevelt laughed and laughed. He slapped Muldoon on the back and said, "That's good, I must remember that one." He removed his spectacles and wiped his eyes, repeating under his breath, *"Speak softly but carry a big stick."*

" '*Walk* softly,' sir," Muldoon corrected.

"Eh? Ha! '*Walk* softly,' then. It's a bully remark all the same. Blast, but I hope you're telling me the truth, Muldoon."

Muldoon did too; by now he was beginning to doubt his story himself. Well, he thought, as he followed the Commissioner from the Fellowship building into the heavy air of the August night, he'd find out soon enough.

VII.

It was a small mark of Theodore Roosevelt's boundless energy that he usually walked everywhere in Manhattan he wanted to go. In the early days of the Strong administration, reporters used to gather around the steps of Police Headquarters to see the Commissioner end his daily eighty-odd-block walk from his sister's house on Madison Avenue and Sixty-second Street to his office at 300 Mulberry Street by *sprinting* up those steps. On the first day of Roosevelt's tenure, the reporters were invited to run up with him—not many ever tried it again.

Lately, though, the Commissioner had taken to riding in cabs. It wasn't that he still didn't prefer walking; it was that he saw the cab-riding as a part of his job.

Crime in hansoms was a chronic problem. A hansom cab was a perfect trap for an unsuspecting swell with a bulging wallet, with its lockable doors, and its trap door to the driver's seat. It was almost proverbial wisdom that one should never get into a hansom with two men on the trap, but people, especially out-of-towners, continued to do it all the same.

So, when the occasion presented itself, Commissioner Roosevelt went looking for cabs with two drivers. He would just like to see the extra man jump down through the trap into the passenger compartment and try to take his money away.

Apparently, though, all the criminal drivers had their vehicles elsewhere. The driver of the cab taken by Roosevelt and Muldoon was distressingly honest, and courteous as well, wishing the Commissioner a very good evening.

"Actually, sir," Muldoon told him, "I don't think any but an honest hackie is likely to be stoppin' for you. Even if you wasn't the best-known man in New York, you'll never pass for an easy mark, and easy pickin's is what they like."

"I suppose you're right, Muldoon," the Commissioner said, as the cab approached Muldoon's beat.

Judging from what he could see through the small window, a person would never think anything out of the ordinary could happen in that neighborhood. There wasn't a cop to be seen, and the crowds had gone to seek excitement in other places.

Muldoon had calmed down considerably. In little bits, Roosevelt had put the patrolman at ease by asking him questions about himself.

"Actually, sir," Muldoon found himself saying, "it was me own idea to join the Force. Me mother intended me for the priesthood, God rest her. That's how I come to be a high school graduate, you see. Many's the time I was for leavin' school and goin' on to a better job at the brewery, drivin' a wagon, maybe, like me father did, instead of workin' the blasted graveyard shift loadin' those gut-bustin' hogsheads onto the drays."

"Well, Muldoon, I believe life must be lived strenuously; with vigor. And hard work has done you no harm. On the contrary, it has left you the legacy of a magnificent muscle structure.

"You know, Muldoon, as a wealthy man's son, I led a soft life in my early years, and I was a sickly, asthmatic child because of it. It wasn't until I put myself on a schedule of vigorous exercise that I began to enjoy good health. Hard effort is a necessity, Muldoon."

"I'm sure you're right, sir," the patrolman replied, "but it'll always be amazin' to me that it hasn't left me the legacy of permanent bags under me eyes. It wasn't the workin' that was so bad, mind, it was the not sleepin' nights." Muldoon sighed. "Still and all," he said, "I'm glad I stuck it out. Seems to me as sensible for a cop to be an educated man as it is for a priest to be."

"How is it you came to change your mind?"

Muldoon made a face and scratched his head. "Well, I *tell* folks it's because just about the time I was to leave for the seminary, me mother and father and me younger brother, Jimmie, all took fever and died, leavin' me alone to care for me three sisters."

Roosevelt held up a hand. "You needn't speak further on the matter, Muldoon. I quite understand. My sincere sympathies." On Valentine's Day, 1884, Theodore Roosevelt's mother and his wife both died. He wrote that day in his diary, "The light has gone out of my life." And though he was very happily remarried, it was obvious much of the grief remained. Muldoon had heard it said that in the twelve years that had passed since the tragedy, Mr. Roosevelt had never once been able to bring himself to utter his first wife's name.

"I thank you very kindly, sir," Muldoon said softly, "but since you've been so square with me, my bein' anything less than square with you would be an insult. And I don't intend to be insultin' the only man I've met tonight who doesn't want to parcel me straight off to the loony bin.

"No sir. It goes without sayin' the loss of me family members was a horrible blow, but I could have taken me Orders and still seen to the welfare of Katie and Brigid and Maureen. I hope, Commissioner, that you haven't taken the notion that the Holy Roman Catholic Church would stand to one side watchin' a priest's family starvin' to death!"

"No, no," the Commissioner hastened to assure him. "I never had a thought like it."

"Thank you, sir," Muldoon said. "The real reason I left off tryin' to become a priest—and I know it does me no credit to have to say it—was females."

"Females?"

Muldoon shrugged helplessly. "They like me, sir. And I can't live without 'em. All that summer I was tryin' to prepare meself for a lifetime of service to the Lord; but everytime a colleen would lower her eyelashes at me, I'd be overcome with an unholy yearnin' to fall from grace."

Muldoon's voice dropped to a whisper. "And, Commissioner, sometimes—well, sometimes I went farther than yearnin'."

"I am *ashamed* of you, Muldoon. That is disgraceful. Men are to protect and care for women, not take advantage of them. Women are not called the weaker sex on the basis of physical strength alone, you know."

"Oh, I agree with you completely, sir. But in all fairness to meself, I feel I should be tellin' you that these particular women didn't seem to be in need of any serious protectin'. And sometimes, I'm thinkin' their weaknesses are stronger than our strength, if you follow me, sir."

"I do *not* follow you!" Roosevelt was angry, now. "You are not absolved of responsibility for a wicked deed because the woman was equally wicked!"

You'll never learn, will you? Muldoon asked himself. Now he had Mr. Roosevelt mad at him. He was doomed.

"I know that, sir. But I knew that as long I was like to fall from grace, and worse, enjoy the fallin', I had no business bein' a priest of God."

"If your behavior is still the same, Muldoon," the Commissioner barked, "you have no business being an officer of the Law! The Police Department of the City of New York is to consist of men of clear grit and finest moral fiber! I mean to have it that way, and I shall not allow anyone's animal appetites to interfere!"

"Sir," Muldoon assured him, "if ever I find meself in a position where I'm like to be disgracin' this uniform, I swear I'll take it off immediately."

For the first time on record, Theodore Roosevelt was struck dumb. He sputtered for a second, then said, *"Muldoon!"*

Muldoon was bewildered. "Sir?"

The Commissioner looked at him, opened his mouth, changed his mind, and closed it again with a snap of his teeth. He polished his spectacles, replaced them, and said, "You should be married, Muldoon. It's not unnatural for a healthy young man to think about such things. That is why God created marriage. Get married, Muldoon."

"I'd like to sir, but—"

"That's an order. See to it as soon as possible."

"Yes, sir," Muldoon said, but he wondered if the Commissioner really had the authority to give an order like that. The Mayor, maybe.

The cab horse clopped around a corner into the block where the murder (or whatever it was) had occurred.

The evening's strange events ran through Muldoon's mind, and with them the gnawing fear that despite his best efforts, he had done something wrong, or unworthy. Or worse yet, that he actually had gone insane.

He fixed his eyes on the front of Mrs. Sturdevant's building as though he expected it to gather up its foundation and run away. It didn't, but something happened that surprised him as much.

"I'll be a blasted Chinaman!" Muldoon exclaimed.

"What is it, Muldoon?" his superior demanded.

"Old Mr. Harvey is goin' out again. I don't believe it."

"Harvey? The drunkard?"

"Yes sir, if you'll recall me tellin' you, I had Mrs. Sturdevant pour him into bed before I went to Listerdale's."

"I remember," the Commissioner said. "But how can you recognize the man at this distance?" He squinted through his spectacles.

"It's the height of him, sir," Muldoon replied. "He's such a little bit of a man. And his clothin'. I'm sure you agree there's no mistakin' *that* jacket."

"No indeed," Roosevelt said. "Ha! And the press calls *me* a fancy dresser."

The figure in the loud coat walked strangely, even for an old man, but there was nothing of the usual stagger about it. It was a faster walk than Mr. Harvey usually managed; the coat was around the corner and out of sight within a few seconds.

Muldoon assumed the first stop would be Crandall's flat, but Roosevelt let the driver keep going until they came to Listerdale's Literary Emporium.

"We'll confirm that part of your story first, Muldoon," he said. They went upstairs to Listerdale's quarters, above the Emporium, and knocked on the door.

Listerdale was still awake and dressed. "A new enterprise demands a lot of extra planning," he explained. Muldoon performed introductions.

"Roosevelt!" Listerdale exclaimed, echoing Muldoon.

Roosevelt laughed. "Certainly I'm not cause enough for all that astonishment, am I?"

"What? Oh, no, forgive me. It's just that I've heard so much about you. I've read many of your books. I sell them in the store. I must say, as a former schoolmaster, you make history, especially military history, horribly real."

"Horribly?" The Commissioner was upset.

"I'm sorry. No reflection on your writing intended, as I said, you make it live. But I'm in agreement with General Sherman when he says 'War is hell'."

"Sometimes, hell must be endured, Mr. Listerdale. It is glorious to conquer, even to die, in the defense of Right. It is base to ignore that responsibility. It is shared by all, and it is the sternest of all tests: the test of righteous war."

"Eloquently put, Mr. Roosevelt. You have carried your point." The Commissioner acknowledged with a bow. "Tell me," Listerdale went on, "when will Mr. Putnam publish the fourth volume of *The Winning of the West?* I have one customer who says he can't wait to discover how it turns out."

There was general laughter, then Listerdale asked how he could be of help. The Commissioner told him what he wanted, and the bookseller obliged with an account of his meeting with Muldoon. He confirmed the patrolman's story, up to the time Mrs. Sturdevant screamed, in every particular. Listerdale went on to say that he was acquainted with the victim, because Crandall once or twice ordered a high-quality drawing paper from him.

"Thank you," Roosevelt said on leaving. "I'll see you get a copy of my book when it appears."

Outside, he turned to Muldoon and said, "Now we'll see if the rest of your story holds water."

VIII.

Muldoon showed the Commissioner to Crandall's rooms and reenacted his discovery of the bodies, first the dead one in the sitting room, then the lively one in the boudoir. The Commissioner listened intently, silent except for an occasional loud, hissing inhalation.

Muldoon guessed Mr. Roosevelt made that noise because his

asthma still caused him some trouble, and he preferred to hiss the air in through his toothy grin than to hint at infirmity by panting or wheezing. Muldoon kept his guess to himself, of course.

". . . And there you have it, sir," he concluded. "The seemin' of it is she vanished into the atmosphere like a human camphor flake."

Commissioner Roosevelt sniffed, as though testing the air for fumes. "Let's first make sure she was here at all, Muldoon." Slowly, being careful of the fabric of his trousers, he knelt beside the canopied bed.

Not knowing anything better to do, Muldoon knelt, too, but it struck him as an odd hour to be saying his prayers. "Mr. Roosevelt?" he said.

"Be still, Muldoon."

"Yes, sir. I was just wonderin' what it is we're at."

"I have no idea what *you're* doing. *I* am casting for a trail."

"Under the mattress, sir?"

For the first time, Roosevelt looked up from his work. "Officer, I know you are aware of my ranch in Dakota. Listerdale told me you have at least perused my book, *Hunting Trips of a Ranchman;* were you also aware that in my time in the Bad Lands I have served as a deputy sheriff?"

Lord, Muldoon thought. Thirty-eight years old, and already he'd been a state legislator, a Western rancher and lawman, a book writer, and the Head Policeman of all of New York City. Whatever was he going to find to do with the rest of his life?

"In fact, sir, I wasn't aware you'd done any sheriffin'. But bless me, if you'd taken the trouble to talk it up more, I'll warrant you'd have made a better showin' when you stood election for Mayor in eighty-six."

"That's irrelevant, Muldoon," Roosevelt snapped. The Commissioner had finished third in a three-man race, behind Abram Hewitt, the Democrat, and Henry George, the radical originator of the single-tax movement. It was not Roosevelt's favorite memory.

"The point is this: If I am not too proud to kneel in mud to look for traces of a cattle rustler, I am not too proud to kneel on the carpeting to look for traces of a missing woman." He gave his attention back to the bed. "*Aha!*" he exclaimed. "See this, Muldoon."

The Commissioner was pointing a strong, square finger at a juncture in the bed frame. A strand of stiff fiber was caught there. Roosevelt plucked it free. "Hemp," he said. "You described a coarse rope, did you not, Muldoon? Tied around the woman and the bed? Well, here's evidence of your sanity. A coarse rope *has* been tied on this bed, and tightly enough to force a strand of it between the wood."

For the first time in hours, Muldoon drew an un-sour breath. "I thank you, sir, with all me heart. 'Twas a work of genius; you've saved both me honor and me hide."

"Nonsense," Roosevelt barked, though he looked pleased. "It's simply a matter of experience. Having been in the West, I know something of rope. In fact, if I can find a few more fibers, I may be able to say precisely what sort of rope this is, and that in itself may be the start of a trail."

"I hope so, sir," Muldoon said. "And if you don't mind, you've started me thinkin'. There's something else I'd like to be checkin' if I might."

"Bully for you! It's high time someone showed some initiative in this matter. Go to it, Muldoon."

Muldoon went to the window, leaned backward out over the sill, and surveyed the wall above the fire escape for marks of the bullet the Pink Angel had fired at him, but to no avail. What with the effects of age, weather, and previous trouble in the neighborhood, those bricks might once have stood at the back of a shooting gallery.

Muldoon sighed, and looked down at the spot in the alley where he'd last seen the girl. He remembered the kiss she blew him, and wondered what that would have felt like without sixty yards of air between her lips and his.

An urgent whisper cut short Muldoon's reverie. "*Muldoon!*"

The constable turned to see the Commissioner standing with his back pressed to the wall alongside the door. He signaled Muldoon to join him.

Someone was creeping across the outer room. Muldoon could hear it now, too. He reached for his revolver, then cursed silently when he remembered it wasn't there.

The footsteps drew nearer, then stopped just outside the door. Roosevelt set his jaw. Muldoon held his breath.

The doorknob wiggled and started to turn, but the intruder's nerve failed, and running footsteps in the opposite direction could be heard.

"Stop him!" bellowed the Commissioner, who immediately followed his own order. He threw the door open, catching Muldoon neatly on the point of the chin, and sprinted after the prowler.

Muldoon shook his head to rattle the stars away from his vision, then ran to follow. From the hallway just outside the sitting room came a great angry sputtering from Mr. Roosevelt, and equally great angry screams from a very indignant landlady.

Muldoon broke it up. "Mrs. Sturdevant," he began.

"Please, madam, I—oof!" said Mr. Roosevelt.

"Take that!" said the landlady.

"Mrs. Sturdevant, please. Stop this. It's me. Officer Muldoon. Dennis. Look." She finally did, but only after Muldoon took her by the chin and twisted her neck to a position where she had to see him.

"Dennis!" she exclaimed. "I demand you put this . . . this *monster* under arrest!"

The Commissioner made a choking noise.

"I'm afraid I can't be doin' that, ma'am," Muldoon said.

"I'd like to know why not! He *attacked* me! He attacked a decent, God-fearing woman in her own house!" She shook a meaty fist. "You arrest him, Dennis. I demand it!"

Muldoon took a deep breath. "Mrs. Sturdevant, I'm afraid we've all been laborin' under a bit of a misapprehension," and he presented the Commissioner to the landlady.

"Delighted, madam. Hah! Pardon me. I shame to admit it, but I took you for a criminal, as I suppose you did us. I do apologize. Muldoon and I wanted not to disturb you."

"Not disturb me! Sneaking in and rummaging around that way? Still, you've been more civil, I have to admit, than that *captain*. Hmpf, I hope Dennis told you about *him*."

Commissioner Roosevelt promised to speak to Captain Herkimer, and informed the lady he needed to return to Crandall's rooms. She grumbled some, but at last gave her blessing.

He was only there a moment, removing the last of the hemp fibers from the bed, and placing them with the rest in the back of his pocket watch.

"Tell me, Mrs. Sturdevant, how did you happen to know Muldoon and I were here at all? As I implied, we tried not to make any undue noise."

"If you made noise, I wouldn't have taken such a fright! I heard you only because I happened to pause just outside the door. You see, I have a batch of bread going—I like my bread fresh on a Sunday morning—and I thought I'd come up and check on poor Mr. Harvey."

"An excellent idea. Have you," the Commissioner grinned, "managed to accomplish your mission?"

"Why, no."

"Then let's see to it immediately."

Mrs. Sturdevant preceeded them across the hall. She paused outside the old man's room. "Hear him whimpering?" she asked.

Muldoon sniffed the air. "I hear somethin' cracklin' in there, too."

When she pushed the door open, the landlady immediately uttered a short, choking scream; Muldoon could only gasp. It seemed to him like total madness.

On this hot August night, Mr. Harvey was sitting, Indian-style, before a bright fire that burned on the hearth. Seemingly mindless of the flames and the way they scorched his hands, he was trying to pull something from the fire. He was crying; in between sobs, he spoke.

"Why couldn't you have at least left me *that?* Why couldn't you *stay?* My love, if you had to go, why couldn't you have left me that to remember you by? Why?"

He buried his face in his blackened hands. Mrs. Sturdevant went to see to him. Muldoon was stupified; he leaned against the door frame. He jumped at the sound of a voice.

"Hah!" said Mr. Roosevelt. "I expected as much!"

Muldoon looked at him.

"Don't just stand there, Officer," Roosevelt told him. "Help me get this poor man to a hospital."

IX.

The small figure in the houndstooth jacket was apprehensive as she looked behind the portrait of George Washington on the papered wall of the Devereaux Hotel. She prayed that the extra key would be there. She trembled with relief when she found it.

She opened the door across from the portrait and entered. As she closed it behind her, she said, "Thank heaven!" It was relief to be able to talk. She'd been afraid to say a word since she left the old man's room. She'd been afraid to come straight here—she'd walked the streets for hours. She smiled at the irony. She'd never been one who'd had to walk the streets.

That cab *would* come by just as she'd decided it was safe to leave. And the passenger would have to be the only man who had seen her and could recognize her. Along with some barrel-chested figure, but she didn't think he mattered.

She had to make sure she wasn't being followed. She'd walked downtown as far as Sixth Street, then walked up Broadway to Tenth, where she joined the bread line at Fleishmann's Vienna Bakery. For some reason, they'd started their famous charity a little earlier than midnight—she'd even received her one-third loaf of bread along with the rest of the homeless and destitute.

But she was home now. The suite was hers, at least until September first—the rent had been paid till then. She had no idea what would happen after that. At the moment she didn't care. She tore off Mr. Harvey's hat, and shook free her long, black hair. She called for her maid, but got no reply.

"Vangie, you lazy thing, wake up!" she called, with the same result.

She went to the maid's quarters, her anger growing. Vangie wasn't there, but there was a note pinned to the pillow. There was trouble, apparently, in Coontown, up in the Seventies around Tenth Avenue, among members of Vangie's enormous and complicated family, that only Vangie could straighten out.

The woman sighed, and went to draw her own bath. While the water ran, she went to the boudoir to undress, as she always did, in front of the tall French mirror. Her feet slipped easily out of the too-large men's shoes. She shed that impossibly loud jacket and the soiled, collarless shirt. She leaned close to the mirror, giving her neck, her shoulders, her more intimate parts a close but businesslike examination. No permanent harm done, she decided. Even now, the red marks from the ropes were fading.

She yawned, then unbuttoned the trousers. They fell to the floor with a heavy thud. She jumped; she'd become used to the weight of it and forgotten it was there. She bent, removed the officer's revolver from the pocket, then kicked the pants away with a flick of a shapely limb. She put the gun in a vanity drawer, then covered her nakedness with a frilly white robe.

She went to her bath, and settled slowly into the tub. The warm water felt good. She rubbed herself lazily with the sponge, then touched the strange birthmark on her thigh. How fascinating the young policeman had found it.

Men had always found it fascinating. Why should the policeman be any different?

And yet, different he was. So shy, and still so gallant, like a character out of Dumas. She'd used him badly. But then, that was the nature of things. Men used women; an intelligent woman could only use them right back.

But she felt strangely guilty all the same. He seemed nice. She hoped a new gun wouldn't be expensive for him to buy. She smiled. If they ever should meet again, she would make it up to him.

She smiled again, leaned back, and closed her eyes, musing about the handsome officer. Why, she'd make him forget she'd ever taken the gun.

The door to the bathroom opened, and the draft of cold air it let in startled her. A man, formally attired, stood in the doorway.

Despite his dress, there was something about the way he held his lanky body that said he was no gentleman. And the way he pointed the policeman's gun at her said the same.

"I believe I've let you soak long enough, Miss Cleo. Come with me, now."

Cleo looked at the man's face—it terrified her. The features were perfect, taken one by one, but the woman had the fancy that each had been intended for a different face. The whole impression of strangeness was reinforced by his ears. They were almost perfectly round, and they had no wrinkles in them.

"How do you know my name?" Cleo demanded.

"The fact that I know it is enough for now. Are you coming, or do I have to—"

The man's words seemed to be swallowed up in anger. He stepped rapidly toward the tub. Cleo wanted to scream, but before she could the man's big hand forced her head below the surface of the water.

SUNDAY
the twenty-third
of August, 1896

I.

His sister woke him by pinching his nose. One of Dennis Muldoon's earliest memories was his resentment of Katie's waking him that way. Restless sleep had gummed Muldoon's right eye closed, but with an effort, he managed to pry the left one open. He closed it again immediately. The morning sun came slantwise through the parlor window of the Muldoons' Sixteenth Street tenement, bathing the cot where Dennis slept with a warm yellow light. It gave him a slightly nauseous sensation of being covered in melted butter.

Muldoon pulled the pillow over his face and counted chimes. "Lord save us, Katie," he said when they finished. "It's only seven o'clock."

"Those bells are from the Italian church on Twelfth, as you are well aware, brother darlin'."

"Katie, think what you like about Italians, but they do know how to tell the time." He groaned again. "And I hate to be tellin' you what time I come in last night."

She knew what time he'd come in last night. She'd been worrying about him, though of course it wouldn't do to say so. Dennis was the Muldoon, now, the man of the house, and a good man he was, at that. All the same, he was her little brother, and all her life she'd been used to minding him and wiping his nose for him, and it was a hard habit to break.

Kathleen Theresa Marie Muldoon had a sure sense of family responsibility, and it was all the more important to her because she realized this was all the family she was ever likely to have.

She pinched her brother's nose again. "I'll be havin' no more excuses from you," she said. "We're goin' to the eight o'clock mass at Saint Mary's, so you'd best be bustlin'."

Muldoon sighed. "You know, Katie, I'm sure Ma is lookin' down from Heaven and smilin'. I'll wager she made you promise before she passed on you'd follow in her footsteps and never let me get a minute's rest."

"Up with you!" Katie said, in her I-shall-brook-no-nonsense tone. "Brigid and Maureen are up already, and they'll be wantin' to come through the parlor on the way to the privy. It won't do for you to be lyin' here like one of them other Saturday Night Irishmen we left behind in Mackerelville."

Mackerelville started at Fourteenth Street and ran southward, so the Muldoons had left it all of two blocks behind them, on Avenue C. Dennis told his sister he resented the word "other," but she ignored him.

"Besides, they'll be wantin' to use the big lookin' glass—I told them they could wear the pretty bonnets you bought for them Eastertime."

"And will you be wearin' yours?"

Katie sniffed. "I'm too old by several years to be wearin' frills the likes of that. I've told you more than once buyin' me that bonnet was a foolish extravagance."

"Sure, you've one foot and three toes of the other in the grave. Listen, Katie me darlin', this isn't Ireland, where a girl who isn't three times a mother by the age of twenty just ain't tryin'. You're a handsome woman, and a good one, but you're givin' up too much of yourself to the family. What are you, all of thirty-one, for cryin' out—"

"I'll not hear another word of it!" Katie snapped. Muldoon shook his head and shut up.

"Will you be takin' Holy Communion today?" Katie asked.

Muldoon examined his conscience. Between holding naked women in his arms, finding dead bodies, and being thought daft by all and sundry, he was sure he must have sinned in thought and word, if not in deed.

"No," he said," I don't expect I will be."

"You'll be wantin' your breakfast then," said his sister, and went off to fix it.

She grumbled as she stirred the porridge. Dennis was always going on about her staying home all the time, and never seeing anybody whose name wasn't Muldoon. But that was her place, wasn't it? It was where she wanted to be, making a home for the family.

But how long would the family stay together? Katie tried angrily to put the thought by in the instant it came to her, but it stayed in her mind and insisted on an answer.

One of these days, one of Dennis's women would reel him in, and neither of the girls was destined to stay single long. Brigid was seventeen, Maureen fifteen, both small and dimpled and dark haired the way Ma had been, not big and fair and loud like Da and Dennis and herself.

It might be happening already. Just last week, Dennis had had a talk with Brigid's beau in the parlor with the door closed. Just a matter of time. And when the rest of the family were all out on their own, what would become of Katie?

Some steam came off the porridge and clouded Katie's eyes. She wiped her face on her apron, and called her brother in to breakfast.

After mass, Muldoon brought the family home, announcing he had to go to the precinct for a little while. Maureen protested. She was a budding young woman now, but she still showed displeasure with a baby's pout. "You promised you'd help me with my reading," she said. Of all the Muldoons, Maureen alone had lost her brogue.

"I'll be comin' back in no time," he promised. "Besides, can't

Brigid be helpin' you? I'm not the only one in this family with an education, am I?"

"I'm goin' to be workin' this afternoon, Dennis." Brigid Muldoon had a beautiful, sweet voice, which she used all the time except when she was at work, where they made her speak in a terrible whine.

"I thought," her brother said, "I'd made it clear I don't like for you to be workin' Sundays. Mr. Alexander Graham Bell may be a heathen Scotchman, but you ain't."

"I'm doin' a favor for a girl," Brigid said. She didn't tell him she wanted to go to work to have a chance to see her fellow, a cracker-jack telephone maintenance man, but he suspected it all the same.

"Well, all right today, but don't go makin' a habit of it." He turned to his youngest sister. "I'll help you as soon as I get home, Little One. What is it you're readin'?"

"Shakespeare," said Maureen. She was always reading one play or another, but she had some trouble with the hard words.

"Ah, Shakespeare," Muldoon echoed. "A genius. An immortal. I go so far as to say there aren't ten men in New York the equal of Shakespeare. What's the play?"

"*Macbeth*."

Muldoon smiled. "Another heathen Scotchman, eh? Well, we'll deal with him. I've just a trivial bit of straightenin' up to do at the police station first."

II.

At the precinct, Mr. Theodore Roosevelt was conversing with Captain Herkimer.

"I—ah—I wasn't aware you had taken an interest in this case, Mr. Roosevelt," the captain said. Herkimer twisted a finger in his beard. He was trying to figure the Commissioner's angle in this. He didn't like Roosevelt; Roosevelt didn't like him. Still, one drunken patrolman wasn't enough to get the President of the Police Board to come to the precinct Sunday morning. Herkimer would play it cautiously—the promotion hearings were coming up.

"I take an interest in anything that concerns the Department,"

Roosevelt replied. He glared at the captain for even daring to ask the question.

"Oh, I didn't mean that, sir—"

"I'm sure you didn't. Now, let's make certain we have understood each other. What are your plans concerning this Muldoon. You plan to suspend him from duty?"

"To have him dismissed, sir."

Roosevelt cleared his throat and hissed.

"Is anything the matter, Mr. Roosevelt?" the captain asked. "Can I get you some water?"

"No, Herkimer, blast it, everything is fine. To avoid delay, I will make the order dismissing Muldoon now, if you wish."

"I'd be grateful if you would, sir," Herkimer said. Damnation, he thought, what is Roosevelt's game?

The Commissioner looked up from his writing and asked if he might have another piece of paper and an envelope. He wrote for a few more seconds, then folded the paper in half, covering the writing.

"Would you be so kind as to witness my signature, Captain?" He signed, and Herkimer signed as witness. Then Roosevelt sealed the document in the envelope and put it in his breast pocket.

Just then, the sergeant poked his head into Herkimer's office. "Officer Muldoon to see you, Captain."

"Wait a moment," said the Commissioner. "Now, Herkimer, I must leave. I'll use the other door. The sight of the man—well, I would find it unsettling. Now, you know the sort of story he can tell, so don't listen to him. Is that understood?"

Captain Herkimer said it was, and the Commissioner took his leave. Muldoon was allowed to enter the captain's office.

III.

Cleo awoke with a roaring in her ears. She was still underwater, still drowning. She sobbed, and came to her senses when she heard herself. She couldn't have sobbed underwater.

She opened her eyes to see the sunlight streaming through a small window high up on the wall. She was in a bed, a perfectly comfortable bed, in a small but well appointed room. There were curtains on the windows. There was a wooden door. She ran to the door and tried it. As she somehow knew it would be, it was locked. She was imprisoned again, and she didn't like it.

She was naked again, but at the foot of the bed she could see her very own calfskin grip. At any rate, her captors were getting more considerate.

She had a terrible headache. That seemed, to be sure, a natural result of being nearly drowned, but how had she *not* been drowned? She had been brought here (wherever that was) unconscious, but not, she was sure, from being underwater. Who could tell how long one person or another could withstand being immersed? If he'd kept her under somehow while he'd packed her grip, she would cerainly have died.

The sunlight was very strong, and Cleo wasn't about to let it mar the pink clarity of her skin. Carefully, she dressed herself (the man who'd nearly drowned her had brought a hat as well) before she looked out the window.

She was, she observed, in a gabled room of a huge four- or five-story house in the country. No, in the suburbs, rather, because over the trees, she could see the roofs of similar buildings not far away.

Then, looking south along the house, she saw the corner of a massive stone structure. And as soon as she did, she knew where she was. That was the Croton Reservoir, the source of the city's drinking water, the one they were going to tear down soon to build the new public library. So the house and its land were on Forty-second Street, between Fifth and Sixth avenues.

If it had been possible for Cleo's face to show ugliness, it would have been ugly now, contorted as it was by anger and hatred. She knew who lived here, and she would stand for no more nonsense.

She became aware again of the roaring that had awakened her. It was getting louder. Down below, she saw a strange vehicle rolling up the private drive toward the rear of the house. It was a horseless carriage, or, what was that other word? An auto mobile. She knew he owned one, but catch him giving *her* a ride in it, no matter how much she begged.

As the auto mobile drew closer to the house, Cleo could see the two men in it, both wearing dustcoats, caps, and goggles. She had no idea who the gaunt gentleman with the white beard was, but she recognized the dapper figure gripping the tiller. She knew the cap covered a bald spot, and that his money belt never contained less than three thousand dollars. His name was T. Avery Hand, the financier all the newspapers called "The Boy Whiz of Wall Street" or "Lone Hand." He was the man who paid the rent on Cleo's suite at the Devereaux; the man who had bought the calfskin grip and everything Cleo might ever put in it. And he was also the man who six weeks ago had sold her into the perverted slavery of the late Mr. Evan Crandall.

All her young life, Cleo had lived by her wits as well as by her beauty, but those wits deserted her now. Leaning dangerously out the gable window, she shook her fists at the men below, screaming threats and imprecations with such passion they could scarcely be understood.

She screamed so loudly, she never heard the lock. She never heard the footsteps behind her, until she was pulled from the window. The tall man in formal attire stifled her screams with the same hand that had held her underwater just hours ago.

IV.

T. Avery Hand brought the auto mobile to a stop at the rear entrance of his home. "Here we are, Reverend," he said. "I'll have Baxter put it in the carriage house later."

Soft spoken and small boned, T. Avery Hand was often mistaken for a minor clerk among his own board of directors. He'd never intended to be one of the 'ruthless financial manipulators of the Nation's economy,' and didn't especially enjoy being one. It was just the way Fate had decided to deal with him. Fifteen years ago, when he was quite a young man, he was thinking about steam engines, when he happened upon an idea for a valve that could cut the cost of running a locomotive by some 30 percent. With the price the coal industry was obliged to pay him to suppress his invention, he was able to lay the foundation of what was now a truly impressive fortune.

In amassing that fortune, however, he'd learned that of all the proverbs his mother had taught him, only two really applied: "Anything worth doing is worth doing well"; and "Render unto Caesar the things which are Caesar's." It took, he had discovered, an extraordinary amount of rendering to do business well.

"Do you trust him with such an expensive piece of machinery, Avery?" his companion asked. "I must say, this is a daisy of a machine; a *daisy*."

Hand smiled shyly for a fraction of a second. "Good of you to say so, Reverend. This was made to my order by the Duryea Brothers. It is twin to the one that won the Chicago to Waukegan fifty-five-mile endurance race last winter. The gasoline engine stood up to the cold better than Benz's electric could."

The clergyman was proud. "That's American handiwork for you," he said. "That," he repeated, "is American handiwork."

White haired, bright eyed and bearded, the Reverend Mr. Lewis Burley might have resembled a prophet from the Bible, had he taken himself that seriously. As it was, he resembled only himself—a good natured, if somewhat pompous, Nebraska clergyman with the annoying habit of repeating himself every time he spoke. It was something he'd started doing back at the theological seminary, where his assigned sermons always seemed to be twelve minutes short. Then one day, it occurred to him to repeat phrases at random, and it had worked so well, he had never stopped.

"No, Reverend," Hand said. "I don't worry about the well-being of my machine. Baxter is quite as good a driver as I am It's a pity men of his station will never be able to purchase their own. Though they may want them badly enough. That's why I purchased a mastiff to protect it. The dog has the run of the property at night."

Reverend Burley was a staunch believer in Progress. "Oh, surely, Avery, with time, the common people . . ."

Hand shrugged. "An auto mobile is a work of art. There's a fellow named Ford who has some scheme to mass-produce them, but I told him what a dreamer he was, and sent him on his way."

The Reverend removed gloves and goggles, cap and duster. "I know nothing of business, nothing at all. But perhaps, perhaps Avery, after the election, and you are—"

A woman started screaming horribly.

"What was that?" the clergyman demanded. "What was it?"

Hand couldn't breathe. He wanted to rush into the house, to make sure nothing had happened to Cleo. But he couldn't with Burley there. Burley mustn't know about her, ever.

Hand took control of himself, and with the same alertness

that had helped him corner the market in india-rubber last year, improvised a story.

"One of the servant women, Reverend. The poor woman was putting up preserves, knocked over the pot, and scalded herself quite badly with hot wax, or whatever it is they use. The doctor refused even to let her be moved to a hospital. She is in great pain, and sometimes she cries out."

"The poor soul," Mr. Burley said. "The poor soul. Take me to her, Avery. Take me to her."

Even as he said it, the screaming stopped.

Hand sighed with relief. "She—ah, wouldn't see you, Reverend. She is of the Roman faith. Superstitious. A good woman, but sadly, ah, misguided in spiritual matters."

"Ah, I see. Well, then, I shall pray for an end to her pain. I shall pray fervently."

"You are a good man, sir," Hand said. "It will be an honor to join your family." It wasn't pleasant, Hand reflected, to string the old gentleman along this way, but it was necessary.

"It will be our honor to have you. Our honor. And I have news, excellent news, from William. He says he will try to re-arrange his schedule so that he may be here next Sunday when you and my daughter are wed. He is my dear, dear friend, as you know. As he is yours."

"Oh, yes, Reverend," Hand said. He knew it, all right. "Perhaps we might change the wedding to a date in March, and Mr. Bryan will let us marry on the lawn of the White House."

"Ho ho," laughed Mr. Burley. "I'm afraid you will be too busy by then, Avery, far too busy."

He laughed; Hand joined in. It would indeed be out of the question. If things went according to plan, by March, T. Avery Hand would be Secretary of the Treasury of the United States, and too busy by far for frivolities like weddings on the White House lawn.

V.

"In short, Muldoon," Captain Herkimer concluded, "you are dismissed."

"*Dismissed!* What is this, a flamin' *joke?* I was standin' right next to Mr. Theodore Roosevelt himself when he was sortin' out evidence. The girl was there, Captain! Mr. Roosevelt said so! She went down the fire escape, just like I said. Then, durin' the confusion, while the landlady and me was callin' for reinforcements, she climbed back *up* the fire escape, only this time she went into old Mr. Harvey's rooms. Don't you see, that's why she couldn't be found durin' the searchin' of the streets.

"Now, I don't know what she was plannin' to do with him— she was carryin' me gun, though I can't believe she'd go harmin' the old man—but she got a stroke of luck, what with Mr. Harvey mistakin' her for the ghost of his wife."

"The ghost of his wife," the captain said.

"Yes, sir. I've seen a daguerrotype of the late Mrs. Harvey, and there's a passin' resemblance."

Herkimer nodded slowly. "I presume this Mr. Harvey was holding a seance? He's an Egyptian, perhaps? A professional spiritualist?"

Muldoon explained about Mr. Harvey's drunken visions. "And last night bein' the anniversary of his wife's passin', he'd be all the more ready to believe it was her he was seein'."

"Go on, Muldoon," Herkimer said. Let the young fool hang himself, he thought.

"Not much more to be tellin'. She waited till the coast was clear, then started the paintin' of her to burnin' in the fireplace, and made her getaway in Mr. Harvey's clothes. The two of 'em are of a size; he's a very small man.

"Mr. Roosevelt and I saw her leavin'! Of course, we didn't realize it at the time."

"Muldoon," the captain said, "have you ever thought of consulting an alienist?"

"A what, sir?"

"An alienist. A mind man. A crazy-doctor, Muldoon."

"I never," Muldoon said with restraint, "have felt an overpowerin' need to see one, Captain."

"Uhh," Herkimer grunted. "Mr. Roosevelt was with you. That is your position, is it not?"

"It is."

"And he will support your word?"

"Sure as we're standin' here. They're mostly his words, after all. He be tellin' them to you himself, as soon as he gets here."

"He will, will he?" Herkimer's voice suddenly exploded. "I'm weary of you, Muldoon! Roosevelt has been here and gone, and this is what he left!"

He thrust the order at him. Muldoon took it and read it, paralyzed with disbelief. "What kind of blasted crooked game are you runnin' here?" he said at last.

"You are dismissed, Muldoon. I hope never to be inconvenienced by your presence again."

"You'll be a damn sight more than inconvenienced, and this Roosevelt with you!" Muldoon told him. "I'll be nobody's patsy. I'll get the truth of this thing if I have to tear the city down rivet by rivet. Then we'll see what Mr. Hearst will be makin' of it, or Mr. Pulitzer, or one of the others."

"Now, see here, Muldoon—"

"How clean are your skirts, Captain?" Muldoon waited two seconds for an answer that didn't come. He leaned over the desk and shook a finger under the captain's nose. "Beware the fury of a patient man, Herkimer. An Englishman said that, but it's true all the same. And that's me one and only warnin'."

Muldoon stalked out, mumbling. Try to do your duty, and look what happens. Might as well have stayed at the brewery. What could he ever do about this ungodly mess?

He cussed under his breath all the way home. He paid little attention to where he walked. Even the incredible clamor of traffic at Union Square failed to distract him. The place where Broadway, Fourth Avenue and Fourteenth Street met was one of the city's busiest intersections. Muldoon was almost crushed between two horse cars at Dead Man's Curve, that section of track at the south end of the Square where the trolleys and horse cars whipped around at such speeds they frequently tipped over.

Muldoon jumped out of the way, considered the state of his life, then thought of jumping back in. After reflection, though, he decided it would be just too much to commit suicide on a Sunday, and proceeded home.

VI.

His sisters had some interesting news for him when he arrived.

"Well, it's himself," Kate said. "A gentleman came callin' for you while you were out."

"A very important gentleman," Maureen added. Her eyes were bright.

"Dennis, you should have let on to us how you've been movin' in such elevated circles."

Muldoon narrowed his eyed. "Are you tryin' to tell me *Roosevelt* was here?"

Katie nudged her baby sister. "Mind, Maureen, how well your brother does in hobnobbin' with the upper crust. He don't even have to give the man a 'Mister'."

"Of all the chrome-plated *nerve!*" Muldoon threw his hands in the air. "I don't believe it. I don't believe it!"

Katie and Maureen wanted to know what the matter was.

"Never mind that, for the moment," Muldoon said. "Just let it rest at this: After what happened this mornin' at the precinct, I'd sooner expect to be seein' the Grand Sultan of the Ottoman Turks come knockin' at that door than I would *Mister* Theodore Roosevelt. When was he here?"

"About an hour ago. Katie said we wouldn't mind his waiting for you, but you were an awful long time coming home."

"I was takin' a walk. I had a lot on me mind."

"He stayed for a little while. He—he helped me a bit with my Shakespeare. He said you were a good boy."

Muldoon rubbed his chin. "Called me a boy, did he?"

"I don't think he meant any offense, Dennis."

Muldoon snorted. Maureen went on, "Anyway, after a bit, he pulled out his watch, said he had an appointment, and left. He said he'd be back sometime early in the evening."

"Ah, so he's comin' back." Muldoon smiled shyly and sat in his favorite chair. He slipped off his Sunday shoes and leaned back with his hands clasped behind his head.

"But tell me, me darlin's," he said, "how did you know this was the real Theodore Roosevelt come callin'?"

Katie sniffed. "He ain't hard to recognize. You've been talkin' about him enough since you joined the Force, and I see the newspapers, too. A big walrus of a man with a moustache to match, dressed like a dude, wearin' spectacles, and all the time goin' '*hsssssst!*' through his teeth, who else should I be takin' him for? Besides, he had a visitin' card. I've saved it somewhere."

She opened her sewing basket and removed the card. Muldoon took it, looked at the engraving on the front. There was a message on the back, as well: "*Muldoon, I must speak with you as soon as possible—T.R.*"

It had been the genuine article at the door, all right. That was the same handwriting that had dismissed Muldoon from the Force. He told his sisters all about it.

Maureen was close to tears; Katie was as angry as Muldoon himself. "What are we goin' to do about this, Dennis?" she asked grimly.

"We're goin' to have a pleasant Sunday afternoon," Muldoon said. "Just the three of us. And we're goin' to wait until Mr. Theodore Roosevelt decides to return."

VII.

"Sit down, Baxter," said T. Avery Hand to his employee. "Reverend Burley has left."

"It wouldn't be proper, sir."

"Hang what's proper. I realize there is a certain set of standards a man of substance is expected to adhere to, but most of them are silly, and I will not be held to them in private."

Baxter sat on one of the chairs around the ornate dining table (a French king had once eaten off it) where Hand was having his second breakfast. Hand ate seven meals a day. Sometimes he ate to the point of nausea, and hated the whole process. But one of the things the public expected from a man of substance was that he have as good a corporation between his suspender-straps as he had on Wall Street. And since Hand's was a nervous constitution, it was all he could do to maintain the minimum corpulence for respectability.

"Did you want me for anything special, sir?" Baxter inquired through a smile. Hand frowned. Baxter was often smiling at things Hand didn't find amusing in the slightest.

The millionaire conveyed a bit of steak to his mouth with a gold fork. He had once calculated that the cost of one of those forks would pay one of his factory hands for a week. That, by God, was Wealth.

"You know perfectly well what I want you for, Baxter," Hand said.

"What's that, sir?" Baxter asked. He pointed politely at Hand's moustache. "A piece of egg."

"Curse it," Hand said. Eggs fried in ambergris had been the favorite food of Napoleon the Great, and Hand was fond of it, too, but it tended to make his moustache smell for the rest of the day.

"The woman, Baxter. The woman. I know that voice, though it scream the house down. Where did you find her? How did she come to be here?"

It was hard to read Baxter's smile. Baxter had come to him over a year ago, with excellent references from his previous employer, an American living in London, and had made himself indispensable to the industrialist. Still, there was something reserved about him, something Hand found made him uneasy.

"I wish I could say I found her. Someone else did. He told me Crandall was dead—"

"Crandall dead!" Hand hardly dared believe it. Crandall had held the millionaire's future hostage.

"Yes, it was in the papers. I suppose it's just as well you and the Reverend didn't stop for one coming in from your outing in the country."

Hand finished his eggs. "I never could have restrained myself." Hand lowered his voice. "I love her, Baxter," he said simply. "But for the accident of birth, she might . . ."

"She doesn't think kindly of you at the moment," Baxter warned. "She doesn't understand the bargain you struck with Crandall."

"I would have gotten her back, curse it. Couldn't she have had a little patience? Dammit, Baxter, I'm going to make her the mistress of the richest man in the world. These things take time."

Baxter regarded him with what Hand took for wonder. At last the butler said, "I'm sure she'll come around, sir."

Hand leaned back, patted his swollen stomach, and stifled an eructation with an embroidered napkin. "Of course, she will. She's . . . ah . . . a smart girl." He paused a few seconds. "Ah . . . do you really think so?"

"I haven't told you how she came to be here," Baxter said, cracking his knuckles.

"Ah, yes, please do."

"It was a mysterious telephone call. Someone calling himself 'Rabbi'."

"A Jew?" Hand snorted. "How much money did he want?"

"He didn't mention money."

"I am astonished," Hand said, and rose from the table. "Well, if he calls back and asks for some, give it to him."

"He did mention something else, Mr. Hand."

"Yes?"

"He suggested you speak to the young lady about the bill of sale."

Hand sat back down. "The bill of sale? D-didn't she have it with her? Didn't she take it along?"

"No, sir," Baxter said flatly.

Hand turned white, and stared blankly ahead of him. Without the bill of sale, his plans were still in grave jeopardy.

Sometimes, just sometimes, the opulent mansion of T. Avery Hand would slip from his eyes, and Hand would perceive how much his life had been and still was a figment of his own imagination. At such moments, he was amazed at his own audacity. To even *think* that he could capture the command of the Treasury of the United States and run it as a branch of his business enterprises, when such a tawdry thing as love (and oh, he did love her) could cause such complications. It seemed to be the scheme of a lunatic.

But dammit, he had been born too late. The money and the power that came easily had been gobbled up by Gould and Morgan and the Van Derbilts years ago. His whole empire had been based on long-shot gambles, and this was to be the greatest.

Suddenly he had an idea. "Baxter, bring me the telephone."

When he had received the instrument, he told Central to get him a certain police precinct. When the precinct answered, he asked for Captain Herkimer.

"Yes, Herkimer," he said. "Avery Hand, here. I just wanted to tell you, friend to friend, that if I owned a few shares in bicycle pumps, I'd expect to be a happy man in a couple of months. Don't mention it."

"Now, I understand there was rather a bizarre . . ." He looked at Baxter.

"Suicide," whispered the butler.

"Suicide," Hand said. With two fingers he drew patterns on the tablecloth while Herkimer told him of the death. "Renegade officer, eh?" he said after a while. "Good, slap him down, make an example of him.

"Now, this Crandall, I understand, kept some odd things, something a—a friend of mine may have lost. What's that? No? Well, my—my friend will be grateful to whoever finds it. Do you follow me, Herkimer? Good. Good day."

He dropped the earpiece. Baxter retrieved it and put the telephone together properly. Hand was back to staring into space.

"He doesn't have it, Baxter. He doesn't have it. If he'd found it, he would have used that information to squeeze me, and he didn't."

There was a rather long silence.

"Baxter?" Hand said at last.

"Yes, sir?"

"What am I going to do?"

Baxter shrugged. "Fate sir. All I can see to do is follow this Rabbi's advice."

VIII.

Hand took hold of himself as he climbed the broad, carpeted stair. He reminded himself of all he'd achieved already, of the obstacles that had been already overcome. After all, Crandall had first been placated, and now somehow, was no more. Problems could be dealt with.

Wasn't he, after all, the richest Democrat in New York, saving only, perhaps, William Randolph Hearst himself? And he'd only been a Democrat a short time, since June, when Bryan had been nominated. Then he'd switched. Been converted, he'd told the press, to Free Silver.

What he'd actually been converted to was the scent in the wind, the one that told him he could be one of the few (if not the only) industrialists in the country to back Bryan. It was the same wind Hearst had sniffed, and it had brought them together in the hierarchy of the Bryan campaign.

Bryan needed money. McKinley had Hanna's war chest, Bryan had only Hand. It was costing Hand a fortune, but if it paid off, the gamble would be worth it many times over.

And anything that would help the gamble pay off must be done. Early on, Hand had met Reverend Burley. The parson was supposed to be helping his young friend, the candidate, with speechwriting, but if there was one thing William Jennings Bryan needed no help with, it was speaking.

But that wasn't important. The parson had a daughter. The daughter was homely. She had prepared (and privately published) *A Child's Study Guide to* The Pilgrim's Progress, *With Elucidation of All Moral Teachings and Explanation of Allegory;* which was more unreadable than the original work of Bunyan's; something Hand hadn't imagined possible. She was nearing forty and suicidal desperation at the same rate.

Hand volunteered to relieve the desperation. The parson had made noises about a proposal coming so close after a first meeting, but Essie May screwed up her face and cried, and said she'd do terrible things if she couldn't marry the handsome little millionaire from New York. Confronted with that, the parson said there, there, patted his daughter's shoulder, and relented. So it was a settled thing.

Cleo was supposed to make it all bearable. How could Hand know Crandall would come along with his blackmailing ways and take her from him? And now Cleo was even holding him responsible for it.

For a long time, Hand had had problems coming to grips with the idea that he was actually in love with Cleo. It was a weakness. Anything a man wanted could be used against him; Crandall knew that; he had used Hand's desire for power to get Cleo away from him.

Now, though, somehow, Hand had Cleo back. And come hell or high water, there'd be no getting her away from him again.

Hand took a deep breath, and knocked lightly on the door of Cleo's room.

Cleo had been thinking, too. At first, she had thought that at first sight of T. Avery Hand, she would claw his eyes out. She soon realized, though, that her strength was not violence, but guile. She was not yet twenty, but she could never have survived as long as she had if she hadn't learned to wait, watch, and listen—and be nice to men, especially men with money.

Then too, the waters here were deeper than they seemed. One thing she remembered from her near-drowning last night was Smooth-Ears warning her not to tell Hand about any of it, or he would see to it her face wouldn't be fit for the bottom of a cuspidor. She would heed that warning, at least for now.

"Who is it?" she said, though she recognized the sound of the knock.

The door opened, and Hand walked in. He looked such a schoolboy, Cleo could never understand how he made a penny on Wall Street.

"Darling?" he said.

She turned her back to him. She could almost feel him wince behind her.

"Cleo, please." More silence. "You're back now, and I swear, may I lose all my holdings if I lie, that I never meant for it to be this way. It's over for you—your ordeal, I mean. Can't you be nice?"

On hearing that, Cleo felt her calm resolve vanish. She spun on him. "*Nice?*" she cried with a loud, synthetic laugh. "Nice? After you sold me, like some black slave, to that *maniac?* Do you have any idea what he *did* to me?"

From the contortions of Hand's face and hands, Cleo could tell the millionaire was suffering. And that suited her fine.

Hand was almost unable to meet her eyes. "Wh—what did he do?" he whispered.

Hand and Cleo were precisely the same height, so it wasn't easy for the young woman to look down her nose at him, but somehow she managed it. "Why do you ask, Avery?" she said haughtily. "Are you afraid your goods have been damaged in handling?"

"Oh, darling, don't torment me this way," the millionaire moaned.

Cleo had heard of Charles Darwin, most people had, but aside from people being just some new kind of monkey, she didn't know much about his theories. She did, though, have her own ideas about the Survival of the Fittest, and it had nothing to do with who your grandfather was. Cleo knew there were many ways to be fit, and she picked one to suit each occasion. Sometimes she ran like a rabbit, or hid like a turtle. With Hand, it was best to be meek and wide-eyed, like a fawn the hunter can't bring himself to shoot. She had almost forgotten.

"He—he tied me up, Avery," she whispered.

"The brute!" Hand ran to the woman and wrapped his arms around her. "I should have killed him myself, if he hadn't committed suicide."

Cleo said nothing.

"You are trembling," Hand said. "Now, don't think any more about it."

Hand broke off his embrace, and started to pace the room. He paced six steps one way, then six steps the other, all the time holding his hands clasped behind him. He gave the impression that if he were picked up and set in the middle of the Desert of Arabia, with nothing but flat emptiness separating him from the horizon, he would still continue to pace those six steps.

Just when Cleo thought she would go mad from watching him, Hand stopped pacing and said, "Cleo?"

"Yes, Avery?"

"Then what did he do?"

"Then what did who do?" Cleo asked.

"That swine, Crandall. What did he do after he . . . after he tied you up."

"Oh, Avery, must I? It is torture for me to even think of it."

"I know, darling. But I must know. Just this once. Please?"

Cleo suppressed a smile. She might not fully understand what was going on, but she could still make Hand dance to her tune.

"He *painted* me, Avery," she said. "Or drew pictures of me, with charcoal. Or just stood, looking at me. Day and night. Hardly any time for meals, and when he *did* feed me, he said it was to 'maintain my glorious form.' He—he tied me again," Cleo started to sniffle, "any time he left the room."

Cleo's tears were tears of anger. The very memory of it made her itch for revenge against the dead man. In her lifetime, Cleo had been bought, sold, given, and borrowed, but no way she'd ever been treated, and nothing she'd ever done, had made her feel as low as what Crandall had made her do. He'd made her feel like a *thing*, a still life, a bowl of fruit, or a piece of driftwood. She'd been suffered to exist because the artist had found her pleasing to look at.

She was trying to find the right words to impress this on Mr. T. Avery Hand, who, after all, had had no small part in her humiliation. But Hand had other things on his mind.

He was thinking of Crandall's death. Suicide, as it seemed, or murder, as that patrolman Herkimer had mentioned insisted, that bill of sale was not to be found in Crandall's room.

Unless Herkimer had lied to him. But why should he have? At least in so subtle a fashion? No, Hand was convinced Herkimer was playing it square. The captain had a reputation as an honest man—once bought, he stayed bought.

Who had the paper then? And what did they plan to do with it? For certain, it wasn't the Republicans who had it. Hand shuddered at the thought. If Hanna, or any other McKinley man had gotten that paper, the extras would be on the street even now— BRYAN BACKER'S LOVE-SLAVE SOLD TO DEAD MAN. Oh, wouldn't Pulitzer have loved to have gotten hold of that.

A shrewd grin that usually meant trouble for Hand's business opponents crossed his face. The corpse must be the key. The patrolman, whoever he was, must be right. Whoever had the paper must have killed Crandall, for some reason as yet unknown to Hand.

The industrialist smiled. The biggest, sharpest political dagger of the campaign, and it was too dirty for either side to pick up and stick in the other. So far.

He nodded, then reached tentatively for one of Cleo's soft hands. Hs smiled when she did not pull it away.

"I," he said, "have missed you more than I can say, my darling."

Cleo looked him straight in the eye. "And I you, Avery," she lied. Well, perhaps it wasn't a lie. Whatever Hand's shortcomings, at least he didn't tie her up.

Too few minutes later, there was a knock on the bedroom door.

"Mmmmff," Hands said. "What is it, Baxter, damn it?"

"Someone," the butler said, "to see you, sir."

"Tell him to go away."

"He calls himself 'Rabbi', Mr. Hand."

There was a silence. Then Hand said, "Have him wait a moment, Baxter. I'll be right down."

IX.

It was twilight when they heard the cab. They knew it must be Roosevelt—cabs weren't frequently heard this close to Mackerelville. Most things with wheels on them around here were to be found under a load of fish.

Muldoon looked out the window of the second floor flat, and sure enough, there was Mr. Theodore Roosevelt, just alighting to the street. Muldoon saw the Commissioner speak a few words to the driver, then enter the building.

"Here he is, darlin's," Muldoon said. "Now, remember the plan. Keep him here five minutes. That's all the time I'll be needin'. And don't be lettin' on there's anything up, mind."

"You just put your mind to the handlin' of your end of the business," Katie told him. "Maureen and I know what we're about."

"I'm glad to be hearin' it," Muldoon replied.

"Now go on with you," Katie said. Dennis kissed his sisters, then left the flat and ran down the hall to hide in the privy.

If the Pink Angel could play tricks with doors and stairways, so could Dennis Patrick Francis-Xavier Muldoon. He waited until he heard Katie answer the door and welcome Roosevelt inside (laying it on a mite too thick, to Muldoon's thinking), then raced quietly downstairs.

About now, Muldoon thought as he reached the bottom,

Maureen should be telling the Commissioner that her brother had stepped out for a few minutes, and in the meantime, would he mind explaining if Macduff chopped off Macbeth's head in a fit of pique, or if it was a regular thing for Scotchmen to be doing to each other.

Outside the tenement, Muldoon walked jauntily up to the hansom with his hands cupped together in front of him.

"Evenin'," he said politely. Muldoon was pleased to see the driver (the Commissioner had found another honest one, apparently) had a decent size to him; it was all the better for his plan.

"Engaged," the driver said.

"Nope," Muldoon replied. "Not even keepin' steady company at the moment."

"Well, I should smile," the driver said, with no humor at all. "I mean the *cab* is engaged, you chowderhead. I'm waiting on a passenger."

"Don't you think I *know* that?" Muldoon asked. "Mr. Roosevelt, right?" Muldoon held up his cupped hands. "Here. He sent me down to show you this."

"What?"

"Are you deaf, man? Mr. Roosevelt wants to know what you think of this I've got in me hands. Bend over and take a look."

The driver, who had lots of things he'd rather be doing of a Sunday evening, shrugged, and leaned over the box as Muldoon raised his hands.

The young officer then grabbed the man by the collar and pulled him from the box. Muldoon was spared further effort by the way the man hit the sidewalk. For a moment, Muldoon's victim was powerless.

The moment was all Muldoon needed. He caught the driver under the arms, and dragged him into the alley alongside the fishmonger's.

"I'm sorry to be doin' this," Muldoon told the driver. "But it's got to be done all the same." He'd brought a piece of clean rag from upstairs. He tied it now around the driver's mouth, then stuffed the whole driver into an empty fish-barrel. The smell was atrocious, but the fellow would be able to work himself loose before he stifled. Besides, Katie and Maureen were under orders to see to the poor man's welfare as soon as Muldoon and Roosevelt were out of sight.

Muldoon went back to Avenue A and mounted the box of the hansom. Even as he thought over what he would do next, a part of his brain was pleased to be holding the reins of the animal now relieving herself on the cobbles. She was no beauty, but it would be a lark to drive her after the burnt-out wrecks he'd had to deal with during his few turns on the beer dray.

Theodore Roosevelt came out of the building, grumbling under his breath. He barely looked at Muldoon as he got into the cab. "Uptown, driver," he barked.

Uptown was fine with Muldoon. He took the cab uptown and east, to one of the Consolidated Gas Company's coal yards hard by the East River.

Muldoon took a deep breath. Roosevelt sought a confrontation in a cab, did he? Well, here's where he found one. He brought the horse to a rapid halt, and leapt from the box.

Just as Muldoon grasped the door handle, Roosevelt's voice boomed from within. "Decided to stop at last, have you, Muldoon? Bully idea. For a moment, I was afraid you planned to take me clear out of the city and into Brooklyn." With a wide grin on his face, the Commissioner opened the door and jumped out.

"You knew it was me?" Muldoon demanded. "When?"

"When you turned east instead of west off Avenue A, of course. I may have been preoccupied, but really. What have you done with my driver? He's a lout, but he didn't try to jump me."

"He'll be all right," Muldoon told him.

"For your sake, Muldoon, he'd better be."

"You have," Muldoon said severely, "me word on it. And now, Mr. Theodore Roosevelt, we'll be gettin' down to our business."

"Excellent, Muldoon. As you know, I've been trying to talk to you all day."

Muldoon made a noise. "Oh, we'll be havin' a talk all right. And it had best be one daisy of a talk, or I expect to be resumin' our little boxin' tournament. And this time, only one of us will be leavin' standin' up."

MONDAY
the twenty-fourth
of August, 1896

I.

Any reporter who'd remained at the Mulberry Street
front stairs vigil would have had a treat. A second person came
walking fast around the corner and went sprinting up the stairs
to Police Headquarters. So determined was she, in fact, that she
was in the anteroom to Mr. Roosevelt's office before anyone
thought to try to stop her.

"Ma'am, I'm afraid I'll have to announce you," said a young
woman at a desk.

"Fine!" said Katie Muldoon. "You do the announcin', and
I'll do the talkin'. Who are you, the secretary?" The Commissioner had caused a bit of a sensation in the press last year when
he hired a girl secretary—the first in the Department's history.

The girl replied meekly that that was indeed who she was.

"He ought to be ashamed of himself for exposin' you to a

bunch of men, not to say criminals. And you ought to be ashamed for puttin' up with it." Katie looked at the secretary. "Well, announce me. Me name is Kathleen Muldoon. We've met."

The girl looked at Katie's red face and decided it would be best for Mr. Roosevelt to attend to her after all. She rose to meet Katie's demand.

"Wait!" Katie snapped. She took her bonnet off (it was the one Dennis had bought her for Easter) and brushed a piece of ash. "Damned elevated trains," she mumbled. "Belchin' monsters."

The secretary, happy to find a bit of sisterly feeling with this mad Irishwoman, made sympathetic noises. Katie finished brushing, put the hat back on, then said, "Thank you for your indulgin' me. Now, I mean to see Mr. Theodore Roosevelt right away."

She got her wish. The door to the office opened, and the head of Mr. Roosevelt appeared, asking what all the noise was about. Katie went for him like a robin for a worm, pushing him inside the office and closing the door behind her.

The Commissioner reflected that he'd been having a wretched time with angry women over the last day or so. Against his nature, he decided this time he must forego gentlemanliness.

"See here, Miss Muldoon. I have been having an important meeting, and I cannot allow—"

It didn't work.

"Where's me brother, you blinkin' walrus?" Katie demanded.

At that moment, Roosevelt reflected, he had rather been back face to face with the grizzly bear. Her attitude was fully as menacing, and her cheeks, pleasantly rosy yesterday, were now sufficiently red with anger to enrage a dozen bulls.

"Why, ah, ask me where your brother is, Miss Muldoon? You may remember, I failed to see him when I tried yesterday."

"He was waitin' for you downstairs!" Katie said. "And don't try to be lettin' on like you ain't aware of it! He went down to wait for you, and he ain't been seen hide nor hair of since. And don't be tellin' me he's out carousin', because the whole world and New York City both know Dennis Muldoon is no carouser, and furthermore, even when he does do his tipplin', he tells us first, so I won't be worryin' about him, and this time he didn't tell me anything, and by the Lord, I *am* worried, and I aim to know where he's at and whether he's alive or dead before I'm leavin' this room!' "

Katie ran out of either aims or breath, and stopped talking. Roosevelt took a second to savor the silence.

It was a second too many. "Well?" Katie demanded.

"Well, what?" The Commissioner was at a disadvantage and knew it. Curse it, but he hated deception.

"Here you are, callin' yourself a reformer," Katie sneered, "and go stoppin' a poor man as has a thirst from gettin' a simple glass of beer on a Sunday, when you're as bad as any of them.

"Well, you just listen to me, Mr. Theodore Roosevelt. If Dennis isn't home and safe, and almighty soon, I'll . . . I'll go to the newspapers and tell them what comes of a man just doin' his duty when he runs afoul of the likes of you. Then we'll find out who's doin' the reformin' and who's doin' the corruptin' around here."

"Katie, for Jesus's sake, stop it," moaned a loud and somewhat embarrassed voice.

"Dennis!" Katie cried. "Where the devil are you?"

Muldoon replied by emerging from the closet. "I'm right here, so you needn't be yellin'. I'm thinkin' you owe Mr. Roosevelt an apology."

Even as she embraced her brother, Katie managed to fix the Commissioner with a wary eye. "I'll do the decidin' about whom I owe apologies to. And where have you been learnin' to hide in closets like somebody in a French stage-play?"

Muldoon made an exasperated face; this whole scene brought back uncomfortable memories of his boyhood. "Mr. Roosevelt and I have been *tryin'* to do a man's work in a man's office, where we'd be safe from meddlin' females comin' in and takin' over."

Katie sniffed. "Well, that's a fine way to be talkin'! Here I am, dealin' with the two little ones, pinin' away the night over you—"

Muldoon held up a hand. "I know, me darlin', and a lucky man I am to have you all to worry about me. But it seems I've stumbled into some dark doin's, and Mr. Roosevelt needs me help. So you apologize like a nice girl, and go home and tell Brigid and Maureen I'm still breathin' fine, but not a word to another soul. Will you do that? That's me girl!"

Katie sniffed again, but she said, "I'm sorry, Mr. Roosevelt, if I have been hasty in referrin' to you as a crook, and implyin' you was a murderer. I'll just ask you to be keepin' in mind I was wrought up over the absence of me brother." There, she thought, an apology, and a very pretty one if she did say so, though it pained her to have to do it. Still, Dennis had commanded it, and he was the man of the family.

"No offense taken, Miss Muldoon," Roosevelt assured her. There was a twinkle behind his spectacles.

Katie looked at her brother. "Will you be comin' home for supper?"

"I don't know, Katie," Muldoon said softly.

"Ah, well, it's only a bit of a stew. It'll keep." She straightened her bonnet (the Commissioner complimented her on it), and gathered up her things. "I'll be goin' now," she said. "Mind you take care of yourself, Dennis."

"I'll do that, Katie."

Katie left.

When she was gone, the Commissioner clapped Muldoon on the shoulder. "You are a lucky man, my boy. I hope you appreciate that."

"I do, sir."

"Bully. But Muldoon, from now on, I will tolerate no more profanity."

"Sir?"

"The name of the Savior is reserved for prayer. Is that clear, Muldoon?"

"What? Oh, yes, sir. Now, what kind of work was it you said you had for me?"

II.

"Blast it, Muldoon, we've been up the whole night talking of nothing else."

Muldoon scratched his head. "I know, sir, and don't think I ain't appreciatin' your patience with me. But walkin' a beat, you don't get much practice at deep thinkin'. I want to be absolutely for certain what the situation is."

Roosevelt sighed. "Very well, Muldoon." He reached into his breast pocket. "Now that I think of it," he said, "it's better for you to carry the original of this letter."

Muldoon took it and read it.

"I wrote that at the same time I wrote that 'dismissal', and as you can see, Herkimer himself witnessed the signature."

" 'This is to state that my order dismissing Dennis P. F.-X. Muldoon from the Police Department of the City of New York is countermanded,' " Muldoon read, "and so on and so forth, and, here it is, '. . . said Muldoon is still and has continuously been, an officer in good standing of the Police Department of the City of New York, and has, since this date, been acting directly under my orders on my authority. Signed . . .' "

Muldoon looked at the Commissioner and blinked a few times. "Curse me for a flannel-headed idiot," Muldoon said. "I—I just hope I can be worthy of your trustin' me so. And to think I was plannin' to knock your block off for you—"

"Muldoon," Roosevelt said.

"—And all the time, you plannin' to fix it up like this—"

"Muldoon, confound it, stop!"

"And I—" Muldoon looked up from the letter. "Sir?"

"In another moment," the Commissioner said, pointing a finger at the officer, "you would have been blubbering. I shall never understand how the Irish, so manly in most regards, can still be so sentimental."

Muldoon straightened up. He *had* been about to blubber. "Sorry, sir."

"It's all right, Muldoon, but try to control yourself. A display like that is disconcerting."

Muldoon thought it might be best to change the subject. "What about the other letter?" he asked. "The one you gave to the photographer fellow."

"It was a copy of the letter I gave you, along with an explanatory note."

"You see, sir, that's one of the things I don't get. What's this Riis fellow want with a copy of my letter?"

"Jacob Riis is one of my closest friends, Muldoon. More than that. He is one of the finest men, one of the finest Americans I know, though he did not come to this country until he was nearly a young man. Did you read *How the Other Half Lives*?"

"I've heard of it. Listerdale stocks it, I think."

"Read it, Muldoon. It was Jacob Riis and his book who opened my eyes to the plight of the poor in this city, and he's opened the eyes of many others as well. He is in large measure responsible for what progress has been made in helping the poor. I trust him without limit, Muldoon. And, since I have temporarily placed your good name in jeopardy—something I do not take lightly—I have trusted Jacob Riis to redeem my promise to rescue it in the unlikely event something happens to prevent me from doing so.

"Something dark and evil is gathering in this city. It may have something to do with this police force. I don't know, but I hate the very idea. Whatever it is, we, you and I, are about to come to grips with it. Mark my words, Muldoon, Crandall and that woman are only the tip of the iceberg. This looks like the spoor of bigger game, and it's possible I may not be in at the kill."

At this point, it occurred to Muldoon that anything that might happen to Mr. Roosevelt was equally likely to happen to him, in which case the restoration of the luster to the name of Muldoon became all the more important.

Mr. Roosevelt went on. "Now, if anything *does* happen to me, Riis will see to it the truth is made known. If you will look at his book, you will see he has a passion and a talent for doing just that."

"I've got that much," Muldoon said. "And thank you again. But about this dark and evil business, and Crandall and the woman and all. What was it, now, you were tellin' me last night? The boys have found out Crandall was E. Noon, the cartoonist for the *Journal*?"

"That's right," the Commissioner told him.

"Well, there's an example of me slow thinkin'. I found a bit of a drawin' of Mayor Strong when I found Crandall's body. I thought he was having' a go at *copyin*' E. Noon."

"No, representatives of Hearst's have seen the body. They were one and the same."

The Commissioner rose from his desk, adjusted the fine louvres of his wooden blinds, walked from the window to the fireplace, read the glass-domed clock, then returned to the desk. He straightened some papers that didn't need straightening, then said, "Blast it, Muldoon, this murder upsets me. Crandall was a powerful weapon. Did you see that blasted insulting cartoon Hearst had him do of me when—well, never mind that.

"The point is, the campaign is in full swing, and Crandall's work could go a long way toward making Governor McKinley and the rest of us Republicans appear fools, or worse.

"But now, someone has silenced him."

There was a pregnant pause.

Muldoon was horrified. "Surely, sir!" he exclaimed. "I can't bring myself to the point of believin' that somebody would pull a dirty trick like this to influence the Presidential election. I mean sir, really, in the United States of *America*?"

"I shudder to think it myself, Muldoon, but there it is. My belief is that we can defeat Bryan and his blasted Free Silver at the ballot box."

"But somebody else that thinks Republican might not be feelin' so confident," Muldoon said.

The Commissioner looked at him. "Your brain isn't so slow as you like to pretend, Muldoon. Yes, blast it, that's exactly what I'm afraid of."

Suddenly, Mr. Roosevelt exploded. "But I won't stand for it! No matter who is responsible, Democrat or Republican, Progressive or Anarchist, let him beware."

Muldoon, who without thinking about it much, had always assumed he was a Democrat, smiled. "Well spoken, sir, if I may say so." Then he frowned. "I still can't see, though, why the death of Crandall, bewilderin' as it may be, is weighin' so heavily on you. I mean, folks are all the time gettin' themselves murdered for reasons that have nothin' to do with politics and such."

Roosevelt polished his spectacles, replaced them, and started to pace once more. "Muldoon," he said, "when I am in the Bad Lands, and I ride out to the herd, and I think an animal might be missing, I get back in the saddle, and track it down.

"But if I go to the herd, and I discover *fifty* animals are missing, I ride to town, get the sheriff, join the posse, and make sure we have plenty of rope.

"Because, Muldoon, a strange thing or two may happen of itself from time to time, I grant you that. But when queer event follows queer event in the same place, over a short time, you may rest assured that someone is *making* them happen.

"Let me list some of the strange things that have been happening lately.

"First, there are the Mansion Burglaries.

"Second, as you know, Franklyn and Libstein have left New York."

"The Anarchists?" Muldoon asked. "I'd think we'd be happy to see the backs of them."

Roosevelt shook his head. "You may recall, Muldoon, when the current Police Board was first appointed, how in one day, we ran all the quack doctors out of town."

Muldoon grinned. He was new on the Force when the operation took place. Roosevelt had ordered every patrolman and roundsman to take down the names on every doctor's shingle on his beat. Then men from the licensing board in Albany checked the names against the official rolls. Muldoon had been on the docks then, so he hadn't the opportunity to arrest any of the quacks himself, but he was proud of his part in the operation, however small it had been. He told the Commissioner as much.

"Yes, Muldoon, and I am pleased to have thought of it. My point is, anarchists do not oblige us by hanging out shingles—most don't, at any rate. Except for public figureheads like Franklyn and Libstein, *their* membership list is a dark secret. The two of them may be gone, but you can wager their minions are at work in their absence.

"Where were we, now? Oh, yes. Third, E. Noon, or Crandall, if you prefer, is not only found dead, but found dead under circumstances that make even a decent dedicated officer doubt his sanity."

It took Muldoon a moment to realize the Commissioner meant him.

"Fourth. That woman, the one you call the Pink Angel. Everything about her, blast it, is a mystery. Who is she? What was she doing there? Why was she bound? Why did she leave?"

Muldoon said, "Hmmm," and stroked his moustache. He tried to think of a connection between the naked lovely and politics. He failed, and shook his head over the matter.

Roosevelt barked a laugh. "Shake your head once for me, too, Muldoon; I don't hesitate to say I find it too many for *me* as well. But that leads us to the *fifth* puzzling event. Someone promises to shed a little light on the matter."

"I'm afraid I ain't followin' you," Muldoon said.

"Just before your sister entered—spirited woman, isn't she?—an aide gave me this note. It had been delivered downstairs."

He handed Muldoon a piece of cheap, soft, greyish-white paper. Pieces of wood were still visible in the grain.

"This is for Mr. Roosevelt," Muldoon read, *"and for him alone. If he desires information concerning the death of Evan Crandall, he is to stand at the corner of Mulberry and Houston streets at quarter past ten."*

Muldoon felt constrained to make some remark, so he pursed his lips and said, "Nice handwritin'."

The Commissioner grinned and hissed. "I'm looking forward to meeting the man who wrote it."

"I'm comin' along," Muldoon said. "It might be a trap."

Roosevelt's eyes twinkled behind his spectacles. "So it might," he said. "So it might."

III.

It was one of the interesting peculiarities of the newspaper business, William Randolph Hearst had discovered, that everyone thought he would be good at it.

T. Avery Hand, for instance. The dapper, intense little industrialist was saying, ". . . and I am having flowers of the tropics shipped in ice from the Hawaiian Islands, so that Essie May may wear flowers that no bride in New York City has ever worn before."

"That is interesting, Avery," Hearst said, politely, "but I'm sure our society editor has the coverage planned down to the last detail. *Our* meeting, correct me if I'm wrong, was to concern the campaign."

"This does concern the campaign," Hand told him. "I've just learned that Bryan is definitely going to attend. In fact, since the Reverend Mr. Burley will perform the ceremony himself, Mr. Bryan has consented to give the bride away."

"Yes," Hearst mused. It might be a good headline for the *Journal*'s readers to see: BRYAN UNITES INDUSTRIAL EAST WITH AGRARIAN WEST; *Brings Nation Together.* One month before the election; it could be effective.

"Very good, Avery, I'll put my people to work on it. Thank you for bringing this to me." Hearst rose, to indicate the meeting was over. He expected Hand to try to drag things out, but today he seemed distracted, on edge about something, despite all his pretended enthusiasm over his marriage to the homely Essie May Burley. Hand had something weighing heavily on his mind.

As did Hearst himself. The publisher and the industrialist shook hands and said goodbye. Hearst reflected that if he weren't such a practical man, he would find it ironic that politics had forced him into bed with the likes of William Jennings Bryan, and even more ironic that an opportunist like Hand should be so successful at leaping under the covers with them.

Still, the object was to get Bryan elected, and thereby top Pulitzer and the rest. Especially Pulitzer. And, he was surprised to realize, there seemed to be no end to the strange people and events he would endure to do that. He gave Hand plenty of time to leave the building, then told his secretary to have his carriage meet him at the loading dock.

IV.

Hand had to blot sweat from his brow as he emerged into the street, and it wasn't because of the hot August sunshine. He must have sounded like a babbling idiot in there. But then, he supposed not. He was a businessman after all; self-made, self-taught. And he had done his business. He could take pride in that, he thought. Whatever else may transpire, T. Avery Hand could still attend to his business.

His visitor of the night before had told him to do just that. Hand made futile fists just thinking about the man. The Rabbi. Angrily, Hand expectorated into the gutter. He wiped his bearded lower lip with the back of his hand, and remembered.

Baxter had accompanied Hand into the library, where the visitor had been waiting. He was, or perhaps he contrived to look like, a gnarled old man. He did it well, too. He had clouds of fluffy white hair on his face and some spilling out from under a shaved beaver hat, long out of fashion. Gloves of kid-skin covered his hands, and green-tinted spectacles hid his eyes. He had gone so far as to wear an ill-fitting pair of grey spats, the mother-of-pearl buttons cracked where they weren't missing altogether.

Hand was stunned by this apparition into momentary silence, enabling the visitor to speak first.

He spoke in a thin whisper that fluttered the white beard like a cold wind. "I've been admiring your library, Mr. Hand."

"The—the best in New York," Hand replied. It was true. He'd paid plenty to auctioneers and experts to make sure that it was.

"Not harmed by overreading, I should say." There was a ghost of a smile discernible behind the beard as he took an uncut volume from the shelf.

"I am a busy man," Hand said. "What do you want?"

"Why, to show you this," the visitor said. "Your servant was most impressed." He took a few slips of paper from his pocket and presented them to Hand.

As Hand read them, a scarlet curtain of anger descended in front of his eyes. The papers were word-for-word transcriptions of the bill of sale and other documents Crandall had forced him to make. Hand began to tremble; his worst fears had been realized. He had traded one blackmailer for another.

Without knowing what he hoped to accomplish, Hand saw himself rip the papers to pieces, then wad the shreds into a ball, which he flung into the old man's face, saying, "Damn you and your papers!"

The visitor merely clicked his tongue. "If that is the way you treat my poor fac-similes," he whispered, "I dare not trust you with the originals, do I?"

With an effort that cost him nearly all his strength, Hand brought himself under control. He must not panic. He must not play the other's game.

"I think you will give me the originals, after we have talked, Mr. . . ?"

Again, the ghost smile. "You may call me 'Rabbi'."

This time Hand returned the smile. "Ah, yes, Baxter told me. Well, I have dealt successfully with your kind in the past. I think, then, money is what you chiefly want."

The visitor chuckled somewhere deep in his beard. "Don't be so hasty to form opinions, Hand. I daresay I shall prove to be the most un-Orthodox Jew you have ever met.

"But my faith is of no importance. Let me tell you, Mr. Hand, what is expected of you."

Hand's voice took on a cutting edge. "No, *Rabbi*, I will tell you what I expect of *you*. I expect you to take me immediately to the originals of those documents."

The Rabbi raised a hand. "Then it seems one of us must be frustrated in his expectations, doesn't it? Now, in return for . . . *dealing* with Mr. Evan Crandall, and thereby making possible the return of your Miss . . . Cleo I believe is her name?"

"How dare you bring a woman's name into this?" Hand's fury killed the last of his caution. "Damn you, I'll make you *beg* to tell me where those documents are. Baxter!"

The huge butler advanced on the visitor with such a look of deadly purpose, that Hand was afraid the intruder would be dead before he could speak.

He needn't have worried.

It was over in less than a second. At Baxter's approach, the visitor stood straight, and it was evident he was far younger than he appeared. Then Baxter grabbed for him with a meaty right hand, and the Rabbi did *something* with his own right hand, under Baxter's chin. It was less a blow than the merest gesture, but it sent the larger man crashing to the floor as though he had been clubbed, straining for breath and grimacing as though posing for a death mask.

"Baxter!" Hand's voice was half surprise and half rebuke.

"He will be all right," the whispering voice said. "Leave him be."

For all the exertion the visitor showed, Baxter might as well have lay down of his own volition. The bent posture and feeble appearance might never had disappeared.

"Now," the Rabbi said again, "in return for dealing with Crandall, and making possible the return of—since you forbid names, shall we just say the object of your lust?"

"Damn you . . ."

"Then let us say, as the French do, your *belle aimée*." The old man nodded, as though pleased to have the matter settled. "For the service I have described," he went on, "I want five thousand dollars."

"I—I don't have that much in the house."

"The famous T. Avery Hand?" The voice managed to be whisper and sneer at the same time. "You have at least half that in your wallet, or your reputation is richer by far than your estate." The Rabbi lifted his right hand a fraction of an inch. "Shall I take it from you?"

Hand had swallowed his pride (and almost bit off his tongue in the effort), and sent the now-recovered Baxter for the cash.

The "old man" received the money with a bow. "I thank you, sir. I'll be in touch with you. Now, I must be on my way."

"Wait a minute!" Hand exploded. "What is the meaning of this! What's your game, old man?"

"I have said," the Rabbi whispered, "that I will be in touch with you. In the meantime, here are some preliminary instructions." He gave Hand a slip of paper. "See that these are carried out, but otherwise, just go about your business. Good evening."

And he left Hand standing there, wondering what to do.

Much, in fact, as he was standing now, in front of Hearst's New York *Journal*. The "preliminary" instructions had put in motion things Hand would never have contemplated doing just a few months ago. He'd had to call in Eagle Jack, and his services came dear. With a shake of his head and a sigh, Hand engaged a cab for Wall Street, and continued to follow the Rabbi's instructions.

V.

Two generations ago, a Muldoon had been able to buy a watch. Hard work, good character, and most of all the avoidance of the infant mortality that had eliminated all the other male Muldoons of his generation, had enabled Dennis's father to inherit it. It had come to Dennis on his father's demise.

It was a grand old turnip of a repeater, wrought in gold with heavenly trumpet-players inlaid in silver and ivory. It had a heavy gold chain, with double-square links. It's ticking sounded like someone beating a bass drum, and it kept excellent time. It was easily worth more than everything else Muldoon and his three sisters owned put together, but due to a Muldoon family tradition of extorting promises on the death-bed, it had never seen the inside of a pawnshop, even at those times Dennis and the girls had no idea where their next bowl of porridge was coming from.

Dennis Muldoon hauled that watch from the pocket of his Sunday suit, clicked back the lid, and consulted it. "Twenty-five past ten," he said. "I think, Mr. Roosevelt, that someone's been havin' a bit of a tug on our leg."

"The traffic is heavy, Muldoon. Monday morning deliveries to be made, you know. I'm confident our man will be here."

"Beggin' your pardon, sir, but you're actin' like you've a notion who's comin'."

Roosevelt rubbed his hands together, cracked his knuckles. "Ha! I'll wager I do know who it is. Didn't you see the note, Muldoon? Why, it stands to reason—But here comes our secret correspondent now. I recognize that phaeton. You there! Driver! Over here!"

As the Commissioner's voice piped merrily over the din of traffic, Muldoon risked being trampled to death following him through traffic to approach a handsome closed phaeton drawn by an equally handsome bay gelding. The inside of the carriage was made invisible by heavy curtains across the windows.

"You Roosevelt?" the driver inquired.

"I am *Mister* Roosevelt," the Commissioner replied scornfully.

"Good."

"Say it," Roosevelt demanded.

"Say what?" the driver countered. Muldoon, meanwhile, was beginning to think those Spaniard bullfighters in the funny costumes had nothing on him when it came to dodging big dangerous objects moving at high speed.

" 'Mr. Roosevelt'," said Mr. Roosevelt.

"Oh," the driver said. "Sure." He said the required words.

"Much better," the Commissioner said. "You must respect me as a guest of your employer, if for no other reason. Now, is Mr. Hearst inside, or are you to take us to him?"

The driver goggled.

"Well, man, don't sit there gawking," the Commissioner told him. "This is a busy thoroughfare, and we are holding up traffic."

The driver looked straight ahead. "I ain't supposed to say who's inside. Sir," he added, remembering to be respectful.

"I believe that aswers my question. Ha! Come along, Muldoon. There is no danger, but I believe this will be an interesting meeting."

The driver, who normally earned his bread by driving a delivery wagon for the morning *Journal*, shook his head and promised himself he'd have nothing more to do with driving people around, no matter how politely Mr. Hearst asked him.

Roosevelt bustled from the front to the side of the vehicle, opened the door, and bounced in. Even before Muldoon had a foot up on the sill to follow into the darkened interior, he heard his superior say, "Good morning, Hearst."

"Good morning to you, Mr. Roosevelt," replied a voice even higher than the Commissioner's, though still not unpleasant. Muldoon still couldn't see him. "If I recall correctly," the voice went on, "the note specified a private meeting."

Muldoon's eyes had adjusted enough for him to see the publisher's round, blond head swivel in his direction. "So," Hearst went on, "if you would be so kind, sir . . ."

"This is my associate, Dennis Muldoon," Roosevelt said. "I answer for his discretion." Muldoon felt proud.

"I have your word?" the publisher asked.

"You do."

"Then that is all I ask. You and I have our differences, but I know you are a man of your word. I am pleased to meet you, Mr. Muldoon."

"Likewise," Muldoon said. "I read the *Journal* daily."

Muldoon could see perfectly well, now, and he caught the smile below the publisher's sad eyes.

"Then I'm even more pleased." Hearst settled back on the plush of his seat. "How did you learn I was the one who sent that note, Mr. Roosevelt?" His tone implied a bad time for the unwise employee who had leaked the news.

"It seemed likely. I have trained as a naturalist, you know. I can draw inferences from artifacts. In this case, I had a piece of cheap, low-grade paper bearing words and writing that could only be the work of an educated man. The two are commonly found together only in a newspaper office.

"And when the note specifies Evan Crandall, it is your office that comes to mind. He did, after all, work for the *Journal*."

"An excellent bit of reasoning," Hearst conceded, "but if you knew all the facts of the matter, you would think of other newspapers when Crandall's name is mentioned."

Roosevelt stroked his moustache. "You don't say so?" Hearst nodded. "It is your duty as a citizen," Roosevelt reminded him, "to tell me all about it."

Not, the Commissioner thought, that the duties of a citizen meant a whole lot to the newspaper crowd. During the Sunday saloon battle of '95, not one of the city's dozen top dailies had backed enforcement of the law. Many of them, especially Hearst's paper, had characterized the Commissioner as a Puritan and a kill-joy, out to rob the workingman of his recreation, when the issue had simply been one of the superiority of the law over that of private interests. Relations between the press and the President of the Police Board had been strained ever since.

"Before I go into details, I must have your word the conversation will go no further than the walls of this vehicle." Hearst shrugged apologetically. "As the publisher of a great newspaper, I have responsibilities."

He was, Muldoon could tell, perfectly sincere. It was obvious Mr. Hearst had a lot of power and liked using it, but it was equally obvious he was convinced that power was being used in the best interest of the common folk. And Muldoon couldn't argue with the fact that when the *Journal* made enough noise, things got done.

Roosevelt and Hearst engaged in some further pleasantries while Muldoon, out of idle curiosity, hooked a finger around the window curtain and peeked out through the isinglass.

"You put me in a position I cannot occupy, Hearst," Roosevelt huffed. "If what you tell me includes evidence of a crime, I am compelled by duty and by honor to report it."

Hearst made a small humming noise and rubbed his nose.

"Ah, excuse me for interruptin'," Muldoon said. "We've been ridin' down Mulberry Street, and we're gettin' mighty close to Five Points. I know it's broad daylight and all, but the mugs there don't often see a fine rig like this one, and I'm thinkin' the temptation might prove too much for them."

Five Points made Mackerelville look like the Promised Land. It was a pentagonal area not too far east of Police Headquarters. It was, quite simply, the worst slum in New York. Criminals held sway; it was worth a policeman's life to stroll through the neighborhood with fewer than two comrades. The jaded of the city could indulge any desire. Strong, and knowing of the life of the slum as Muldoon was, he feared Five Points, and avoided it as much as he could.

As it was, there were signs that the worst days of this blight on the city were past—the ancient, abandoned brewery, which had sheltered the worst of the scum since the 1840s, had been demolished, and there was talk of doing the same to the whole neighborhood, and planting it as a park.

Hearst had no more desire to tour the Five Points than did Muldoon. He rapped on the wall of the phaeton, and told the driver to change course. He turned with a sigh, and regarded Roosevelt intently. He thought of how the death of Crandall was inconveniencing the *Journal*, and how spreading that inconvenience around was the least he should do about the situation. He thought of how whoever had killed Crandall had made the task of electing Bryan more difficult. He thought of how humiliating it would be to have to make public the fact of Crandall's resignation. And he remembered how enjoyable it had been to score this same sort of humiliation against Pulitzer.

"Were you aware, Mr. Roosevelt," Hearst asked, "that Pulitzer's editor was tried for murder a few years ago in St. Louis? That he gunned a man down right in the offices of the *Post-Dispatch*?"

"I was aware of it. Were you aware that the gentleman in question was acquitted on grounds of self-defense?"

Hearst nodded, and thought some more. At last, he sighed more deeply than before. It was unprecedented to have news and not to print it, but it was the only thing that could be done.

"I'll take a chance my information won't effect your sense of duty or honor, Mr. Roosevelt. Aside from those considerations, may I have your word?"

Roosevelt had already committed himself to the (equally unprecedented) course of secrecy. If it could be done honorably. "Yes, Hearst. If my conscience allows, I will keep your confidence."

"Thank you," Hearst said politely. He told Roosevelt and Muldoon the story of the employment and resignation of Evan Crandall and E. Noon.

VI.

The Commissioner took Muldoon for an early luncheon at the dining room of the Fifth Avenue Hotel. That establishment, at the northeast corner of Madison Square, was New York's foremost political meeting-place, and Muldoon recognized many of the early patrons as he followed Mr. Roosevelt past the fluted marble columns and onto the bold checkerboard floor of the dining area.

It was easily the most elegant place Muldoon had ever seen the inside of, and he would have enjoyed it immensely, had not some trick of his perception caused him to see the public figures present not as flesh and blood, but as E. Noon cartoons.

The headwaiter recognized the Commissioner, and led him and Muldoon to a good table. Muldoon was a little taken aback when he saw the menu—why a man with a bit of a hunger could spend *seventy-five cents* on lunch without half trying. Muldoon concentrated on clams, which came by the dozen, and managed to keep his tab considerably below that.

Theodore Roosevelt seemed to be digesting Hearst's story along with his chop. "We must," he said, "be grateful for the information, regardless of his motive in giving it to us, ha, Muldoon?"

The young officer was so surprised at being consulted, he swallowed his clam without tasting it. "Huh?" he said. Then, "Oh, yes, sir. That is, if your meanin' is that Hearst is sore he won't have E. Noon to help Mr. Bryan get elected, and that he'd like to be tyin' one to Mr. Pulitzer's tail.

"But sir, may I be askin' what may be an impertinent question?"

"What's that, Muldoon?"

"Well, what's so terrible about that?"

"About what? Fixing Pulitzer? Ha! Nothing! There's no great love between him and me, either."

"No, sir, I mean Mr. Bryan gettin' elected. I heard him speakin' at the Garden, and to me own mind, he was mighty impressive. He had a lot of energy to him, certainly more than Governor McKinley. I hear *he* spends the whole day sittin' on his front stoop out there in Ohio, and only leaves when he has to . . . Well, he hardly ever leaves.

"And Mr. Bryan is for the poor folk, instead of the big interests, and he's plannin' to reform them. Now, I know you're a rich man yourself, and a member of the other party and all—"

"That's quite enough, Muldoon. I will answer your question. It is true I am rich by most standards, but that alone does not make me oppose Bryan. I am far less rich than Hearst, or Hand, the industrialist, and they support him. As I have said in the past, my father left me provided with my bread and butter, but if I wanted jam, I would have to provide that for myself. I have never been over-fond of jam, Muldoon. That is why I have chosen a career of public service.

"Now, as for being a member of the 'other' party. You forget, Muldoon, that the very administration which we both serve is a *fusion* administration—we are committed to fighting corruption in *both* parties. Mayor Strong is no politician—he is a merchant of dry goods, and a banker. But he is a man of honor and goodwill who is ready to back his ideas with his actions; in short, a *true* reformer.

"Bryan *claims* to be a reformer, Muldoon, but his reforms may be worse than the conditions he seeks to cure. Of *course*, monopolists and trusts must be fought and fought hard, and of *course* the poor, in the country or in the city must be helped, but not at the cost of destroying the very economy from which their help must come!

"Muldoon," he said, and took a deep breath. The officer noticed that the Commissioner's audience had grown to include diners at nearly half the tables in the room. The Commissioner's voice carried. "'Muldoon," he began again, "there is, at the edge of all reform movements, a group of dangerous men—a 'Lunatic Fringe,' if you will. Men who go to extremes, and beyond. Madness, Muldoon, madness. These men reason that if it is healthful to bathe, it must be more healthful still to drown. That kind of man must never be President of the United States." Mr. Roosevelt lowered his voice, but not much. "You know, Muldoon, sometimes I think the only way to deal with these people is the way the French dealt with theirs—take them out, stand them against a wall, and shoot them."

Muldoon wasn't quite ready to go that far with Mr. Bryan, but the Commissioner had given him some new things to think about. He mused about the "lunatic fringe" for a few moments, then said, "Mr. Roosevelt, did you ever consider runnin' for President?"

Roosevelt hissed and leaned across the table as though he intended to bite Muldoon's nose off with his strong even teeth. "Don't ever say that again, Muldoon. Don't even think it."

"B-but why not, sir? I'm sure I ain't the first to be thinkin' of it."

"No," Roosevelt conceded, "you're not. But I prefer not to hear such things. The temptation, man, the temptation! To have *any* of one's fellow citizens think of you in that office? Who would *not* want to be President?"

"I wouldn't—" Muldoon began.

Roosevelt ignored him. "But it's hopeless. After the debacle of eighty-six, I fear my public service must continue outside of elective office."

"Well, I'm thinkin' it's a shame, sir. You could at least try for Mayor again. We're doin' that fool merger with Brooklyn and those towns up north come ninety-eight. You might be givin' it a try then."

"Muldoon . . ." the Commissioner intoned. Muldoon subsided, and the rest of the meal was eaten in silence.

"I think I should explain to you," the Commissioner said over coffee, "why I am conducting this investigation in the way I am."

He told Muldoon that the main reason was Captain Herkimer, who was up for promotion. His handling of the whole affair had been suspect, but there could be various reasons—overconfidence, incompetence, or something worse.

"I know his wife has an extensive art collection, but they say she's in the way of bein' an heiress," Muldoon said.

"If you're hinting that Herkimer seems to live beyond his salary, I agree, Muldoon, but gossip is vulgar, and I won't stand for it.

"The point is, I must get to the bottom of this. As it stands now, Herkimer will not be promoted, but if his character cannot withstand the light of day, I want him off the Force. He must be treated squarely, but if he's guilty of wrongdoing, I mean to see him punished for it."

Muldoon remained silent for a few seconds, then he stuck out his chin and said, "Every man is deservin' of square treatment, Mr. Roosevelt. Even Herkimer."

The Commissioner grinned. "That's what I'd hoped you'd say. And since that woman is the key to the whole affair, it's imperative that we find her as soon as possible."

Now Muldoon grinned. He even twirled his moustache. "And that's what I hoped *you'd* be sayin', sir. I've been givin' the matter some thought, and this is how I plan to go about findin' her . . ."

VII.

"I am an art dealer," the man in the morning suit said through a very long nose, "not a procurer."

Muldoon sighed. This was the fifth place he'd been to, but for all the difference between them, he might as well have kept walking around the block and going back to the first. Apparently, every art dealer in New York had the same long nose (for looking down), a sarcastic and slightly soiled sense of humor, and no use whatever for an Irishman. It was a shame.

Muldoon looked at the walls, but they offered no relief. He was getting mighty sick of paintings of ladies in bonnets having picnics by a lake, which seemed to be the only kind of painting they hung in the showrooms. He wondered just where Crandall had expected to peddle his nude of the Pink Angel, unless these art guys had a back room for special customers, the way "Frenchy" Moriarty did to show his postal cards.

Things had not gone well for Muldoon since he'd parted from Mr. Roosevelt outside the hotel—his ignorance had shown him up badly at the first place he'd gone to. He'd had to pretend he was still on the Force to get any cooperation at all. Or rather, he had to pretend he wasn't pretending not to be still on the Force, and he was beginning to confuse himself. It was bad strategy, in any case.

It would have been worse, though, if he'd tried the same trick at the second shop—Captain Herkimer and his wife had shown up while Muldoon was trying his luck with the proprietor.

Muldoon couldn't run, and he was too big to hide, so he just brazened it out, taken no notice whatever of the captain, even after the art dealer had run off to see to Mrs. Herkimer.

Mrs. Herkimer was a large, loud, handsome woman, who, it seemed, *loved* those paintings of the men and women in silk suits picnicking on the riverbanks. Muldoon could tell neither the artists nor Mrs. Herkimer had ever tried to remove grass stains from clothing. If Katie ever got a look at these paintings, she'd have a fit.

Muldoon pretended to be interested in the dealer's pitch, but he was really pitching a notion to himself. His whole search was based on the assumption that the woman he'd found Saturday night was at least a part-time artist's model, and that someone in the world of Art would know who she was. And here was Herkimer, apparently at home in that very world. Of course, it could just be coincidence, but a connection between them would lead to some interesting speculation . . .

Herkimer, meanwhile, was doing some speculation of his own. What in Time was *Muldoon* of all people doing in an art gallery? Did he think he could follow the captain around? Herkimer thought that even though Muldoon had been in the store first. The captain wanted to approach the ex-officer and have the matter out, but since Muldoon was no longer on the Force, he didn't want to start what promised to be an unbridled and loud conversation in the presence of his wife.

So Muldoon left, after being assured no one at that gallery could help him.

By now, Muldoon realized he needed another kind of help. His plan had been to visit galleries, starting with those closest to Crandall's flat, working on his assumption that the Pink Angel's statement that she was "not usually" a figure model actually meant something.

But he hadn't made much progress, and he hadn't many steps to retrace before he arrived at Listerdale's Literary Emporium.

Listerdale greeted him warmly, and offered consolation over Muldoon's dismissal.

"Ah, then you've heard, have you?"

Listerdale nodded sadly. "The whole neighborhood knows."

"They think I'm a grafter, then."

"Only the fools. The rest of us know you for what you truly are. Frenchy Moriarty from the saloon was saying he'd stand you to a drink—any day but Sunday."

Muldoon laughed. "I've run him in more than once for it."

"He also hinted he could use another bouncer."

Muldoon was touched. "I'll be thankin' him proper when I have the chance. But before I go takin' him up on the bouncer's job, I'm goin' to have a try at clearin' me name with the Force. You can help me, if you've a mind to."

Listerdale raised his eyebrows. "Of course, Muldoon. How?"

"Would you be havin' any books about Art?"

"I surely do, Muldoon. Several. Why do you want them?"

"Well, it's lookin' at them I'm really after. But the reason is I want to be learnin' something from the art dealers in this town, but from the way they've been begrudgin' me a blasted second of their time, I'll be at it until Saint Paddy's Day."

Listerdale saved his life. He looked through the books with Muldoon, and picked out a few key words for him, like "chiaroscuro" (which he also told him how to pronounce), "brushwork," "balance," and since it was a figure model he was looking for, "flesh tones."

Listerdale also helped Muldoon improve the story he'd been giving the dealers. Muldoon thanked him.

"Nonsense!" Listerdale smiled the way a parson would at a Sunday school pupil who'd been able to tell him why the Poor in Spirit were blessed. "I'm glad to do it, believe me. I wish I were able to do more."

"Well," Muldoon said sheepishly, "if you put it that way . . ."

Listerdale threw back his head and laughed. "Out with it, man. What can I do to have you back on the beat?"

"When the Force threw me out, they told me they didn't want to be seein' me face around the precinct any more, so they give me me back pay. Now, I'm not sure where me questionin' will be takin' me, and I'd like to be sure me sister Katie had this money safe under the mattress. Do you think you could be takin' it to her this evenin' after you close the Emporium?"

"Glad to do it," Listerdale said again. Muldoon thanked him and gave him the money and the address. Listerdale said, "Now, just go about your business, Muldoon, and don't worry about a thing."

So Muldoon went, with a lot more confidence, though with no more success. Still, it was something to be able to reply when long-nosed art dealers made remarks about "procurers."

"See to the launderin' of your mind, sir," Muldoon told this one. "I am in the employ of an artist of, as the *Outlook* is fond of sayin', 'no mean repute on the international scene when it comes to depictin' the charms of the female form'!"

"And who is that, might I ask?"

"You might, but I might not be answerin'. Me employer is bound and determined to paint this young woman, whoever she might be, and he swears he'll switch all his shows to the gallery that helps him find her. The last time that happened, the fellow who lost him went jumpin' off—but perhaps I'm saying too much."

Had Muldoon been telling the truth, he had indeed been saying too much, since he had identified a very fashionable artist. Muldoon could almost hear the wheels turning in the dealer's brain. He blessed Listerdale for his help.

The dealer now listened eagerly as Muldoon described the Pink Angel, from her shiny black hair to her small pink feet. He mentioned everything in between, too, including the birthmark.

The dealer's mouth was fairly watering—Muldoon couldn't tell if it was over the girl or the painter—but he couldn't think of a model that matched Muldoon's description. Muldoon thanked him, and asked him to get in touch if he saw, heard, or remembered anything that might help.

The dealer was reluctant to let him go. "But tell me," he said. "How came Mr.—"

"Ah, ah, ah," cautioned Muldoon, waving a finger.

"Yes, of course. How came your *employer*—heh, heh,—to

know of this woman without being able to find out who she is?"

Muldoon was glad of a chance to practice this part of the story. "He come across the paintin' in a small shop in Philadelphia. It had been done by a fellow who'd left New York one step ahead of the sheriff if you get me meanin'. The artist was dead, and he left no friends or relatives to tell him who the girl was, except that she had to be in New York 'cause that's where the paintin' was done."

"If I could just see it," the dealer suggested.

Muldoon shook his head. "The paintin' was unfortunately destroyed in a small fire." That much was true, anyway. "That's why me employer is so anxious to be findin' her. He wants to capture the chiaroscuro of her flesh tones, and like that."

The dealer nodded wisely. "He's just the man to do it, too." He scratched his nose. "Ah . . . could you describe that birthmark for me again?"

Muldoon did better. He took out his memorandum book (the one thing he hadn't turned in to the Department) and sketched it.

"How odd," the dealer said. "I have some little knowledge of Egyptian art—it's all the go with certain of my customers, you know—and this looks just like an *ankh*."

"A what?" Muldoon demanded. He was after information, and he was damned if he was going to settle for goose noises.

"An *ankh*," the dealer repeated. "A-N-K-H. It's an Egyptian symbol of life, of good luck."

"Good luck, eh?" Muldoon muttered. He put on his hat, a smart yellow skimmer. The Commissioner had insisted he buy it. "I don't believe I'll be takin' up any more of your time, sir. I bid you good afternoon."

VIII.

There was a warm yeasty smell that transformed the dim hallway from the distressing entrance to a tenement to the welcoming foyer to a home. Someone was baking bread. Hiram Listerdale's life had, for many years, been a lonely, unsettled one, and he had forgotten how comforting that smell could be. It told him someone was working with the products of nature to care for a family.

Yes, Listerdale thought, you can keep your Fifth Avenue mansions. It's people like the ones who live here who are the backbone of the world.

Second floor, second door on the right, Muldoon had said. Listerdale found it and knocked. He took a deep breath and smiled. Unless his nose deceived him, this is where the bread was being baked.

"Who is it?" demanded a voice that Listerdale thought might be very pleasant if it ever wanted to.

"Miss Muldoon?"

"Never mind who I am. I'm askin' who *you* are!"

"My name is Hiram Listerdale. Your brother sent me."

"Why would he be doin' that?"

"Well, I don't really know . . ."

"A likely story."

". . . Except he said he was going out to try to clear his name, and didn't know when he'll be home. He asked me to bring you his pay."

Silence. She was thinking it over.

"You the fellow owns the book emporium?"

"I am," Listerdale assured her.

"You're friendly with Dennis? Spend time talkin' with him?"

"Why, yes." Listerdale wondered what she might be driving at.

"What's me name?" Katie demanded.

"Pardon me?"

"You heard me well enough. What's me Christian name?"

"Oh, Kathleen. Your Christian name in Kathleen."

Silence again, but only for a few minutes. Then Listerdale was inundated with icy cold water. She'd dumped the icebox pan over the transom on him.

"Get away from me door, you lyin' skunk! You're no friend to Dennis, and you're no friend of mine! I don't know what you crooked coppers are up to, but you'll not be gettin' away with it!"

Listerdale sputtered, and rubbed his frozen eyes. There was nothing he could do about the glacier of chills that was running down his back. "Madam, are you *insane*? For the love of God I—" Suddenly, he realized what he'd done wrong. "Katie!" he exclaimed. "Katie! Muldoon always calls you that. Not Kathleen. Katie."

"Lord have mercy," said Katie Muldoon.

Listerdale stopped rubbing his eyes in time to see the door opened by a tall, sandy-haired woman with an embarrassed look on her face and a white smudge of flour on her nose.

"Oh, you poor man," she said, as though Listerdale had been the victim of some natural disaster.

Listerdale looked at her.

"Well?" Katie said at last. "Are you just gonna stand there drippin' in me hallway, or are you comin' in and lettin' me give you some of me brother's dry clothes?"

Listerdale could do nothing but laugh. Katie Muldoon could do nothing but join him.

IX.

"More tea, Mr. Listerdale?"

Katie spoke loudly enough for her voice to carry through the open kitchen door in case any of the neighbors were about. After all, Brigid was at work, and Maureen was at a girlfriend's, and Katie was a respectable woman. So the door stayed open.

"Yes, thank you," Listerdale said. Muldoon's clothes were long on him, and baggy, but he managed to look presentable nonetheless. He smiled. "It helps take the chill off," he said.

Katie blushed. "I'll never get over bein' sorry for that, Mr. Listerdale. Have another piece of soda bread."

She cut a thick slice, spread it with butter, and placed it before him. He took a bite, washed it down with tea.

"Ambrosia," he said.

"Oh," Katie said. "Likewise."

"Food fit for the gods, Miss Muldoon. I would gladly take a daily dousing for bread as good as this."

"Pity I have no raisins this week; then you'd really be tastin' somethin'." She cut a piece for herself.

"You know, Mr. Listerdale," she said, "I'm worried about Dennis."

Listerdale raised an eyebrow. "He specificially instructed me to tell you not to be." But he seemed uneasy himself.

"Ah, well," Katie said, "I can't be helpin' it. I seen him with Roosevelt this mornin' . . . Yesterday, Dennis was set to dip the man in molasses and feathers, but today, he's tellin' me they've got it all worked out. I don't know what to think. Sure, you see Dennis as a great, stout man, but I cleaned his little —beggin' your pardon—bottom for him, and he'll always be me own baby darlin'. It's me *duty* to worry about him.

"Then you showed up referrin' to me as 'Kathleen.' Well, that's the name on me baptismal certificate, and in the police files as Dennis's next of kin, but I can't think of another place you might be seein' it. So I thought you were up to no good."

Listerdale put his napkin to his lips, and brushed crumbs from his hands. "My fault, entirely. I once asked your brother what 'Katie' was short for. Kathleen is such a lovely name, I simply substituted it in my thoughts whenever he spoke of you. With your permission, I shall continue to do so."

Katie blushed again. "Why, Mr. Listerdale . . ."

The former teacher stood up. "This has been a delightful afternoon, Miss Muldoon. Please tell your brother he may retrieve his clothes at the Emporium, if he likes, but I would much prefer it if I might have the honor of returning them in person."

Katie looked at her hands. "I—I'll tell him."

"Thank you." They stood by the open door. Listerdale loosened a collar that was already ridiculously loose. "Ah, Miss Muldoon?"

"Yes?"

"In any event, I should like to see you again."

Katie felt positively giddy. She kept looking down, as though she wanted to make sure her feet were still on the floor. Why couldn't she look at the man?

"Well," she said, and swallowed. "You'll have to speak with me brother."

"I see," Listerdale said.

"But if Dennis approves, I—I've no objections."

"Thank you," Listerdale said. He pressed Katie's hand warmly before he left. It was a liberty, but Katie didn't seem to mind.

X.

Muldoon walked toward home with his hands in his pockets and his head down. There was no lack of people on First Avenue—there seemed to be even more than usual for this time of the evening—but Muldoon still felt terribly alone.

He'd tried about a third of the art schools and galleries, and made no more progress than you could hold in a thimble. He was angry with himself, not so much because he hadn't found a lead today as because he couldn't think of a single thing to do if he couldn't find one tomorrow or next day. The population of New York City numbered one-and-a-half million; that many and more lived in Brooklyn, just a short walk across the bridge. Half of them were women. Even with the full resources of the Department, it wouldn't have been easy. Muldoon had just himself.

Suddenly, he wasn't alone anymore. Someone had fallen into step beside him. "Evening," said the man. The voice was high and raspy, like that of a child with a cold.

"Evenin' to you," Muldoon replied, touching the brim of his skimmer. He looked at his new companion. The fellow was middle-aged and too burly and muscular for even his expensive tailoring to hide. His suit, made from some rich, brown fabric, was wonderful enough, but his derby, spats, and gloves were enough to make Muldoon drool.

Strangely enough, the fellow's shirt was open at the throat, but the end of a necktie peeped out of his jacket pocket, and a circular bulge told Muldoon his collar was in there with it.

He sported a salt-and-pepper moustache fully as magnificent as Muldoon's own, but his head was completely bald.

Even that was muscular. When the man talked, mounds moved under the shiny scalp, and the derby wobbled as though it had a notion to jump off and run away.

Muldoon recognized the man, and wasn't happy about it.

The rasping voice spoke again. "You Muldoon?"

Muldoon nodded. "And you'll be Mr. Sperling."

"Heard of me, eh?" The man was pleased.

"I have indeed. May I say, I am totally flabbergasted to be makin' your acquaintance."

That was true. "Eagle Jack" Sperling was currently New York's most prominent strong-arm hoodlum. There were smarter racketeers, and more daring thieves, but for sheer efficiency in bully-boy tactics and just plain violence, Eagle Jack and his boys were without peer. His talents were recognized, and in demand, and were available to anyone who could pay the price.

"You shouldn't oughta be surprised," the bald man said expansively. "The minute the coppers done you dirty, you should of been expecting me. Or one of my men. I don't do much recruiting myself, these days."

Muldoon stopped and looked at him. "Recruitin'? Me?"

Eagle Jack adjusted his derby to a jauntier angle. "Sure, a lot of my boys are guys got booted off the coppers. That Roosevelt character don't know a valuable man when he sees one.

"In fact, I got an old colleague of yours works with me."

"Who's that?"

"Tommy Alb. Remember him?"

"I do indeed," Muldoon said grimly.

Eagle Jack ignored his tone. "He put in a good word for you."

"Nice of him," Muldoon said. "Before we go any farther, I'd like to ask you somethin' that's got me aflame with curiosity, you might say. Why is it you always carry your tie and collar in your pocket?"

"What? Oh, that. That goes back to the time my Wall Street clientele threw me a dinner on account of I busted up a couple strikes, you follow me? Anyways, after the dinner, some hothead trade unionist or somebody jumps me, and damned if he don't grab hold of the tie and nearly choke me blue.

"Now, see, in situations like that, I don't like to go killing guys—no money in it, teach 'em a lesson is enough—but then I had to. I felt bad. Ever since then, I decided I don't wear ties no more."

"Why do you even put up with the bother, then, of carryin' them around?"

"Hey," Eagle Jack said. "I move with the upper crust these days. You want they should think I'm a slob?"

"Oh," Muldoon said. "No, we can't have them thinkin' that." Somewhere in the back of the officer's mind, a dim little foreboding that said he might be in danger was growing bigger and brighter by the second.

"Now, here's the thing. Tommy tells me you're good with your fists, good with a club. I like that in a guy.

"I'm in the *negotiating* business these days, you follow me? It's a good business. I work for these respectable guys. You read the papers? These are the guys they call 'giants of industry.' I handle some of their troubles with the trades, and anarchists, and Reds, and like that, and they treat me good. A guy as is good with his dukes is a sap to go into any other line of work. Besides, I pay good."

Muldoon didn't know what to say. Under ordinary circumstances, he would have told Sperling to go chase himself, but these weren't, he suspected, ordinary circumstances. A lot of that extra traffic had stopped walking when Muldoon and Eagle Jack had, a while back. Muldoon suspected he'd better try to be charming.

Eagle Jack took silence for encouragement. He clapped Muldoon on the back, stuck an El Primo Havana cigar between his lips, gave one to Muldoon, produced matches, and lit them.

"Here," the bald man said. "Have a see-gar." He puffed. "Know something? I never tasted one of these things till I gave up grafting and like that and went into legitimate business. Delicious, ain't it? They tell me they got teen-age Cuban girls as rolls these. Small hands, you follow me?

"Another thing I wanted to mention is dressing nice. You're a guy as likes to dress nice, I can see that, but how many suits you got, three?"

Muldoon, who had two, said nothing.

"Know how many I got? Twenty-six. I got a hundred-thirteen silk shirts. Never wear the same thing two days in a row." He pulled his collar and tie from his pocket. "Why, I never so much as used to own *none* of this stuff, not so much as a collar. And now I worked my way up to be a Man of Substance—they say that in the papers, too.

"You could do it, if you got the Moxie. The garment workers is having a rally Sattidy, and I could use all the help I can get on it. How's about coming along?"

"Well," Muldoon said, "I'm sure it isn't everybody who finds himself bein' offered a job by you, personal, Mr. Sperling."

"Damn right it ain't" he said, around his cigar. "Call me Eagle."

"Ah—all right, then, Eagle it is." Muldoon was scanning the crowd. He spotted three men who had the look of thugs. Four to one was bad odds. He'd better be careful with his words.

"I'm afraid, Eagle, that I can't be acceptin' your generous offer, as I've got a project of me own in the works."

"Yeah," Eagle Jack said, no longer smiling. "Well, since you're coming to work for me, you're gonna hafta let that go, ain't you?"

Muldoon shook his head sadly. "I've given me word to a lady."

Eagle Jack snorted. "Dames. You know what dames are for, Muldoon. They ain't for keeping promises to, that's for sure."

"Well, I've given me word to meself, as well."

"It ain't healthy, Muldoon. Never mind how I found out, but I know you're looking for some skirt's got wings on her back like an angel or something stupid like that. Drop it. She don't wanna be found. You don't wanna find her, and, if you follow me, I don't want you to find her."

Muldoon was still afraid, but he found he could no longer bring himself to kow-tow to this hoodlum. "So that's the way of things, is it, Eagle? And who might be payin' you not to want her found?"

"Don't worry, I handle the business end of things. That's what I mostly do these days." He stuck out his hand. "Come on, Muldoon, give up on it. Join up with me. Whaddaya say? You'll never regret it."

Muldoon looked down the street, stuck his hands in his pockets, and said, "I think I'll be wishin' you a pleasant evening," and walked away.

"The hard way," Eagle Jack Sperling muttered behind him with genuine regret. "Nothing can't ever be the easy way no more. Okay boys!" he yelled. "Get him!"

XI.

Hand kissed Cleo softly on the forehead. "Thank you, darling." He got up. "I must go now. Rest. I know it's been a trying few days for you."

Cleo's face stayed serene, but her mind sneered. A trying few days indeed. Her neck was still sore from the grip of that monstrous butler. Even Hand had noticed the bruises and asked her how she'd come by them. For a moment, she had thought of telling him what sort of man he had working for him, but she held back. Judging from what she'd heard this afternoon, she'd never even known the sort of man Avery himself was.

"I will rest now, Avery," was all she said. He left her.

Cleo was glad to be rid of the sight and smell and touch of him. Nothing was right. He used to be kind, used to consult her wishes. Today, he came talking of Washington, and how he would buy her a house there, how nothing need change just because he was getting married and becoming Secretary of the Treasury. Cleo hated Washington, especially in the summer-time. A gentleman had taken her there once, and all she could remember of it was mosquitoes, limp dresses, and air too heavy to be breathed.

Then there was what Avery was out to do to that dear Officer Muldoon.

She was no longer kept locked in her room, though her movements were restricted to the second floor and above. Still, she took advantage of what freedom she had.

Late this afternoon for instance, a telephone call had come. She heard the bell ring in the niche at the bottom of the stairs. She paid no attention to it until she heard Avery's explosion of anger. Cleo decided it was in her best interests to find out what he was angry about—perhaps she could learn what was going on.

She crept silently to the top of the stairs to eavesdrop. Avery was one of those persons who couldn't learn that the telephonic cable was not a speaking tube, and that one didn't have to yell into it to be heard, so the matter was easy.

Avery was talking to a Rabbi, it seemed, which surprised Cleo. Avery was not fond of Jews, and judging from what she'd heard and seen from this vantage point the night before, he wasn't fond of this one, either. She could now catch glimpses of the dapper little millionaire as he paced back and forth, waving the telephone and receiver in angry little circles.

"Muldoon?" Hand exploded. "Nothing is to happen to Muldoon?"

Cleo stifled a gasp with the back of her hand as she recognized the name.

"Listen, you Hebrew assassin," Hand said bitterly. "I never heard of this Muldoon before last night, when you gave me that slip of paper that said he was looking for the girl and must be stopped at all costs!

"What? No you damn well *didn't* express yourself properly! I have *Eagle Jack Sperling* on the job, damn you. What do you *think* his instructions are? To stop this Muldoon character at all costs! No, he had some idea or other of his own, it seemed, but he won't shrink from killing him if he has to."

Cleo stifled a gasp. She put a knuckle between her teeth and bit to keep from crying out. It wouldn't do to be discovered now.

"Yes," Avery said bitterly. "I hope so, too. But there's no reaching Sperling now. All right! But I won't be able to get to him until tonight. Now you listen to me, Rabbi. You will be sorry you ever crossed me. T. Avery Hand will be pushed only so far. Good day to you, and may you fry in Hell!"

Cleo heard footsteps, and went rushing back to her room just in time to avoid being caught by Baxter, who had come silently up the back stairs.

Later, she heard Avery tell Baxter he would have to go meet Sperling tonight, but how the matter was hopeless. Muldoon was sure to be dead already. She'd heard that, because the encounter had occurred outside her bedroom door, just before Avery had come to her. God, how she hated him!

Now, alone again, Cleo lay in the dark for a long time. Then she did something she couldn't remember ever having done before without at least one man for an audience. She cried.

XII.

Muldoon had been right about the extra traffic on First Avenue. He'd had no time to run far; no time, even, to spit out his cigar, when he found himself surrounded by seven men, not including Eagle Jack Sperling, who stood a little outside the circle.

The seven men, (who, incidentally, included only one of the three Muldoon had speculated about—a barrel-chested, one-eyed character) were all sizes and shapes, but they were identical in degree of ferocity. The young policeman felt like a mouse who's stumbled unawares into a cat convention.

He recognized one of them. "Hello, Tommy," Muldoon said.

Tommy Alb, former patrolman of the Police Department of the City of New York, showed his pretty teeth. Alb had always been a rarity among adult males of the day, and a downright freak in the Department, because he chose to go completely clean shaven. Muldoon always thought it was so people who wanted to look at the classic lines of his jaw and chin, or appreciate the fullness of his lips, wouldn't be cheated. Tommy had enough shining yellow hair on his head to make a moustache or beard superfluous. He was, without a doubt, the handsomest man, in an unwholesome sort of way, Muldoon had ever seen.

"Hello, Dennis," Tommy said. "It's been a long time. Too long. It's closing time, Dennis." Tommy gently rubbed the tip of a nose as delicate as the Pink Angel's. "We're going to close you down," he said, "like a saloon on Easter Sunday."

"To my recollection," Muldoon said, challenging Alb with his gaze, "you was never any great shakes at accomplishin' that sort of thing." Muldoon tried to sound casual, though his back itched in anticipation of the attack of the unsavory characters lurking behind him.

"In fact," he went on, talking around his cigar, "you were kicked off the Force for that, right? For takin' money to close your eyes to that Raines Law hotel on the Bowery that was keepin' those little colored girls as prostitutes. Weren't you?

What's the matter? Thought it didn't count because of their bein' colored?"

"To *my* recollection," Alb snarled, "you were the one who told the captain."

"No, but I bleedin' sure would have, if only I'd had brains enough in me head to look behind the pretty face of someone I was thinkin' was a square guy and me friend besides."

"You're something, Dennis," Alb said. "You're a regular saint. You're out of touch with this life. Lucky for you you'll soon be leaving it."

"No more gabbing," Eagle Jack said. "Let's do what we gotta do."

Muldoon's eyes grew wide, and he began taking short, deep pulls on his cigar. The coal glowed cherry red.

Eagle Jack Sperling looked on in disgust. "Good thing he let my offer go by at that," he said. "Lookit him, he's yellow. You first, Tommy, what the hell."

The ex-copper stepped forward, as the two men behind Muldoon made a move to grab his arms. Muldoon spit the cigar at Alb's face. It flew straight and true, and its bright red coal branded Alb's handsome face under the left eye.

"Aaaa! You son of a—" The tough grabbed his face and bent over with the pain. Muldoon's aim had been better than he hoped, but he didn't intend to stay around and admire it.

Instead, he lowered his shoulder and bulled into his former comrade, knocking him sprawling, and, more important, breaking the deadly circle.

He couldn't run away--there were some mighty fast runners among them—they'd caught him unaware before, but now he could make a fight of it. He had surprise on his side.

And, it occurred to him, he had a weapon. He took his father's big, heavy watch from his pocket, and pulling the chain free, he laid about with it like Samson among the Philistines.

Two more of the thugs went down before him, but it was Eagle Jack who ended the fight. He might not do much of the strong-arm work himself anymore, but it was obvious the bald man hadn't forgotten how. And he too had a weapon. Sperling fetched Muldoon a lick in the brisket with his gold-headed cane that made the young man sink gasping to his knees.

Before Muldoon could recover, he was held immobile by two thugs, and Tommy Alb was before him holding a great, sharp bowie knife to his throat.

Muldoon's reading about the Wild West had led him to learn quite a bit about bowie knives. He wished it hadn't. If Mr. Theodore Roosevelt had found one sufficient to kill a grizzly bear, an Irishman should be short work for it.

"This is going to be a pleasure," Alb said. The yellow flame of the street lamp cast deep shadows on his face. He looked like a banshee come to claim the dead.

"A pleasure," Tommy repeated, and pressed the tip of the knife just the slightest bit more forcefully against Muldoon's throat. Muldoon felt a warm, wet trickle begin.

Muldoon tried to speak, but no sound came. Instead he spat. He had hoped his last act on earth might have been something more refined, but spitting would have to do.

Tommy pulled back the knife for the final thrust.

"Stop it," said Eagle Jack Sperling.

"What?" asked Alb.

Muldoon suddenly felt sweat flow on his forehead like the blood flowed now on his throat.

"No, Tommy," Eagle Jack said.

"But boss—"

"No, dammit! You done too many knife jobs already. When they find this guy, they ain't gonna pin nothing on us. Because we ain't gonna be the ones that done it. He's going out with the rest of the garbage."

The thugs laughed. Muldoon didn't get it, but a second later a blow on the head knocked him unconscious, so it didn't really matter.

XIII.

Hand was shaking as he left the saloon. A horror. A den of thieves—of worse than thieves, animals. He never should have gone there. Even Sperling was mad to stay in the place.

Hand wasn't wearing his best clothes, by any means, but it hadn't mattered. The minute he crossed into that notorious hellhole of a neighborhood, he had drawn every eye. They could smell money, Hand decided, the way naturalists tell us a shark can scent blood.

He had been challenged and mocked by toughs who kept demanding to know "the weight of his purse," which struck Hand even through his fear as a rather quaint way of putting things.

Things might have gotten ugly, but Hand had had sufficient wit to mention the name of Sperling. Eagle Jack was his safe-conduct pass to the back door of the establishment called Max's, a dismal place fragrant with the smell of sour beer.

Sperling was happy to see the millionaire. "Hey, Mr. Hand," he said softly. "Come sit down, have a drink. Let me get rid of my boy first, though. I don't want nobody to see you. You could go, Roscoe," the hoodlum said to a barrel-chested, one-eyed grotesque in a striped shirt. Hand was glad he wouldn't have to be in the same room with him.

"Right, boss," Roscoe growled, but he withdrew just as far as the other side of the door.

Hand entered, crossed an uneven wood floor, and sat at a scarred table across from Eagle Jack. "Sperling," he began.

"Just a second," Sperling said. "Roscoe!"

The voice of the one-eyed man came through the door. "Yo?"

"Make sure the neighborhood knows Eagle Jack says all his friends get home safe, you follow me?"

"I follow you, boss," the voice said.

"New man," Sperling explained. "Buttering me up. Just come down from up the river. Let me pour you a drink." A greasy-looking bartender appeared with what he claimed was a clean glass, and Sperling poured out a faintly brown liquid. "Applejack," he explained. "They keep it for me here, special. Ain't got the time to freeze my own no more. I go traveling around.

"Now, what brings you down to Five Points? I mean, I know I told you you could find me here, but I never thought you'd do it personal. I hope nothing ain't wrong."

Hand told him Muldoon wasn't to be hurt.

Sperling cocked his head. "Aw, c'mon, you can't do business that way. Your previous order . . ."

"Yes?"

"We already filled it."

The only movement Hand permitted himself was to pinch the

bridge of his nose and close his eyes, the way people do when suffering a headache.

"He was a hard-headed Irishman, sir. You can't do nothing with that sort, though God knows I give it a try. Why do you change your mind about it?"

And though he never meant to, and would have called the man insane who had suggested the possibility, T. Avery Hand found himself confiding part of his story to Eagle Jack Sperling.

"Rabbi, eh?" Sperling had never heard of him. "By the way, I hear Cleo turned up. Sorry me and the boys was no help on that one."

"What? Oh, it's all right, Sperling." Hand was thinking it might have been better if Cleo had not come back after all. "Cleo is a large part of this whole business."

"Oh. Anything I can help you with?"

"No," Hand said. "No, Sperling, I don't think so."

"Okay. Let me know. Always happy to work for a man pays as good as you do. Take care."

"Thank you, Sperling."

"Don't mention it. Wait a minute. Roscoe!"

"Yo!"

"Your errand done?" Through the door Roscoe assured his employer that it was.

"All right," Sperling told the millionaire. "You oughta be safe going home."

But Hand still shivered.

XIV.

Avery was gone from the house, and more importantly, so was Baxter. That should have left no one home but Cleo and the servants, and Cleo hadn't seen a servant since she'd been there.

She was going to escape. She had to. She realized that it had been only natural for Avery to sell her into slavery. She had been a slave of one sort or another all her life, but a pampered one, so that she had been able to hide from herself the truth of her condition. But no longer.

To think that Avery had been the best of those who had

come to visit her at Mother Nanette's. To think that she had voluntarily enlisted herself as his love-slave. It sickened her.

In that mood, she was on the verge of writing off the race of men altogether, but something, perhaps the memory of that Officer Muldoon (and what had Avery done to him? she wondered) stopped her just short.

She listened again, listened hard, to make sure she was alone in the house. Other than the baying of a dog somewhere nearby, she could hear nothing.

She rose from her bed and dressed quietly, in a dark cotton dress she had worn only once, to a funeral. It was ugly, and she hated it, but it was black, and it didn't rustle when she moved about. Besides, it was the only thing she owned that wouldn't hang too long on her without a bustle. Cleo had had some experience leaving places abruptly, and she preferred to travel light.

Cleo carried her shoes in her left hand and kept her right hand on the banister as she crept slowly down the main staircase.

She would have loved to be able to open the grand front door, walk down to Forty-second Street, and vanish. Unfortunately, since Avery had announced his intention to go out, it was safe only to steal the back-door key as he lay stuporous by her side. Avery would need the front-door key to leave, and she wanted him gone.

Luckily Avery was methodical, and the keys were plainly labeled. Cleo was worried that it all was going so easily. She'd ignored the keys for Main Entrance, Pantry, Kennel, Gun Cabinet, and Carriage House, and found the one she wanted without making a sound.

She made her way through the house. The night was chilly for August, and the stone tiles of the kitchen floor were cold on her stockinged feet after the warmth of the thick red carpeting in the main hall.

Cleo felt herself go all goose-flesh, whether from the chill or from anticipation of freedom, she didn't know.

It was going well. She breathed evenly, silently. Once outside, she'd cross the grounds, keeping to the shadows of the trees, just in case Avery or (God forbid) Baxter were to come back. She'd proceed past the carriage house, where the auto mobile was kept, and exit through the back gate, the key to which she had also managed to obtain.

The house was so *silent*. She couldn't believe there was *no one* stirring. So she listened. She listened until listening became almost a kind of madness. She could hear the house creak; soon she could hear her own heartbeat. After a while, she thought she could hear the very blood running in her veins, and possibly the grass growing just past that kitchen door.

And still nothing. She went on. She opened the back door, hastily donned and buttoned her shoes. She leapt over the gravel walk, landing on the soft, silent grass. She headed for the shadows of the trees.

There was a moon, and it gave her plenty of light to see by. Why, she wouldn't even have to worry about her footing. It was going to be as easy as it seemed . . .

Then she heard the noise, a rustling, slapping, panting sound that got louder and closer by the second.

The dog. Cleo had cursed herself for a fool. She had forgotten about the dog. A mastiff, Avery had told the Reverend. To protect the auto mobile. It had the run of the grounds every night. Baxter had told her once of the prowler it has savaged.

Cleo abandoned her plan of silent escape. She ran with all the speed she could summon for the back gate.

Even as she ran, she knew it was hopeless. The kennel was near that gate—she would be running right into the mastiff's jaws.

She'd come too far from the house—if she tried to go back, the dog would catch her, and she'd be torn to pieces.

Then she saw the carriage house. She sprinted for it, dashed inside, and slammed the door behind her. She was surprised to find a lantern on inside, casting a dim light over the Duryea Brothers' creation and the interior of the building.

The dog was still outside, growling and scratching at the door. Cleo put a hand to her throat, and felt the breath rasping its way into her.

She couldn't go back out, so she picked up the lantern, and explored the building. She saw that the walls were lined with boxes, fifteen or twenty wooden crates, about the size of orange crates. One was open, but tilted away from her. She walked around so she could see inside.

Candles, she thought. Red candles. The dim light of the lantern also showed her a slip of paper that had been tucked in between two of the narrow cylinders. She took it out, unfolded it and read it: 20 MILL GALS. There were some dates and figures on the paper as well, but Cleo could make no sense of them. Her mind was too taken up trying to figure out what twenty factory women would want with fifteen crates of red candles. Most factories she'd heard of had gas lights.

She got no opportunity to puzzle it out further—someone was coming. She could hear the crunch of footsteps on the gravel walk, and the dog started to bark again.

The barking stopped though, at a command from a male voice. Baxter's voice. "Well done, Caesar," Baxter said, with the mocking undertone Cleo feared and loathed. "Let's see what kind of coon you've treed for us."

Cleo could feel her heart stop as Baxter opened the latch. The door swung open, and the tall, bony man stood behind the growling dog.

Baxter seemed surprised at the sight of Cleo. "You!" he said. "I'm surprised you had the brass to try to leave the house."

"What . . what are you going to do? Are you going to tell Avery?"

Baxter smiled. "No. And neither will you. Outside, Caesar." He scratched the huge dog behind the ear, and it ran away happily.

"It's not good for trollops to be curious," Baxter said. Cleo sniffed; she wouldn't dignify that with a reply.

"Come here," Baxter commanded, but when Cleo ignored him, he came to her. He grabbed her about the waist, tried to kiss her. Cleo, like a cat, tried to claw for his eyes. She managed to scratch his cheek, but he was far too strong for her. He bore her beneath him to the dirt floor.

But even as she fought for—well, if not her virtue, as least her self-respect, Cleo noted with confusion that on this hot summer night, the sleeves of Baxter's jacket were cold and damp.

TUESDAY
the twenty-fifth
of August, 1896

I.

There was a Monster outside—Master Theodore Roosevelt III was sure of it. He could hear the sound of heavy, half-dragged half-slapping footfalls climbing the stoop of the Madison Avenue town house Papa was renting from Aunt Bamie.

Ted wondered if he should wake Papa or shoot the Monster himself. Ted was nine years old.

He wasn't supposed to be awake at this hour (the clock was just striking three), and even if he were, he shouldn't be in the parlor. But it was a good thing he was too excited about his trip to visit relatives in the South tomorrow to sleep. It was a good thing he'd come downstairs, or the Monster would have gotten in unmolested. It was a *very* good thing Mama and Lee and the babies were safe out at Sagamore Hill.

The Monster groaned.

He'd better wake Papa. But he wasn't *absolutely* sure it was a Monster. Policemen sometimes came to call, and they all had heavy feet, and a lot of times they groaned.

But they didn't *smell* like that. And they didn't squish when they walked.

The Monster groaned again and pounded on the door.

"Go away! I have a rifle!" Ted picked up and shouldered one of Papa's little-used walking sticks. The Monster *might* think it was a rifle. Monsters weren't known for their eyesight.

Then the Monster said, "Roosevelt," in a slow, horrible voice, and Ted hollered at it to go away again. But it didn't go away, it just kept pounding on the door.

"What is all this racket?" asked the perturbed but welcome voice of Ted's father. The boy ran to him, pointing the cane at the door and telling him about the Monster.

The elder Roosevelt took the news *cum grano*, to say the least, but after a few tentative sniffs, his game-tracker's nose told him that whatever was outside that door required some investigation.

He told his son to keep behind him, and, adjusting his spectacles and grasping the walking stick like a club, he advanced on the door and flung it open.

Ted was startled into crying out. The Monster had been leaning against the door, and he now fell staggering into the house.

The Commissioner raised his stick, but the Monster rolled over, showing two shining grey eyes surrounded by a mass of filth that probably had a face under it somewhere. Ted realized that the Monster was only a man; a big, wet, dirty, smelly man.

The Commissioner looked closely into the man's eyes, and half lowered the stick. "Muldoon?" he inquired in disbelief.

The erstwhile Monster struggle into a sitting position with a horrible attempt at a grin on his face. "By Jesus, Mr. Rossevelt, we've got the bastards worryin' about something, now," he said. Then he collapsed back to the floor with a thud.

Ted tugged at his father's sleeve. "Papa, did you hear—?"

"Yes, son. But sometimes, in extreme circumstances, a man's use of profanity may be overlooked."

II.

Muldoon decided he wanted to spend the rest of his life (after thanking God again that he still had the rest of his life ahead of him) right there in Mr. Roosevelt's bathtub. After twenty-odd years of having to dip in and out of a galvanized tub in the kitchen, with water heated on the wood stove, it was heaven to relax in a proper bathroom, without having to worry someone might want to be entering or leaving the house.

"Muldoon?" Mr. Roosevelt called from the other side of the door.

"Hah?" Muldoon exclaimed. "Oh, yes, sir. I must have been dozin' off for a second. It's been a tryin' day." Muldoon ached all over. Mr. Roosevelt had a frontiersman's rough-and-ready knowledge of medicine, and had used it to tend to Muldoon's cuts and scrapes. The Commissioner then pronounced the officer fit, and told him to go take a bath. Muldoon was all for the bath, but he would just as soon have had a proper doctor. He'd have said so, but he didn't want to hurt Mr. Roosevelt's feelings.

"You may come out any time, Muldoon. I've gotten some clothes for you from one of my men on the Broadway Squad."

The members of the Broadway Squad were the elite of the Department. Every man of them was Muldoon's size and a cracker-jack officer to boot. Muldoon's most cherished aspiration as a policeman was to be named to the Broadway Squad.

Ha, ha, he thought, sounding in his thoughts very harsh and sarcastic. Fat chance of making the Broadway Squad there is for a pudding who let himself be taken by a bunch of toughs, and left for dead under a pile of garbage on one of the scows docked on the West Side, he thought.

Big hero, lying unconscious with a banana peel astride your nose, dumped unceremoniously into the Hudson like the carcass of one of the dead horses Sanitation Commissioner White's men always have to be picking up.

It's a good thing for you, a flaming miracle, if the truth be known (he told himself), that the water of the Hudson River stays cold, even in the summer-time, and that the shock of hitting it brought you to. You're lucky you managed to ditch your shoes, before they brought you to the bottom like two water-filled anchors. You're luckier still gals of a certain age like to go out to Coney Island, or you'd never have learned to stay afloat long enough for that passing boatload of touring Methodists to fish you out.

Muldon shuddered. No, he concluded, if any of those pieces of luck hadn't come through for you, you wouldn't have been found for three-four days, and then you'd be floating belly-up, food for the gulls. Broadway Squad, indeed.

Muldoon made a noise, grabbed the bath-brush, and washed himself some more.

After he dried and dressed, he went with Mr. Roosevelt to the kitchen, for some hot tea with honey and conversation.

"I've been considering your report, Muldoon," the Commissioner said. Roosevelt was as enthusiastic as a hunter on the track of a twenty-point stag. "You have put it precisely right." He rubbed his hands together. "We *have* got them worried. For the first time, they've shown themselves. For the first time, we have outside confirmation that that woman exists, and that she is in some way important. Now for tomorrow—"

Muldoon gripped his cup. "Tomorrow," Muldoon said, "with your kind permission, I'm goin' to devote meself to the settlin' of recent debts. There's a particular bruisin' I'm owin' Mr. Tommy Alb, and I can hardly wait to get square up on it."

"In good time, Muldoon, I promise. But tomorrow, I want you to be dead."

"To be what?"

"Dead, Muldoon."

Muldoon stood up, wincing. "I'd rather not. Death and me have been flirtin' tonight, and I'd just as soon be lettin' the relationship cool off."

"Nonsense, Muldoon. Don't be obtuse. I want them to *think* you are dead, as they undoubtedly do now. They don't know you are working with me—they think you are working alone, or they would never have tried to kill you. Now, they think they are in the clear, and my experience has shown an animal is much easier to trap when he thinks the hunter has given up.

"I detest them, Muldoon, all of them, the ones we know and the ones we must find. The Sperlings, Albs, and the rest think they are strong, but they are cowards, Muldoon, with no more back-bone than a chocolate eclair."

From the satisfied look on the Commissioner's face when he said that, Muldoon judged that Mr. Roosevelt felt he had paid back for the "Big Stick" remark of the other night.

"We have a wedge in, Muldoon. We are closer to the source of the corruption. Tomorrow, we'll be closer still."

"But what will I be doin' in the meantime?" Muldoon wanted to know. "Playin' cow-boys and Indians with Master Theodore?"

"He'd be dee-*lighted*," the Commissioner laughed, "but I have something better for you. You are going to Maine. Lovely country up there. Good hunting."

"I've never been huntin' an animal in me life," Muldoon protested.

"You won't be hunting an animal. You are to beard Joseph Pulitzer in his lair."

Muldoon was puzzled. "Pulitzer?"

"Yes, Muldoon. Hearst has all but accused Pulitzer of being the power behind Crandall's death. I think Pulitzer should have a chance to give his side of the matter."

III.

"My service," Avery said.

Cleo thought she must go mad from boredom. *Ping!* went the tiny celluloid ball as it hit the clumsy little wood-and-skin tambourine held by T. Avery Hand. *Pong!* it went off Cleo's. It was easy to see where the Parker Brothers of Salem, Massachusetts, (whoever *they* were) had gotten the trade name of this new pastime. Table tennis, enthusiasts like Avery called it.

It was all the go these days; it was reputed to be an exercise suitable for men and women to enjoy together. Cleo hated it. Her only consolation was the knowledge that Avery had decided against taking up lawn tennis, where one was actually expected to run around under a hot sun. Even ladies did it, regardless of the fact that it could make them perspire. And in public, too.

Cleo would never run anywhere, ever again. She had done all her running last night, and that had taken her nowhere but into the unholy embrace of Peter Baxter. Cleo closed her eyes tight to blot out the memory. The ball brushed her sleeve and went by her for Avery's point.

"Don't be afraid of the ball," he told her. "It can't hurt you."

"Yes, Avery." The monotony of sound resumed. Ping. Pong. Ping. Pong.

Baxter had taken liberties, extreme liberties, and he had not been gentle. She had, at some time, been unconscious, but whether she fainted, or Baxter had in some way caused it, she had no way to tell. She could not breathe when she tried to imagine what might have happened while she was helpless.

Baxter had ordered her to tell Avery her bruises were the result of a stumble down the stairs. Baxter said he would kill her, painfully, if Hand ever heard so much as a *whisper* about the inside of the carriage house or anything that had happened there. Cleo believed him. Baxter terrified her. She could feel his presence in the house, and she could feel the fear he carried with him.

What could it mean? Did Avery not know about the red candles? About the tweny mill gals?

She wanted to be alone, but Avery wouldn't let her be. Almost a third of her life had been devoted to pleasing men, to making them feel the way they wanted to feel, and what had they ever done for her in return?

The little ball clicked off the green surface of the table. Cleo swung wildly with her tambourine, and smashed it the length of the parlor.

Hand smiled the first smile Cleo could remember seeing on his face in days. There was still worry behind it, but it was genuine nonetheless. He is smiling, Cleo thought angrily, because the ranks of men he must fear has been reduced by one. Rabbi or no, Avery is happy poor Muldoon is dead.

When the ball came to her again, she smashed it harder than before.

"Now you're showing spirit, darling," Hand told her, "but you've got to try to keep the ball on the table."

"I'm afraid I'm not skillful enough, Avery," she said.

"There, there," he said. He laid his tambourine on the table. "I must go to the study and sign some papers—property closings and the like. Why don't you practice with Baxter? *Baxter!*"

"Oh, Avery, no!"

"Yes, Mr. Hand?" Baxter had already appeared in the doorway.

Hand indicated the table. "Keep the young lady occupied while I attend to some papers, won't you?"

Cleo was fervent in her protests that it wasn't necessary. But Baxter smirked at her and told Hand it would be a pleasure.

He picked up the ball and tossed it to her. "Your service, Miss Cleo," he said.

IV.

The news of Muldoon's "death" made its way along his beat even faster than the news of his "dismissal" had. A tearful Mrs. Sturdevant relayed the news to Hiram Listerdale early in the afternoon. Listerdale shook his head sadly, gently pushed Mrs. Sturdevant from the Emporium, locked up, climbed to his rooms above the store to get his hat and a few other things, and went calling on the survivors.

It was much easier, this time, for Listerdale to gain admittance to the Muldoon flat. He simply knocked, identified himself, and was admitted as if he were a family friend of a generation's standing. He found that gratifying. He hoped someday that would precisely state the case.

"Mr. Listerdale," Kathleen said as she admitted him. "How kind of you to be comin' to see us."

"I—I felt it my duty." Listerdale stood playing nervously with his hat, while he searched for the proper words. "I cannot tell you how sorrowful I am to learn of your brother's passing . . ."

"Ah," Kathleen said quietly, "I can imagine. Come in, sit with us, won't you please? Take a cup of tea with us?"

So Listerdale was escorted to the parlor, where he was introduced to Maureen and Brigid. He found them perfectly charming, and as courageous as their sister. Not many women, he thought, could have withstood such a loss with such quiet dignity. Simple people like this—well, all he could do was make a silent vow to continue to do what it was in his power to do for the Muldoons and everyone like them. They were the true Royalty.

Katie Muldoon, bustling about the kitchen making tea, had a decidedly lower opinion of herself. She felt like a liar, and a fraud.

So much so, in fact, that her mourning dress seemed to itch her like a hair shirt.

For a moment, she tried to tell herself that it might have been better if Mr. Theodore Roosevelt (and Lord, how Katie was beginning to hate the sight of that man) hadn't come around this morning with his astounding news of Dennis's near-drowning; and with his intimations of great doings in progress; and especially with his warnings of secrecy. It wasn't fair to put an honest, God-fearing woman through this sort of play-acting. Why—

Katie brought herself up short, made the sign of the Cross, and asked herself how she could ever have been so foolish. If, for one measly second, she had believed her Dennis was lying dead at the bottom of the Hudson, her heart would have broken, and she would have died herself.

Dennis was alive, that was the important thing. And if subtlety was the coin required to pay for that comforting knowledge, then subtle she would be. If she could.

Katie put the tea things on a tray and carried them off to the parlor.

". . . And," Listerdale was saying to the little ones, "while I only knew your brother these few weeks my Emporium has been open, I count myself his friend. I shall always treasure our talks. We shared a love of literature, particularly Shakespeare, so, if I am not presuming, Miss Maureen . . . I mean, I know I can never replace . . . What I'm trying to say is this: If I can be of any assistance in your studies, of Shakespeare or anything else, I would be honored if you would allow me to do so."

"You used to be a schoolmaster, didn't you, Mr. Listerdale?" Katie asked.

"Why, yes, I was. But it was decided—that is, I decided I could achieve greater good for greater numbers here in the big city."

Maureen smiled uneasily. Brigid said, "That's very interestin', Mr. Listerdale," and announced she had to leave for work. Katie could see the girls didn't like play-acting any better than she did.

Maureen assured the bookseller that she would come to him if she needed assistance.

"Thank you," Listerdale said. "I never never tell you how

—how *deeply* I regret your brother's passing." And Katie could see his eyes beginning to mist over.

Listerdale rose to go. "But I have intruded on your grief long enough.

"Before I go, I would like you to have this." He reached into a coat pocket. Katie thought he was going to try to give her money, and sought desperately for a way to turn him down without wounding his feelings.

She was relieved to see it wasn't money.

"This," he said as he handed it to Katie, "is a vial of water from the Sea of Galilee. I extracted it myself, when I visited the Holy Land."

Katie breathed a big, round, Oh. This was even more precious than money. Brigid and Maureen stood breathless, as though they expected the none-too-clean liquid in the vial to glow.

"I hope you all may find comfort in it. It—it has helped me. If, as chemists have it, matter can never truly be destroyed, it may be possible that some molecules of this water knew the touch of Christ; it is possible that some of this water may be the very water He walked on."

Katie started to cry.

Listerdale looked bewildered. "If I have offended you in some way . . ."

Katie took his hands in hers. "No, of course you haven't been offendin' us, you silly man." She sniffed. "How could you be offendin' the likes of *me*? I'm not worthy to touch this vial, let alone be trusted with the keepin' of it. You take it back now."

Listerdale wouldn't hear of it. "I am the one who is unworthy," he said. Katie just cried all the harder and insisted he take it back.

"I don't understand," Listerdale said at last.

Brigid Muldoon has not figured largely in these pages; as a young woman soon to be off on a life of her own, she was occupied during these August days with other concerns. And, being the calm, quiet girl she was, her very nature would isolate her from intrigue and adventure.

But she had wisdom, and a good heart, both of which she used to deal with the situation before her. She embraced her older sister and comforted her. At the same time, she took the vial from Katie's hand and spoke to Listerdale.

"Sir, I can see how much you want Katie to be havin' this water at the moment. And you can see how reluctant she is to be takin' it."

"I do want her to have it. I want all of you to have it."

"I understand. But there are things, that, if you were to know them, might be keepin' you from feelin' that way."

Katie wailed.

"So with your permission, I'll take the vial with me, and on me way to the telphone company, I'll be leavin' it with Father Dominic at the Italian church nearby. Then, when all the circumstances are known to all of us, either Katie or yourself can be retrievin' it from him."

"Bless you, Brigid," Katie sobbed.

"That will be fine with me, Miss Muldoon," Listerdale said. "Thank you." He turned to go. "I just don't understand," he muttered.

His tone was so forlorn, Katie simply couldn't help herself. "Hiram!" she called. "Wait!"

Listerdale stopped halfway down the stairs. "Yes, Miss . . . Kathleen?"

"You deserve to be knowin' the truth, but I've given me word not to tell you, so I can't. But try not to be hatin' me when you do find out."

Listerdale looked at her. Katie thought no man ever seemed more miserable, more tormented than Listerdale did. Look what I've done to him, she thought.

Finally, Listerdale's lips moved. "I could never hate you," he whispered.

V.

Muldoon hated Maine, especially after the misery he had to go through to get there in the first place. It seemed the only train leaving reasonably soon from New York to Ellsworth was a "special" that had been booked up long ago. Muldoon had to use a goodly portion of the expense money Mr. Roosevelt had given him to bribe a young man out of his seat.

He was sorry he'd succeeded as soon as the train started. Sea breezes or not, the train was hotter than the inside of Satan's kerosene stove.

And once they'd made it halfway through Connecticut, it had been like entering a big outdoor asylum. The people didn't speak English—at least not as Muldoon knew it, but they kept making remarks about *his* "accent."

He couldn't get anything to eat but fish, or so it seemed. Once the sun came up (and Muldoon was awake to watch it— tired as he was, he could never sleep well on a train), every time the train stopped, someone was there waving a lobster under his nose. He might as well have been back in Mackerelville.

Bar Harbor was a town on a small bay on the east side of something called Mount Desert Island. "Desert" was pronounced like running away from the Army, instead of like sandy places in Arabia.

He had to take a ferry from Ellsworth to get there. The place looked like a wilderness, covered with trees, except for some scaly-looking pink patches on Mount Desert itself.

The town of Bar Harbor, though, was nice, as far as the look of the place went. There were gingerbready little shops running up a hill from the bay.

But the place was rich folks through and through. It seemed nobody in that town could make a living for two weeks if the rich folks were to stop coming there in the summer and spending money.

Why, Muldoon saw five auto mobiles within a half hour of the time he stepped off the ferry—only the Lord himself knew what kept them from crashing into each other. There hardly seemed to be room for them all.

Muldoon had some questions to ask, but he didn't much like stopping rich folks on the street, even the ones that weren't chugging by in auto mobiles. Unfortunately, the natives would hardly give him the wiggle of a lip. He'd ask someone in a plaid shirt where "Chatwold" was, and they'd always tell him he meant "the old Bowleh place." Muldoon had learned enough of the language to know that "Bowleh" was supposed to be "Bowler," but knowing who had owned the place before Pulitzer didn't help him any. He'd try to say so, politely, but they just went back to doing whatever people in plaid shirts did. It made Muldoon angry.

Chatwold was the name of Mr. Joseph Pultizer's "cottage." Muldoon snorted every time he heard the word. All the nobs had cottages south of town, fronting the ocean for the breeze. Any one of those cottages would have sheltered a hundred and thirteen families from Muldoon's old neighborhood.

Muldoon finally hitched a ride to Chatwold—in a wagon, not an auto mobile. He had convinced some natives that he was leaving town. Like in most summer resorts, people in Bar Harbor thought you were just taking up space if you didn't have money to spend.

Muldoon walked up a private road to the cottage. The place was enormous, built of stone and plaster and timber, every bit as much a mansion as those that clustered around Fifth Avenue back in New York.

Muldoon strode up to the heavy front door and grabbed the gold knocker, then thought better of it. He took out his handkerchief, wiped his neck above his new celluloid collar. He straightened his tie, and made sure the crease in his trousers was sharp. He mopped the sweat from his face, and combed his hair and moustache.

Muldoon was still worried about how he was to gain access to the publisher. His first idea was to pose as a reporter looking for work, but that was hardly an inspiration, what with Pulitzer's newspaper three hundred miles away. His next couple of ideas were even sillier.

His best course he decided, would be to assert himself. He would simply announce himself as an investigator, giving the impression (without actually saying so, if he could help it) that he was still with the Force.

That was his best course; he didn't try to deceive himself into thinking it was a very good one. Pulitzer was not known for allowing himself to be pushed around. What he was known for was sending telegrams, and it would be the work of a moment for him to wire New York to find out about Muldoon and get the reply—Sweet Jesus, Muldoon thought, he'll get the reply that I'm dead.

He grinned. If I'm dead, they can't jail me for impersonating an officer, he thought. He squared his big shoulders, and grabbed the knocker.

A butler opened the door. He dressed like a penguin-bird, and he was built like one. And despite the weather, he looked as cool as a penguin floating to the Pole on a cake of ice.

"Afternoon," Muldoon said. He tipped his new skimmer—the old one hadn't survived Eagle Jack and the boys. "I—"

"You are the young man from New York, I presume," the butler said.

Muldoon was somewhat taken aback. It always bothered him when he went to all the trouble of steeling himself to lie, then found out he didn't have to. Because, somehow or other, they were expecting him.

"I am that," Muldoon said.

"You are late."

"Sorry. The train moved as though it was burnin' ice shavin's for coal." The butler nearly smiled, Muldoon would swear it. "Say, how did you know I was comin'? Did Mr. Roosevelt wire you after all?" They had discussed wiring Pulitzer in advance, but had decided against it, so as to take him by surprise if something really were amiss. Or so Muldoon had thought.

"Wire?" the butler intoned. He waved a hand. "Well, no matter, Mr. Pulitzer and his staff are in the Tower. You are to see his secretary, Mr. Smithers.

The door closed. Muldoon got one last look at the carved lions and the huge staircase and the expensive rugs before it swung shut. Muldoon was tempted to knock again, to get another look at the opulence, and to ask directions. He didn't, because he didn't want to take a chance of saying or doing something wrong. He wanted to get inside that Tower. He had read about it, but not in any of Mr. Pulitzer's publications.

The Tower of Silence—a square structure, four stories high, was sound-proofed from top to bottom. And most astounding of all, the basement of the building was a bathing pool. Muldoon could hardly believe it—a whole man-made pond for the old geezer to go swimming in.

The Tower of Silence was attached to Chatwold itself on the sea side. Muldoon decided it was more impressive to read about than to see. It looked like it had been plopped down next to the mansion by mistake. It was just a few feet too tall to be a perfect cube, and it was so plain as to be practically featureless. After all the elaborate architecture he'd seen in New England, Mr. Pulitzer's retreat reminded him of a nun in the middle of the Fifth Avenue Ladies' Cotillion.

It took a while for anyone to answer Muldoon's knock. He worried for a second that the door might be sound-proofed; that he'd be standing there and knocking all night.

Eventually, though, they let him in, and showed him to Mr. Smithers. Smithers was a pleasant young man, not much older than Muldoon himself.

"How do you do?" he said, extending a hand. His voice was very soft.

"Me own pleasure, entirely," Muldoon told him. "I'm Dennis Muldoon, I understand you've been expectin' me."

Smithers raised an eyebrow. "Why, er, yes—that is, we were given to understand your name was *Moulton*. Is something funny?"

For Muldoon was laughing. Moulton was the name of the college boy he'd bought the seat on the train from. The similarity in names was an added stroke of luck.

"No," the officer said. "I was just thinkin' of somethin'. No, Muldoon is the proper pronunciation of me name."

"Please," Smithers said. "Speak quietly. That's a habit you must begin to cultivate immediately, if you are to work for Mr. Pulitzer."

"Sorry," Muldoon whispered.

"That's better," Smithers said, but without enthusiasm. He pursed his lips, stroked his chin. "You," he told Muldoon, "are *Irish*."

"*I*," Muldoon began, with some heat.

"Quietly," Smithers reminded him.

"I," Muldoon said again, with reduced volume but no less intensity, "am an *American!* I've got a document as says so. Have you?"

"Heh, heh," said Smithers. "No offense meant. After all, Mr. Pulitzer is himself a naturalized citizen. It's just that your voice . . ."

"And what, pray tell, is the matter with me voice?"

"Well . . . Have you any education?"

"Good Lord, man!" Muldoon was getting angry now, and kept his voice low only with difficulty. "Haven't we been talkin'? Can't you see me intellectual ways? And in case that's not enough, I've got another document as says I'm educated. All right?"

"Hmm," Smithers said. "Wait here a moment." He disappeared through a doorway and returned after a few seconds, bearing a two-day old New York *World*. "Read this," he said.

"I read it two days ago, in New York," Muldoon replied.

"No, no. Read it aloud."

About this time, Muldoon was deciding that the Tower of Silence should be renamed the Tower of Silliness, but he began to read aloud. Smithers listened, nodding approval for the most part, but occasionally breaking in with a comment such as "More quietly," or "There is too much expression in your voice," or "For God's sake, don't rattle the paper!"

Finally he said, "That's enough. I'll take you to Mr. Pulitzer, now."

At last! Muldoon thought. "I'm beholden to you," he said.

Smithers was suddenly brisk. "Well, let us see what transpires. You have a pleasant voice; he may like you. I don't believe he's ever had an Irish one before."

VI.

Muldoon was firmly resolved to start swinging at the first sign of funny stuff. He didn't care if Mr. Choe Bulitzer (opposing papers often rendered the publisher's name that way, to make fun of the man's accent) had ever had an Irish one or not. He didn't like the sound of it, and he wasn't about to let himself be the first, whatever it was.

It was dimly lit inside, and quiet. Muldoon followed Smithers's lead along the poolside to where the slight, bearded figure reclined, wrapped in a thick robe.

"This is Mr. Muldoon, sir," Smithers said.

Pulitzer peered through thick lenses at the young man, or at least toward him. "So?" he said.

The rumors are true, Muldoon thought. The man is stone blind.

"You are applying for a job as one of my secretaries? Let me hear you read."

"No ,sir," Muldoon said softly. He was glad to know reading was all the old man wanted. "I'm afraid I've been a little slow correctin' a misconception. I'm not applyin' for a job—I have one already. What I'm doin' is interrogatin' you on behalf of the Police Department of the City of New York."

Muldoon heard Smithers gasp. The young officer had heard rumors of Pulitzer's hysterical outbursts at the most trivial of irritations. Smithers was apparently ready for one now.

But it didn't come. The old man looked somewhere past Muldoon. "So that's what you are doing, is it?" His accent was that of the vaudeville East European, but his manner was patriarchal, at the moment, gentle.

"Yes, Mr. Pulitzer," Muldoon said. "I'll ask me questions and be on me way."

"Why do you come to ask me questions?"

"Evan Crandall has been killed."

The publisher's voice took on a hard edge. "I know that, young man, I publish a newspaper."

"Yes, sir. And a fine one it is, at that. We have heard that you've had dealings with Mr. Crandall—a business deal that fell through."

"I never met the man."

"But I wouldn't be wrong in supposin' one of your famous telegrams gave the order to hire the fellow away from Hearst, would I?"

"You've been talking to Hearst?"

"We're goin' about our investigations," Muldoon said.

"He worked for me you know, Hearst did. After he was thrown out of college. Harvard. He is an ambitious bastard. He wants power to go with his money. You are young, you'll see. What did he tell you? That I sailed my yacht to New York and killed Crandall, then sailed back to Bar Harbor?"

"It has been suggested you might be interested in seein' that E. Noon wasn't drawin' cartoons for Bryan durin' the campaign."

"And what do you think of that charge, Officer?"

"It's not me proper place to be havin' opinions, Mr. Pulitzer."

"Not as an officer, then." Pulitzer laughed. In some perverted way, he seemed to be enjoying himself.

Muldoon wasn't. Still, if the old man insisted . . . "As a man, then," he said. "It seems to me that backin' Mr. McKinley is a strange thing for all these Democrat papers to be doing, especially the *World*."

"God *damn* it!" Pulitzer exploded. He shook his small, spare frame with his anger, raised his fists and brought them down heavily on his couch. "The *World* is not a Democrat newspaper!" He screamed. "The *World* is *independent! Inde-goddamn-pendent!* Do you hear me, you young fool? How dare you—"

Smithers was beside himself. He looked daggers at Muldoon, then bent to soothe his employer. Muldoon was embarrassed, and sorry that he'd upset the old man, but he was a bit angered, too. He said so.

"Hold on a minute," Muldoon commanded.

"Hush!" Smithers commanded.

"Hush yourself," Muldoon told him. "Mr. Pulitzer!" he barked, trying to cut through the publisher's tirade. "Mr. Pulitzer!"

"What? What, goddammit? What do you want?"

"You ought to be ashamed of yourself," Muldoon scolded him.

"Are you mad?" Smithers hissed.

"I ain't been askin' anything worse than I've heard reporters for the *World* ask lots of folks. Granted, their job is askin' the questions. So is mine. I'm not askin' for more respect than a reporter gets, but by Jesus, I aim to be gettin' that much.

"What do you say? You're a fair man. Am I right, or ain't I?"

"You—Goddammit, Smithers, let go of me!—You're right, young man. I—Well, you're right, that's all. I'm telling you, Smithers—Good.

"But my answer remains the same, Officer. The *World* is independent—it will back whomever it pleases, yes? And it will answer to no one but the Public. If you will but read the *World* you would know why Bryan is unacceptable as a Presidential candidate."

Pulitzer was calming down. He adjusted the lenses before the feeble eyes and leaned back. "I saw Lincoln, you know. He reviewed my regiment."

This was the first Muldoon had known that Pulitzer had even been in the Army. He said so.

Pulitzer laughed. "I hated it. But I was penniless and spoke little English, and the Army fed me, in exchange for going to war."

He was silent for a few moments. Muldoon waited for the old man's thoughts to lead him somewhere besides hate and warfare.

"Hearst," Pulitzer said at last. "Hearst is so ready to accuse, is he? I will tell you about Hearst. He has stolen my circulation lists, my distribution reports. This past week. All the secrets I have built since I came to New York, how many papers will be for sale, where and when, he has stolen. Oh, he claims they at his paper 'recovered' them for me but I know better. You tell that to your superiors, hey?"

"Yes, sir." Something else for Mr. Roosevelt to consider, Muldoon mused. Did Crandall have anything to do with the missing circulation information?

"Anything else you want of me, young man? Are you through wasting my time?"

"Yes, sir. I'm sure I can be gettin' the rest of the information I need from Mr. Smithers here."

"Yes, you can," Smithers said. "I'll join you in a minute."

Muldoon waited outside, digesting, speculating. When Smithers joined him, he got from him a list of persons to talk to in New York that might be of help.

Muldoon was relieved when he could shut his notebook at last. He was returning to New York on the next train.

"You are lucky to have caught Mr. Pulitzer on one of his more mellow days," Smithers told him.

Muldoon clicked his tongue. "Can't be an easy life for you secretary fellows. Or for himself, either."

"He's a great man, Muldoon," Smithers said. They shook hands. Smithers said he'd have a car take Muldoon to the ferry in Bar Harbor. Muldoon thanked him and turned to leave.

"Oh, Muldoon," Smithers said.

"Yes?"

"He liked your voice. If you think you may have had enough of police work . . ."

"But I haven't though," Muldoon said. "Not yet."

WEDNESDAY
the twenty-sixth
of August, 1896

I.

There were still several hours of daylight remaining when Muldoon arrived at 689 Madison Avenue. The servant told him Mr. Roosevelt wasn't home, and was going to close the door on him, until young Ted came along and vouched for him.

Muldoon was glad of it, but he wouldn't have been surprised if the boy had had him pitched into the street. It would have been consistent, Muldoon decided, with the last few days.

Muldoon's opinion was that he'd been through an awful lot— a beating, a near drowning, and two long and nearly sleepless train rides—for precious little help from Joseph Pulitzer.

Even when he'd returned to the family flat, he'd found things in an uproar. The womenfolk were in a panic over deceiving "poor Mr. Listerdale" about Muldoon's death.

"For cryin' out loud," Muldoon had said to Katie. "I'd have

told him meself I was alive if I'd thought of it. Water from the Holy Land, eh?" Muldoon was impressed. He'd known Listerdale to be an educated man, but not a World Traveler.

Muldoon resolved to speak with Listerdale at his first opportunity. He was likely to be pretty busy, and it would make him feel a lot more secure if he knew a man he could trust was coming in from time to time to make sure the girls were all right.

Having gotten that settled, Muldoon took a nap, then sent word to Roosevelt at Police Headquarters that he was back in town and ready to report.

He sat around the Commissioner's parlor, waiting for him to arrive. When he did, Muldoon thought he was seeing things.

"Watch out, Mr. Roosevelt!" he exclaimed, then rushed the doorway. Standing right behind Roosevelt, on the stoop, was the one-eyed man from Eagle Jack Sperling's gang. He recognized the thick ears, the barrel chest, and the close-cropped, bristly hair that marked the professional brawler. Muldoon couldn't understand how the Commissioner had let him get so close behind him, on his own stoop besides.

The one-eyed man dropped into a fighter's crouch, but that wouldn't help him against what Muldoon had in mind. After his treatment the other night, he was going right for the throat with this character.

The Commissioner, to Muldoon's astonishment, stepped between them. "Muldoon!" he said, placing both hands hard against the young officer's chest. "Dee-*lighted* to see you again. I'd like you to meet Roscoe Heath." He indicated the one-eyed man.

"We've met," Muldoon said. "Look here, sir, this is one of the mugs that almost did for me!"

"Hey," Roscoe growled, "I'm mighty sorry about that. I did my best. I was on trial with the gang, they watched me careful."

Roosevelt sighed. "I suspected this might happen. I must apologize, Muldoon. I suspected this when you described the members of the gang."

"What's goin' on here?" Muldoon wanted to know. He was more than a little perturbed.

"Roscoe is working with us, Muldoon. You may recall I mentioned his name to the Reverend at the Christian Fellowship. He's the fellow I used to spar with in Albany. I'm going to see the Reverend gives him a job." He looked at Muldoon, who was still wary, and at Roscoe, who was sheepish.

"Shake hands," Roosevelt commanded.

Roscoe had a grip that could powder a billiard ball, but Muldoon gave as good as he got, and seemed to pass some sort of test.

"I am really sorry about the other night, Denny," Roscoe said. "The boss is giving me more of a break than I deserve, and I don't want to muck it up." Roscoe's growl was low and friendly.

"I'm through cracking houses," Roscoe went on, "and before I got dragged into this business, I *thought* I was through cracking heads. They made me in charge of loading you on the garbage scow, which was lucky, cause I'm a trainer, and I know a lot about bringing guys to. You was supposed to wake up before you got dumped in the drink, but I guess I lost my touch in Sing Sing."

Muldoon grinned in spite of himself. He found it impossible not to like the fellow. "I'm glad you've reformed," Muldoon told him. "I wouldn't like to be arrestin' the likes of you."

"Haw, haw," Roscoe said. "Don't worry, Denny," he added, clapping Muldoon on the back. "I just fell in with bad companions. Now the boss has me doing it again."

Muldoon looked inquiringly at the Commissioner. "Sir?"

"A fortunate co-incidence, Muldoon. These Mansion Burglaries have all had a slight flavor of what the criminals call an 'inside job.' It occurred to me that Sperling has had dealings with quite a few of the victims, so I set Roscoe to infiltrate that gang and see if he could learn anything. I knew they would accept him—"

"All I done," Roscoe said, shrugging modestly, "was let my record speak for itself."

"That record is nothing to be proud of," Roosevelt reminded him.

"No, sir," he said. "But it done the job."

Roosevelt ignored him. "That idea, unfortunately, proved to be unfounded. Eagle Jack, Roscoe has learned, is far too protective of the rich men who hire his services to try to rob them. So that remains a mystery. However, he has heard some other things, provocative things."

"Yes, sir?" Muldoon asked.

"In good time, Muldoon. First tell me of your interview with Pulitzer."

Muldoon told him. "I'm sorry, sir," he concluded, "but the poor old daffy was so sick and miserable I didn't have the heart to press him."

"Don't worry, I'm sure you did your best." Suddenly, he laughed through his teeth. "Besides, you have the consolation of knowing a job awaits you.

"Now to bring you up to date. For one thing, you are alive again."

Muldoon yawned and rubbed his eyes. "Thank you, but it strikes me as a bit of a pity. What with the company I've been keepin', and the paces I've been through, I've been feelin' deader and deader all the time."

"Nonsense!" Roosevelt told him. "There's work to be done." He hissed. "To pick up Roscoe's story, then. He found Sperling at his hideout in a foul saloon in Five Points—"

"It wasn't so bad, considering," Roscoe said.

"Be quiet. Roscoe was accepted, provisionally, almost at once."

"They asked me what made me think I was good enough to join the gang. But this is where the boss had them outsmarted. Nobody is smarter at this sort of thing than the boss is."

"Go on with the story, Roscoe," the Commissioner said, trying to behave as though he weren't pleased.

"Yeah," Roscoe said. "I just told them what the boss said to tell them. I says, 'What makes you think your gang is good enough for the likes of me?'

"Well, then a couple of them says they're gonna show me how good they are, but Eagle Jack said I was just talking tall, and the time was coming when they'd be able to find out if I was blowing hot air or what.

"Then, couple days later, he comes to me and says 'There's some fellow named Muldoon might need a little persuadin'. This is your chance to see if you got the makings of a business man.'

"That made me laugh, but I told him okay. I didn't know then you was working for the boss too, but I done my best to keep you from getting hurt. I never hit you all I got, and I sort of got in the way of anybody had a real good shot at you. I'm sorry you got hurt."

"We've been through all that already, Roscoe," Roosevelt said. "Tell him what happened afterwards."

So Roscoe told about the mysterious visitor to the back room of Max's. "Eagle Jack never said his name and I never seen him," Roscoe explained. "But I listened." When he finished, the Commissioner's eyes were bright. "The plot thickens, eh? We'll just have to widen our search to include this Cleo and this mysterious 'Rabbi'."

"Cleo," Muldoon said. What could these people have to do with my getting killed, he wondered.

"Yes, Muldoon?" Roosevelt asked. "Does it mean something to you?"

"I don't know, Commissioner," Muldoon replied. "A thought went whizzin' through me brain like the Third Avenue Express, and I wasn't quite able to flag it down. Can you tell me anything else, Roscoe?"

"Nah, I hung around some more, hopin' somebody'd let drop what Rabbi they're talkin' about, but then somebody comes in the saloon that knows me from upstate, knows I'm friendly with the boss. So before I knew it, I had eighteen mugs trying to kill me."

"My Lord," said Muldoon, remembering his recent experience with a few of those mugs. "How in heaven's name did you get away?"

"Fought my way out, what do you think? Crack a few heads, break a few arms, it's easy when you got the knack. Course, you can't expect to get out untouched from a spot like that." Casually, Roscoe pulled up his shirt to reveal a hairy belly partially covered by a bandage the size of the pillow they carry the wedding ring to the bride on.

"I was still trying after I left," Roscoe went on. "I come across Willie Du Pré in the street, grabbed him, and done horrible things to him, but he still couldn't tell me nothing about the Rabbi or about Cleo."

"It's a shame," Muldoon said.

"Yeah," Roscoe agreed. "One thing you'll be glad, though. I sort of pushed Tommy Alb's nose off center for him. He ain't gonna be so pretty in the future."

"That's enough, Roscoe," Roosevelt commanded. The one-eyed man was smiling at the memory, admiring it, Muldoon thought, exactly the way Mrs. Herkimer had admired the works of art the other day at the gallery.

The express whizzed by again, but this time it stopped. The gallery. The works of art. Angels. *Ankhs.*

"Cleo," Muldoon said.

"Yes, Muldoon?" the Commissioner barked anxiously. "What is it?"

"I know who it is."

"Who? I shall order the search for him immediately!"

Muldoon laughed. "You already have, sir. I've been doin' the searchin'. Only Cleo isn't a him. It's Cleopatra, I'll wager. It's the woman we're lookin' for. It's the Pink Angel."

II.

Muldoon walked the familiar streets of Mackerelville for hours searching for Brian O'Leary. The boy had, since Saturday last, taken Mr. Roosevelt at his word and visited him at Mulberry Street once or twice.

The Commissioner remembered the boy's home address. Muldoon had gone there. The dark windowless flat he'd found, and the drunk and the shrew inside, were all Muldoon needed to tell him why Brian O'Leary spent most of his time on the streets.

The boy's name had come up as the solution to a problem. Cleo had to be found. As Mr. Roosevelt had pointed out, now that they had a name for her, the searching would go that much more easily.

But not for the police. It pained Muldoon to have to insist on that, but he was adamant. "Look, Mr. Roosevelt," he'd said, "I don't like this sneakin' around any more than you do. But the fact is there for all to see: Captain Herkimer met me searchin' for Cleo that afternoon, and before the day was out, I was tossed in the drink like I was personally chummin' for sharks."

Roosevelt had to face the truth, though it irritated him. He mumbled something about keeping closer eye on Captain Herkimer.

So the police were to be left out. How to find the woman's trail?

Surprisingly enough, it was Roscoe who inspired the idea. Roscoe had a taste for sensational literature (acquired in prison) that was the rival of Muldoon's own. While the patrolman and the Commissioner discussed the problem, the ex-pugilist wondered aloud what Mr. Sherlock Holmes would do in a situation like this.

Muldoon (and Mr. Roosevelt too, if the truth be known) gave out with a cry of astonishment. It was *obvious* what the hero of Mr. Arthur Conan Doyle's detective romances would do.

So Muldoon strolled the streets of the neighborhood where he had grown to manhood, looking for the newsboy who counted Mr. Roosevelt his friend.

He found him at twilight in the midst of a game of hide-and-seek. The boy was so intent on the game, he never noticed Muldoon standing near home base until he'd "tap-tapped" everyone from his hiding place.

"You've got the makin's of a good detective," Muldoon told him. "I never thought you'd find the one under the ash-pile."

"Ahh, that's Filthy Larry. He always hides under the ash-pile." He regarded Muldoon. "Ain't I met you before, Mister?"

"You have. The same time night you met Mr. Roosevelt."

The boy brushed red hair from his eyes, and narrowed them at the officer. "Mulroy, ain't it?"

"Muldoon."

"I ain't done nothing," Brian said quickly.

"I ain't sayin' you did. I'm just a messenger. I've got a note here for you from Mr. Roosevelt."

The boy took it, after wiping his dirty hands on his knickers. He studied the note. "Uses a lot of big words, don't he?"

"I'll explain anything you can't understand," Muldoon said.

"Who's this Doyle fellow? He the one lives on Delancey Street?"

"He's an Englishman. We're goin' to borrow an idea he wrote in a book. You ought to read one sometime."

"I'm too busy with my papers. It says here you're supposed to give me a dollar."

"Understood that part all right, didn't you? You only get the dollar if you take the job." Muldoon reached into his pocket. "Well, boy, what is it? Are you willin' to serve as Captain of the Mulberry Street Irregulars?"

Brian made a face. "What are you talking about? We ain't nowhere near Mulberry Street. And as for the other part, if that nasty cod liver oil they make us take in school don't keep us reg—"

"Never mind," Muldoon interrupted. That was what came of trying to deal with illiterates. "Just do what it says in the letter. Get a bunch of your hoodlum newsboy friends together, and tell Mr. Roosevelt and me where to find this Cleo woman. Will you do that?"

"Sure, for Mr. Roosevelt, I will."

"Good."

"Yeah," the boy said. "Gimme the dollar."

III.

Thursday night—servants' night off. Peter Baxter and a companion walked slowly along a city street.

The voices came loudly through the ground-floor window. "A dollar and forty cents? For a little scrap of rag!"

"It's genuine silk, Harry!"

"Dammit, Marie, do you know how long I have to work to earn *a dollar and forty cents?*"

"It's not like I spend it every day." The woman was near tears. "My sister is getting married. I'm matron of honor. I have to look respectable."

"Oh, so now we're not respectable, is that it?"

"Harry, you are so . . . *ooh!*"

"Genuine silk. I suppose you'll be wanting diamonds next, or a kerosene stove. Well, wool, glass, and coal is all we can afford, Marie!"

Silence, then a quiet, "I know."

"What—why, I ought to belt you!"

"If you do, Harry, I warn you, don't go to sleep when I'm around. Or so help me I'll take a knife and—"

Peter Baxter and his companion walked by the window, the angry voices receding into inaudibility behind them.

"Damn the rich," Baxter said. "Damn them for keeping the poor poor, and even more for dangling their riches before them."

"Not in public," his companion, the individual known to T.

Avery Hand as "Rabbi" hissed. "How many times must I tell you?"

The two stepped inside a building, then a room. A make-up kit lay on a mirrored vanity that was the most expensive thing there.

"Better lock that away," Baxter said. He rubbed one of his smooth ears.

"I intended to." The Rabbi locked the make-up kit in a drawer. "You know, Peter," the Rabbi said, "I've been thinking that it might be more advantageous to our cause to wait."

Baxter sat on a windowsill and snorted. "We've waited long enough. What we've done in this country is nothing to what they've done in London, Paris, Vienna, or St. Petersburg. They've come near to killing *kings*. We can be expected to do no less."

"There is more to life than killing, Peter."

"Not for capitalists. Not for kings."

"We could *control* a king!"

"What are you talking about? We have no interest in controlling a government. 'Government is the yoke of Slavery on the neck of Mankind.' You yourself made me see that."

His companion smiled sadly at him. "And you learned well, didn't you? But look, Peter, my friend and comrade, how this all has grown. We put you in with Hand to tell us how to retrieve the riches he has stolen from the poor, just as we did with the others.

"But Hand has turned to politics, and worked his way into the confidence of that imposter Bryan. Bryan is coming back to the city. Vulnerable. And Franklyn and Libstein and you and I evolved the plan for this great gesture."

Baxter bit his tongue. If the Movement didn't frown so on personal glory, he would have pointed out that the plan was his. He was the one with the opportunity, and he was the one with the expertise.

"It will be a master stroke," he said. "It will show the slave masters that they can't escape justice, even in their mansions."

"It's a good plan," the Rabbi said. "Haven't I worked for it? Didn't I kill Crandall to make sure Hand stayed high in Bryan's regard until he could come here? Haven't I put fear into Hand's heart, to keep him in line?"

"Look here," Baxter said. If the other could break the rules, so could he. "You killed Crandall, but you took no notice of the woman."

"Who would have thought the fool would keep her in his own flat? I told you immediately when I saw her leave the building."

"You *should* have thought it. She could have been fatal to our plan. But *I* tracked her down, and *I* brought her back."

The Rabbi patted the servant on the shoulder. "You've done well, as always, Peter. Perhaps we don't say these things as often as we should.

"But that wasn't the point. Don't you see that the document Hand gave Crandall, the document we now possess, puts Hand in our power for as long as it serves the purpose of humanity to keep him there? If Bryan wins, Hand becomes Secretary of the Treasury; and since we control Hand, that puts us in command of the loot of the capitalists. We can build schools, decent housing —yes, and libraries as well."

Baxter smiled.

"We can use the power of the currency to bring the capitalists to their knees," the Rabbi went on, "first in this country, then in others. We could—"

"Rule the world?" Baxter interrupted. "Is that what you were going to say, Teacher? Power? Command? Strange words, my friend, from the person whose lips taught me the truth of things in the first place. Wasn't it you who said, 'Power is a powerful drug, and those who taste of it are soon little better than madmen'?

"Why this sudden tenderness toward the Enemy? You know as well as I do that Hand is better dead, Bryan is better dead. They will all have their finest hour as corpses. And it will happen like a bolt of lightning striking them down, turning the stolen palace into a mausoleum. The world," he concluded, his eyes bright, "will never forget."

"Peter, please try to take a longer view. Don't you see how we could—"

"Yes, we could, but the People *will*. When they see what we've done, they will *take* their freedom. They will know how."

"Faith."

"Have you lost yours? Perhaps we should put the matter to

the Committee, Franklyn and Libstein and the rest. Perhaps they will see fit to make a change."

"Perhaps. But until a change is made, I am still the one who was chosen to lead this mission. Pray remember that."

Baxter was silent. His companion took that for consent. "Very well. I will consult the others. I'll wire Franklyn and Libstein in Philadelphia immediately I finish dinner. In the meantime, Peter, the plan will proceed. What are we to do with this woman Cleo?"

"What do you mean?"

"She saw the dynamite?"

"Well, yes. But she took it for candles. She had no idea what we mean to do. And I've made sure she won't talk."

"How? With threats? Threats only work with a woman so long. She is dangerous, Peter. I'm afraid you must kill her." The Rabbi's voice was sad, but resigned.

Baxter choked. "I—I disagree," he said.

"Why this sudden tenderness?" was the mocking reply.

"Nonsense," Baxter said through clenched teeth. The Committee must definitely hear of this behavior. No one, not even an old, dear friend like his companion, could endanger the Movement with so cavalier an attitude.

"Hand is unstable enough," Baxter explained. "Of all the trappings of his wealth, he values this . . . this *whore* the most highly." He had to pause a moment to regain his temper. He hated that woman, because the only thing worse than the capitalists were those who indulged them in their corrupt pleasures.

"And Hand is afraid," he went on. "Your melodramatic visit—"

"It was necessary."

"Necessary or not, has made Hand fearful and wary. If the woman dies, he will not be able to function. He could no longer deceive his fiancée. The wedding would be postponed, perhaps canceled. Bryan wouldn't come."

"Enough, Peter, enough. You convince me. Let her live."

Baxter was astonished, and somewhat annoyed, at his own relief. "Besides," his companion went on, "if the council decides your course of action is best, she is very likely to die with the rest of them."

THURSDAY
the twenty-seventh
of August, 1896

I.

Before Muldoon's arrival at the Christian Fellowship last Saturday night, Theodore Roosevelt had told the boys a tale of a man lost in the Bad Lands without food or water, and how he had been pointed in the direction of both by one tiny paw-print.

The name "Cleo," young Brian O'Leary reflected, had apparently done the same. He was proud of himself for accomplishing what the grown men could not. He had picked up the trail of the Pink Angel.

Brian O'Leary knew every newsboy in New York, having tangled with a significant number of them. He had fought (literally) his way up to a choice corner on Wall Street, and he stood always ready to defend it.

He had called on his acquaintances, and told them what to do. He had the information in five hours, and he still had thirty cents of the dollar Muldoon had given him, an amount some grown men couldn't earn in a day. He'd saved the money through shrewd bargaining among his comrades.

With the homing instinct most street boys seem to develop, Brian found the Muldoon flat. He was admitted to the parlor, where Mr. Roosevelt, Muldoon, and some guy named Listerdale were talking.

"Ah, Brian," the Commissioner said. "Have you news?"

"Yes, sir. Good news." Muldoon's sister, or wife, or something, a nice-smelling lady called Katie, brought Brian a glass of milk from the kitchen, asked him was he related to some O'Learys he's never heard of, patted him on the head, then left.

"It was Stinky McGonigle told me what we wanted to find out, so I give him an extra nickel. He used to work the block where this Cle—"

Listerdale raised a hand to stop him. "Just a moment, young man, if you please." He turned to the Commissioner. "Mr. Roosevelt, this seems to be police business, and I am not a policeman. Since I am here only because Officer Muldoon has honored me with the request to help him look after his sisters, perhaps I should pay them my respects in the kitchen, then see to my Emporium for the rest of the afternoon."

Roosevelt chewed his moustache. "Yes, perhaps that would be best. Thank you, Listerdale."

The balding man left. The Commissioner told Brian to go on.

"Who was that guy?" the newsboy wanted to know.

"A friend. You must learn, Brian, to follow orders immediately they are given. Now, give me your report."

"Yes, sir." Brian took a sip of milk, licked his lip, and began. "This Cleo you're looking to find—I found out she's a *hooer*. Why are you looking for a hooer? Ain't you mar—"

"That's pronounced *hor*, Brian," Muldoon said hastily. "W-H-O-R-E." Muldoon was probably the only Irishman in New York who pronounced that word properly—it was one of the marks of his education—but it wasn't his intention to show off. He'd just said the first thing that popped into his mind, in order to drown the boy out. He shuddered to think what the proper Mr. Roosevelt would have made of the implication that the

Commissioner desired to see Cleo in connection with her profession and not his.

Muldoon needn't have worried. The word itself had been enough—the Commissioner doubtless hadn't even heard the question. He hissed through his teeth and waved his finger at the boy. "Master O'Leary, if one of my men dared use such a word to me in reporting, I would fire him on the spot! I only excuse you this time because of your youth and ignorance.

"But *you*, Muldoon, have no such excuse. Speaking such a word, even spelling it out! A police officer must be upright in appearance, behavior, *and* speech. You should be ashamed of yourself."

Muldoon hung his head. "I am, sir," he said. "Would *prostitute* have been better?"

"*It would not have been one particle better!*" The Commissioner's steam was way up, now. "Not in the presence of the boy!"

Muldoon was meek. "Harlot?" he asked in a small voice.

Roosevelt nodded grimly. "The word is in the Scriptures. I prefer, however, 'lady of the evening.' It isn't nearly so coarse. You must strive to be a gentleman, Brian. Please remember that."

"Yes, sir," the boy said. He went on with his report. "This Cleo is a lady of the evening," he said. "She used to be the star trick at Madam Nanette's cathouse on West Fifth."

Muldoon worked on not laughing. There was a delay of several minutes while Mr. Roosevelt instructed Brian in the proper words to use in Society. In the interval, a great sadness had come over Muldoon. Cleo had used him. All that talk about her shame and her tears and all that. Shame my eye, he thought. Why, nakedness was probably her natural state!

He was still pondering that one when Mr. Roosevelt finished. "Boy," Brian said, "this gentleman stuff isn't easy, is it, Muldoon?"

Muldoon, still thinking of the woman, agreed. The boy resumed. He didn't have to give them the background of Madam Nanette's. Until a year ago, it had been the best-known bawdy house in the city. All the swells had gone there, and many an underpaid copper had supplemented his income with a little something at the back door.

Then, what with the reform administration coming in, Madam

Nanette had decided to retire. She was old, and, thanks to Cleo and women like her, extremely rich.

Unfortunately, neither Stinky McGonigle nor any of the others had been able to say what had become of Cleo; some thought she'd taken up with one of the foreign noblemen or rich millionaires that made up the bulk of Madam Nanette's clientele; some said she might even have married one. Based on his knowledge of hooers—of ladies of the evening, rather—he didn't think it likely.

Muldoon was not happy. Something inside him told him he would never be at ease until he saw and spoke to this Cleo, this misnamed Angel. "So you don't have any idea of where she might be hidin' then? Or who she might be with?"

"No," Brian admitted. "But Madam Nanette might. And *everybody* knows where *she* is."

II.

It was the third hotel they'd stayed in since their arrival in Philadelphia some five and a half days ago. This was the best one yet—it had a view, more or less, of Independence Hall. What revolutionary history had been made there. Franklyn tangled his hands in his bushy beard as he looked out the window and nursed a dream that just as his misspelled namesake had gone down in history for helping end the tyranny of a mad monarch, he too would earn immortality by freeing mankind of the tyranny of government of any kind.

It was his favorite dream, and Philadelphia his favorite place. Libstein didn't know it, but Franklyn had engineered matters so that they would stay in this particular hotel the longest. Their frequent moves were supposed to be at random, to avoid, as Libstein put it, "attempts by the corrupt power-structure to still the voice of Freedom," or as Franklin translated, "We don't want any goons to come in and beat us to death."

It was a surprising but verifiable fact that no one had ever tried. It was also a little disappointing. Part of the romance of being a leading anarchist was how dangerous you were to the Privileged, and how they'd stop at nothing to wipe you out.

Franklyn chuckled. The Privileged would find out just how dangerous, very, very soon.

Libstein was seated at a desk working on a speech to be delivered to the stone cutters tomorrow morning. With his glasses pulled down his patrician nose, and his sleeves held clear of the wet ink by black garters, he looked like apotheosis of Capitalism. Franklyn had to chuckle again.

Libstein was very short tempered when he was working on a speech. He looked up at his companion and said, "What the devil are you laughing about? Is there no work you can be doing?"

"I'm sorry, my friend. I was reflecting on the times I have argued with you against playing musical hotels when we're in this country. Now I'm glad we've had the practice. When Bryan and the rest die Saturday, they'll be after us for sure—and all their lip service about fair trials will vanish." That was one thing about Europe, Franklyn reflected. They were not so hypocritical as to pretend it wasn't open war on the forces of Anarchy. "Come Saturday, it *will* be necessary to be hard to find."

Libstein clicked his tongue at his disheveled colleague. "It has always been necessary," he said flatly.

"Oh, come now," Franklyn began, when a loud pounding on the door caused him to stop.

"Franklyn?" a loud voice bellowed. "Libstein? You in there?"

"Were you expecting anyone?" the distinguished Mr. Libstein hissed to his partner.

"No," came the whispered reply. "We don't meet with the Philadelphia Inner Circle until tomorrow."

"What do we do?"

"What can we do?" Franklyn gave a shrug and bowed to fate. "What do you want?" he demanded of the door.

"Telegram," the loud voice said. "Two of them, in fact."

"It's a trick," Libstein insisted. He went to his valise, opened it, and took out, to Franklyn's dismay, one of the things Cleo would have taken for a red candle.

"What are you doing?" Franklyn croaked.

"We're doomed, comrade. We will take them with us."

Franklyn swallowed hard, but at last he admitted it was all they could do. Libstein lit the fuse, which sparked and hissed like an Independence Day firework.

"I can't wait here all day, you know," came the voice from outside. Franklyn opened the door.

To his astonishment he found, not an army of large-muscled, small-brained minions of oppression, but one, small, old, irascible delivery boy, who handed him two yellow envelopes.

"Uh—thank you," he said. The delivery boy stood with his palm out.

Still holding the dynamite, Libstein walked over and placed a pamphlet in the open palm.

Oblivious to the dynamite, the Western Union employee sputtered for a time, then said. "What the hell is *this?*" He gave every indication of going on indignantly, at length, until Franklyn reached into his pocket and presented the aged boy with a ten-cent piece.

"That's more like business," said the recipient. He nodded brusquely, handed Libstein back his pamphlet, and left.

"Why did you do that?" Libstein demanded. "It degrades the worker."

"Until the Revolution, he still has to eat. Now would you please extinguish that thing? There is very little fuse left."

"Thing?" Libstein was very absentminded. "Oh," he said as Franklyn indicated the explosive. Hastily, the taller man plucked the fuse from the stick and let it sizzle harmlessly out on the floor.

Franklyn sighed deeply. Dedication was one thing, but sometimes Libstein went too far. "Very well," he said. "Let's see what the telegrams say."

The wires were from Baxter and the Rabbi. They were in code, one Libstein had devised, and Franklyn needed a little help in deciphering them. But when all was clear, the two men were in perfect agreement.

"Baxter is right," Libstein said. "Maybe he should, as he suggests, replace our old comrade on the Committee."

"He does sound as though he's getting soft," Franklyn conceded.

"Perhaps we should retire him from the Movement altogether."

"After all he's done?"

"Franklyn, the Movement is larger than any of us."

"I know that. But—well, it's too late to do anything about the current operation except to send him a stern wire ordering the operation to continue. He follows orders. Didn't he drop his religious friends at our insistence."

"Yes, but . . ."

"Listen to me. I've known him for a long time. When the dynamite goes off, and he sees Bryan and the others literally washed away from the face of the earth. And—" Franklyn chuckled. "And, when he sees how much money the people of New York have saved on the planned demolition, why, he'll come around. I'm sure of it."

"I hope you are right. I just wish—"

"Yes?" Franklyn said. Libstein did often wish things.

"I wish we could be killing McKinley, too."

A grin split the forest of Franklyn beard. "There's plenty of time for that, Comrade," he said. "Plenty of time."

III.

Brian O'Leary had been exaggerating when he said "everybody" knew where Madam Nanette was, but a considerable number of people did know. It was a favorite local joke around Five Points that one of that neighborhood's leading citizens had gone uptown to mingle with the rich and well-born in Mrs. Fenwick's Home for Widows and Single Ladies. Madam Nanette's whereabouts were also known to those of her wealthy former customers who had volunteered (or had been persuaded) to write letters of reference for her when the time came to retire.

Roosevelt and Muldoon traveled to Forty-fifth Street to pay her a visit. Mrs. Fenwick's Home was a large, colonial building that had been a school for young girls in a previous incarnation. Mrs. Fenwick, in fact, had attended it. When her husband died, she used the money to buy the building and begin the Home.

Muldoon was surprised at Mrs. Fenwick's appearance. She was, apparently, the youngest woman in the building. She was very busy, and had no time for them.

"Madam," Roosevelt said, "this is official police business. We must see Mrs. Le Clerc as soon as possible." It had taken two hours for someone back at Headquarters to find the ancient arrest report that included Madam Nanette's last name.

Mrs. Fenwick lifted her square, competent face from a column of figures. "I'm afraid that will be contrary to regulations. She has a visitor with her at the moment, a Mr. Meister, and our guests are not allowed more than two visitors at a time. Saving only immediate family, of course."

"That is a ridiculous rule," the Commissioner told her. "Any old person who has an immediate family would be living with that family. They would have no need of this institution."

"Be that as it may, Mr. Roosevelt, that is the rule."

It all seemed rather academic to Muldoon. "Listen here, ma'am, and tell me if I'm makin' a mistake. She's allowed two visitors, and she's got this Meister fellow in there already, right?"

"That is correct."

"Well, then, I'll just be goin' down there and knockin' on the door to ask this Meister fellow to hurry up."

"I don't think that's such a good idea . . ."

"Now, now," Muldoon told her. "Rules is rules. You don't want to go deprivin' the poor woman of her rightful two visitors, do you? So tell me the room number."

The Commissioner grinned and said, "Bully for you, Muldoon," and Mrs. Fenwick told him the room. Muldoon walked down a quiet, carpeted hall, and knocked.

"Yes?" asked a sweet voice. "What is it?"

Muldoon opened the door and entered. "Mrs. Le Clerc?"

"I am she." The old woman was as far from Muldoon's idea of what a brothel keeper looked like as Mother Superior at Saint Mary's was. She was petite and charming, with gleaming silver hair and soft blue eyes. She was dressed modestly in a light-blue dress. "Come in, young man, please. This is my lucky day."

She raised a hand to gesture the young officer into the room. She moved as though she knew herself to be something both fragile and precious, almost, Muldoon thought, as though her skeleton were made of the same china as the fine plates on the tray before her.

"Sorry to be interruptin' your lunch," Muldoon said.

She waved that away. "Don't give it another thought. As I told Mr. Meister, here, the service in this establishment is characteristic of the decline everywhere. It is a topic," Mrs. Le Clerc said primly, "of which I have some little knowledge."

Muldoon smiled. "I mean to be askin' you about that, as soon as you and Mr. Meister are through." Muldoon bowed at the old woman's visitor, a remarkable-looking old man who peered at the world through green spectacles surrounded by fluffy white hair.

Meister rose. "I—I was just leaving, in any case." His voice was a toneless whisper. "It was nice of you to have me in, Madam."

"It was nice of you to come. I am truly sorry I don't remember you. I had so many clients during the years of which you speak."

"I understand, fully. Here, let me take your tray with me."

"That is very kind, but the help here do little enough as it is. Besides, I have not finished my tea, nor touched this lovely almond torte you've brought me."

It was indeed lovely, a masterpiece of the baker's art. Muldoon could smell its fragrance across the room.

"I wasn't sure," the green-spectacled man said, "that your diet would permit—"

"As an old woman, I have had to give up many pleasures. I thank God eating is not one of them."

"I go now, then," Meister whispered. "*Adieu*, Mrs. Le Clerc."

The old woman smiled in a way Muldoon supposed had once been irresistible. "Say rather, *au revoir*, Mr. Meister."

He answered with only a mumble from somewhere underneath the white whiskers, and left. Muldoon introduced himself more formally, then went to fetch Mr. Roosevelt.

It was all the Commissioner could do to be at all civil with the woman. She extended a hand when he entered the room; Roosevelt pretended not to see it.

"You are the Nanette Le Clerc," he said without prologue, "who, known as Madam Nanette, kept a notorious brothel on West Fifth Street until a short time ago?"

She looked at him for a few seconds, then sipped at her tea. "I have no desire to talk to you." To Muldoon, she said, "This man is a boor. I am disappointed in you for bringing him here. Now get out, both of you."

Roosevelt began to redden. "You will talk to me, madam, whether you desire to or not."

"I think not. What are you going to do, place me under arrest? I am an old woman, sir, and in my current state, I am well thought of. I have friends, and I read newspapers. I cannot believe that you feel you have not made yourself sufficiently ridiculous over the Sunday liquor business. I cannot believe you wish to be known as a persecutor of harmless old women."

For the first time, Muldoon was able to see the steel underneath the china. He was no longer astonished by the fact that this woman had made a great success in a very difficult and dangerous business.

"The opinion of others," Roosevelt said, "has never and shall never stay me from my duty. You shall answer my questions, madam. Where is the woman known as Cleo?"

Mrs. Le Clerc drew back as though she'd been struck. "Cleo!" she exclaimed. "What do you want with Cleo?"

"You know her, do you? Where is she?"

"I—I will tell you nothing to help you hurt that girl. I love her as I have loved nothing in my life before or since."

The Commissioner snorted. Prostitution and those involved with it were Evil. Love was Good. There could be no connection between them.

Muldoon's background had given him a different perspective. "Is that the truth of it, ma'am?" he asked softly.

"What?"

"Is it true you love this Cleo? She is a beauiful creature, that's for sure."

"You've seen her?"

"That I have."

"How is she?"

"In good health, but that was the better part of a week ago. No one's seen hide nor hair of her since. Now look in me eyes and see if I'm lyin'. Cleo is in trouble. There's bad business about, and Cleo's stumbled right in the midst of it."

"And you want to help her, is that it?"

"I do. Mr. Roosevelt, too."

The old woman looked at the Commissioner. "Do you?"

"She is young. She can reform. She can aid us in our investigation of a murder, and make amends for her past wickedness. Yes, I want to help her."

Mrs. Le Clerc sipped her tea, cut a forkful of her almond torte, but did not eat it. She looked out the window and watched Mrs. Fenwick's trees swaying in the August breeze. At last, she said. "I curse you both if you are lying to me. Very well, here is my story.

"It was eleven years ago, eleven years this past January. It was an awful night, with sleet and wind and bitter cold. Most of our regular customers would stay home on a night like that, so business was slack. A few of the girls took the opportunity to wash their hair; some were in the kitchen, baking cookies. That was an extra treat—usually, they only had a chance to do that on Christmas, when the house would be closed."

She ignored the look of incredulity on the Commissioner's face. "One of the girls—she was a Bohemian, a big, good-hearted girl, I remember—heard something making a noise with the garbage cans in the alley. It might have just been the wind or a stray cat, but it might also have been a tramp." She looked at the two men. "Tramps were a constant problem. I don't think I flatter myself unduly when I say my garbage contained the remains of some of the best food to be found in this city. Far better than the food in *this* place. My customers would have expected no less."

"Caterin', so to speak," Muldoon said, "to all a man's hungers."

Madam Nanette looked pleased. "Precisely. I opened the door to chase away the cat, or tramp, or whatever, but I saw it was a child, filthy and dressed in rags, hunched over against the elements and chewing on an old bone."

She sipped again at her tea. "It tore out my heart. There are thousands of homeless children in this city, Mr. Roosevelt. They sleep in alleys, or in the parks or on hay barges, and they are prey for persons far worse than the likes of me. Why haven't you great reformers done something for them?"

"That's not fair," Muldoon said. "Mr. Roosevelt's been doin' all kinds—"

"Not now, Muldoon," Roosevelt said. "You are quite right, madam. The situation is a disgrace. Please go on with your story."

"Very well. I called to the child to come in, and we would fix a proper meal, but my words couldn't be understood above the wind. The child started to run, but got only a few steps before slipping on the ice, and collapsing in a heap. The poor thing had fainted.

"I got several of the servants to carry the child inside.

"A physician of sorts lived nearby, an Egyptian named Dr.

Fahmoud. I had him summoned immediately. He had to come, because I had him on a large annual retainer to see to the, ah, medical needs of the girls."

"Indeed," was all Roosevelt trusted himself to say.

"Fahmoud looked at the child," the old woman went on, "and called for clear broth and a hot bath. The child was near death, he said, from starvation and exposure.

"It wasn't until he removed the clothes for the bath, and sponged it off a little, did we see it was a little girl. Her face, when I cleaned it, was the most beautiful face I've ever seen, the face of an angel. Is something wrong, Mr. Muldoon?"

"Ah, no, ma'am," Muldoon said, though he knew he'd felt a twinge in his heart when the old woman had said "angel."

"The doctor found a strange pink birthmark on her limb. He seemed to give it great significance, said this was a joyous occasion, because the mark was a symbol of life. One of the girls dubbed her Cleopatra, but we all called her Cleo.

"It appeared that it would be the only name she'd ever had. She was only eight years old, or so Dr. Fahmoud estimated, but she'd been abandoned and alone for such a long time, she couldn't remember her own name.

"We had her baptized into the Church, in case she—she died, then we kept her in a room in the house until she was well. Everyone loved her, the girls and the gentlemen alike. She was bright and quick-minded, and she would hear the gentlemen speak of books and music and the like, and she'd pick it right up. More than once, I arranged for her to be adopted, to stay with a decent family and live there, but she always ran away from them and came back to me. Once, she looked at me with those big brown eyes and said, 'Mama Nanette'—that's what she called me—'why do you send me away? Don't I love you good enough?' After that, I never had the heart to do it again.

"Cleo blossomed into a beautiful young woman, as you have seen. I dreaded it, but I have found dreading something never prevents its occurrence. Then, about three years ago the day I had dreaded most of all came. Cleo wanted to go to work in the house.

"I forbade it, of course, but she was stubborn. She said I was the only mother, and the girls were all her sisters, and the only friends she had ever known. That she loved us all, and was nothing loath to do anything we would do, for she knew we were . . ."

The old woman began to cry.

"You are a wicked, wicked woman," Roosevelt said, his voice tight and dangerous.

"*What would you have me do?*" Madam Nanette exploded. "Throw her back into the street to starve, rather than expose her to my wickedness? Reject her love, the only love that offended little, loving heart could find it safe to give?"

"You allowed a child to prostitute herself!"

"What would her fate have been on the street? She prostituted herself to be like her friends, the only friends she had ever known! She wanted to pay me back—that's what she said! Pay *me* back, for giving her a life out of the gutter. As though she hadn't paid me back a hundred times, just by being herself.

"Yes, Mr. Roosevelt, I am, by your standards, a wicked woman. And I allowed that beautiful, trusting, holy child to follow me in my wicked ways, and when my days are through, I shall pay for it.

"But my defense shall be this: Where were the good Christians? Where were the righteous who condemn me? How came an innocent child to spend so many years living in gutters and eating from garbage cans that she forgot her own name?

"God knows I was not the best woman to raise a daughter. And He knows I should have been stronger in keeping her from following my ways. But He also knows I was the one He placed there to find her the night she almost died, and He knows I and my girls did our best, because there was nobody else. Nobody else."

Muldoon looked at the Commissioner. Roosevelt was silent, but he didn't look convinced. Muldoon didn't know how *he* felt. He used to think telling right from wrong was easy.

"In any case," said Madam Nanette, after drinking tea, "I have been punished already. Last May, when I decided to retire, I announced my decision to all the girls at once. I had assumed that Cleo would know I intended for us to live together, as a mother and daughter, quietly and respectably. I am quite a wealthy woman, you know.

"But I hadn't known the scars of her early childhood had gone so deep. She thought that, by my retirement, I was abandoning her, just as the unknown woman who bore her had abandoned her so many years ago.

"Within the week, she had gone, leaving in the middle of the night. Her note said she had gone with one of the customers, who would treat her kindly and keep her clothed and well. She—she thanked me for—for being like a mother to her." Madam Nanette was crying copiously, now. As he had done for Cleo, Muldoon gave the old woman his handkerchief.

"Thank you," she said. "The man had left something, too. A chest containing two hundred double-eagles. Four thousand dollars. Four thousand dollars for the dearest thing in my life!"

She cried into Muldoon's handkerchief. "There, there," Muldoon said. "We'll find her, you'll be havin' a big reunion. Everything will be all right."

"Will you, really? I am not usually this emotional. I advise you not to toy with my feelings."

"We've got to be findin' her anyway, so why not? Here, eat some of this lovely cake the old geezer brought you. Cryin' makes you weak."

The old woman's face broke into a smile. "I'd quite forgotten about the almond torte. You don't mind if I—"

"Please do," Roosevelt said, with a hint of a shrug. He was not enjoying his afternoon.

Madam Nanette took a bite of torte, and frowned. "Strong," she said.

Muldoon took out his notebook. "Now, could you be tellin' us, ma'am, exactly what customer or customers would be most likely candidates for Cleo to be runnin' off with?"

She took another bite of cake, then put the fork down. "I don't believe I care for any more of that. Do you know, it actually burned my tongue?"

"What?" Roosevelt asked, horrified.

"There were sev—several . . ." The old woman's voice trailed off into silence. A look of horror and acute discomfort came to her face. She made a croaking noise, and fell from her chair to the carpet.

Muldoon went to the door to shout for a nurse. The Commissioner went to the old woman. "It's no use, Muldoon," Roosevelt said. "The torte burned her tongue. That's when I knew. Curse the *fiend!*" he spat.

"Sir?"

"He killed her under our noses. The woman is dead—"

"Oh, no!"

"And I should be hanged for a fool. Fiendishly clever of Meister, or whatever his real name is, wouldn't you say? To use an almond torte to disguise the fragrance. I—I passed him in the hall. I shall see him executed for this, Muldoon. I swear it!"

"What fragrance, sir?" Muldoon was hopelessly bewildered.

"The fragrance of bitter almonds, Muldoon. That torte was literally filled with prussic acid!"

IV.

Baxter had to work to keep his face suitably grim as he handed the telephone to T. Avery Hand.

"It's the Rabbi, sir," he said.

"What now? Baxter, did he say? Did he say anything?"

"I didn't think it my place to ask," the butler replied.

Hand was a coward, he thought. It disgusted him. All the capitalists were cowards—they gathered wealth to gain power, because only with their power could they assuage their fear. The Giants of Industry were no giants at all, which, Baxter thought, was a bit of a shame, since they would make that much less noise when they toppled.

"Excuse me?" Baxter said.

"This is a fine time for your mind to be wandering, Baxter," Hand said. He had the mouthpiece tightly covered. "I said, as soon as I have done with this, I intend to get in touch with Sperling. I'm going to have him and a few of his men stay here until after the wedding. Have rooms prepared for them, and notify the cook, so that she may do any additional shopping. I no longer intend—that is, the next time this Rabbi pays a call, he won't find us unprepared."

Baxter bowed and left. Inside, he was shouting with laughter. The next time the Rabbi called, Baxter knew, neither Hand, nor Bryan, nor anyone else would know what had hit him. And all the hoodlums in New York couldn't stop it.

Hand uncovered the receiver. "Yes?" he said.

The voice he had grown to hate whispered to him. "How could you ever have expected to be safe with the brothel keeper still in this city?"

Hand was confused. "What—what do you mean?"

"Don't worry, I got to her before the police did. You are far luckier than you deserve to be, Hand."

"You got to her? You *killed* her? But she didn't even know it was I who—"

"Perhaps not. But your name would have been on the list. Her death is your fault. If you had told me before, we could have gotten her safely out of town."

"How did you find out?" Hand's head was spinning.

The person on the other end clicked his tongue. "Perhaps you talk in your sleep, Hand." There was another click in the millionaire's ear as the connection was broken.

Hand was afraid he would lose the use of his senses. What in the name of God was happening to him? First, this Muldoon, now Madam Nanette. Hand seemed to be trapped in the middle of a spider's web of death that was being woven ever wider by forces beyond his understanding. He was afraid, so afraid he even had to admit it to himself.

The telephone rang again. Hand watched it as a man would watch an adder coiled to strike, then, with a half scream, he snatched the instrument up.

"*What?*" he demanded. "What do you want of me now?"

There was silence for several seconds, then the startled voice of the Reverend Lewis Burley. "Avery? Is that you? Is that T. Avery Hand speaking?"

Hand closed his eyes and breathed deeply. "Reverend?"

"Yes, Avery. Are you feeling all right? You gave me a fright, just now, a severe fright."

The industrialist thought he would make himself laugh, but once he started, he found it took an effort to make himself stop. "I'm fine, sir. I'm sorry I snapped at you. There is a promising young man I am trying to train to be office manager, but he—he calls so often for advice and instructions that he vexes me to death. I thought you were he."

"Ah, you must have patience with him, Avery. Your office

is no trifling enterprise, after all. You have trusted the boy with a responsibility that must be awesome, awesome. I would find it so. Not as awesome, of course," the clergyman continued, "as your *own* responsibility."

Hand went cold. His voice was the voice of a dead man. "What did you say?"

Reverend Burley guffawed. "I said awesome, Avery, not fatal. Marriage, my dear boy, marriage. Surely you haven't forgotten. You can't have forgotten our darling, darling Essie May."

Hand had forgotten. "Of course not," he said. "I can hardly wait for the happy day."

"Yes, well, that is the purpose of my call. My daughter is arriving late Saturday, or early Sunday. Though of course, you may not see her before the ceremony Sunday afternoon. Women must have their way," he added. "When it comes to the wedding day, women must have their way."

Hand mumbled agreement.

"Well, I just wanted you to know all was proceeding according to plan. William has been heading east, campaigning, and he will arrive with Essie May. It's going to be a glorious day," he concluded. "A *glorious* day."

"A glorious day," Hand echoed. He said goodbye to the Reverend and replaced the receiver. He stood for a few seconds and rubbed his eyes, then climbed slowly up the big staircase to find what comfort he could in the arms of the woman he loved.

FRIDAY
the twenty-eighth
of August, 1896

I.

"It's simply astonishing, Muldoon," Theodore Roosevelt said, discarding yet another morning newspaper. "I expected by now to be the laughing stock of the city. Yet none of these has any mention of me whatsoever. Only the *Journal* even goes so far as to hint Mrs. Le Clerc might have died of anything other than old age and general debility. It—oh, I am sorry, Miss Muldoon." Katie had come in from the kitchen and swooped down on the discarded papers. "I know I am somewhat eccentric in my reading habits. I am accustomed to picking up after myself, however." "Eccentric" was an understatement. Roosevelt was known to read magazines by ripping out each page as he finished it, crumpling it up, and throwing it to the floor.

"I do the pickin' up in me own house, thank you," Katie replied. She was not used to having visitors dropping in at quarter past eight in the morning, before the housecleaning was half done. Apparently, the Commissioner had led Dennis into some damn-fool embarrassing situation yesterday, and had spent the night roaming the streets, taking out his wrath on unsuspecting police-men. She was pleased to note that Dennis had had enough mother wit to leave the old walrus to it, and come home and get some sleep.

Roosevelt picked up the *Times*. "Nothing here either," he said after a short time (he was a rapid reader). "Frankly, Mul-doon, I am at a loss to account for it."

Muldoon took a bite of a red New York State apple from the basket the Commissioner had brought with him. We're getting to be real lace-curtain Irish, he thought—fruit in the house when nobody's sick.

"Perhaps," he said, replying to Mr. Roosevelt's implied ques-tion, "somethin' made them see there was no benefit in embar-rassin' a high official of the Administration as was tryin' to do his duty."

"Ho," Roosevelt laughed. "After the things they've said of me, I'd like to know what that something could be."

Muldoon knew; but he had come to understand his superior well enough to realize he could never tell him. It had been Muldoon, practicing a little ward-level politics that had kept the news of "Meister's" daring murder quiet. A little judicious good-will buying among the staff at Mrs. Fenwick's Home, and a phone call to Hearst, with intimations that keeping confidence and faith went both ways, had effectively cut off the story. Muldoon had guessed, rightly, that if Hearst's *Journal* were to hint the old woman's death had not been a natural one, the other papers would all but ignore the story, hoping to make Hearst look foolish.

Muldoon finished his apple, went to the kitchen to dispose of the core, then returned and said to the Commissioner, "Have you anything for me to be doin' today, sir?"

"No, unfortunately, I can't think of anything useful. Perhaps the normal investigation of Mrs. Le Clerc's death may yield some results."

"Mmmm," said Muldoon, not optimistically. "I suppose it's back to the art galleries, then." Muldoon sighed. "At least I know who it is I'm lookin' for."

The kitchen door opened, and Katie reappeared. "I don't know," she said, "why I just don't open a blasted cafe and have done with it. You've got a caller, Dennis. A Mrs. Sturdevant she's callin' herself."

Muldoon and Roosevelt looked at each other. "A strange time to come calling," the Commissioner said. He seemed not to hear Katie's snort.

Muldoon said, "Show her in, Katie, if you please."

Mrs. Sturdevant, as usual, was red faced, but it seemed to Muldoon she was quite a bit more red faced than usual.

"Dennis!" the landlady panted. "Ah, and Mr. Roosevelt as well. Well, Mr. Smarty-Pants Police Commissioner, if you weren't here to beg this poor boy to take his job back, you soon will be."

"Ah, Mrs. Sturdevant . . ." Muldoon began.

"No woman indeed." The big blond landlady muttered to herself as she rummaged through the carpetbag slung over her arm. "Don't you worry, Dennis. Here it is!"

With a flourish, she pulled an envelope from her bag. To Muldoon, it didn't seem worth the fanfare, until she handed it to him. The envelope was postmarked Rochester, New York, and the return address was that of the Eastman Company. It had been mailed to Mr. Evan Crandall, of New York City. Muldoon remembered the Kodak he'd found in the dead cartoonist's desk.

Roosevelt remembered, too. "May I have that envelope, please, Muldoon?" he asked. "Madam," he said to Mrs. Sturdevant, "how did this come to be in your possession?"

"It was brought to my building," she said. "In the second post. By the postman. I never bothered to tell them about Crandall's death because I can't recall a single piece of mail he ever got besides this. Though I can't say that surprises me any longer, now that I know what kind of man he was." She shuddered. "When Mr. Sturdevant was alive, he used to say, 'Ethel—' "

"You've opened the envelope," the Commissioner said. He hated to interrupt a lady, but he had an intuition that with this one he had no other choice.

"That's right. And when I saw what was inside, I knew I had to tell Dennis right away, never mind I left my kitchen floor half unscrubbed."

"It's a serious offense to open someone else's mail, Mrs. Sturdevant," Roosevelt said.

The landlady gave him a look that indicated a decided lack of faith in the intelligence of the Police Department of the City of New York.

"Then I'm guilty," she said. "Let Crandall press charges."

"Madam—"

"Ah, Mr. Roosevelt," Muldoon put in, "since the envelope's already been opened and all, and no one can say *we've* been up to anything wrong, how about our havin' a little peek at the contents?"

"Ha!" said the Commissioner, falling in with the spirit of the gathering. "Bully idea. Since this kind lady has presented us with a *fait accompli*, as the lawyers say, let's have that little bit of a peek."

He tilted the envelope and let the contents spill out into his hand. Photographs, twenty of them, taken at various places about the city, under a variety of weather and lighting conditions, at various differences, but all of the same subject.

"Have a look at these, Muldoon," Roosevelt invited. "I believe the subject will not be totally unfamiliar to you."

Mrs. Sturdevant beamed; she gave the impression of being just seconds away from starting to dance with joy.

Muldoon looked at the first photograph the Commissioner showed him. It showed a young woman emerging from the shop of a fashionable dressmaker. Her face, though shaded by a lacy parasol, was clearly discernible.

"Oh, my yes," Muldoon breathed. He gazed at the picture. By Christ, she was just as beautiful with her clothes *on*. "That's her. That's Madam Nanette's little Cleo."

II.

Mrs. Sturdevant made them tea and muffins. Muldoon and the Commissioner had been in the landlady's flat for close to an hour and three quarters, studying the photographs—with unsuccessful side trips to Crandall's flat to look for more. If the woman had been one little bit less attractive, Muldoon thought, he would have long since gotten sick of the sight of her. Cleo coming out of the shop. Cleo going into another shop. Cleo alighting from a carriage with some kind of light-colored smudge on the door. Cleo adjusting her hat. The woman's picture started to swim before his eyes.

Even the indefatigible Roosevelt showed signs of weariness. He removed his glasses and rubbed his eyes, then replaced them and reached for his cup. "This is excellent tea, Mrs. Sturdevant," he called. "Quite the best tea I have had in months."

He turned to Muldoon. "There is something in these pictures. I know there is. Something we are overlooking."

Muldoon sighed, and began leafing through the photographs once again. Strictly for a change of pace, to keep himself from going mad, he held them upside down this time.

The Commissioner consulted his watch. "I only have a few more minutes to spare, blast it. There's a meeting of the Police Board at Mulberry Street in half an hour."

"Do you have to go?" Muldoon asked.

"Yes, I do. We have to discuss promotions—Parker is determined to promote Herkimer, you know."

"Why?" Andrew D. Parker, another member of the Police Board, for no apparent reason other than a dislike of its President, had adopted the policy of opposing Roosevelt in anything he tried to do.

"Sheer perversity," the Commissioner said. "Of course, it is within my power to cancel the meeting, but then Parker will say I did it because I was afraid to face him, and I shall never give that sinister snake the opportunity to say I am—"

"It's a *palm* print, for cryin' our loud," Muldoon said.

"I beg your pardon."

"Oh, sorry for interruptin', sir. But I've been wonderin' what this smudge on the carriage in this photograph could be—see it there?—but I couldn't make anything out of it. The focus ain't too good. But when I turned it upside down, I could sort of make out the thumb.

"Only thing I can't figure is, why would a fellow with a carriage this nice let it be driven around with a big, dusty handprint on it."

Mr. Roosevelt was examining the photograph. "That is a palm print, but it isn't dust. It is painted on. Muldoon," he said, rising to shake the constable's hand, "you have done it. I know now why the photographs struck a chord in my brain. I know that carriage. I recognized it both by its shape, and by the hazy outline of that palm-print. That is the carriage of T. Avery Hand."

III.

What ensued was Muldoon's first argument with Mr. Roosevelt. The Commissioner wanted Muldoon to wait until the Police Board meeting was over. Muldoon had two points in rebuttal: First, if Hand knew about the Pink Angel, there was not a second to lose in finding out what. Second, T. Avery Hand was a solid citizen, one of the city's foremost industrialists. He probably had nothing whatever to do with Cleo, except maybe to give her a ride in his carriage the day Crandall happened to be taking his photographs, so it would be just as well for Muldoon to attend to him without the Commissioner's having to bother himself.

"Curse it, Muldoon, you contradict yourself as thoroughly as Parker does!"

"Beg your pardon, sir?"

"Forget it, Muldoon. Your points are contradictory, but they are well taken. Go and speak with Hand, but if you may be contradictory, so may I. Remember that Hand is indeed an eminent and respectable citizen, and remember as well that a man of sound money principles who can desert the Republican party for a man like Bryan is capable of anything. In either case, mind where you put your feet, if you catch my meaning."

"I do, sir."

"Bully for you, then. Take care, Muldoon," the Commissioner said, then left for his meeting. Muldoon, meanwhile, took the elevated train uptown, then walked west to the Hand mansion.

Judging by the sun (his watch had been ruined when he'd been dumped in the river with the garbage—something else he owed whoever was behind this) it was about two o'clock. Muldoon's plan was to avoid flunkies, and speak to Hand directly when he returned from downtown. So, if the millionaire kept normal banker's hours, he should be arriving in an hour and a half or so. Muldoon would use the interval to scout out the situation, the way any good cop would. He noted the fence that surrounded the house and the smaller buildings—the kennel and the carriage house. He circled the building twice, then returned to the Forty-second Street side, crossed the street, and took up a position in the shadow of the reservoir, with his back against the twenty million gallons that was the city's water supply.

An Italian came by, selling peanuts. A few days ago, Officer Muldoon would have given him the bum's rush for peddling in this high-class neighborhood. Now, he simply made a purchase, and calmly ate peanuts while he waited for the millionaire to come home.

IV.

Cleo was looking out the window, because that was all it was safe to do in this house. At least, it was for her, as long as that Baxter was about. She pulled her little straight-backed chair to the windowsill, spread a towel over it to avoid soiling the elbows of her frock, and leaned out, gazing at nothing in particular, and thinking thoughts that were either vain hopes or bitter memories.

If she turned her head just right, she could see between two trees to a little patch of sidewalk at the front of the house. It was her habit to look that way whenever she heard footsteps. She didn't know why. Perhaps it was sheer boredom, perhaps a wish that it would be someone who could help her.

She was wishing precisely that, and dismissing herself as a romantic fool at the same time, when the young man with the moustache walked across her patch of sidewalk. It pained her to see him, he reminded her so of the young officer who had gone to his death because of her.

She was a wicked woman. She had tried to draw a limit, to only certain wicked things (which in truth didn't seem so bad) and no others. But now she knew wickedness was a Monster with a life of its own, a Frankenstein's creation that turned first on the innocent, then on its author.

More footsteps from in front of the house. She didn't, in her melancholy, even bother to look at their source. She couldn't even bear to raise her head when those steps were joined by others.

But then she heard the voices.

"Pea*nuts!* Getta some hot peanuts!"

"I think I'll be havin' a bag, there, Mario."

It was his voice. Cleo could not breathe.

"*Tony* issa my name," the peanut seller replied.

"Sorry," said the Irish voice. "I was meanin' no offense. Call me Paddy if it'll help your feelin's." The Italian laughed, and said that wasn't necessary. The young Irishman bid him good afternoon.

It was him. It had to be. Somehow he wasn't dead, somehow he had traced her to Avery's house. She had to let him know she was here.

Cleo closed her eyes for one second, all the time she was willing to spare. She could only hope that would be prayer enough to make the Almighty keep Baxter downstairs while she did what she had to do.

Moving as quickly and as silently as she could, Cleo ran down the second floor hall to the small guest room at the front of the house. She had to call to him before he went away.

But he hadn't gone away. He was across the street, lounging up against the dark stone of the reservoir. She couldn't call to him now, because any call Muldoon (and the more she looked at his handsome form, the more certain she became it truly *was* Muldoon) could hear from across the street could also be heard from within the house. She'd have to attract his attention some other way.

She opened the window, stuck her head out, and began to wave both her shapely arms rapidly. She might as well have been the wind vane on the roof for all the notice she drew. The young man who had freed her from the mad artist didn't even look in her direction—he was too involved in watching the afternoon traffic on Forty-second Street.

Cleo kept up her efforts until her arms ached, until she wanted to cry.

Then she saw Muldoon begin to cross the street toward the house. She was going to call to him, but her voice stilled when she heard the familiar hoofbeats of the horses that pulled the carriage of T. Avery Hand. She could see now Muldoon was going to confront him. She couldn't let that happen—it would mean his life for certain, this time.

There was only seconds before the carriage would arrive. Cleo snatched a pen and a piece of paper from the writing desk by the window. She scribbled a hasty note, then removed the crucifix and its fine gold chain from around her neck. It was the first time she had removed it since Mother Nanette had given it to her ten years ago.

She wadded the note as small as she could, then wound the gold chain tight around it, knotting it so it wouldn't come undone. She took aim, and planned her throw so the note would land at Muldoon's feet.

She had just finished the act of throwing when the guest room door opened.

"What are you doing here, slut?" demanded an angry Baxter. "Will I have to lock you in again?"

Cleo did not scream, an act of self restraint that amazed her even as he stood there. Instead, her voice remained calm. "I desired a different view," she said. "Unlike prisoners in a penitentiary, I get no exercise in the yard, or constructive work to perform."

Cleo never saw where her letter landed; she was sure that by making her jump at the moment of release, Baxter had spoiled her aim.

Baxter looked at her strangely. "I'm sorry," he said, almost, Cleo thought, as though he actually *were* sorry. "You must not be seen. Come back to your room."

He led the young woman back to the room on the side of the house, and locked the door behind her. Inside, Cleo threw herself down on her bed, and cried tears of frustration and despair.

V.

Cleo couldn't know it, but she let go a cry of just the right volume for Muldoon to hear when Baxter had startled her. The young policeman couldn't see who'd made the noise, but he saw the golden arc described by the sunlight on the chain. He saw a trailing loop of it hook on the top of the iron spikes that made up the fence surrounding Hand's house. And he saw the whiteness of the paper wrapped up in it.

Muldoon had to investigate—even if it hadn't been his clear duty, it would have been his nature to do so. He left his position at the base of the reservoir, and started to cross Forty-second Street.

Before he could though, Hand's carriage arrived. Muldoon was pleased. It was still some time before the banker was due home; arriving early had paid off.

Muldoon took up a position by the carriage gate—he didn't want Hand disappearing inside before he could get his questions in. When the driver alit and opened the gate, Muldoon blocked the way.

"Mr. Hand," he said, showing a palm to the person in the carriage. "I know this is a strange way to be approachin' you, but I've got some questions of what you might call a delicate nature to put. Dennis Muldoon is me name, and—"

"*What!*" The startled, angry face that poked out the carriage window wasn't that of T. Avery Hand. "Blast you, you're *dead!*" shouted Eagle Jack Sperling. "Get him, boys, dammit!"

The driver, and another bully-boy who had been inside with Sperling, started to move. Once again, Muldoon felt the necessity to run from Sperling and his men, but this time, he managed to shorten the odds against himself.

He still had most of his bag of peanuts left. It had been a long time since he had played base-ball, but his arm and eye were as good as ever. He wound up and threw his peanuts through the window right into the ruffians eye, then fetched Hand's handsome roan a wallop on the rump that sent it charging off like a fire horse to a four-alarmer.

That left only the driver to deal with, and Muldoon turned on him, ready for action, but he was already running away nearly as fast as the horse.

Muldoon wouldn't have to run away so rapidly after all. He spent a few seconds to retrieve the note, read it, let out a long, low whistle, and read it again. Commissioner Roosevelt would have to know about this. Immediately.

It occurred to him that he was wasting time. That horse wouldn't run forever. He tucked the note and the cross in his pocket, then struck a brisk step eastward to catch the El.

VI.

Muldoon looked at the note once again, at the bottom of the steps at Police Headquarters. *"Officer Muldoon, the Cross will tell you who I am. I am a prisoner again. Forgive me. Help me. —One you have helped before."*

It would raise a commotion, Muldoon knew, to burst into the meeting room, interrupting the Board members as they sat at the massive oak table, with its rim scalloped to accommodate the bellies of prominent men. Still he had to do it. He planned what he would say as he climbed the steps to the entrance.

He never got to say anything.

"May I help you, sir?" asked the desk sergeant.

"No thanks, I know the way." Muldoon headed for the stairs.

"You have to state your business. Come here."

Muldoon approached the desk. "Sorry, I'm in a bit of a hurry."

"Is it a violent crime that's now going on?" the sergeant asked. He was a portly, white-haired man with a nose the size, shape, and color of a pomegranate.

"No," Muldoon admitted. "I want to see Mr. Roosevelt."

"He's in a meeting. Name, please?"

"Muldoon. I know that, but I have to be seein' him all the same."

"All I can do is let you leave him a note." The sergeant's hands shook as he offered pen and paper. He had used to stop the shaking with frequent doses of "medicine," but he hadn't been allowed to have it for a long time. He was close to his pension, or he would have quit long ago. "We've got a lot of coppers here, you know. Somebody ought to be able to help you."

"It's Mr. Roosevelt I've got to be seein', and right away!"

A staunch-looking uniformed policeman appeared on the stairs. "Dennis," he said. "It is you. I thought I recognized your voice."

Muldoon looked at him with joy. "Ed Bourke! Thank the Lord for sendin' you." Ed was the fellow "King" Calahan couldn't intimidate—he'd know a man had to be allowed to do his duty. "Ed, help me convince the sergeant here to let me see Mr. Roosevelt."

The sergeant rubbed his great red nose. "You know this mug, Ed?" he asked.

"I used to," Bourke replied. He reached the bottom of the stairs, then walked across the wooden floor to stand face to face with Muldoon.

The taller man extended his hand. "Good to be seein' you Ed. Have you on Headquarters duty now, do they?"

Bourke stared at Muldoon's hand, then looked away. "You've got a lot of nerve coming here. You were thrown out for a reason, you know."

The sergeant slapped a meaty hand on the desk with an impact that rattled the glass globes on the poles at either end of it. "So it's that Muldoon, eh?" he intoned.

"What did you want the Commissioner for, Dennis?" Bourke asked. "Out for revenge for his throwing you off the Force?"

"Maybe we better frisk him, eh, Ed?" the sergeant asked.

"Oh, for cryin' out—" Muldoon took hold of his temper "Look, Ed, I don't know how you can believe it of me. I ain't on the bent, never was. I'm—"

"Lots of guys I believed," Bourke said. His blue eyes were cold as ice. "Tommy Alb for one. Look at him now—a bully-boy for Sperling's bunch. How do I know my judgment is going to be any better with you?"

"Dammit, I'm workin' undercover. For Mr. Roosevelt himself! I got a letter as says so!"

"Do you really?" Bourke's tone said he didn't believe it.

"Bet your mother's rosary I do!" Muldoon replied.

"Well, that's a letter I'd like to read."

"Now you're talk—" Muldoon left off in the middle of the word. He had the letter all right. It was back in the flat, locked up in Katie's jewelry drawer. And he'd been just too blasted stupid to stop on the way here and pick it up. He kicked himself mentally. Hard. Many times.

"I—ah—don't happen to be carryin' it with me at the moment, but I'll tell you what's goin' on." And he tried to. In a better hour, Muldoon would have seen the futility of the effort, but now, he was so disheartened by his fall from grace in the eyes of his friend, he didn't see, until it was much too late, that he could only make his position worse.

"Let's lock him up," the sergeant said. "Or get him hauled off to the booby hatch. He's a rum one."

"I'd as lief," Bourke said, "call a few of the boys and kick him downstairs."

"Ed, will you listen to me, for cryin'—"

"Shut up, Muldoon! You stink in my nostrils. You know what one bad cop does to the whole Department, but you come here anyway. Talk about brass! Get out of here, before I *do* call the boys."

Muldoon spoke quietly, between his teeth. "When this is all over with, Ed Bourke I'm comin' to look you up. Not because you don't believe me. Because you never left an inch for the *possibility* of believin' me. And I think a friend deserves that much. And I'm comin' back when me name is clear, to kick your flamin' teeth down your throat. And that, you can believe."

Muldoon turned and stormed from the building.

VII.

"Of *course* I recognized him," Eagle Jack Sperling protested. His salt-and-pepper moustache fluttered and his muscular bald head flexed with the force of his argument. "You don't go dumping a guy in the river without taking a good look at his phiz to make sure he's the right one, if you follow me. Hell, that's only good business practice." Sperling ran a finger around the neck of his shirt, as though loosening the collar he didn't wear.

"Then he's alive after all," T. Avery Hand mused. He stroked his dapper moustache to remove the crumbs of the French pastries he'd just eaten. The events of the last few days had caused him to fall sadly behind in his weight-gaining schedule, and the wedding was sure to upset things even more, so he ate when he could to keep up.

"At least," Hand mumbled, "this will make that blasted Rabbi happy."

"Mr. Hand?" Sperling said. "Hey! Mr. Hand, pay attention, will you? This is serious!"

It occurred to the millionaire that for all his talk about becoming a Man of Substance, Sperling was just as uncomfortable and out of place in his ornate parlor as he himself had been in the tough's hideout. "Yes, Sperling, I was thinking of something. Please go on."

"Well, Mr. Hand, I was saying it ain't so much I recognized him, it's that *he* recognized *me*. He wouldn't have done what he did if he didn't. Hell, hadn't been for your man Baxter running out of the house and pulling the horse to a halt, I would have been minced meat, and my man, too. That Baxter's a strong one. Too bad you seen him first.

"Anyways, that Muldoon has seen too much. This time I got to kill him. You follow me? Bad business, otherwise."

Hand nodded. He could see Sperling's point—Muldoon's stories of the attempts on his life could make things very uncomfortable for Eagle Jack. And he'd be happier with the Irishman out of the way, too—Cleo had been in the front room today, according to Baxter. If only he could make the Rabbi see all this. If only he even knew how to make contact with him.

As if in answer to this unspoken thought, the telephone rang. He could hear Baxter answer it. Sperling looked at him while he waited for the butler to summon him. It was a short wait.

"Telephone, sir," Baxter said expressionlessly. "I think it's the Rabbi."

The millionaire took a deep breath, and went to answer the phone.

He returned a few minutes later, shaking his head.

"Sir?" Baxter asked. "What's the lay?" Sperling wanted to know.

"That Hebrew bastard," Hand said, "is a hateful, blackmailing scum, but he has a brain. He does have a brain. This is what we'll do."

The Rabbi's suggestion had indeed been brilliant. Peter Baxter, alone in his secret, could barely keep from smiling as he heard it.

The heart of the story was to be true—that T. Avery Hand, eminent industrialist, had hired Eagle Jack Sperling, for protection. This was to be told to the police—Captain Ozias Herkimer for preference, though it was not his precinct, and strings would have to be pulled. Herkimer (or whoever) was to be told, however, that the protection was not for Hand's person, but for his property. He was after all, a wealthy man the Mansion Burglars had not yet victimized, and he was leaving town overnight to be sure a present that was in preparation for his bride-to-be—a custom sidesaddle a craftsman in Riverdale was making—was finished and true to what he had wanted.

No sooner had he hired Sperling than a man known to the security expert as Dennis Muldoon had stolen his carriage. Chase had proven futile.

"I don't get it," Sperling had said.

"Don't you see? Muldoon is already in disgrace with the police over the woman. When they catch him as a carriage thief, what matter what he says? They'll think he's lying to protect his own skin. And now, we needn't care who knows you and your ten men are staying here."

Baxter noted that in his enthusiasm for the plan, the millionaire had forgotten completely that it was to protect him from the Rabbi that he had hired Eagle Jack in the first place.

"Well, I must get things started. I'll call Herkimer, then go up to Riverdale in a spare carriage and find a sidesaddle somewhere. Baxter, you take the damaged carriage and dispose of it. Sperling, you stand guard."

"I still think I ought to kill him," the bald man said.

"This is better. I want no more killing before my wedding. Whatever else she may be, Essie May is very sensitive."

"Mr. Hand?"

"Yes, Baxter?"

"After I dispose of the carriage, may I have the rest of the evening off?"

"Of course. Sperling, no one is to bother the young lady upstairs, do you understand?"

Eagle Jack was hurt. "My men are hand picked, Mister."

"Very well. On your way, Baxter."

And Baxter had gone, ditching the carriage somewhere along the Boulevard, north of Coontown. Walking back now, he smiled. His comrade *did* have a brain, a brain that not only had calmed the fears of Hand and Sperling, but had seen to it that Baxter got the night off.

Now he had plenty of time.

Time to check the placement of the dynamite, to see that his measures to keep the water from seeping in had been effective. Time to test-run some lengths of fuse. Time to place the final charges.

Time, most of all, to imagine what it would be like Sunday afternoon, when he set off those carefully shaped and timed charges to blow a large chunk out of the north wall of the Croton Reservoir. When the underwater charges behind them would lift the twenty million gallons or so of water into a veritable tidal wave. When that massive wall of water would go crashing across Forty-second Street onto Mr. T. Avery Hand's front-lawn wedding, washing him, his bride, Mr. William Jennings Bryan, and all the other capitalists into oblivion, the way a thunderstorm washed dead leaves and horse leavings into the sewers.

VIII.

"What are you gonna do with it when you finish, Muldoon?" Brian O'Leary asked.

"It's not for me to say. I paid for it with Mr. Roosevelt's emergency money. I hope he doesn't take a mind to flay me alive for it later." Muldoon had been busy in the house since he'd left Headquarters. The first thing he'd done was recruit some help.

"Roscoe, can't we be gettin' there a bit faster? The boy is drivin' me crazy with his questions."

The one-eyed man looked down from the trap into the rented carriage. "Sure we could; this is a good nag they give us. But, in my experience, you want to crack a crib, you wait till the sun goes down. Won't be long now."

Muldoon could see he was right. Fifth Avenue was visible, but only in the purplish light of dusk. He could hear crickets chirping, and he saw the lamplighters at work. They reminded him of Mr. Harvey. He had learned from Mrs. Sturdevant that Harvey was going to be kept at a sanitarium on Staten Island until they got him dried out. It struck Muldoon as a good idea.

"You know," Roscoe's voice rumbled down, "I don't want to keep harping on this, but I think I'd feel a lot better if the boss knew what we was doing."

"Don't you think I do, too?" Muldoon punctuated his remark

by worrying another fraction of an inch off the end of his finger-nail. There wasn't much of it left. He'd be reduced to nibbling the ends of his coat sleeves before the night was over if things kept up at this rate.

"But blast it, Roscoe, there's no way out of it. They won't let me in to see him, they won't let you in to see him, what with your havin' a record and all. We tried sendin' Brian, and that didn't get anywhere, either. They take those meetin's seriously."

"We could have set fire to the building," Brian said, reproach-fully. "You should have let me do it. I know how. All you have to do is—"

"Shut up before I whip your bottom." Muldoon had another go at his nail. "Roscoe, let's at least get to where we're parkin' the carriage so I can stretch me legs. It's uncomfortable with this thing in here."

The "thing" was a tandem bicycle, the Zephyr Double Jewel, forty-five dollars, cash on the barrelhead. ("I can't believe it," Brian had breathed later, "you just opened your purse and plunked down *forty-five dollars*.") The salesman had told Muldoon it'd been made by a couple of brothers named White or Bright, or something like that, out in Dayton, Ohio, but that cut no ice with Muldoon. All he cared about was that it was solid built and quiet.

"I bet," Brian mused, running his grubby hands over the shiny black enamel, "that Mr. Roosevelt's kids all have bicycles already."

"Even if they do, what the blazes would you be doin' with a tandem?" It was an inane topic, but Muldoon needed something to keep his nerves from feeding on themselves.

"Rich Danny Frey has one of these. He rides girls uptown on it, you know, all the way to Central Park and like that. Then they let him—"

"There is never," Muldoon pronounced, "goin' to be any makin' a gentleman of you, I can see that." Muldoon proceeded to lecture the boy—he felt he had to carry on the work started by the Commissioner. Muldoon told Brian about his own misspent youth, using his own exploits as Bad Example. Brian listened carefully, discarded the morals, and wound up with an excellent collection of new techniques to try on the neighborhood girls next time he had a chance.

"Okay," Roscoe said, bringing the carriage to a halt. "Here we are, Fifth and Fortieth." The southeast corner of the Croton Reservoir loomed high above them.

Muldoon and the boy got out, and lifted the bicycle to the ground. The officer looked up at stars twinkling in a rich indigo sky. "Dark enough, Roscoe?"

"Too much moon for my taste, but I guess it'll do."

"Okay," the young man said briskly. "Let's get goin' then. Brian."

The boy could sense the time for banter was over, "Yes, sir," he said.

"Do exactly what I told you before. Guard this carriage, get the horse turned around, then keep him happy and ready to go. Give us a half hour. You got that watch?"

"Yes, sir." Brian reached into a pocket and showed it to him.

"Good. Take care of it, it's Roscoe's. If I ain't back in a half hour, get out of here, as quickly as you're able. Take the carriage if you're up to handlin' it, but one way or another, get downtown and get hold of Mr. Roosevelt, pronto, because all hell will have broken loose by then."

"I can handle the carriage."

"Good," Muldoon said. Roscoe said, "Sure he can, nothing to it."

"But what if they don't let me in to see him, like last time?"

"Then," Muldoon said grimly, "you have me personal permission to light fire to Headquarters. Burn down the whole damn Mulberry Street if you've a mind to, but get him out of there, get to him, and get us help, 'cause we'll be needin' it. That's a half hour from right now. Look at the watch. Good. Thirty minutes. Got that?"

"I've got it," the boy said, closing the watch.

"Good. We're countin' on you, son," Muldoon said.

"I won't let you down," Brian said.

"We know you won't. Don't we, Roscoe?"

"Damn right. Kid could work a job with me any time."

Brian's thin chest swelled with pride. He felt prouder still when each of the two men solemnly shook his hand before they climbed on the tandem and pedaled silently into the night.

IX.

The bicycle was leaning against the fence on the Fifth Avenue side of the property of T. Avery Hand. Roscoe was picking the lock of the side gate. Muldoon was standing guard. Every once in a while, he'd cast a nervous glance down the block at the handsome home Captain Ozias Herkimer had bought with his wife's money. All Muldoon needed was for Herkimer to catch him in the midst of a burglary.

"They got a dog," the one-eyed cracksman whispered.

"I don't hear anything," Muldoon replied.

"Me neither. But anybody with a lock this cheesy on their gate got a dog. It's like a rule."

"Well, I'll see to the handlin' of any dog." Muldoon pulled something from his pocket, something he thought he'd pick up while he was spending the Commissioner's money that afternoon.

It was a pistol, a beauty, a .38 caliber blue-metal Hopkins & Allan Shell-Ejecting, Double-Action, Self-Cocking, Hinged Revolver, seventeen ounces, three-and-a-half-inch barrel. Four dollars and fifteen cents, but worth it if he needed to use it. Plus sixty-nine cents for a box of cartridges.

"No you won't," Roscoe said. "All we need is a gun shot out here. That poor gal is dead the minute you was to shoot. *I'll* handle the dog. If there's only one, that is. If there's more, well, you got to shoot. And we got to face the consequences."

"If you don't mind me sayin' so, Roscoe, this is one hell of a time to be tellin' me all this."

"Well, I'm used to workin' with professionals, know what I mean? No offense. Ah, got the lock. Okay, follow me. Walk soft."

Muldoon obliged, wishing as he entered the grounds that he'd thought to bring along a big stick while he was at it.

"Here, doggie," Roscoe crooned. "He-e-ere, doggie."

"Are you out of your everlovin' mind, man?"

Roscoe shrugged. "We gotta face him sooner or later." He let out a low whistle, then began crooning again.

It worked. Muldoon could hear heavy panting and low ominous growls. He thought he could make out a massive, grey shape crouched against the darkness.

"He's got to spring at me before I can do anything," Roscoe explained. The explanation did nothing to help Muldoon's disintegrating nerves. Give him a good, old-fashioned street fight any day.

"Why don't you," the patrolman suggested, "make a noise like a cat?"

Roscoe turned to him wearing a look of disgust. "You mean, say 'meow'?"

"*Look out!*" Muldoon snapped.

"What—?" That was a dog who hated cats. He sprang, coming at them with fangs like icicles and paws like manhole covers. To Muldoon, it looked like a flying rhinoceros, or an omnibus with claws.

Roscoe was almost taken unawares, and he almost died for it. As it was, one of the mastiff's fangs caught his prominent nose and ripped it open up the left nostril.

But Roscoe, meanwhile, had managed to grasp the animal's paws while it was still on the rise. He then lifted his arms straight up as he pivoted on his heels, adding the strength of his boxer's arms and the speed of his spin to the already considerable momentum of the dog's charge.

Then, when the bewildered mastiff was lifted high above Roscoe's head, the one-eyed man whipped his arms down and bent his body, slamming the dog on the ground across the protruding root of one of Hand's willow trees.

There was a sickening crack. The dog yelped, then lay motionless, its back broken.

Muldoon had never seen anything like it. He gave his companion his handkerchief to hold to his bleeding nose. "And hardly a sound, either. You'll have to be teachin' me how to do that, friend."

"Nothing to it," Roscoe said, grinning around the reddened cloth. "I won't teach you the nose part, though. Fellow's gotta have some secrets."

"You all right?"

Roscoe waved a hand. "Got lots worse than this in the ring and come back to win the bout."

They made their way across the grounds to the house in silence.

X.

They had agreed there was to be no talking once they entered the house, so Muldoon tapped Roscoe on the shoulder and pointed in the direction he should go to leave the pantry-kitchen area and find the stairs. If they could leave the house with the girl without alerting anyone else, so much the better.

There were voices in the house, voices Muldoon recognized. Eagle Jack's men, apparently making free with the host's liquor. Muldoon heard them talking about how this was the easiest job they'd ever done. If they'd had a sentry at the back door, Muldoon reflected, it would have been.

As it was, they were bunched in the parlor, so the intruders had a clear path to the staircase. Muldoon had some idea of the layout of the house, from the daylight study he'd done earlier, and besides, he was the one Cleo would recognize, so he climbed the stairs to the top while Roscoe pulled a weighted sap from his jacket pocket and stopped just above the shadow line to keep watch.

The hoodlum guards hadn't been completely remiss in their duty—one had been posted outside what had to be the girl's door. The man, just past a boy, really, one of Sperling's newest recruits, was seated on a wooden chair; there was a bottle of something red and a glass on the floor beside him. He was a big kid, with a low forehead and shoulders as wide across as those on Monsieur Bartholdi's statue out in the Harbor. He wouldn't be a pushover in a tussle.

Muldoon decided to employ strategy. The officer was still standing in a dark patch, below floor level, and the guard wasn't paying any mind to anything but his dime novel, anyway. From the way he was reading it, you might have thought it was the winners of next week's races instead of one of Mr. Horatio Alger's Luck-and-Pluck stories. Muldoon squinted and read the title—it was one he hadn't seen yet. He'd have to ask Listerdale to get him a copy.

Muldoon shook his head to clear it. It was time to get down

to the matter at hand. The young officer reached into his trouser pocket and clenched his fist tightly around his change, so it wouldn't jingle, then pulled it forth. He slowly opened his hand, then selected a dime from the coins and replaced the rest, again taking care they shouldn't jingle.

As quietly as possible, he ascended the remaining few stairs. He held his breath—to be detected now would be fatal. Muldoon bent his legs slightly, to gather strength for a quick start. Then, with an almost casual flick of his thumb, he sent the dime sailing down the corridor. It landed with a quiet "plink" a dozen feet on the other side of the door the guard was watching.

The guard, quite naturally, started at the noise, and turned his head in the direction from which it came. That was the instant Muldoon sprang.

"Hey!" was all the wide-shouldered boy was able to say before Muldoon knocked the wind for any further speech out of him with a hard right to the belly. He followed that by clapping a hand over the boy's mouth and the pistol to his head. The young thug's eyes danced with fear as they saw the gaslight of the hall lamp gleaming dully from the blue metal of the revolver.

"One word," Muldoon whispered urgently in the boy's ear, "and you'll be whistlin' through your temples on windy days."

Perspiration began to bead the hoodlum's forehead.

"Where's the girl?" Muldon demanded. "In here?"

The boy nodded.

"Good. Open the door. Just give me the key to it, I mean."

The hoodlum started fumbling through his pockets.

"*And don't be makin' so damned much noise about it!*" Muldoon hissed.

The boy produced the keys. Muldoon took them. "That's bein' smart," he said. "I'm goin' to let go your mouth now. Not a sound, mind, or you're as dead as I'll be. Which won't be doin' you any good."

He let go; his prisoner remained quiet. Muldoon gagged him, effectively but gently—he didn't want the poor fellow suffocating to death—then pulled the boy off the chair and around to the railing over the stairway. He laced his prisoner's arms through the bars, and reached over to cuff them behind him. A quick frisk showed the boy had a watch, some gold money (a McKinley man, thought Muldoon), and a little silver-plated two-shot derringer —more a toy than a weapon, but still deadly enough under the right circumstances. He left the rest, and put the derringer in his pocket. Patiently, he fitted keys in the lock until he found the one that fit. Then he opened the door.

XI.

Cleo lay on the bed, just as when Muldoon first saw her. There were some differences this time, however. She lay face down, crying into her pillow. And, except for her bare feet, she was fully clothed.

It mattered not at all; she still took Muldoon's breath away.

Cleo spoke without looking up. "You *monster!*"

Muldoon was startled. These were the first words he'd heard spoken aloud in some time, and he had somehow expected a warmer reception.

Cleo went on. "What do you want of me? Whatever I may be, you are worse, you degraded—"

Her voice, he was sure, was still too quiet to be heard downstairs, but she was just getting warmed up. "Miss Cleo," he said softly.

It was Cleo's turn to start. Her head and upper body twisted wildly, looking for the source of the voice. She saw her rescuer, and she felt hope well up within her. "*Officer Muldoon!*" she cried happily, her eyes shining behind her tears. "I thought you were Baxter!"

"Shhh!" Muldoon scolded her with a look. "Quiet."

"Oh, you *have* come, I didn't dare hope you would. You got my message?" Her voice was quieter, but still excited.

"I did."

"But how did you get in here? Avery's assassins are guarding the house."

Muldoon had dozens of things to worry about at that moment, but the thought that insisted on his full attention was, So it's "Avery" is it? Cursing himself for a fool, he dismissed the question from his mind.

"Questions for later," Muldoon said. "Right now, we're gettin' shut of this house while we still can."

"Oh, bless you, Officer Muldoon. I don't know how I can ever repay—"

"Can it, you prevaricatin' little bitch! I'm doin' me duty, just like before. I may be stupid enough to fall for that line of yours, but I'm not stupid enough to fall for it more than once."

He might have slapped her. No one had ever taken quite that tone with her before. It stunned her. "I—I'm sorry."

"I'll be content to take your word for it. We'll get out of here now, and do our talkin' later. And if we can get our talkin' done without me takin' you over me knee, I will be one surprised copper. Now get your blinkin' shoes on."

Cleo complied, and they tiptoed back into the hall.

Disaster struck just as they reached the head of the stairs. Muldoon had just exchanged signals with Roscoe, and had started to descend with Cleo, when the front door opened and Eagle Jack Sperling entered, accompanied by Tommy Alb and still more rum characters.

"Idiots didn't even have my brand," he muttered under his breath. "Best Havana see-gars made, and this poor excuse for a tobacconist don't even have any. After I walked all that way. That's no way to run a business, if you follow me."

"We follow you, boss," one of his henchmen replied.

"And another thing—*what the hell's the big idea?*" He had stumbled onto the liquor-sampling party in Hand's parlor. "Put them bottles down! I swear, I'll skin every worthless man jack of you alive for this."

The tirade went on, but this was the sentence that worked its way into the tiny brain of the boy handcuffed to the railing. He had tried to do his job. He didn't want Eagle Jack to skin *him* alive. So he had to do something to stop the man and the lady from getting away. So he began to kick his feet on the floor.

Three times. He only made three thumps on the carpeted hardwood before Muldoon scampered up there and stopped him. But it was enough. Eagle Jack was still standing in the hallway, and the thumping caused him to look up the stairs, where he saw Roscoe.

"It's that one-eyed bastard as was spyin' on us!" he yelled. "Get him."

Hand's men began to pour from the parlor and run for the stairs.

"Sweet Jesus," Muldoon said, as he returned to the top of the stairs. He turned to Cleo. "How can we get out of here?"

"The back stairs! Hurry!"

"Come on, Roscoe!" Muldoon called.

"Beat it," the one-eyed man replied. "I'll be all right." He took a firmer grip on his sap. Roscoe hated guns, and wouldn't carry one.

"Are you daft, man? There's five of them!"

"I know, and someone's got to hold 'em off. You got to take care of the female, and I gotta stay. The boss would want it that way. Now *get!*"

The mob was upon him. Muldoon hesitated, unwilling to leave his friend. Then he heard Cleo's voice screaming "Dennis!" in real terror, the first unfeigned emotion he'd ever heard from that woman.

With tears in his eyes, he turned and ran. The last thing he saw before the stairway was around a bend and out of sight was Roscoe still laying about him with the sap, laying villains low, even as some of them clawed at his legs, bringing him down through weight of numbers.

XII.

"Here!" Muldoon said, handing his new revolver to Cleo. He knew he didn't have to ask her if she knew how to handle it. She led the way to the back stairs, then recoiled as she looked down them. "They've cut us off!" she said.

Two of Sperling's men, at least, had used their brains to anticipate the move Cleo and Muldoon would make. They clambered up the stairs now, with wide grins on their faces, thinking their quarry trapped on the landing.

They didn't anticipate, however, that their quarry would be armed. Cleo raised the revolver, and Muldoon his borrowed derringer. Two shots sounded at once, and the men went down, the one in front shot by Cleo in the leg, the one behind by Muldoon in the shoulder.

Despite the situation the young officer smiled. "Like we been practicin' for years," he said. "Fancy shootin', girlie."

They proceeded down the stairs, climbing over the wounded. Cleo raised her skirt and slips to avoid letting blood stain their hems. Muldoon started to mutter apologies to the wounded, then thought of what Roscoe was probably going through, and choked them off.

The two sprinted through the kitchen and out through the back of the house. "This way," Muldoon said, pointing toward the gate where he'd entered.

Cleo entertained a frightful thought. She froze in her tracks and clutched Muldoon's sleeve. "The *hound!*" she said.

"Been taken care of," Muldoon assured her. "Now move! I can't be carryin' you."

Cleo ran behind him. It was only a few seconds before Eagle Jack Sperling's voice sounded again. "There they go, blast them! Where's the goddamn dog? Well, don't just stand there, catch them! Kill them!"

But by the time they heard this, they had reached the bicycle.

"Get on!" Muldoon said, then watched stupified as Cleo handed him the revolver, gathered up her skirt, and climbed aboard the front seat.

"What are you doin', woman?" the young man demanded. "I'm drivin'."

Cleo tightened her lips and shook her head. "It's better this way. I have my own bicycle, so I'm used to steering. And we'll get more power if you pedal in the rear."

"This is a hell of a time for an argument!" Muldoon said. He stood in angry frustration for a split second, then hopped aboard the rear seat. It wasn't any of Cleo's arguments that convinced him; it was his own sudden realization that his body would make a good shield for hers against bullets fired as they fled.

"Let's get goin'," Muldoon said.

Cleo twisted her neck to face him. "Time your strokes to mine. I'll count, all right?" Before he could answer, she leaned back and kissed him, with open mouth. Muldoon nearly forgot about escaping.

Before he knew it, though, her lips were gone, and Cleo was

singing out in a strong, clear voice, "One! Two! One! Two!" The bicycle pulled away from the gate, and began to pick up speed.

"We're goin' to the southeast corner of the reservoir," Muldoon told Cleo's graceful back. Never breaking her cadence, she nodded her understanding.

The wind whipping past the now-speeding tandem blew a delicate whiff of Cleo's perfume to Muldoon's nostrils. It occurred to him that the whole excursion would have been very pleasant, if it hadn't had such a desperate purpose.

That thought reminded him to wonder what had happened to the pursuit. They had made it the better part of a block now, and there was still no sign of Sperling or his men.

No sooner had he finished thinking this, when he heard an ominous roaring from somewhere on the grounds of Hand's estate.

"Oh, no!" Cleo said. She no longer had to call cadence; their rhythm had become almost second nature by now.

"What's the matter?" Muldoon demanded. "What the hell's that noise."

"It's the Duryea," Cleo said. "I was afraid of this." There was a grim fatality in her voice.

"The what?"

"Avery's auto mobile. We're doomed. Leave me, I can't run with these skirts. Save yourself. Run between buildings, or into a house, where the auto mobile can't follow."

The roaring was louder. Muldoon turned his head to the side as they sped by Forty-second Street, and saw the twin acetylene lamps of the self-propelled vehicle.

"Pedal faster!" he said. "*One! Two! One! Two!*"

"It's no *use!*"

"Nonsense, girlie. If we can just get to the carriage, we've got a fightin' chance."

"You have a carriage?"

"What do you think, I was expectin' you to *swim?* Now let's get a move on!"

They pedaled mightily. Muldoon could see a sheen of perspiration on his pretty pilot's neck, and he himself finally appreciated the nights he'd spent loading heavy barrels on brewery trucks and the muscles they'd given to his back and legs.

The tandem fairly flew; they might have been an entry in the Six Day Race.

But it was no good. The auto mobile couldn't go as fast as they could, but it would never get tired. The roar of the machinery was like a banshee's wail behind them.

Then there was a noise above the roar, like someone slapping a razor strop across a table. It was followed almost immediately by a buzz past Muldoon's ear.

"They're shooting at us," Cleo said, matter-of-factly.

Muldoon's admiration for the girl was growing by the second —*he* hadn't figured that out yet.

"Right you are, me darlin'," he said. "Keep a good hold, now. I'm gonna let go one hand, give these buggers something to be thinkin' about."

He took his right hand from his fixed handle bar, and took his new revolver from the pocket of his jacket. There were still four shots left in it. At the speed they were traveling, he daren't turn to aim, for fear of throwing the bicycle out of control. Instead, he raised his arm straight up, then bent it at the elbow until the gun, upside down, was aimed directly behind him. He adjusted as well as he could from the sound of the engine, and began to squeeze off his shots.

XIII.

Eagle Jack Sperling ran a hand over his bald pate and cursed under his breath. He could kill that idiot Hand for leaving them with no transportation but this belching monster. What kind of fool would neglect a good, honest horse for something that sounded like it was going to explode into flaming pieces in the next second?

They weren't going to get away, that was for sure. Not if he had to ride in this hunk of junk, crammed in with three of his men, including Tommy Alb, (who *claimed* he knew how to steer the thing). Not, in fact, if he had to ride with the chickens on a livestock dray. Muldoon was dead. No more orders, no more business, except personal business. Nobody messed up Eagle Jack Sperling that many times and lived.

The auto mobile continued to bound along over the cobbles.

Eagle Jack leaned over the side (he was in the back seat) and was sick. While he was at it, the car swerved widly. Eagle Jack nearly pitched out of the vehicle.

"You son of a bitch!" he gurgled. "Are you trying to kill me, or what?"

Tommy Alb swerved the vehicle again. "He's *shooting* at us, boss! Can't you hear the bullets?" The handsome blond man's voice came strangely through the white bandage on his nose. It was a souvenir from that Roscoe mug. Tommy was happy they'd gotten him.

"I don't care," Eagle Jack began, building in volume with every syllable, "if he makes a goddamn *Switzer cheese* out of you! You keep this thing on a straight line!"

Tommy had his doubts about complying, until the man on his right, a human gorilla called Big Knuckles, who spoke about once a year, said, "He ain't shooting no more."

Tommy looked, and sure enough, Muldoon had put the gun back in his pocket. "It's okay, boss," he told his employer gaily. "They're getting tired, slowing up. We've got them, now."

It was true that the strain of running through Hand's house and grounds, followed by the forced sprint on the tandem, had taken their toll on Cleo and Muldoon, but that wasn't why they were slowing down. They had nearly reached the rented landau.

"Hurry up, hurry!" Brian O'Leary piped up. "You've only got half a block on 'em!"

They brought the bicycle to a halt, and ran to the horse-drawn vehicle. "Get in!" Muldoon ordered.

"And just leave the tandem?" Brian's voice said he couldn't believe it.

"GET IN!" roared Muldoon. Brian complied, just as gunshots began to whistle past them once again and the auto mobile picked up ground; the boy was helped along by a healthy shove from Muldoon. The officer then vaulted to the driver's perch, only to find Cleo sitting there already.

"Saints give me strength," he intoned. "You fixin' to drive this thing, too?"

Cleo's dark eyes were bright as she took his hand and put the reins in it. "No. I just want to be at your side in case we don't make it."

"I appreciate the gesture," Muldoon said, "but you'd be safer inside."

A bullet knocked splinters loose from the side of the carriage. There was no more time to argue. Muldoon cracked the reins, and the horse began to run down Fifth Avenue.

XIV.

Now the roar of the engine sounded in counterpoint to the hoofbeats of the big bay. Muldoon constantly whistled and shouted, coaxing it to greater speed. The bullets still flew by, but, it seemed to Muldoon, less frequently. The men in the auto mobile were probably getting low on ammunition.

There was a bit of traffic around Thirty-ninth Street—some function or other at the Union League Club. With skill he never suspected he had, Muldoon guided his vehicle around two pedestrians and a hansom that had stopped to discharge a couple of swells.

A brief glance backward showed him that his pursuers had been as adroit—he could hear cursing and shouts for the cabbie to get his obscene vehicle out of the way.

Crowds, Muldoon knew, were his best chance to lose the hoodlums, and the shortest distance to a crowd was right down Fifth Avenue. The horse continued to gallop.

Brian O'Leary was pounding on the inside of the carriage.

"What do you want?" Muldoon yelled.

The boy said something. Muldoon turned to Cleo. "What did he say?"

The girl leaned back and listened, then pulled some wind-whipped strands of hair from her face and said, "He wants to know where Roscoe is."

Muldoon blew out a breath between tight lips. Then, in a hearty voice, he said, "Don't you remember the plan, boy? Roscoe wasn't supposed to be comin' back with us. He was supposed to take off on foot, headin' west. For a decoy."

"That ain't," Brian O'Leary said, "what I asked you."

Muldoon was unable to speak.

"*Well?*" Brian insisted.

"They got him, all right?" Muldoon spat. "Are you happy

now that you know? The goddamn motherless bastards got him while I ran away." Muldoon felt a soft hand on his shoulder. A look from the corner of his eye told him Cleo was crying. Suddenly, his own eyes started to burn, and Fifth Avenue started to blur. Blasted wind, he thought.

They galloped by clubs and mansions, but they never managed to leave the drone of Hand's machine behind. Muldoon had an idea. "Cleo," he said, "take the derringer from me pocket."

She had to reach around him to do so, and a bump in the road almost caused her to drop it, but she held it, just as they passed the Presbyterian church on the corner of Thirty-seventh Street.

"Now grab something, and hold on tight! Brian! Secure yourself in there!"

Everything makes a difference, Muldoon thought, everything pays off. The days, the weeks, really, he'd spent exploring this island when the Muldoons first landed. It would come in handy, now.

Because the road dropped off rapidly from Thirty-sixth Street to Thirty-fifth, a steep grade, with wooden planking across it to make ascent and descent easier.

But of course, only a madman would take the hill at these speeds. The horse, seeing the road disappear before him, took it at a leap, and the landau flew behind him, landing with a clatter that must have startled all the guests at the huge Waldorf-Astoria in the next block. Muldoon decided that if he were ever to be flush enough to buy a carriage, the fellow who'd made this one would get the business. He was surprised it didn't fly to flinders.

He was surprised *he* didn't fly to flinders, but he didn't waste time thinking about it. He had only seconds to tell Cleo what he had in mind.

"There's one shot left in the derringer," he told her. "We're out of their sight, at the moment. So as soon as they appear at the top, before they go flyin' through the air, I want you to shoot it at them. Maybe their landin' won't be as safe as ours."

It worked better than Muldoon expected. The man next to the driver (who Muldoon saw was his old chum Tommy Alb) ducked so energetically when Cleo raised and fired the tiny pistol that he fell clean out of the auto mobile while it was in midair. He hit the wooden planking on the grade with a wet crack, and rolled to the bottom of the hill.

Angry people came running from the hotel, going to help the hoodlum, and shaking fists at Muldoon. The young officer wished he had time to explain.

The ride reached a point where it ceased to be real—the angry people who had to dodge for their lives, the helmeted policemen who tooted their whistles and began to give chase, even Eagle Jack and the threat he represented, became secondary to the sensation of New York City whizzing by as he sat next to the most beautiful girl he'd ever seen.

He felt almost nostalgic on the block between Thirty-second and Thirty-first, as the carriage passed Tooth's, Marcotte's, and Duveen's, three art galleries where he'd tried to pick up Cleo's trail.

Muldoon had thought all during the wild ride that the streets had been oddly deserted for a warm Friday evening. As they approached Madison Square, and the city's night life, he knew the reason: everyone had gone to the theatre.

The traffic at Delmonico's, on Twenty-sixth, was so bad that for the first time, Muldoon had to rein in the foaming, panting bay, coming almost to a dead stop. He cursed softly while Cleo at his side fretted as the auto mobile gained on them.

They got close enough, in fact, for Cleo to fairly count Tommy Alb's pretty white teeth, and when, almost by a miracle, there was a break in the traffic, Muldoon snapped the reins, and the horse took off again.

"No shots," Muldoon said.

"Maybe they're out of bullets," Brian O'Leary suggested from within.

"Or else they just don't feel like havin' to explain shootin' an innocent bystander." Muldoon's voice was bitter; the reality of the situation had returned to him.

"Muldoon," Cleo said. She managed to give the impression of intimacy, even though she had to shout above the noise of traffic, "Dennis. I want you to know that however this turns out . . ."

Muldoon swept into the wrong side of the road to pass two carriages, evoking the wrath of yet another traffic patrolman.

". . . whatever happens, I think you are a wonderful man."

Muldoon mumbled a somewhat confused thanks as they crossed Twenty-third Street, and emerged into Madison Square.

XV.

Madison Square. The heart of New York's social life. Hotels. Theatres. Eating places. Mr. Edison's electric light.

Muldoon and company crossed it in fourteen seconds. The horse was sure to go insane, Cleo thought. Muldoon had had him run such a zigzag course, it made her dizzy, but it got them through the worst of the traffic, though now, they had switched roads, and were heading, instead of due south on Fifth Avenue, south by east on Broadway.

And the auto mobile was right behind them, still. It had simply followed Muldoon's path. Cleo closed her eyes. What was she, to cause all this suffering? It happened to all she met, those she hated and those she liked . . .

"Why are we slowing down?" she asked, just past Nineteenth Street.

"Well, it ain't my blinkin' idea! The horse is done for. If we get three more blocks out of him, it'll be a miracle." She could see him shake his head ruefully as he reached for the whip. Now she was even making the horse suffer.

There was a new sound added to the noise of the motor car—the whizzing sound made by bicycle squad policemen. Muldoon heard it too, and cursed. Cleo knew the worst part of all of this, for the man at her side, was having to run from his comrades.

Muldoon's arm was moving constantly, now, up and down, cracking the whip on the poor horse's body. They had gotten the three blocks and more, but at a constantly decreasing speed.

The auto mobile was only a few carriage lengths behind as they entered Union Square, where the traffic and the din were even worse than at Madison Square.

The men in the auto mobile were grinning now, two of the three remaining ones shouting taunts. And they were close enough for the taunts to be intelligible.

"Give up, save the horse," they shouted. "We'll have you by Twelfth Street."

Muldoon's face was a bitter mask. Fifteenth Street. Cleo reflected that this was the first time she'd ever passed Tiffany & Co. without looking in the window.

Then Muldoon had an idea. Cleo could see it in his face; he had a wonderfully expressive face.

"Get us by Twelfth Street, will they, the bastards? *Hee-yah!* Move, horse, dammit. One more block, I promise!"

He was standing now, whipping the horse with all the strength remaining in his arm. And getting results. The horse picked up the pace, and she could hear the auto mobile's throttle being opened more to try to match it.

Then Cleo looked forward. "Dennis!" she cried. He was going to kill them all instead of letting them face capture. "Don't!" she pleaded. For Muldoon was whipping the horse full speed at an impossible tangle of trolleys and cable cars whipping around Fourteenth Street at Dead Man's Curve. There seemed to be no way to avoid being crushed.

The horse kept running, while Muldoon whipped him toward a rapidly diminishing opening between two of the huge cars. The horse was too bewildered with pain and fatigue to shy away, or even think of it.

They would never make it. The space was too small already. It would be like trying to thread a needle with a clothes line. Cleo covered her eyes.

"*Jump!*" Muldoon yelled. "Cleo, Brian, *JUMP!*"

Without even opening her eyes, Cleo jumped. There was a thunderous crash, and then silence.

XVI.

Brian O'Leary bounced up like a rubber ball, and surveyed the damage with true appreciation. The auto mobile had been pinched between the two cars, and the hoodlums lay sprawled on the sidewalk in varying stages of stupefaction. Police and bystanders, he saw, were already coming to their aid. He climbed down from his perch on the overturned landau (it had been clipped on the rear corner by one of the cable cars), and rejoined Muldoon and the girl, who were just getting to their feet.

"Let's get movin'," Muldoon said. It seemed to him he was saying that quite a bit, recently. It also seemed to him that he was getting to be a terror on clothes. This latest suit was ripped at one elbow and both knees, and had dust and bits of gravel ground into it. As he started to scurry with his two friends away from immediate police interest, it felt like he had bits of gravel ground into him, too.

He noticed, to his surprise, that he had quite automatically taken Cleo by the hand. She looked fine, as though she had somehow managed to fill her skirts with hot air and float down from the landau like an aeronaut. Of course, the fact that she had landed full on top of Muldoon might have something to do with it.

There wasn't mark on the boy, either, but kids were made of india-rubber, anyway, so that was no surprise.

Just around the corner, walking back up Fourth Avenue, Muldoon stood stock-still, grasped his forehead, and gasped.

"What's the matter?" Cleo demanded.

"I should be hanged," he said. "I should be hanged. I've gone and killed Roscoe, went riskin' both your lives . . ."

"No, no," Cleo said softly. Brian asked Muldoon what he was talking about. The young woman took a lace handkerchief from her sleeve, and touched it to Muldoon's face—that was the first he realized he was crying.

He pushed her hand away. "No, by God. I'll face it like a man. Brian, I'm a mite beat up and sore. Would you please go see Mr. Jacob Riis, at his newspaper, or at this address," he handed the boy a slip of paper Mr. Roosevelt had given him, "and have him get Mr. Roosevelt out of that meetin' and bring him to me?"

"Hey," Brian said, "that's a good idea."

"Sure, it is," Muldoon said. His voice was full of self-hatred. "It's a corker. If I'd only had the wit to think of it a couple hours ago, Roscoe'd still be breathin'." Muldoon closed his eyes and breathed deeply. When he finished, he said to the boy, "Well, are you back yet?"

"I'm going now. But where are you going to be waiting?"

"Waitin'?"

"Yeah. You stand right here, the coppers are gonna get you."
An ambulance went by, bell clanging, horse galloping to the scene
of the crushed auto mobile and its injured occupants. "Where are
you gonna be?"

Muldoon couldn't seem to understand the question. Finally,
the young woman gave his hand a squeeze and spoke for him.
"We'll be at the Hotel Devereaux, Brian. Miss Le Clerc's suite."

The boy looked at her and scratched at his red hair. "You
Cleo?" he asked.

"Yes."

"Hmmm," he said. "Father Brannock is wrong. You're nice.
See you later. Take care of the big mick, okay?"

"I shall, Brian," she said, and led Muldoon back uptown to
the hotel.

XVII.

This is marvelous, Muldoon thought. This is one for the
Police Gazette. He had invited Mr. Theodore Roosevelt, who, if
he were ever to meet God Almighty face to face would probably
tell Him the Ten Commandments was a good idea, but didn't go
far enough, to meet him in the hotel suite of a Kept Woman.
Well, he'd report to the Commissioner, then turn in his shield
(figuratively—Herkimer still has his real one), and after that, it
wouldn't matter what anyone thought of him. It wouldn't even
matter what he thought of himself.

Lord, his head hurt—not from a bump, his head had somehow
managed to escape the crash unscathed—but from fatigue, and
from failure. Trying to see the bright side, he reminded himself
that the pain in his head doubtless kept him from feeling the full
effects of the pains in the rest of his body.

He was sitting on something of carved wood, lace, and pink
satin that was too wide to be a chair, and too narrow to be anything else. Cleo was in a different part of the suite, doing something or other.

"Cleo?" he called. He didn't like the thready sound of his
voice, so he tried again. "Cleo?"

"Yes? I am just getting some hot water. Please bear with me

a moment. Apparently, my maid has despaired of my ever returning and has left me."

Of course she would have a maid. A fancy place like this, she'd need one. Katie didn't; probably wouldn't have stood still for one.

"I seem to recall," Muldoon said, "durin' the course of the evenin', lettin' words slip me lips that I should never have said in the presence of a lady. I apologize."

Cleo reentered the room, bearing a small basin of hot water, a sponge, and a towel. When she heard Muldoon's words, she felt very strange. It had been so long since anyone had cared about her sensitivities (not, she told herself, as though she had any), or had considered her to be a lady, that she almost blushed.

"I especially wish to apologize," Muldoon continued, "for snappin' at you back at Hand's mansion. What I said was unforgivable, and I—"

"It was *not* unforgivable," Cleo said. She sat the basin down on the floor and knelt beside it in front of Muldoon. "It was totally justified. I was trying to play on your feelings, as I had when we first met. That has been on my conscience. It was only a wicked habit that made me simper and whine as I did when you rescued me tonight. My only excuse is, well—I am not accustomed to being treated squarely. My misfortune has been to fall in with those who think only of themselves. In all my life, I have met no one who didn't betray my trust in the end."

Muldoon knew she was talking of Madam Nanette. His memory showed him a picture of the elegant old woman eating the poisoned almond torte he'd so gaily urged on her a moment before. God, Muldoon, he thought, you're a walking menace.

He also remembered about the mixup when the brothel keeper had decided to retire. "You're wrong, you know," he told Cleo. "There *was* somebody who—what are you doin' to me feet, girl?"

"I'm taking off your shoes. You landed heavily, and I believe you have twisted your ankle. Yes, you have, and cut it, too."

Gently, she bathed the wound with the hot water. "You may take off your own jacket and shirt," she said while she dressed the ankle.

"Listen," Muldoon said, "I am in no mood for it, do you understand?"

He regretted it the instant he said it, as he saw Cleo's lovely dark eyes moisten, and start to run.

"I suppose," she said, flicking the tears away with a finger, "I deserve that. But I—"

Muldoon reached out a big hand (wincing, for his shoulder hurt) and patted Cleo's head. "I'm just a big, beat-up, stupid, thickheaded Irishman. Pay me no mind." He began to take off his jacket and his shirt. She seemed to know what she was about.

Cleo suppressed a gasp when Muldoon was done. Not at his torso, though it was strong and manly—she had seen one or two better—but at the state of it. The men she'd known had been rich, and pampered. She'd never seen a man in a state like this.

For Muldoon's right shoulder, and much of his chest, was a bloody mess, the result of a series of long parallel gashes at the shoulder, not deep or dangerous, but nasty and painful. Muldoon winced as she touched them with the sponge, no matter how light the touch.

And as the blood disappeared, she saw the bruises, new and old, on the young man's body. Cleo wondered what Muldoon had been through for her sake.

"I'll be back in a moment," she said. She went to the bathroom cabinet, and got the bottle of laudanum. She had wanted to ask Muldoon what her ordeal (and his) had been all about, but that could wait. His mind and body were in pain, and that had to be eased first.

"Take this," she said, handing Muldoon the dose of narcotic. He drank it and made a face. "Have you any whiskey lyin' about? God, what a nasty taste."

"I have some brandy," Cleo said.

"That'll do."

She got him a glass of brandy, which he took in his left hand while she dressed the wounds on his right shoulder. She had him lean forward, and did his back, which wasn't so bad.

"You must lie down," she said.

"Indeed I must," Muldoon agreed. "Whew, me head is spinnin' like a phonograph cylinder."

He tried to stand, then made it. Cleo led him by the hand to her boudoir, where he lay on the bed. Cleo sat at her vanity bench.

"Hey," Muldoon said dreamily. "Do you know a rabbi?"

So much had happened since she'd seen him, Cleo thought for a second Muldoon meant an actual Jew holy man. "Oh," she said when she remembered. "Yes, I do know of him. I'll tell you later."

"Nope." Muldoon giggled. The laudanum and fatigue were taking effect. "You'll tell Teddy. Good old Teddy. You'll tell him. I'll be off the Force by then. Work as a bouncer in Frenchy Moriarty's saloon. What happened, damn it? I was *tryin'* to do me duty, but I, but I, I . . ."

His voice broke into quiet sobs. Cleo rushed to his side. "Shh," she said, stroking his brow. "You did your best. You were very brave. Commissioner Roosevelt will understand. He'll be proud of you."

"You . . . you think he will?"

"I'm sure of it. Now, let yourself go to sleep, Dennis."

Muldoon obliged. Cleo left him, went to the other room, and arranged with a corrupt but discreet bellboy of her acquaintance to get Muldoon something to wear. As she crossed the sitting room on the way back, she saw that the satin love seat was ruined, stained with water, linament, ointment, and Muldoon's blood.

She didn't care. The furniture here had been a gift from Avery, and if she'd ever felt any warm emotion for Avery, she felt it no longer. She would gladly sacrifice *ten* Averys for one Dennis Muldoon.

She returned to the boudoir. Muldoon was sleeping soundly now. Carefully, Cleo removed his trousers, and attended to the injuries on his legs. Then she covered his dear, naked body with a clean sheet. She smiled to think how their roles had been reversed.

How comforting it would be, Cleo thought, to prepare for bed and join him under that sheet, just to hold him in her arms, and feel all night the concrete evidence of the existence of a Good Man. How wonderful it would be to spend the night with a man because *she* wanted to, and not because someone had paid money. To enjoy the unprecedented freedom of staying with a man, and having the option not to do *anything*, if that was her wish.

But not tonight. Not when he was unconscious and helpless. Besides, she had work to do.

She looked at Muldoon for a second longer, then bent, and

burrowed softly through his moustache until her lips found his for a tender, lingering kiss. Then she turned out the light, and returned to the sitting room, where she took pen and paper and filled page after page with a detailed account of her life since Evan Crandall had appeared in it.

She left out nothing. There was no telling what Mr. Roosevelt might find important.

SATURDAY
the twenty-ninth
of August, 1896

I.

"Thank you, sir," the reporter said, closing his notebook. "This will make a ripping good side-piece to the story of your wedding. MAN OF PRINCIPLE; Thwarts Thieves, Weds To-day; *T. Avery Hand, Man of Courage.*"

Hand smiled and nodded. He liked the sound of it himself. It was the Rabbi's suggestion, of course. Another of those mysterious phone calls had come this morning, just when Hand was toying with the idea of putting a bullet through his head because of the mess last night. But the Rabbi had a plan to make it all come out right. He would be a handy man to have around. If he weren't a Jew, of course.

Hand figured that as long as he was here, he'd drop in on the boss. "Hearst around?" he asked the reporter.

The fellow adjusted an eyeshade on his bald head and said,

"Oh, I almost forgot. He's in his office, and would like to see you if you have the time."

"Almost forgot, eh?" Hand said, rising to his full five feet four inches. "It ill behooves a journalist, I would think, to *forget* things." Ah, well, he wouldn't have the fellow fired. Despite the fact that he'd lost his dog and his auto mobile, he felt good. It had been more Baxter's dog than his, anyway, and he'd pretty much lost interest in the motor car. The vogue would soon pass, and besides, he was about to have the Treasury of the United States to play with. He could buy *hundreds* of motor cars, and have the Government build roads to drive them on. He laughed at the thought of such foolishness.

He didn't laugh, though, when he remembered that he'd also lost Cleo. The ungrateful trollop. He'd apparently lost her quite thoroughly, to judge by the stories told by Sperling's men. She'd been quite eager to run off with that Muldoon character. Well, he was taken care of now; Cleo was welcome to him. She'd come back, but it would be too late. To hell with her, Hand decided. I can buy women as easily as motor cars. And there's always my dear Essie May. He chuckled again, though not at all heartily, this time.

Hearst rose to great the industrialist, putting a folded newspaper down on his desk as he did so. Hand saw it was a copy of the *World*.

"Keeping track of the opposition, eh? Sound business practice."

"Yes, thank you for seeing me. It appears Mr. Pulitzer doesn't appreciate the *Journal's* efforts to recover his lost circulation figures. But that's not what I wanted to see you about. I wanted to ask you about your close call last night."

"Yes, I just spoke to your man about it. The burglars finally got around to me. I'd suspected they might, and I had men ready for them. It appears a rogue policeman named Muldoon is their ringleader, but I must request again that you not publish that information—and I thank you for omitting it from today's editions —until he is apprehended. My good friend Captain Herkimer advises me an overconfident culprit is the more easily caught."

"I'm dreadfully sorry, but I cannot promise to suppress the news indefinitely, Hand. I have a duty to my readers." Hearst made a helpless gesture, but there was a shrewd light in his pale blue eyes.

Hand smiled to himself. The Rabbi wasn't the only smart one. He knew if he appeared reluctant to have that swine Muldoon named, he would have Hearst drooling.

"It's fortunate, isn't it," the publisher went on, "that you were not at home when the burglars struck."

"Oh, I wouldn't have minded getting in my licks at them." Hand stifled a mild belch with his small hand, then patted his stomach. "Philadelphia scrapple," he said, smiling. "My man received some from friends, and kindly offered it for my breakfast. It is delicious, but I fear too spicy to allow social intercourse afterward."

Hearst ignored him. "It is even more fortunate that William Jennings Bryan was not present. Last night, I mean. We wouldn't want him in any danger, would we?"

"No, that's true, Hearst. William is arriving tomorrow, by the way, on the Limited. Reverend Mr. Burley has traveled to Utica to meet the train and ride back with them—my fiancée is also traveling with them."

"Fortunate," Hearst repeated. "Extremely fortunate." Hearst began to drum his fingers against his desk. "There is something I wish to say, Mr. Hand. I urge you to listen closely to it."

Hand wondered what the publisher had on his mind. The request was courteous, but something in the tone commanded attention. "I'm all ears," Hand said.

Hearst stood and began to pace. "I have," he said, "much time and effort, to say nothing of money, invested in the person of William Jennings Bryan and in his candidacy."

This was not news to Hand. "So have I," he said.

"My point exactly. Our interests in this matter are identical, or should be. We would take it badly if anything were to happen to embarrass him, to hurt his chances. Wouldn't we?"

"I'll say." Hand had a tendency to slip into vulgar speech when agitated, as he was now with curiosity. What was Hearst driving at?

"Yet, the—ah—burglary at your home last night had a potential to become an embarrassment. If, for example, it happened tonight, instead of last night.

"We have managed to avoid that—you by having men at the ready, and foiling the—ah—thieves, I by playing up your story. But it must not happen again."

"How . . . how would you have me stop criminals? They don't consult me when they plan to rob me." Hand could feel sweat start on his forehead. Hearst knew something.

"I'm sure you are astute enough to think of some way to prevent a similar incident from occurring, at least between now and election day. Don't you agree, Mr. Hand? Please say you'll agree. All I can do is see it goes hard on the offender if it happens again, but you can do so much more. Please agree, Mr. Hand."

"Of course, I agree," Hand said. "I—I'll do everything in my power. I always do."

Hearst smiled. "Excellent. I think this election will be a close one. We can't take any chances, you know. Good day, Mr. Hand. I wish you and your bride every happiness."

"Thank you, Hearst," Hand said. He was still very puzzled. He stifled another explosion of scrapple gas, put on his homberg, and left the office.

Hearst sat back down and drummed his fingers on his desk as he watched the smaller, older man go. The burglary ring, indeed. Whom was Hand trying to deceive? The burglary ring struck only at houses that were deserted. That was their invariable pattern.

And claiming that someone named Muldoon was behind the whole business. Nonsense. His reporters had been to the Waldorf and found witnesses who had seen part of the mad escape. If their descriptions could be relied upon at all, then that man with the flying carriage had been the same Muldoon he'd met the other day—Roosevelt's man.

Hearst was good at sizing people up. If that big Irishman was a burglar, Hearst was a printer's devil at the *Tribune*.

No, Hand was up to something, something that could embarrass Bryan, and therefore Hearst. Worse, it was something Theodore Roosevelt had gotten in his bulldog teeth, and Hearst knew he'd never let go until he'd worried it to death.

Hearst's newspaper-ink blood was in a ferment. He would give a lot to know what was going on.

II.

Earlier that morning Theodore Roosevelt had finished reading the last page of Cleo's manuscript, crumpled it, thrown it on her flowered rug, leaned back on the blood stained love seat, and polished his spectacles. I know the "red candles" are dynamite, blast it, he told himself, but what have "mill gals" to do with anything?

"Have I offended you?" Cleo wanted to know. Roosevelt remarked once again (to himself) that she was indeed a lovely gir.. Neither her life of sin, nor her ordeals of the past few weeks, nor the fatigue of her adventurous night had marked her features. There was hope for this woman.

"Not at all," the Commissioner said.

"Then why have you crushed and discarded my final page?" Cleo wasn't hurt, just curious.

"Ha!" Roosevelt grinned, somewhat sheepishly, and retrieved the paper from the floor. "Force of habit. My apologies." He placed the paper on an occasional table and pressed it as flat as possible with his muscular hands. Then he added it to the rest of the manuscript, which he remembered *not* to crumple.

"This is a very valuable document, miss," he told the young woman. "And as a professional writer, I must say it is clearly and elegantly expressed."

"Oh, do you really think so?" Cleo had expected many things from this meeting, but not praise; especially not praise of that nature.

"A fine job."

"I met Nellie Bly once, when I was a little girl. When she was traveling around the world for Mr. Pulitzer. I sometimes think I would like to be a journalist." Cleo couldn't believe her own ears—she had never breathed a word of this to *anybody*, not even Mother Nanette, and here she was telling this Civil Servant. But he thought nothing of it, it seemed.

The Commissioner looked at his watch. Not quite six in the morning. He had been here a little over an hour. The Police Board meeting had broken up, and he had left the building frustrated and upset with the obstinacy of his colleagues. He had decided to go on one of his patrols, be Haroun-al-Roosevelt again, something he hadn't been able to do properly for several days.

Unfortunately, he left just as young Brian O'Leary arrived to look for him. Learning what the Commissioner was up to, the boy doggedly wandered the streets of New York, looking for him.

He didn't find him until four-thirty or so. Brian told Mr. Roosevelt the story of the escape, of the loss of Roscoe, and of Muldoon's going off with Cleo.

The Commissioner hadn't liked the sound of that. After ordering Brian to go home and get some rest, he hastened to the address the boy had given him. Brian had wanted to come along, but this, he suspected, was to be a trip to the apartments of a lady of temporary affection, and that was no place for a teen-aged boy.

It really was no place for him, either, but he refused to go sneaking about his business. He marched up to the desk and asked the way to Miss Le Clerc's room. The clerk had no reaction at all. Either he didn't recognize the Commissioner, or he was trained not to recognize callers. Roosevelt resolved to investigate someday soon the nature of the business at the Devereaux Hotel.

He marched boldly up to the door and knocked. He felt miserable to think Muldoon had disregarded his admonitions and succumbed to the woman's charms. He would dress Muldoon down—if not dismiss him—then interrogate him thoroughly. He hadn't decided what he would do about the woman.

But it hadn't turned out that way at all. Muldoon had been injured, and she had tended to him. She had gone a little farther, perhaps, than propriety would allow, but she had thought it best to keep the secret among as few as possible, and avoid calling in a doctor.

And, the Commissioner had to face the fact that the sight of a man's body was no novelty to her. Besides, she had written that manuscript; she had a sincere desire to help. Now, if he could only trust it . . .

"Miss, if you aspire to journalism, you must have heard this: 'Accuracy is to a newspaper what . . .' oh, blast."

Cleo laughed, a good, hearty laugh. " 'Accuracy is to a newspaper what virtue is to a woman,' is that the quotation you mean?

You needn't worry about offending me, Mr. Roosevelt. I am through with that life, and need to learn to be a respectable woman."

"Bully for you!" the Commissioner said. "Bully! Still, it was a poor choice of words. What I meant to ask is simply this: how accurate is this report?"

"I think it is very accurate, sir," she said. "I have a very good memory. I have only described things I have seen with my own eyes, and I only record as quotes conversations I remember word for word. For the rest, I recorded the substance of them as best I remember. I gave as much detail as I could for everything but," here she dropped her voice, "everything but the indignities that monstrous Baxter forced me through at gunpoint. Though, if you think it necessary, I could bear to relate them to you now, if you could bear to hear them."

Roosevelt assured her it would not be necessary. He did have a few questions to ask about the butler, however.

"How did he come to find you so soon after you got away from Muldoon and me?"

"I don't know, sir." Cleo had been wondering about that herself. "Unless he killed Crandall himself. But I did hear voices, talking about a 'paper,' that 'bill of sale' that sold me into slavery, no doubt, and the voice didn't sound like Baxter's. I'm sure it wasn't a disguised voice, either—though I didn't hear too clearly."

"Just what did you hear?"

Cleo touched her hair and shrugged. "I can't say much more than I already have. There was a door between the conversation and me, and the way Crandall tied me invariably forced my head deep into the pillow, muffling sound all the more."

The Commissioner hissed through a grin. "Can you remember anything more about the conversation and what followed? Anything at all? This is, after all, the only link we have with the killer, and your testimony is invaluable. You did justice a great disservice in running away, young woman."

Cleo lowered her eyes. "I know that, Mr. Roosevelt. I think I have done myself one just as great." She looked at the stocky man across from her again, and saw approval in his eyes. She went on with her story.

"There was a knock at the door of Crandall's flat. Crandall told the caller to wait while he tied me up. He had done it often, and it took hardly any time at all. Then he locked me in the bedroom, and went to answer the door.

"If they exchanged names in greeting, they were too far to the other end of the flat for me to hear. I heard their footsteps, though, returning to the center of the room, and I heard just a few sentences. Crandall said, 'Is that the paper?', and the other man said, 'Of course, that's why I have come.' Then money was mentioned, but I didn't hear how m—"

"Wait a moment!" The Commissioner's voice was strident; he held up a hand as though to stop Cleo's words physically. "Is that the way of it? It was *Crandall* who said 'Is that the paper?'"

"Yes. I knew *his* voice very well. I shall hear it in my nightmares."

"But Hand gave the paper, the bill of sale, to Crandall when the foul transaction was made, didn't he? How did the other man come to have it, I wonder."

"Perhaps he was an accomplice," Cleo suggested.

"That's possible, but the tone of the conversation, or at least the part we know, doesn't seem right for a talk between accomplices. I get the impression it sounded almost like an act of everyday commerce."

Cleo clapped her hands together and nodded rapidly. "That's exactly what it seemed to be. That's why I was so frightened when I heard the conversation stop so suddenly."

"There were no sounds of a struggle, then."

"None. One minute they were speaking, and the next, they weren't. And Crandall never returned to untie me. I lay there helpless, afraid I was to starve to death. Then, I began to smell the gas, as it seeped around the door, and I knew it was only a matter of hours before I would be asphyxiated."

Cleo shuddered. The next place she lived would have the electric light, no matter what it cost. Coal-gas would always smell of death to her.

Mr. Roosevelt rose, and patted her on the shoulder. This was a brave girl, whose sins had been as much the fault of others as of herself. "Providence directed Mrs. Sturdevant and Officer Muldoon to act in such a way that your life would be saved. Your duty now is to be worthy of that good fortune. And I must say, you have made a good start with your actions of this night."

"What is to become of Muldoon, Mr. Roosevelt? He feels terrible about Roscoe."

"As do I—it's as much my fault as anyone's. More so. I was so worried about what Parker would say—well, that's past fixing. I mourn Roscoe, and I shall see him avenged. You needn't worry about Muldoon, miss."

Almost as though he'd heard his name, Muldoon interrupted the soft snoring he'd been producing for the last several hours, and made a sort of gurgling noise as he rolled over.

"Ha!" the Commissioner said. "I believe the effect of the laudanum is wearing off." He consulted his watch again. "Half past six. We have work to do. Wait here, miss, if you don't mind. Hand me that bundle of clothes. I will awaken him and tell him the good news."

Cleo wanted to go with him, but Mr. Roosevelt forbade it. Last night had been an emergency; today there was no excuse for that woman's seeing Muldoon in a state of undress.

III.

Tommy Alb was already making plans to take over the gang when they told him he could leave the hospital. Only he and Eagle Jack had survived the auto mobile ride. Big Knuckles hadn't come through after being thrown from the vehicle, and the other man had died in the crash. Tommy, driving, and having seen it coming, swerved the auto mobile so that he was shielded from the worst of the impact. He received nothing worse than the broken nose he'd already suffered at the hands of that one-eyed bastard. He'd get a lot worse back, though, when Tommy got around to him. If he was still alive, that is.

Tommy went to visit Eagle Jack before he left. The former copper was surprised the bald man had lived, but he guessed his boss (of the moment) was pretty near as tough as he always said he was.

The nun tried to keep him out of Eagle Jack's room, but he

told her he was next of kin, and hustled her along. What the hell, he wasn't a Catholic, anyway.

Eagle Jack was in a bad way. Tommy wondered if Sperling himself was aware of how bad. He'd heard a couple of the sawbones talking in the hall. Even if he were to pull through, he wouldn't be walking so straight, let alone beating guys up. What the heck, Tommy would pension him off in exchange for introductions to the Giants of Commerce he was always talking about.

"Hello, boss," the blond man said. His voice was still muffled some by the bandage on his nose. He touched it, experimentally, and winced. Damn that Roscoe.

The bandaged figure on the bed groaned softly and opened one eye. "Tommy," he said. "Good. I was gonna tell them to bring you." The voice was weird, thin. Something flying loose from the machine last night had hit Eagle Jack across the throat.

"How do you feel?" Tommy asked.

"Punk," Eagle Jack said. "But listen, Tommy . . ."

"Yeah?"

"Tommy, Muldoon dies."

"Yeah," Tommy liked the idea. He owed Muldoon a couple. "But won't it get us in bad with Hand?"

Eagle Jack had a vile suggestion for Hand. "It's bigger than Hand," he went on. "Muldoon made a monkey out of us. More than once. Word is getting around, and that's gonna put a big crimp in business, follow me?"

Tommy nodded. He had a very proprietary interest in the business. "Okay. Today. No fancy stuff, we beat in his head, wherever we find him."

Eagle Jack was having trouble making words. He choked a couple of times, then said, "The girl, too, if she's with him. But it's Muldoon I want. Take—" Tommy waited patiently through some more choking, but finally had to say it for his boss.

"I was gonna take Nick, Sammy, and Jersey Red. They're the best of them that are still healthy."

Eagle Jack relaxed, some of the redness of effort left his face. "You take over the boys till I'm ready, Tommy. Tell them I said so. You got b—brains."

Tommy wanted to laugh. He didn't have to do anything, and

they handed him what he wanted. Muldoon was as good as buried.

"Thanks, boss," Tommy said. "I'll get right to it."

He started to leave, but with a sudden effort, Eagle Jack reached out and grabbed his hand. "Tommy," the boss whispered, "I—*I can't feel my legs.*"

"Don't worry about it for a second, boss," Tommy told him. "If you wind up crippled, I'll see you get one of those wheelchairs."

IV.

While Muldoon dressed, Mr. Roosevelt faced the unpleasant task of informing Cleo of the death of Madam Nanette. He hated emotional scenes, but Cleo took it well, surrendering to tears only when she learned that the old woman had not abandoned her, that her last thought, in fact, had been for Cleo's welfare. She cried softly for a while, seemed to be praying. Roosevelt waited in silence. She was through by the time Muldoon entered the room.

"Mr. Roosevelt," he said, taking a deep breath of the still-cool morning air that blew past Cleo's lace curtains, "it seems that you're always bringin' me up when I'm at me lowest. I thank you for it once again. And I want to say, in front of a witness, that Hand and his goons will find I don't hold Roscoe's life cheap. Let me at them, sir. I'm rarin' to go."

"You have been hurt," Cleo said.

"And I've been fixed up, thanks to you. Sir, I won't be sleepin' easy until I've done somethin' to even it up for Roscoe."

"I promise you, Muldoon, you will, and soon. But there are many things you don't know, and must be brought up to date on."

The Commissioner told him of Hand's story to the newspapers and the police about Muldoon's being the head of the Mansion Burglars. "You see, Muldoon, I am aiding and abetting you as a fugitive from justice by not arresting you immediately."

Muldoon turned red. "Blast it, that's goin' too far! You know that for the mess of lies it is, and—"

"Yes, Muldoon, of course I know it!" Mr. Roosevelt shook a fist in irritation. "And I will tell you right now, I shall never,

ever resort to deception again, no matter what the provocation. There is no end to it. I was a fool to act against my inclination.

"Muldoon, we are in an untenable position. Witnesses have seen you fleeing Hand's house, and Hand, a respected millionaire, calls you a thief. If you deny it, and name Hand for the monster he is, the Law will take the word of the rich man, of this malefactor of great wealth, over yours. You have been dismissed from the Police Force. In disgrace."

Muldoon's mouth fell open.

"Please, Muldoon, don't say what's on your mind; your loyalty and courage are reproach enough. I know full well that I was the one who brought the disgrace upon you. I fear it's too late now for even the memorandum I gave you to be of help.

"We need evidence, man! We need just one scrap of evidence linking Hand with this mysterious 'Rabbi.' Or with any of these mysterious events. Then we may proceed."

"Cleo!" Muldoon exclaimed. "Cleo was there the whole time. She must have seen him, or heard him, or heard Hand and Baxter talkin' about him. At least she can get them for kidnapin'!"

"Muldoon . . ." Mr. Roosevelt began.

"Well, *ask* her, for heaven's sake."

"Dennis," Cleo said in a low, sweet voice, "what Mr. Roosevelt has been too considerate to mention—and I thank him for it, though it is unnecessary—is the fact that my testimony would be worthless in a court of law. I am a harlot, and my word is nothing against Hand's. And if I were to accuse Baxter of assaulting me, the judge would laugh me out of court.

"I am sorry, Mr. Roosevelt, if the language is crude, but I am merely facing life as it is."

The news had finally struck home to a stunned Muldoon. "He did *what?*" The officer picked up his hat. "I'm goin' to kill him."

"Sit down, Muldoon! That's an order! That's better. Now, I have a plan that might work much better than mindless action. But, the first thing we must do is to get Miss Le Clerc out of here. They may not know or even suspect that she has come back here, but they took her from this place once, and I won't have that happening again. Do you think your sister would mind having a guest?"

"I'll see she don't mind," Muldoon said grimly.

V.

Muldoon was limping slightly on his twisted ankle, so the three decided to take a cab to the Avenue A flat. The Commissioner, by accident or design, sat in the middle.

He told Muldoon to improve the time of the ride by reading Cleo's narrative, and Muldoon was glad to oblige. At a certain point in his reading, Muldoon growled, so Roosevelt knew he had come to the part about Cleo's ill-fated attempt at flight. Muldoon unconsciously clenched a fist and held it tight until he finished reading.

"Well?" the Commissioner demanded.

"What happened to this last page?"

"Never mind that! What did you think of the narrative."

The clothes the bellboy had gotten for Muldoon fit fairly well, but the hat must have been designed for a pinhead in a side show. The derby sat foolishly on the top of his head. Muldoon removed it to scratch his head, and left it off.

"Well, sir," he said, "if Cleo's been seein' things right, Hand is as much in the dark as we are, and Baxter's up to the funny business. I must be admittin' me surprise over that."

"What about the red candles she mentions?"

Muldoon shrugged. "Smugglin'? Hollow candles with Chinese opium in them?"

"I think not, Muldoon. I think the red candles are dynamite, and I think Baxter is in league with the anarchists. I think Franklyn and Libstein's departure was the signal for whatever Baxter is about."

"That sounds good to me, sir," Muldoon said.

"Then we agree. Anything else?"

"Yes, sir," Muldoon said gravely. "I don't know if you noticed this, but you see here, at the bottom of this page, where Cleo— I mean, Miss Le Clerc—" the Commissioner had reproved Muldoon earlier for undue familiarity. "—Miss Le Clerc got a peek at this Rabbi, and describes him. Tall, sort of? Bent? White, fluffy hair and beard on him? Sir, we spent some time lookin' at this same gent. Didn't we?"

Roosevelt was beaming. "Excellent, Muldoon. I was wondering if you'd noticed that. Yes, I am sure the Rabbi and this Mr. Meister are one and the same. I have thought so, in fact, since I had the sense to speculate on the words."

Muldoon was bewildered. "Beg pardon, sir?"

"I am fluent in German, you know, Muldoon. As a boy, I spent some happy summers there."

Now Muldoon was *totally* bewildered, but he had no time to fret over it, because the cab had arrived at the family flat.

The first sight that greeted them as they entered was Brian O'Leary seated at the trestle table in the kitchen, bent over a steaming bowl of porridge.

"Hi," he said. "I see you found him okay, huh, Mr. Roosevelt?"

"What are you doing here, young man? I distinctly remember telling you to go home."

"I did, but my mother locked me out. She said I was a bum, because I got fired from the *Journal*. I lost my corner to someone who took it over when I was working for Muldoon, and I ain't had time to fight him for it back yet. But my mother ain't much for listening to explanations when she's been drinking heavy, so I come over here to tell Miss Muldoon her brother is all right, and she says, how awful, what an unnatural mother and like that, and says I can stay here. I slept on Muldoon's sofa." He took an enormous spoonful of porridge. "I like it better here, anyway," he concluded.

There were several things in the boy's speech that the Commissioner wanted to delete, add to, or change, but he realized it would have to wait for another time. They left Brian to his spoon and went into the parlor.

Katie was, naturally, joyful over seeing her brother. She was less than ecstatic at the sight of the Commissioner, and downright incensed when introduced to Cleo.

"Dennis," she said, with an ominous rising inflection, "would you mind comin' with me to me room, please? I want to talk to you. Excuse us." Muldoon followed her.

The conversation lasted a long time, but only the first part was loud enough for those in the parlor to hear. It consisted of Katie saying, "What are you thinkin' of, bringin' *that kind of woman* into—" and Muldoon ordering her to pipe down.

Maureen, who had watched all this, (Brigid was at work)

asked the Commissioner if it was Dennis described as the robber in the newspaper reports. Roosevelt conceded that it was, but promised it would all be straightened out soon. After that, they talked about *Macbeth*. Cleo said she thought the language beautiful, but that she preferred *The Tempest*, and Shakespeare's other comedies. Maureen gave her an appraising look, the first time one of the Muldoon women had deigned to notice her at all.

Finally, Muldoon and Katie returned to the parlor. Muldoon pushed Katie to the middle of the room, where she stood with her arms folded, and her lips tight.

"Go ahead," Muldoon grumbled.

Katie looked daggers at Cleo. "You can stay," she said.

"I thank you," Cleo replied.

"You should," Katie added. "You can sleep in me bedroom. I'll move in with the girls. Don't expect a lot of conversation from any of us." Then she looked daggers at her brother, and dragged Maureen off to the kitchen with her.

"She'll be comin' around," Muldoon said. "She's got a picture in her mind she doesn't care for, but she'll soon see you ain't it."

"That," Cleo told him, "is the kindest thing anyone has ever said to me."

Muldoon blushed. He almost jumped when the Commissioner spoke. "I am leaving now—I have something important to do, part of the plan."

"Yes, sir," he said. He tightened up his cravat. "Remember, now," he told Cleo, "just don't go hollerin' back at Katie, and you'll be gettin' along fine in no time."

"No, Muldoon," Roosevelt said. "You are staying here. I'll take a few men from Headquarters."

Muldoon sputtered. The Commissioner was giving him fits this morning. "You promised I could be in on the finish!"

"Oh, this isn't the finish. This is the start of the means by which I hope to bring it about."

"What are you planning to do?"

"As my ranch hands might put it, I am going to light a signal fire under T. Avery Hand."

VI.

"I could have sent a deputation of my men, I suppose," Theodore Roosevelt explained to T. Avery Hand, "but I wanted to express personally my congratulations on your foresight, and for your courage in pressing forward with the plans for your wedding."

The plans for the wedding were busily proceeding all around them. No matter where one might walk on the ground floor of the house, something rich, be it food, costume, or decoration, was being carried by, or put into place.

"And, I wanted to add my best wishes." It killed the Commissioner to be in the presence of the prissy little man.

"I'm glad you don't let politics interfere with civility," Hand said. He was slightly unnerved by the intensity of the Commissioner's stare. He wondered if he might have food in his moustache again. As he brushed at it, he continued, "You said some very unkind things about me when my conscience told me to back Bryan."

"Ha! Heat of the moment!" Roosevelt told himself he'd only have to stand this for a moment more.

A policeman dodged a waiter carrying a plate of tropical fruit, and presented himself. "Ah, Officer Bourke," Roosevelt said. "Did the burglars leave any clues behind this time?"

"I think one or two, sir," Bourke said. As previously arranged, the officer had given a coded message meaning that there was no trace of dynamite on the grounds, though why the Commissioner was looking for dynamite at a wedding was beyond him. Maybe it was the new thing from Europe or something. Like marrying a count, the way all the debutantes were doing.

"Bully, we're making progress. Hand, would it be possible for you to summon your butler?"

"I'm afraid not." Hand was getting more and more suspicious, and he wanted to talk with Baxter before anyone else did. He concocted a lie about Baxter's going to Newburgh to join the train and see to the needs of his wife-to-be, since she had never been in New York before.

Roosevelt smiled, and pretended to believe him. He didn't think that train even stopped in Newburgh.

"Well, then," he said. "Some other time, then. It would aid our investigation, greatly. And, Hand, my earlier offer, extra men to surround your grounds in case the bandits try another raid, still stands."

"Again, no thank you."

"There will be a few guards, of course, with Mr. Bryan on the premises. I insist on that; it is my duty. I might even," he added, with a significant gaze into the smaller man's eyes, "be in the area myself. Do you have any objection to that, Hand?"

"What?" He had been nearly mesmerized. "Oh, of course not. No objection at all." When would he get *out* of here?

Now, apparently. "It's your decision, Hand. Good day."

He left without waiting for the industrialist to say anything. Bourke followed. Outside, Roosevelt considered what he'd accomplished. Hand, (and especially Baxter, who, he was sure, was around somewhere) had seen the search made on the grounds, but not in the house. That had been merest folly if the search were really for clues left by the burglars. They (or Baxter, in the event Hand truly were ignorant) had to know now that the search was for the dynamite. If Baxter truly were gone, he'd learn of it when he returned.

It mattered little no dynamite had been found; the Commissioner had done what he intended. Hand was a man at the edge of an abyss; the fire had been well and truly lit.

Roosevelt ended his reflection, then reared back and bellowed for his men to join him.

And that bellow, in the Commissioner's unmistakable voice, carried around the grounds and through the house. Peter Baxter heard it, on the attic floor, as he guarded the contents of a certain closet against intrusion by a wandering caterer or decorator. He wondered what Roosevelt was doing there.

And inside the closet, Roscoe Heath, battered in his capture, and weak from his several "questionings" by Baxter, was sure he knew why the boss had come—to make a plan to rescue him. Roscoe didn't know what happened to Muldoon and the girl; he assumed they were all right, or the long-armed monkey outside wouldn't keep at him to tell where they were; but he didn't *know* that. What he did know was that the boss would take care of him. That had been what had kept him from talking, even when that bastard . . . but why worry about that? The thing to do was to be ready for when the boss came back. Ignoring the pain it caused him, Roscoe twisted his body and neck so his mouth could work (as well as it could around the gag) on the ropes that bound him.

VII.

Hiram Listerdale came calling about noontime. Muldoon, who had gotten tired of silence, was glad of the arrival of some-one Katie would deign to talk to. Brian had gone to win his corner back, and Muldoon and Cleo had run out of things to say that wouldn't make Katie angry. "Hiram!" he heard her say. "How good to be seein' you, especially this mornin'. But goodness, man, you can't go around neglectin' your business this way. Now you go right back and see to the openin' of the Emporium." Then, in a whisper, Katie told Listerdale about the visitor.

"I am touched at your concern," Listerdale whispered in re-turn. "But this is Saturday, a half day. I promise, I shall concentrate more on my business as soon as I have done what I come here to do. May I speak to your brother?"

"Oh," Katie said; then, as she realized what the man meant to do, she said "Oh" again. "Yes. Only don't go into the parlor, no reason to do that. I'll call him. Dennis!"

Muldoon smiled, and whispered to Cleo, "I've been expectin' this, but not so soon." He went to the kitchen.

"Ah, Muldoon, I am glad to see you safe and home at last." Listerdale was still whispering.

"Glad to be that way," the officer replied. "What's on your mind?"

"Well, ah . . ." The bookseller was twisting his hat between his hands. "I . . . Well, there is something I wish to talk privately about with you. Would you oblige me by taking a walk around the block?"

"Be glad to." He returned to the parlor to inform Cleo he was going out for a few minutes, then left with the bookseller.

The street was crowded, but no one was listening in. The air was warm, but there was a breeze, and people seemed to be enjoying their Saturday afternoon.

"Muldoon," Listerdale began as they walked, resuming his normal voice. "I am not a young man, nor a rich one, nor a handsome one. And I must tell you frankly, that I never thought I would feel myself disposed to settling down.

"But since I have met Kathleen, I have lost whatever compulsion it was that kept me alone. She has made me aware of my loneliness, and soon, I feel I will have freed myself of the things that have bound me to it.

"Have you any idea what I am trying to say?"

Muldoon said he did, in a general way.

"Good. I wonder if most men feel ridiculous at a time like this. Anyway, to continue. I am very fond of Kathleen, Muldoon. Fonder than I have ever been of anyone.

"And so now, I am asking you, in your capacity as head of the family, for permission to court your sister with a view toward asking her hand in marriage."

I should smile, Muldoon thought. He may look like a parson, but he talks like a lawyer. "Do you love the woman?" Muldoon asked.

"I—I realize I have known her only the shortest of times . . ."

"I didn't ask you that. Do you love her? Will you take care of her?"

Listerdale stood straight. "I have told you I am not a rich man, Muldoon. I believe I can make a go of the Emporium. Your sister would not want for—"

"*I ain't talkin' about money, dammit!*" Muldoon snapped. The sudden explosion turned the heads of a few passersby. "Wait, come here. We can talk better." Muldoon and Listerdale stepped into the alley behind the mercer's shop, where a low-hanging fire escape threw stripes across the littered ground.

Across the street, where he had been paralleling their progress, Tommy Alb gave a satisfied smile to his henchmen—*his* henchmen, now. He had known Muldoon would come home eventually; the Irish were like that. And now Muldoon had obligingly bottled himself up in the alley. It was too bad for the other mug he happened to be along. Slowly, the three started across the street.

Muldoon continued his point. "I ain't talkin' about money, Listerdale," he said. "Did you hear me sayin' a word about money? In all me life, and Katie's as well, we've hardly known the feelin' of gold or a paper dollar. We've been gettin' along all right without them.

"But Katie acts tough about life, though she's pure bread puddin' inside, and she knows it. The only reason she's here single for you to meet is she's been afraid of gettin' a drinker or a hitter or a wencher, like some of the mugs we grew up with. Are you any of those things?"

"I have . . . I have done things I now wish I hadn't."

"Will you for cryin' out loud answer the question I'm askin' you for once? Are you a drinker, or a hitter, or a wencher?"

"No. No I'm not."

"All *right*," Muldoon said. Lord, but Listerdale was making it tough for him to do his brotherly duty. "Do you love Katie? Will you take care of her? Will you, and this is what I've been drivin' at, Listerdale, take care that her cantankerous, soft, lovin' Irish heart don't get broken?"

Listerdale looked directly into Muldoon's eyes, and grasped him tightly around the upper arm with a strength that surprised the younger man.

"You must believe this, Muldoon. I would sooner die than see your sister hurt. I would end my life before I would cause her pain. Yes, Muldoon, I do love her, and it is a miracle in my life. I will take care of her. I swear to this, on my love for Kathleen, on all I hold dear, on—on anything you care to name."

"I think you've named enough. Here, seal it with a handshake, and that's good enough for me." Listerdale took Muldoon's hand and pressed it warmly. Muldoon could see the suggestion of a tear at the corner of the bookseller's eye.

"Well, don't be lookin' so miserable over it, will you? If it's askin' Katie you're worried about, I don't mind tellin' you it's a piece of cake. She'll make noises about not knowin' you long enough, but that's just for form's sake. I've been hopin' for her to find a good man for some time. Welcome to the family, Hiram."

They shook hands again. If Listerdale had a reply, he never made it.

"My, my," said Tommy Alb, standing in the mouth of the

alley. "How utterly charming." Tommy had forgotten his intention of striking without warning. Muldoon was trapped, and it was too tempting to taunt him before the end.

Muldoon sized up the situation. Tommy Alb, and three Missing Links, interchangeable except that one had the brightest red hair Muldoon had ever seen. They all carried heavy shillelaghs.

Four against two, then. Muldon laughed at himself. Four professional bully-boys against a fellow who had spent the last week, it seemed, getting beaten up, and one schoolmaster turned bookseller. This was going to be less like a fight than it would be like steak-tenderizing time at Tony Pastor's.

Still, there was one hope. Tommy Alb was the only one of these mugs who could put one foot in front of the other without thinking about it. He was the key to the situation.

"Hiram," Muldoon said softly as the four toughs advanced slowly on them. "Get behind me."

"Muldoon, I'm—" Listerdale sounded worried. Muldoon didn't know how he looked. He was keeping an eye on the approaching men, and at the same time, jockeying for position. It would be fatal for him to look at the fire escape; he had to position himself by its shadow on the ground. Luckily, it was only a few minutes past noon—the shadow should give him an accurate idea of its location.

"*No arguin'*," Muldoon hissed at his companion. "As soon as I've got their attention, I want you to run for it. Do you think you can get over the fence at the back of the alley? Try. Get a copper, then come runnin' with him back here. Got that?"

"I hear you," Listerdale said. His voice was hard. Well, he was sorry if he'd hurt the man's feelings, but Muldoon couldn't allow his sister's suitor to get hurt.

"This time, you die, Muldoon," Tommy Alb said through his bandage. The red-headed troglodyte pounded his club into his open hand with a meaty whack.

Muldoon stood with his feet on the edge of the striped shadow of the fire escape. He could only hope Alb wanted to see to him personally.

He did. "No more backing up, Muldoon? There's still plenty of alley before your back is absolutely pressed against the wall."

"I've done enough backin' up," he said. It was the truth.

"Smart, Dennis," Alb said, still advancing. "At the very end, you're smart. And just because you're making it easy, I'll do this with one blow. Be over before you—*Aaaah!*"

The shadow hadn't lied, and the first part of Muldoon's plan worked almost to perfection. Alb started raising the club about five paces away from Muldoon. At that moment, Muldoon leapt from his position at the edge of the shadow, grabbed the edge of the fire escape with both hands, and swung with all his might at his attacker. He kicked Alb full in the face with his big broganed feet, but he misjudged the distance just enough so that when Alb instinctively ducked backward most of the force of the swing was spent before the feet made contact.

They did, however, land with respectable impact on the point of the blond man's tender nose, pushing it back into the once handsome face. Tommy Alb collapsed in agony, covering his face with both hands. He was out of the fray.

That was the first part of Muldoon's plan. The second went a little differently. Listerdale ran when Muldoon moved, all right, but he ran right *toward* the three toughs. Muldoon picked himself off the floor of the alley ready to wade in and help the foolhardy idiot, but instead he just stood in amazement.

He'd never seen anything like it. The hoodlums were flying through the air, bouncing off the grimy alley walls. They'd rush at the schoolmaster, he'd catch an arm and bend at the waist, and the hoodlums would collide like billiard balls.

Tommy Alb saw this, too, when the haze lifted from before his eyes, and didn't stay for the finish. He got to his feet and ran from the alley. Muldoon never noticed. He was hypnotized.

The whole thing couldn't have lasted for more than a minute. It ended with the redhead, evidently the smartest of them, joining Tommy Alb in flight, and the other two unconscious on the alley floor. Listerdale slapped his hands together and grinned at the incredulous Muldoon. "I tried to tell you, you know."

"Yeah, I guess you did." They left the two men in the alley, and made the best speed they could back to the flat. Muldoon was still wanted by the police, or at least not trusted by them. He didn't want to have to explain this donnybrook. Let them assume the two bruisers had knocked each other unconscious.

"How did you *do* that?" Muldoon demanded of the book-seller.

"On a tour I took, I spent time in Japan. I saw a small Japanese man handle five toughs, nearly twice his size. Some time later, I did him a service which he claimed put him in my debt. To repay me, he taught me some of his art."

"Japanese, huh?" Muldoon shook his head. He didn't like to think so, but maybe the world *was* a bit bigger than New York City.

"Yes," Listerdale went on. "It is known as *jiu-jitsu judo*, which means 'knowledge of the gentle art'."

Muldoon gave a snort that fluttered his moustache. "It may be artistic, but it ain't gentle."

"The name comes from the fact that one uses the attacker's own strength against him."

"Think you could teach it to me?" If people insisted on trying to kill Muldoon, he'd better learn something to stave them off.

"Oh, I hardly know anything. Just a few tricks—" Listerdale cut himself off suddenly. "I'm sorry, I was lecturing. School-mastering is a difficult habit to break."

"You've a right to be lecturin' me, Hiram. Thanks for payin' me orders the attention they deserved, which is to say, none. And the few tricks would be plenty for me. Once again, welcome to the family."

VIII.

"Astounding, Muldoon. Do you think this is more of the Rabbi's work?" Commissioner Roosevelt polished his spectacles as he waited for a reply.

"No, I think this was Tommy Alb workin' alone. He's had a chance to build up quite a bit of a grudge against me. He would have taken care of it, too, if Listerdale hadn't been with me."

"I'm sure you would have given a good account of yourself. You have yet to face even odds in this affair. Still, I am sorry Listerdale has gone back to work at his store."

"He's comin' back to sit with Katie later on. He's fixin' to ask her to marry him, you know." Though the two men were speaking in the hallway of Muldoon's building, the officer still dropped his voice to a conspiratorial whisper. Katie was more than likely in the kitchen, and she had good ears.

"Bully!" Mr. Roosevelt said. His whisper carried as well as some men's shouts. "I have respect and admiration for them both, though I doubt your sister reciprocates."

"Now, sir . . ."

"I am not offended, Muldoon. I have hardly been a cause of easy times for your family. Give her, and Mr. Listerdale when he arrives, my regards. What was that Chinese boxing called again?"

"Japanese, sir. *Jiu-jitsu judo*. It's somethin' to see."

"I'm sure it is. The Orientals have chosen a different path to civilization than we, and have discovered many things along their path we have missed following ours."

"They get some funny notions, too," Muldoon said, remembering his trip to the beach with Blue Jade and its aftermath.

"That's true," the Commissioner conceded. "Well, Muldoon, I must be getting back to Headquarters and make sure our plan is in effect. I doubt Hand will do anything at least until dark, perhaps nothing until after the tradesmen leave, but I expect to have men in position for surveillance by then."

"Yes, sir," Muldoon said. "Please don't be forgettin' to send the patrolman here to watch the women."

"I shall attend to that first thing, Muldoon. And I want you to join me at Headquarters immediately he arrives. Not only because I have promised you will be there at the end of this affair, but because there is no one I would rather have by my side." He clapped Muldoon on the shoulder. "You have done good work, Muldoon."

"Thank you, sir," Muldoon said. Tears came to his eyes, which the Commissioner ignored. He knew how sentimental the Irish were. What he didn't know was that he had clapped Muldoon on his injured shoulder.

IX.

"You are sure now, Peter, that you will have sufficient time to get clear of the explosion and flood once you have lit the fuse?"

Baxter had taken advantage of his employer's confusion over

Roosevelt's visit to slip out for a few minutes to get some air, or so he said. It was actually a prearranged last meeting with the "Rabbi," though Baxter's companion would never be recognized as the white-haired figure.

A few days ago, Baxter would have chafed at the question he'd just been asked, seen it as a slur on his competence. Now, however, he had a note (in code, of course) from Franklyn and Libstein telling him to proceed on his own and disregard any instructions from his superior that jeopardized the outcome of the mission. Henceforth, that note would be one of his cherished possessions; Baxter's long bony finger touched it lightly as it rested safe in his pocket. It was somewhat greasy from the scrapple it had arrived hidden in, but it was his badge of promotion. He didn't mind the grease.

"I will have plenty of time," Baxter said. "I have used slow fuse for this job, and I have found the slowest-burning underwater fuse for the sunken charge. I will have, I estimate, forty-five minutes to get away. Certainly a half hour. I might even hear the explosion as my train pulls out."

"Yes," his companion said. "You are going to join Franklyn and Libstein in Chicago, aren't you?"

"Yes, I am. Aren't you?"

The Rabbi caught a note of mockery in Baxter's voice, but chose to ignore it. "No, I'm not."

Then it was certain, Baxter thought. *The position on the Central Council is to go to me.*

"It's been decided," the Rabbi went on, "that I will be of more use in the position I have established here in New York."

"Oh," Baxter said.

"I think this is goodbye, Peter," Baxter's companion said. "We've known each other a long time. I'll miss you." It was true. During the course of this project, the Rabbi had come to learn things about Baxter that hadn't been nice too hear. But Baxter was still a devoted worker for the people. The Cause needed him.

"Goodbye," Baxter said. "I am grateful for all you have taught me."

The men parted. Baxter returned to Hand's mansion.

X.

It felt good to be back in Police Headquarters again, to be in a private conference with Mr. Theodore Roosevelt in that man's own private office. It would have been perfect, except for the rankling memory of having to sneak past all his brother officers with the aid of Ed Bourke.

There was a bright side. Bourke had met Muldoon outside, telling him, "I don't know what's going on, but Mr. Roosevelt vouches for you, and that's good enough for me. I won't apologize for what I said or did last night, but I will say this: I'm glad to hear you're *not* on the bent. I'll shake your hand, if you still want to shake mine."

Muldoon took it with pleasure. He hoped to see the rest of the Force doing that, and soon.

"Sun's down, now," Muldoon said. "Full dark in no time. If Hand's goin' to receive visitors or go visitin' somebody himself, we ought to be hearin' about it soon."

"Yes, I'm sure we will. We'll wrap this case up tonight, Muldoon. You watch."

"Yes, sir," Muldoon said.

"What's the matter, man?" the Commissioner demanded. "You look as if there were bad news ahead. And don't slouch in your chair that way; if you aspire to the Broadway Squad, your posture must be much better."

Muldoon straightened up, but his handsome face was still twisted in a scowl.

"Blast it, what's the matter?"

"I can't say, sir, specifically. But there's somethin' wrong; somethin' we ought to be doin' but aren't."

"What? I ask you. Hand's house is watched by sixteen men. Anyone leaving from this time on will be followed. If anyone arrives, I will be informed immediately. A telegraph line and a telephone line here at Headquarters are being kept open just so there will be no delay in informing me of future developments."

The news just served to make Muldoon feel glummer. After a long silence, he said, "Mr. Roosevelt, are you absolutely for sure this Mr. Meister we saw and the Rabbi fellow are one and the same?"

"Yes, Muldoon. I thought you were, too."

"Well, I was, until I got to thinkin'. If we hadn't *seen* this guy, wouldn't Captain Herkimer have made a corker of a suspect?"

"Herkimer is a short, stocky man, Muldoon." There seemed to be a sly look on the Commissioner's face. "Are you sure you aren't saying these things simply because you dislike the man."

Muldoon thought it over. "Maybe so," he admitted. "But I can't help noticin'—Hey, he didn't get the promotion, did he?"

"No, Muldoon. That's why that cursed meeting took so long."

"Good. But as I was sayin', certain things have been jumpin' to me mind."

"For example?" Mr. Roosevelt was leaning forward over his desk, as though to pull details from Muldoon's mouth by main force.

"For example, last Friday, when I found Crandall and Cleo in the flat, Captain Herkimer from the very beginnin' was tryin' to sweep it all under the rug. Now, that could have been laziness. You said that yourself, sir. But you also said, it could be somethin' worse.

"And another thing. The way Baxter was there at Cleo's hotel, waitin' for her, practically. Who were the first three people to know she was ever there? Me, Mrs. Sturdevant, and Captain Herkimer, that's who."

"Sloppy, Muldoon. Shoddy thinking. You've left two persons out."

"I have? Oh, yes. Well there's Mr. Harvey, now that I think of it. Cleo was hidin' in his room when the captain arrived. But who else?"

"The murderer himself, Muldoon."

"No, sir." Muldoon set his chin. "It's not established at all that the murderer knew Cleo was there. Cleo thinks he didn't, and she should know. No, if the murderer knew right off Cleo was there, Baxter would have shown up a lot sooner than he did. I said he was practically waitin' for her, but that was hasty on me own part. He didn't get there, accordin' to Cleo's statement, until after she'd arrived, and that wasn't for a couple of hours after the murder of Evan Crandall."

"Ha!" the Commissioner exclaimed. "Excellent, Muldoon. You continually surprise me."

"Thank you, Mr. Roosevelt. I'll wager you were just testin' me out, to see if I could spot your little slip, weren't you?"

The Commissioner harumphed. "Go on with your theory, Muldoon."

"Well, sir, can't you see that this does a good job of explainin' why Captain Herkimer was so frantic to prove Cleo a figment of me diseased imagination? He wasn't only worryin' about a messy unsolved case that might cause him to miss his promotion—which it has, as it turns out—he was worryin' about a witness to a murder. He couldn't tell what she knew; he was afraid she might cause him to walk up thirteen steps and only come down one, if you catch me meanin'.

"And another thing. Herkimer and Hand are thick as thieves."

"Appropriate," the Commissioner murmured.

"Yes, sir. We know from Cleo's narrative how Hand was always calling Herkimer for information." Muldoon gasped as a sudden thought occurred to him. "And he was already acquainted with *Baxter*, too! It was only natural for him to be callin' that house with the news.

"And finally, sir, I think it's just a little bit on the rum side when Herkimer, who'd heard me story, and knew about Crandall's paintin' of Cleo, meets me in an art gallery, and before the day is out, I'm assaulted and left for dead by Eagle Jack Sperling and his gang. Things seem to happen right after Herkimer finds out about them, don't they?"

"Suggestive, Muldoon. But how do you account for the fact that Hand seems to be as baffled by the Rabbi as we are? What of the poisoning of Mrs. Le Clerc? What of the physical dissimilarity? What of the enigmatic note about the twenty mill gals?"

"He could have killed the old lady because Hand was worried I might be closin' in; Hand could have told him about her. Once we knew who she was, she wasn't hard to find." Muldoon sighed. "As for Hand's ignorance of the doin's of the Rabbi, well, maybe it's an act."

"It's no act, Muldoon," the Commissioner said, shaking his

head energetically. "I saw Hand today; his terror was genuine; you may count that as a certainty."

Muldoon shrugged. "Well, maybe Herkimer is deceivin' him, who knows?"

"Why should he do that?" Roosevelt hissed through his teeth.

"There, I must be admittin' you've got me stumped. The Lord never intended for me to make me way through the world by thinkin'. But I've got a word or two to say about the fellow's appearance.

"Now, you've met me sister Maureen. I'm not supposed to know this, but she's not all the time readin' at Mr. Shakespeare's plays because she loves literature the way her big brother does. She's readin' at them, and Ben Jonson, and Oliver somebody-or-other, because she loves the Stage.

"Now, my opinion is, anything that can go producin' a Mr. William Shakespeare can't be all bad, but Katie'd skin her alive if she found out. This'll all be comin' to a head soon. Mr. William Gillette is one of these matinee idols, and Maureen is sweet on him—he's readyin' a play for the fall, and Maureen's got her heart set on seein' it."

"I do not care to go to the theatre, though I do enjoy reading drama," the Commissioner said. "That may be the reason I have no idea what it is you're trying to say."

Muldoon wiped his moustache. "Sorry, I got off the track. The point is this. I read in one of the theatre magazines Maureen is always sneakin' into the house how they make people up to play different parts. Put Herkimer in a corset, some elevated shoes, some false white hair to cover his own beard—the stuff is easy— you put it on with spirit-gum, take it off with ether—let him speak in a whisper to cover that voice of his, and there you have it. I'll wager we could get *Cleo* to pass for this Rabbi fellow, at least from a distance."

The Commissioner sat back in his chair. "Have you finished, Muldoon?"

"Yes, sir."

"Ha! Then it is your position that I should have Herkimer watched?"

"That's what I think, sir," Muldoon said. He was looking his superior straight in the eye. If there was one thing this case had taught him, it was confidence in his own judgment.

"Well, I think so too!" Roosevelt said at last. "This part *has* been a test, Muldoon, though I didn't work it out in as great detail as you just have. Still, Herkimer is being watched, under the same condition as Hand. If Herkimer makes a move from his house, the news will come through on the telegraph or telephone."

"*Telephone!*" Muldoon shouted.

"What?"

"Telephone! That's what we forgot. What we're not doin'. Hand doesn't have to go out to speak to the Rabbi. Hand has a telephone and Cleo heard the Rabbi callin' him—the Rabbi could have one too! He could just call him up, and a bunch of men will have missed a night's sleep for nothin'."

"Blast it, you're right! I think you may have been wrong about the Lord's intentions for you. But what are we going to do? We can't listen in on Hand's phone conversations."

"Maybe we can!" Muldoon was eager and excited. He explained how his sister Brigid worked for the telephone company, but more important, her beau Claude worked there as an engineer. If Hand's phone calls could be listened to, Claude would know how to do it.

"Bully, Muldoon! But there's no time to waste. You must go to the Bell Company immediately. I'll wait here. This is fine, Muldoon. I'm proud of you."

Muldoon beamed, and shuffled his feet.

"Well, don't stand there basking in it, Officer. Get going!"

XI.

Officer Carl Weiss relieved his predecessor on post outside the Muldoon flat on Avenue A. He knocked on the door, told the two ladies and the one young girl inside that he was there, then stood staunchly out in the hall, watching for whatever.

It had been understanding of the first guy to fill in for him until sundown. It was Officer Weiss's understanding that Mr. Roosevelt had assigned him personally to this duty. He wondered what was up.

The last time the Commissioner had personally assigned Carl Weiss to anything was last year, when that *cocker* of an anti-semite preacher had come over from Germany (and I finally learned why Papa left, he thought) to preach a crusade against Jews, that's what he said, a crusade. A lot of leaders of the community wanted Roosevelt to keep the guy from speaking, or at least deny him police protection so that the guys from the cigar-makers' union could get a fair shot at him, but Roosevelt had said he couldn't do that. Instead, he combed the force for Jews, took about forty of them, placed them under the command of a Jew sergeant, and assigned them to protect him.

Weiss smiled to remember how ridiculous the guy had looked, speaking his garbage under the active protection of forty armed Jews. Roosevelt had a lot between his ears all right.

Still, the scuttlebutt also had it that Roosevelt was closing an investigation on a Rabbi. That wasn't too nice to hear. Still, duty was duty. Weiss guarded the door, but he still wondered what the women inside had to do with anything.

The women inside, as Muldoon had predicted, were gradually beginning to acknowledge one another, with Cleo following Katie's lead.

Katie, on her part, felt much too good to be angry at anyone, and it was only stubbornness that kept her aloof. Still, when she saw how neat and polite her guest was, it was hard to think of her as a tramp. And then, Dennis had mentioned to her that this Cleo girl had been led into sin when she was too young to know any better.

Katie took a quick look at the clock in the parlor. Hiram should be here any time now. He was going to ask her to marry him tonight. That is, he had asked her last night, but tonight she could say yes, now that he'd gotten Dennis's consent. Honestly, sometimes Hiram had no idea of the rules and proprieties of anything.

She'd go crazy waiting. Maureen had her nose buried in another one of those plays, and was lost to this world. Katie had to talk to *somebody*.

So she spoke to Cleo. "I'm sorry," Katie said, wiping her hands on her apron, "for the way I acted this mornin'. Me experience of the world has been severely limited, and sometimes I forget it can be any other way than the way I been taught."

The young woman smiled brightly. "Thank you, Miss Muldoon. I know it's difficult for someone to barge in unannounced the way I did."

"Oh, think nothin' of it," Katie replied. The conversation lagged; the clock on the mantel ticked.

Finally, Katie slapped her knee, looked across at her guest on the sofa, and said, "How would you like to learn about the makin' of real Irish soda bread?"

Cleo laughed, and said she'd be delighted. Katie found an extra apron for her, and together they went into the kitchen.

The first thing Cleo learned was how to sift. It seemed to her that everything that went into Irish soda bread had to be sifted, at least twice, with the possible exception of the raisins. And there was something about the domestic work that helped conversation. After talking about Dennis (they both agreed he was wonderful, though Katie had a few reservations) and about Brian O'Leary (they agreed he was a scamp), Katie quite naturally asked Cleo about her life, and Cleo just as naturally told her. The women had discovered they were born to be friends.

"Oh, you poor, poor, child," Katie said. "Can you *ever* be forgivin' me for the way I treated you today?"

"I've forgiven you already. Let's not talk of it any more, all right? I think these are ready. Is the oven hot enough?"

Katie licked the first and second fingers of her left hand, then touched them to the black metal of the stove. She seemed to like the sound of the hissing noise she heard. "Just right," she said. With a master's eye, she surveyed the loaves Cleo had prepared. "Make the next batch a little bigger. These will come out a mite flat. No matter, the eatin's the same." Katie opened the door and popped them in the oven.

About halfway through the next batch, in the middle of an animated discussion on ways to keep feathers on hats from fading, Katie burst in with, "You know, darlin', I'm thirty-one years old and I don't know the first thing about . . ." she blushed to hear herself, but completed her thought. ". . . About *pleasin'* a man."

Cleo smiled. "Judging from the way I saw Mr. Listerdale

looking at you today, I think you please him very well." Cleo had met Listerdale when Dennis and he had returned from their walk. He seemed nice, but very quiet.

"I don't mean that," Katie said. "I mean, well, pleasin' a man as is me *husband*."

"Oh," Cleo said. "Oh." She'd better think for a while before she answered this one. Cleo knew all about pleasing a man, ways Katie would never even hear of, if she were lucky. And then again, maybe Cleo knew nothing. Maybe it was something completely different with a man you loved.

Maybe . . . Cleo sniffed. "Katie, can the bread be burning?"

"Naw," Katie said, "it's way too soon for that." Then Katie sniffed. She made a puzzled face, and opened the oven door. "No, the bread's doin' wonderfully." Still the smell was in the air.

Suddenly, there was a knocking on the door, and Officer Weiss poked his head in. "Ladies, I'm afraid there's a fire in the building. Come with me, please."

Katie went and got Maureen out of her room, and the three females went down the front stairs to the street. Officer Weiss stayed a moment in the corridor, blowing his whistle and knocking on doors, telling people to leave, then he followed.

From a beat-up carriage across the street, Tommy Alb watched attentively. If Muldoon wouldn't come out again, by God, he'd burn him out. There was the girl. And, what the . . . was Muldoon back in uniform? No, he wasn't Muldoon. What was that damn cop doing there so soon, anyway. Nobody's even called the Fire Department, yet. *Where the hell was Muldoon?*

Tommy forced himself to be calm. Every time he got excited, his damaged face began to throb as though it were about to burst. All right. Muldoon got away again. For now. Revenge got better the longer you waited to have it. Like cheese.

If Tommy wanted Eagle Jack's business, he'd have to start acting more like a businessman. He'd do what he could to win back some customer goodwill. He waited for his chance.

It wasn't too long in coming. Tommy hadn't spared the kerosene when he was soaking the back of that building; soon, flames were leaping out all over it.

Carl Weiss was torn between his duty to watch the women and his duty to make sure everyone had gotten safely out of the tenement. The dilemma ended when a woman started to cry that Granddad was still inside. Weiss told the women to wait, then dashed inside the building.

Tommy Alb saw his chance. He dashed from the carriage, grabbed Cleo around the face, stifling her scream, and dragged her to the vehicle. An accomplice on the trap cracked the whip, and the horse took off.

Suddenly, it dawned on Katie Muldoon what had happened. No one could stifle Katie's scream.

XII.

The next time I have a big idea, Muldoon thought, I'll have one that isn't so blasted boring. He yawned. Apparently, Hand had spoken to everyone he wanted to speak to before Claude could be convinced to do whatever it was he had to do to wire things up for Muldoon to hear. It was against the rules, Claude had said. It was an invasion of Mr. Hand's privacy.

"For cryin' out loud," Muldoon had exploded. "What's a man need with privacy unless he's got somethin' he wants hid?"

Claude hadn't been able to argue with that, so he got busy and fixed Muldoon up in a closet with a lot of things that clicked. It wasn't a comfortable closet, because it was too narrow to sit down in, and too low to stand straight in. The ear phone was a trial, too—it had been designed for a woman's head, not his.

All in all then, it was a relief when Claude summoned him from the closet. "Brigid told me to get you," he said. The thing Muldoon liked best about Claude was that he did whatever Brigid told him.

"Here," Muldoon said, handing him the head phone. "You listen to this while I'm gone." He made his escape before the young engineer could protest.

Muldoon skirted the wide floor of the main switchboard room. That was the province of the supervisor, who flitted from board to board on her roller skates, without ever giving any hint she thought that was fun. She had forbidden everything Muldoon had done in that building, and he had only managed to bring it off with an official manner and the showing of his shield. Mr. Roosevelt had somehow managed to get it back for him today.

The officer joined his sister at her board. "It's Katie," Brigid said. "I can't make out what she's tryin' to say."

Muldoon took the ear phone. "Katie?"

"Dennis? What are you doin' there?" Confusion and pique had made her comprehensible. "Do you know how much time I've been wastin' tryin' to find you? The police never heard of you, if you listen to them. I only called Brigid because I don't know what else to do."

"Well, you've found me now. What's the matter?"

"A fire! Someone doused the back of our buildin' with kerosene and lit a fire! And in the confusion, somebody got Cleo!"

Muldoon was sick. "*Got her?* What do you mean?"

"Took her away, Dennis! And the poor thing was standin' right next to me, but I never noticed until it was too late!"

"Katie, where are you?"

"God preserve me, I'm in a low dive called Frenchy's. They use the telephone for bettin' . . ."

"Frenchy's? What in blazes are you doin' there? That's in the middle of me old beat." A horrible thought occurred to Muldoon. "Listen, you haven't got Maureen in that place with you, have you?"

"Now what are you takin' me for, Dennis Muldoon? Of course not. Maureen is with Mrs. Sturdevant in her flat. Hiram arranged it."

"Listerdale?"

"He was comin' to call on me, to . . . Well, anyway, he seen me there, cryin' me fool eyes out over Cleo, and says it looks like dirty work to him, and he's gonna get me and Maureen out of danger. So he asks Mrs. Sturdevant will she put us up, and she agreed. Then he went back to see if he could do anything with the fire, help out with the victims."

"He's a brick," Muldoon said. "Now listen to me; Listerdale did exactly the right thing. So you just go back to Mrs. Sturdevant's and *stay put*. Don't go runnin' off after Listerdale. He's a fellow as can take care of himself. Promise me, now."

Katie was reluctant, but she agreed. Muldoon told Brigid to break the connection and put through a call to the Commissioner.

"Yes?" Roosevelt barked.

"Somethin's happened," Muldoon said.

"Hand has called someone?"

"No, sir, but—" Muldoon was distracted by a noise at the Commissioner's end. "What is Brian O'Leary doin' there, for cryin' out loud?"

"His mother locked him out again. She's thrown out Brian's father as well. Blast it, what has happened, Muldoon?"

Muldoon told him.

"It makes no sense at all, Muldoon, you realize that."

"Yes sir. But you did mention the other day we were dealing with lunatics, sir."

"I am sorry about this, Muldoon."

"They'll get the fire out, sir. It's been a wet summer, the water pressure in the hydrants should be up near full pressure. The r—"

"*The reservoir is full!* Twenty mill gals! Twenty *million gallons!* We have them now, Muldoon, we know their plot!"

"We do?"

"Yes, by jingo, we do. Muldoon, meet me in front of Hand's mansion as soon as possible."

Muldoon scratched his head. "If you say so, sir."

"I *have* said so!"

"Yes, sir!" When Roosevelt used that tone, Muldoon ran.

Claude saw him running. He shouted after Muldoon, but Muldoon just waved. Claude never got a chance to tell him that someone had tried to use the phone at Hand's mansion. Oh, well, he thought, the calls were never completed. Couldn't have been anything too important.

XIII.

The fire was out—the Fire Department had done a crackerjack job. Listerdale wondered if there was anything he could do about, well, about anything. He hadn't been much help here, but at least he had been here. People had seen him. His clothes smelled of smoke.

It seemed to him, though he really couldn't be sure, that Cleo had been brought to Hand, if she hadn't been killed. Listerdale sighed. If Muldoon had just walked by his shop last week, so many things might have been different.

It bothered him to have been the, really, unwitting instrument of a fatality that had meant so much misfortune and distress for people he had come to love, Muldoon and his family. Especially Kathleen.

Listerdale really had no choice. He would go home and change, then head uptown to see what he could do to straighten out the mess.

XIV.

Cleo was doomed; she was as sure of that as she was of her hatred for every man who had ever touched her, for every man who had formed part of the market that made Madam Nanette's house possible, and who had thus twisted her into what she was.

The bandaged man was saying things to her, taunting her. The taunts were all the more cruel because of their truth.

He held a gun on her, for fear she'd try to escape, she supposed. Cleo didn't know whether that made her want to laugh or cry. She wouldn't try to escape; she knew there was no escape for her.

She was going back. It was her fate. So be it.

Cleo closed her eyes.

After a while, the carriage pulled to a stop. She heard the bandaged man, Alb, Muldoon had said his name was, talk to the driver, telling him to drive off, leave a false trail for anyone who might be following.

Then he spoke to Cleo. "Wake up, sister. We're almost there. We'll walk the rest of the way."

Cleo got out and walked. The bandaged man walked close behind her, still holding the gun. Cleo could see the mansion. She'd see the inside, soon. She'd see Avery. She wanted to see Avery, to look into his eyes with the full force of her hatred showing. She'd do that. Then, at her earliest opportunity, with one last, kind thought of Dennis Muldoon, Cleo would kill herself.

XV.

"Can't you reach him, Baxter, dammit?" Hand demanded. Hand was worried; he'd been worried all day about Roosevelt's visit. The housekeeper had told him one of the police had asked her about red candles, whatever that meant. Hand wanted to talk it over with the Rabbi, to hear that whispering reassurance that everything was under control. Hand had lost control of things long ago, he realized.

"I'll try, sir." Baxter went to the telephone alcove, picked up the receiver, and started to operate the machine. Before he finished, however, he let one bony finger rest on the hook, and broke the connection. He returned to the parlor.

"I'm sorry, Mr. Hand," Baxter said. "I can't get through. The telephone seems to be out of order."

Hand couldn't stand it. Last time they had spoken, the Rabbi had given him this number to call, and told him the times at which it might be used. Now, when he had waited patiently for the hour to arrive, his man couldn't put the call through.

"I'm sure everything will be all right, sir," Baxter said. He tried to keep the irritation he felt out of his voice. Roosevelt hadn't been up to anything, he was certain of it. It was too ironic that Hand would crumple under the weight of a purely imaginary danger. No, that wouldn't happen—Fate couldn't be that cruel.

Yet the millionaire kept whining. Baxter was tempted to *let* the blasted call go through, and let Hand's precious "Rabbi" (of all the foolish aliases) reassure him.

No. He wouldn't. His colleague's use to the Movement was over; he seemed to know that himself. Baxter was in charge now; he could hold it together one more day. He would. And Bryan and the rest would die tomorrow afternoon. His biggest worry was the weather, but the latest aerologist's report (Baxter was keeping himself informed) said tomorrow would be sunny and pleasant.

Baxter smiled. He hoped Roosevelt would keep his threat, or perhaps it was his promise, to come to Hand's wedding tomorrow. The more, as the saying went, the merrier.

There was a knock at the door.

"I wonder who that is," Baxter said, rising.

"Whoever it is, send him away. I don't want to see anybody." Hand picked at a plate of cheese and crackers.

The instructions suited Baxter fine. He walked to the door, still picturing tomorrow's triumph. He opened the door.

It was one of Sperling's men, even more grotesquely bandaged than he had been before.

"Hello, Stretch," Tommy Alb said looking up into Baxter's cadaverous face. He pushed the woman with him forward. "Tell your boss I've got a present for him."

XVI.

Brian O'Leary didn't care if he ever went home. Hanging around with these people was a lot more fun than living in Mackerelville with a couple of drunks.

Who would have ever thought he'd wind up being deputized by the Commissioner himself to watch this office? Mr. Roosevelt was just going out the door now.

Then the telephone on the desk rang, and he stopped in the doorway. Brian answered the phone. "Mr. Roosevelt's office speaking."

A pause, then, "Yeah, I know I'm a kid, what of it? You wanna speak to Mr. Roosevelt? Okay, he's right here."

The Commissioner shot Brian an admonishing look, but said nothing as he took the phone away from the boy. "Yes? No, anyone entering the building was to be noted and reported. What is your name, Lieutenant? Very good. You have done exactly right. Take no action until I arrive. Yes. Goodbye."

He turned to the boy. "Remember, Brian, I want you to get your sleep. You may use my couch." Then he turned and bustled out.

Roosevelt's next stop was the police stable. The farrier looked up from the hind hoof of a horse and saw him. "Evening, sir. You want a wagon?"

"No, a horse."

"A what?"

"Saddle a horse for me this instant. That is an order."

"Yes, sir." The farrier hammered one more blow at the horse's hoof, dropped it, and went to work on the Commissioner's order. He carried a saddle to the side of a chestnut mare. "Daisy do all right, sir?"

Roosevelt was looking about the stable. "Yes, she looks a fine animal. Tell me, what is that Winchester doing here?"

"I bought it today, sir, from a fellow on the Harbor Squad. Giving it to my boy for his birthday."

"Excellent choice," Roosevelt said, lifting it and inspecting the action. "The rifle is the freeman's weapon. In fine condition, too. May I borrow it?"

"Sir? What do you want with a Winchester repeater?"

"I have no time to explain. This is an emergency. I will, of course, replace the ammunition."

"Well, sure, Mr. Roosevelt, go ahead." He tightened the last buckle. "Daisy's all ready to go. Just do me one favor, sir, if you don't mind."

Roosevelt mounted expertly to the saddle. "What's that?"

"Bring her, the rifle, and yourself home safe, sir."

Roosevelt grinned. "I shall try," he said. Then he headed Daisy around, and galloped into the streets of the metropolis.

XVII.

Muldoon wanted to scream every time the hansom stopped for traffic. He didn't know what he was going to do when he arrived, but as long as he was en route, he couldn't do *anything*.

"Faster, man, dammit!" Muldoon told the driver, who ignored him. Muldoon never thought he would ever find himself nostalgic for the wild ride he'd made with Cleo *away* from Forty-second Street.

To help pass time, he tried to figure why Mr. Roosevelt had liked "twenty million gallons" better than the "20 mill gals" Cleo had seen written down. It didn't take him long.

"Sweet Jesus," he breathed. "They mean to blow up the Reservoir. Driver, I said *faster*, dammit!"

XVIII.

Roscoe Heath had undone the last knot long ago. The longer he had worked, the easier it seemed to get, perhaps because his mind drifted away, leaving him with no sense of time passing; perhaps because the knots became oiled with blood and perspiration.

In any case, even though he was no longer tied up, he was

still locked in the closet. He had been too weak to do anything about it then, so he had settled back to restore himself with sleep.

Now, the voices from downstairs awakened him.

It was Baxter's voice. Baxter was furious. "You fool," he said. He opened the door for the two to enter. "What did you bring her here for?"

Baxter couldn't believe it. He could not believe it. They were rid of her. Things were going well, if not exactly smoothly. Now, who knew what was going to happen?

"Hey, listen," Alb said. "She got away, I got her back. Stop wasting my time, this is my busy day."

Cleo recoiled in fright as she saw Baxter reach forward with a clawlike hand and grasp Alb by the throat. It was the same grip, Cleo realized, that Baxter had used on her, when she had been kidnapped from her flat.

Cleo screamed as Alb crumpled and sank to the floor. Hand came running to the hall from the parlor. "Cleo!" he said. "You've decided to come back. I knew you would!"

"Oh, be quiet, you idiot!" Baxter spat.

"Baxter, mind whom you are speaking to!"

Baxter's tall body bent over the small millionaire. He spoke in a low, deadly voice, the kind of voice, Cleo fancied, a cobra would use, could it speak.

"I know precisely whom I am speaking to. Now be quiet, do as I say, and you will get out of this. Stay here. Watch the woman. If you let her go, I shall kill you." With long strides, Baxter left the room.

Cleo folded her arms and stared into Avery's face, just as she had planned.

"Dearest," Hand began, "don't judge me harshly. I am—"

"I don't need to judge you. Your actions do that for me. They judge you a coward and a dupe. Whatever your plan is, you can't succeed with it. Muldoon and Commissioner Roosevelt know that something is going on, and they know by now that I have been abducted again. This time . . ." Cleo thought she'd try a wild surmise. Her every word landed on Avery like a whiplash, and she and her friends had suffered enough for her to enjoy it. ". . . This time," she went on, "they will bring a force of policemen with them."

"I knew it! *I knew it!*" Baxter had returned. His face was crimson with frustration and rage. "Well, only you know if you're bluffing, whore—"

"And what does that make you?" Cleo demanded.

Baxter hit her across the face. "If you're not bluffing, you are dead." Baxter lifted Alb's limp form and carried it to the parlor. As Cleo entered, she saw that the butler had gone for a length of rope—and his last nine sticks of dynamite. He threw the bandaged man into a love seat, and forced Cleo to sit next to him. Baxter began to tie them together, and to the piece of furniture.

"Baxter, have you gone mad?" Hand demanded.

"I'm not telling you again. Be quiet."

He *had* gone mad. Hand subsided.

Meanwhile, in the closet upstairs, Roscoe had heard a faint echo of Cleo's scream. Sound carried well on the night air. He gathered up his will, and brought the remains of his strength to bear on the locked door of his small prison.

XIX.

Muldoon paid the driver and alighted. The scene was still quiet as he arrived. He had been afraid he'd land in the midst of doomsday. He didn't know now whether to be glad or frightened he hadn't.

His immediate instinct was to rush into the house to rescue Cleo, but he managed to curb it. What he would do instead would be to try one of the side entrances, and see if he could spot the surveillance. Then he would report to his brother officers, and wait for Mr. Roosevelt to arrive.

To Muldoon's surprise, the first person he met was Listerdale. "What the blazes . . . ?"

"The blazes indeed, Muldoon. The Fire Department had things under control. I came to see if I could help up here. And, I must admit," Listerdale kicked at the ground, "that an . . an almost fateful curiosity led me here."

"Well," Muldoon said, "I know you can handle yourself, but stay out of the way once the gunplay starts."

"You expect gunplay? I hope not."

"Since I got involved in this business, I've given up hopin', to say nothin' of knowin' what to expect. But I'll tell you one thing, Muldoon said, hooking a thumb over his shoulder, "I'd like to be havin' a bit of a look around this reservoir."

"Why?" Listerdale said. "With the woman in trouble and all—"

"*Lower your voice!*" Muldoon hissed, but it was too late.

A uniformed policeman walked up to them and said, "This isn't a good night to be loitering around this neighborhood."

Muldoon said, "It's all right, I'm a copper, too, workin' this case direct for Mr. Theodore Roosevelt—"

"Good work, Officer," came a voice from down the block. "Arrest him. Arrest the lying scoundrel."

Muldoon clapped a hand to his face. It was the booming, unmistakable voice of Captain Ozias Herkimer.

"What are you doin' here?" Muldoon demanded.

"Hmpf. When I look out my window, and see policemen, some of whom I actually know, parading through my neighborhood, I want to know why. I'm glad to discover that it was to capture you, as you return to the scene of your crime. Or should I say, *one* of your crimes, eh, *Dennis?*" The captain smiled.

"It just so happens," Muldoon told him, "that part of the reason the police are in this neighborhood is to keep an eye on *you.*"

"Nonsense!" Herkimer boomed, louder than ever.

"Oh, yeah?" Muldoon wanted to know. "Well, look behind you, and you'll see you got a better tail than a paycock."

Herkimer looked, and discovered Muldoon was right. He looked at the officer. "What is the meaning of this?"

Then Muldoon made a mistake. "And it further just so happens," he went on, rubbing it in, "that I ain't under arrest."

"*Is this true?*" Herkimer demanded of the officer. First he had gotten refused for promotion, and now this.

"Well, Captain, we have orders . . ."

"I order you now to arrest this man!"

"He's got orders from Commissioner Roosevelt, I'll warrant," Muldoon said. He felt Listerdale's restraining hand on his arm, but shook it off.

"He's right, Captain," the officer said. He loosened his collar.

"The lieutenant says we're to take no action until Commissioner Roosevelt arrives."

Herkimer peered at Muldoon, determined not to let the Irishman get the better of him. "This is ridiculous!" he roared. "*I am a captain! I am the highest ranking officer on the scene. I order you to place this man under arrest!*"

The captain was fairly screaming now. Policemen who could do so without leaving their posts uncovered were coming to investigate. The lieutenant was drawn from his command post.

Herkimer was still going. "*. . . Gross insubordination! I want him in irons without delay!*"

There was a sound of hoofbeats. Commissioner Roosevelt, moustache and short hair blown awry by the wind of his ride, reined in his horse near the growing knot of men and dismounted.

"*What is the meaning of this?*" he demanded. "Herkimer, what is going on here? Muldoon, have you arrested the Captain?"

"Not yet, sir."

"Do so." Herkimer exploded into a deafening roar. "Interfering with the police in performance of their duties will do for now. Turn him over to this man. And shut him up, by whatever means necessary."

Captain Herkimer was dragged away. Muldoon smiled. "I think we've got the Rabbi, sir."

Listerdale raised his eyebrows. "Hello, Listerdale," Roosevelt said. "I'm surprised to see you here."

"I've always been drawn to adventure," the schoolmaster said.

"I suppose that's true of all of us," the Commissioner said. "As for you Muldoon, we shall see if you are right. Lieutenant?"

The lieutenant was a competent, middle-aged fellow who'd come up through the ranks. "Yes, sir?"

"Has anyone come or gone from the mansion since the man and woman did?"

"No, sir."

"Bully. Then we haven't arrived too late. Let me reconnoitre, then I shall call the men together for instructions."

XX.

Herkimer's screaming brought Hand to the hallway window. He pulled a curtain aside and looked across the street. "Good Lord, Baxter, she wasn't bluffing. There are policemen out there. And Roosevelt!"

Baxter pushed him aside and took his place at the window. In the gaslight before the reservoir, he could see them gathered, tiny against the huge stone walls, their helmets sticking up like the tops of poisoned mushrooms.

Baxter began to laugh. His laughter came in great jagged pieces, as though it were being literally torn from his lungs. A year of planning. A full *year*. Ruined by a slut, two lovesick fools, and a collection of strong backs with weak minds. Baxter felt his laughter turning to tears.

"Snap out of it, man, for God's sake!" Hand whined.

Baxter had his head buried in his hands. Then he took them away from his face, and regarded the millionaire. Suddenly it was very clear to him what he must do. Something could still be saved.

He knocked Hand unconscious with a single blow of his huge fist. He thought of bringing him to the parlor, but decided against it. Hand was to die in the flood. So be it. Baxter left him where he lay on the cold marble floor.

The woman on the love seat had her eyes closed, but she was not asleep. She sat straight up and her lips were moving. The sight infuriated Baxter.

"Are you *praying?*" The woman's eyes squeezed more tightly shut, her soft lips moved more rapidly. "*There is no God!* God is a myth, used by the Capitalists to keep the poor content with their misery! He . . . He . . ." Baxter couldn't remember the rest of it, just now. It didn't matter. Her God couldn't help her, even if he did exist.

The bandaged man next to the woman groaned and rolled his head. He was coming around. That was good. Baxter slapped him into full consciousness.

"*What?*" Tommy Alb said. "What?"

Baxter flicked a finger against the bandage, causing Tommy

to scream. "I want you both awake for this," Baxter said. *"Open your eyes!"* He reached under Cleo's long hair, grasped one of her delicate ears, and twisted until she complied.

"You are going to die, now," Baxter said. He picked up a coil of fuse from the stack of dynamite sticks, and lit the free end. "Bryan will escape, but you are going to die in his place, you two, and Roosevelt, and the rest. And in dying, you are going to enable me to carry out the plan."

With the coil of fuse still hissing, Baxter picked up two sticks of dynamite. He started to push them down between the two bodies and the ropes.

"Look," the bandaged man said, "I like a joke as much as the next guy, but I don't know as how this is too funny. If you've got something against the gal, here, that's got nothing to do with me."

"Shut up!" The sniveling coward. Baxter would have beaten him senseless, but he wanted him conscious when the dynamite went off.

Still, he had a point. It was the woman who should suffer. It was she, with her soft body and her soft looks who had bewitched Hand, and later Crandall. Yes, and even Baxter himself, that night he'd found her flushed and breathless in the carriage house. She'd soiled him. Just by being what she was, she had doomed the plan before it had ever had a chance.

Baxter pulled the dynamite from the ropes.

"That's better," Alb breathed, almost hysterical with relief. "Shut *up!*" Baxter said again.

Cleo's eyes went wide with horror as Baxter took the hem of her skirt in his hand and lifted. "No, oh, please no, oh, dear God . . ."

Her gentle, pleading voice almost softened Baxter's heart. Until she had mentioned God. He had no more time to waste on these two. He reached beneath the woman's bound limbs, and forced the two sticks of dynamite between her body and the cushion. She'd never be able to dislodge it; at least not in time.

Baxter grabbed Cleo by her long black hair, and kissed her cruelly on the mouth. "Turn your head away, will you? Goodbye then." He picked up the hissing coil, then touched the end to the fuse of the dynamite. He had figured five feet would give him the time he needed. Now that fuse was hissing and jumping on the floor between the woman's feet. Baxter gathered up the remaining seven sticks of dynamite and left.

XXI.

Roscoe had blacked out again, but the sound of the screaming brought him to. It was the woman again, along with a man this time. Screaming for help as though they would go mad. Roscoe wished they'd be quiet and let him sleep, but they wouldn't. Roscoe sighed. He'd have to shut them up himself. He took a deep breath and went back to work on the lock.

Even as she screamed, she knew she was wasting her breath; the last breaths she would ever draw. Already the fuse had disappeared under her skirts. She could feel a sensation like little pin pricks as the sparks burned through her stockings and scorched her legs. She tried to make her peace with God, but each time she closed her eyes, she was presented by a vision of the obscenity the dynamite beneath her would make of her body. And she began to scream again.

Upstairs, Roscoe was making progress; indeed, he had made progress before, but his weakness had made him give up. Now, with his back braced against the back of the closet, he pushed with ever-increasing force with his short, muscular leg against the door, just below the lock.

Soon the wood began to groan; a few cracks showed on the surface.

Now, Roscoe pistoned his leg against the wood in a series of explosive kicks. On the fourth kick, the door flew open, and fresh night air revived him more. Roscoe staggered out into the hall, weary, but triumphant. He was astonished to realize he even knew where he was; he was at Hand's mansion. There was a girl to rescue. He was here with the boss. *No!* he was here with Muldoon, that was it. Where was Muldoon?

Well, that didn't matter. There was a girl screaming. She had to be the one to rescue. Man screaming, too. Maybe *that* was Muldoon. He'd find out soon enough. Now, if he could only find the stairs.

Cleo had a plan. Though her ankles were tied to the lion's-paw legs at one end and the middle of the love seat, there was sufficient slack for her to close her thighs together. If she could stand the pain, perhaps she could smother the fuse, stop the hissing that, she knew, must soon drive her mad. The fuse had burned up to the cushion now; Cleo could smell burning silk and horse hair. She pulled her thighs tight together.

To no avail. The fuse still had oxygen enough to burn. Yet Cleo kept her thighs together. She could stand the pain. She *welcomed* the pain; cherished it. She concentrated on the flesh-searing pain of the fuse until it filled her mind, and blotted out all thought of what was about to happen to her.

Roscoe gave up on thinking—every time he tried to figure out where he was, he got lost. He decided to trust his ears, and follow the sound of the man's screams for help (for the woman's screams had stopped) no matter where they led him.

They led him to the parlor. Roscoe kicked at the door twice before it occurred to him to see if it were locked. It wasn't. He threw open the door and ran in.

Cleo opened her eyes. "Roscoe!" she said.

"You're Cleo, right?" It seemed very important to Roscoe to get things straight.

"Roscoe, listen." It was the bandaged man speaking. It wasn't Muldoon. "There's dynamite under Cleo's dress!" The voice kept breaking with fear.

Roscoe had heard that from people; still it didn't seem like a very gentlemanly thing to say in the woman's presence.

"Really, Roscoe, please look, it's all right. Hurry," the woman said, "or we'll be blown to bits!"

It wasn't her words, so much, that made Roscoe look, as it was the fact that Cleo's dress was smoldering, the smoke drifting upward in a thin grey spiral.

The sight of the actual dynamite cleared the last traces of Roscoe's befuddlement. He had used dynamite plenty of times in his criminal days, and a fuse that short meant trouble.

Indelicate it might be, but Roscoe reached with a rough hand and pulled the two sticks from under the woman. "Thank *God!*" she breathed.

It was a little soon for that. Roscoe sprinted across the parlor toward the window; then the fuse disappeared, and the hissing stopped. Roscoe said a rude word, and hurled the explosive through Hand's imported glass.

XXII.

Baxter grinned as he heard the explosion. The little slut's body had hardly muffled it at all. Baxter waited for the piping voice of Mr. Theodore Roosevelt to command the police to charge the house.

That was all he wanted to hear. He knew the explosion would bring them running. He had clear sailing to the reservoir, now. Of course, it was possible the gates were being kept under guard. Baxter didn't mind; he would make his own gate.

Baxter emerged from the bush he'd been hiding behind. He placed a stick of dynamite under the fence, lit it, then stepped back as it blew. He emerged onto Forty-second Street.

It was in the nature of their characters for Theodore Roosevelt and Dennis Patrick Francis-Xavier Muldoon to be the first on the scene. Hand was just regaining consciousness, but they had ignored him after a quick glance, and left him to the officers who followed.

The Commissioner bent over Roscoe. "Get this man to a hospital," he ordered. One of the officers went to telephone for an ambulance.

Muldoon ran to the couch to untie Cleo. He saw where her dress had been scorched. "Angel," he said anxiously, "are you hurtin' badly?"

"I have been burned, Dennis, but it is nothing to what might have happened. Roscoe saved all of us."

Tommy Alb said, "Muldoon!" Muldoon saw that to Alb's other injuries had been added bruises high on his throat.

"What?" Muldoon replied.

"Muldoon, you've got to stop that Baxter. He's crazy. I don't know what he's planning on, but he's got enough dynamite on him to blow J. P. Morgan's bank. Seven sticks of it." Muldoon gave him a puzzled look. "I want you alive," Alb explained. "I'll be out in ten, fifteen years, and I'll settle with you then."

Muldoon told him he had a deal. He deputized a man to take over the untying. It didn't matter much now, Cleo being fully clothed. He turned to go follow Mr. Roosevelt, who had left, apparently to chase Baxter.

Cleo stopped him. "Dennis," she said.

What is it, me darlin'?"

"Kiss me."

It wasn't seemly, but these seemed extraordinary circumstances. He kissed her, and it was wonderful, and he didn't care if Mr. Roosevelt found out or didn't.

"Thank you," Cleo said. "I had given up hope that that would ever happen. Take care of yourself, Dennis."

Muldoon answered by kissing her again, quickly, then running for the front door.

He caught up with the Commissioner before he was even out of the house. Roosevelt was in the hallway telling Hand he had a lot to answer for.

The lecture was cut short by the sound of the explosion from outside, as Baxter left the grounds.

This much is to be said for Ozias Herkimer: when he saw Baxter blow the fence and run from the Hand estate, he forgot his fury and his being under arrest, and ran forward with other police officers to try to capture him. And with them, he was knocked senseless from the concussion of another stick of dynamite.

Baxter disappeared around the corner of Fifth Avenue. A few yards down the block, he found the metal rungs in the reservoir wall, and began to climb.

Those police who were still able to chase him ran right underneath—it never occurred to them the fugitive would want to get anywhere but away.

Roosevelt and Muldoon and other policemen arrived on the scene. Listerdale was standing under a gas lamp, shaking his head in disbelief at the scene.

"Where has Baxter gone?" the Commissioner demanded. Listerdale pointed to the corner. "Come on, Muldoon," Roosevelt said.

"No, sir," Muldoon told him. Before the Commissioner could

gather enough air for a suitable explosion, Muldoon was explaining. "He's climbin' the reservoir, sir. I'm sure of it. He's plannin' to light off that dynamite he's got, and blow the reservoir."

"Not *that* dynamite," Roosevelt said. "He's been planting a mammoth charge there for days, if not longer. Remember the night he caught Cleo in the carriage house, how she noticed his sleeves were wet?"

"Sir," Muldoon replied, "I don't know nothin' about dynamite except you need a fuse and a match to light it off, but I think that's just what Baxter is goin' to do, if I don't get up there and stop him."

"It's too dangerous," Roosevelt said.

"I haven't been asked," Listerdale said, "but I don't think there's much of a choice. I—I don't want to die."

"Well, blast, don't say that as though you're ashamed of it! I don't want to die either. Very well, Muldoon here's what we'll do: I will have men posted at the base of every ladder to the walkway at the top of the reservoir. You climb the Sixth Avenue side, while my men and I launch a diversionary attack on the Fifth Avenue side."

"Yes, sir," Muldoon said. "I'll be gettin' him for you." Muldoon sprinted down the block, while Roosevelt assembled his men.

Baxter had reached the walkway at the top of the wall, as wide as some Greenwich Village streets. By climbing to this point, he had gotten past most of the length of the fuse—if he lit it where he was now, he would still have some ten minutes to get away. He brought the fire to the fuse, and it hissed to life, showing itself from the fissure at the inside of the low wall that surrounded the walkway. Baxter had hidden it well—at any other time, even by daylight, it would have been invisible.

It was burning well. Now to get down. He looked over the edge, to Fifth Avenue below, saw the policeman, and cursed. Roosevelt himself was down there. And he had a rifle—

Baxter saw the puffs of smoke and felt the shock of a bullet before he heard the reports. There was a horrible, searing pain on his left, where his neck joined his shoulders. He didn't seem to be bleeding too badly, and the bullet hadn't hit bone, but Baxter knew he couldn't get down that way. He wouldn't panic—he'd leave the other way. After all, he could run around the bulk of the wall. And he would delay them further.

Though the pain in his left side made it difficult, Baxter's great strength enabled him to light two more sticks of dynamite, and send them arcing over the wall. Blood was dripping from one of Baxter's unwrinkled ears, he noticed. Roosevelt's other bullet had ruined it. Baxter never felt it.

He raced the burning fuse down the walkway.

Muldoon heard the latest explosions, but tried not to pay attention to them, except to count. That was four. Tommy Alb had said Baxter had seven sticks when he left the building—that meant he had three left. It occurred to Muldoon that lying about the matter would be an effortless revenge for the ex-copper.

Muldoon forced the thought from his mind. Hands and feet. Rung after rung. That's all that was important.

About five rungs from the top, Muldoon pulled his revolver from his pocket. He'd be ready to fire as soon as he reached the top.

But Baxter was waiting for him when he reached the top. Muldoon pulled the trigger almost by reflex, and the same second Baxter kicked the gun from his hand. Served him right, Muldoon thought, the bullet never would have hit him otherwise. As it was, it grazed his side.

Baxter grabbed the new wound (Muldoon saw he had a couple already) but that didn't stop him from kicking at Muldoon's head. Muldoon, made desperate by the prospect of falling to the sidewalk below, switched hands on the top rung, and with the undamaged one, caught Baxter's foot at the next kick and twisted. When Baxter fell heavily to the stone of the reservoir, Muldoon scrambled up.

It did him no good, however, because as he gathered his feet under him, he stepped on something round, and fell backward. He hit his head on the stone, and lay still.

Baxter's laugh was wheezy, because of his wounds. He stooped (because he could not bend) to pick up the cylindrical object the officer had fallen over—a stick of dynamite Baxter himself had dropped when Muldoon tripped him. With the toe of a shoe, he rolled Muldoon's body into the waters of the Croton Reservoir. He gave the wheezy laugh again. Dynamite didn't have to blow a man up to do him in.

Baxter threw back his head to straighten the path for air into his lungs. It still seemed to come raggedly. Baxter faced the fact that he couldn't escape. He didn't want to anymore. He would stay here, with his three remaining sticks of dynamite, and see that no one tried to put out that fuse. The fuse. The flood. The plan. In the name of humanity, it must be done.

Down below, T. Avery Hand had been revived. He was standing (along with the officer who had him in charge) under the gas lamp on Forty-second Street with Listerdale, a shaken but unhurt Captain Herkimer, and Cleo.

There was nothing to see, and very little to hear going on at the top of the structure, but Cleo had her eyes fixed at the edge where the wall met the black August sky. She twisted a handkerchief around her fingers when she wasn't using it to wipe tears of worry from her soft brown eyes.

Hand watched her, saw how she cared for this big Irishman, this hero, Muldoon. Hand had been right all along, to be worried about him. But that was about all he'd been right about, back to the days he thought his locomotive improvement would make him rich, and that being rich would solve all his troubles forevermore.

That was the moment that Peter Baxter, atop the reservoir, made light-headed by exertion, slow seepage of blood from his wounds, and the knowledge that in two minutes or less it would be all over and his job would be at last done, decided to stand up and peep over the wall. He wanted one last look at it. He wanted to imagine the wall of water sweeping it away.

He looked carefully over the grounds. He remembered angrily, but with a touch of pleasure, the lesson he had taught the little slut in the carriage house.

Then he saw the group standing under the gas lamp.

Baxter went insane with rage. He ran stiffly to the point on the wall directly above that gas lamp. As he ran, he lit a stick of dynamite. He noted, without even thinking, that the fuse had perhaps one minute to burn on the main charge. If he'd thought, he would never have done what he did; it made no sense.

For the first time, Baxter reared up above the wall, his black butler's uniform blending with the night sky behind him, only his face visible, floating like a ball of Saint Elmo's fire. Policemen drew revolvers and fired, but none seemed to be able to hit Baxter.

Baxter held the sizzling explosive at arm's length, pointing at the group in the gaslight: Cleo, Herkimer, Listerdale, the patrolman, and Hand.

Baxter's face was opening and closing like a blacksmith's bellows, and he was yelling something, over and over. "The sentence is death!" he cried. "The sentence is *death!*" And he threw the dynamite with all his might at the middle of the circle of lamplight.

No one would ever know why, once the group under the lamp had scattered and the dynamite lay on the pavement, T. Avery Hand tore loose from the grip of the policeman who held him, and ran forward to pick it up.

Those who saw him later said he raised his arm as if to throw it. But throw it where? He couldn't be expected to throw it hard enough to get it back up to Baxter. And if he wanted to throw it away for safety's sake—well, he could have been much safer if he'd just kept running clear.

Perhaps he didn't think of that. Perhaps he didn't think of anything. Perhaps he knew Cleo was watching.

In any event, he did run forward, and he did pick it up, and he did raise his arm as if to throw it, and that was the instant it went off. Between shock and loss of blood, Hand was dead within half a minute.

But while all this was going on, Muldoon had dragged himself out of the water and gone to work on the fuse. Because Muldoon hadn't been badly stunned when he landed on his head. Lord knew, he had sustained worse blows in the course of the investigation. He had been about to rise when Baxter kicked him into the water.

Muldoon could stay under water, but not for long, and, soaked and heavy as his clothes would be, he would be at Baxter's mercy if he tried to climb out. While he was there, though, Muldoon saw the dynamite, attached to the wall in a dull red mass, like a thousand insect eggs.

Then Baxter had seen whatever he had seen, and Muldoon had gotten to work. He climbed out of the water, flopping to the walkway like a dead fish. Then he had run, dripping, to the glowing end of the fuse. There were only a very, very few feet of it to go before it dipped underwater and got to the first cluster of deadly eggs. Muldoon knew that if he didn't stop the first, he needn't worry about any others.

But he couldn't get at the fuse—his waterlogged fingers couldn't get into the crevice and pry it loose. He watched the fuse shorten, chased the little spot of fire down the crack with his eyes, and went mad with frustration because he could do nothing. If only he had something to pry it out with with, a pencil; a pin.

He had a pin! It had just been returned to him that evening, at Headquarters. His shield. That square piece of tin that said he was a Police Officer. The one he'd worked so hard to get.

Muldoon tore open his soggy jacket and detached his badge of office. He almost dropped it when he heard another explosion, though this time from farther away, followed by horrified shouts and screams.

He scrambled down some two feet past the burning part, and started digging at the fuse with the pin of the shield. Behind him, he heard Baxter's voice yelling above all the other noise, "No! No! Not you!" and was afraid the game was up. He took a worried look over his shoulder, but the butler turned madman was still staring over the parapet.

Muldoon gasped with relief as he freed a little loop of fuse from the crack in the rock. That was when Baxter saw him.

Baxter couldn't believe it. It wasn't happening. How often could Muldoon *do* this? Snarling like an animal, Baxter ran to the attack.

Muldoon was concentrating so deeply on pulling up more of the fuse so he could somehow sever it that Baxter was almost upon him before he realized it. Muldoon managed to raise an arm to shunt Baxter's blow from his head to his back, then made the smartest move of his life.

It was something Muldoon had seen Listerdale do during the attack in the alley that afternoon; perhaps it was *jiu-jitsu judo*, Muldoon didn't know. What he did was ignore his instinct, the instinct that told him to stand and put up his dukes—there was no time for that.

Instead, Muldoon remained on his knees, and reached down, not up. He grasped Baxter's left ankle in his right hand, then pushed sharply and suddenly against the tall man's left knee with the heel of his other hand. The move sent Baxter staggering backward.

If he hadn't been wounded, Baxter might have been able to regain his balance. As it was, pain and weakness had affected his coordination; he was unable to find the strength to pull his body upright.

Baxter staggered backward across the width of the walkway, to the low parapet, and over. He was too surprised even to scream. He landed across a curb on Forty-second Street, broke his back, and died. Still clutched in his left hand were two unexploded sticks of dynamite.

Muldoon stared for a second at the spot where Baxter had gone over, shocked that the final confrontation had been so easy. He shook his head, then turned back to his work.

The fuse had burned past his loop. He would have to start all over.

By an act of will, Muldoon forced himself to be calm. There was a good foot and a half of fuse above water level, and another foot or so below. He gave himself a chance, but a small one—at least he knew what to do now.

In seconds, he had a new loop. He folded it (taking care to keep the ends separated with a finger, so that the fire couldn't jump across) then sawed at the top of the loop with his shield.

The spark started to burn his hand, but Muldoon kept sawing away. Sweat was now mingled with the reservoir water that dripped from his body. He had next to nothing to call a loop, now, and he wouldn't get another chance. Then he sawed through. The live part fell to the rock. Muldoon stood and covered it with the sole of his boot until it fizzled itself out.

Then he dropped back to his knees, picked up his shield, and kissed it. Then he raised it high above his head, and watched it shine against the sky like a new square star.

He heard voices; footsteps. He stood again, his instincts back in command, ready to face a new enemy. He relaxed. Police officers, they were, led by a charging, grinning Theodore Roosevelt. Muldoon was all set to salute; instead the Commissioner crushed him in a joyous bear hug. "Well done, my boy," he piped. "A bully job!"

Muldoon began to weep.

SUNDAY
the thirtieth
of August, 1896, and beyond

I.

Clocks around the city were striking one. A hansom cab driver (and still another honest one) was taking Mr. Roosevelt, Muldoon, and Hiram Listerdale back through Muldoon's old beat. The late-Saturday, early-Sunday walkers were at it again, just as they had been a week ago. It had been a long week.

Muldoon snorted. Tonight *alone* had held enough for any one week a man might care to live through. It hadn't ended with Baxter's death, by any means; Muldoon had retrieved his revolver; Roosevelt had arranged for Daisy and the rifle he had borrowed to be returned to the police stable. The dead and wounded had been carted away; Tommy Alb was treated at the hospital, then taken to the nearest precinct for questioning. He talked freely and in detail about what he had done, and about what the Sperling gang in general had done, but none of the real, inside stuff, such as where the Rabbi might be found.

Roscoe was going to be all right, to Muldoon's great relief; so was Cleo. There had been an emotional farewell when Cleo had to be left at the hospital overnight to have her burns attended to.

A search of Hand's mansion and grounds had turned up no more dynamite; apparently, Baxter had died holding the last two sticks. An investigation was under way to see who might have sold it to him.

The Reverend Lewis Burley, his daughter Essie May, and William Jennings Bryan had been told of Hand's death, but nothing more. Essie May had had hysterics; her father and Bryan had comforted her. At this moment, Bryan was making a statement to the press to the effect that the death of T. Avery Hand had been a great blow to his campaign, and therefore to all the working people of America, but that he would struggle on to victory, and so forth.

Katie and Maureen Muldoon (and Brigid, who had joined them at Mrs. Sturdevant's after she finished work), had yet to be told. That's where they were bound now.

The building came into view. Muldoon sighed. "It feels funny comin' back here to where it started, now that it's over with. More or less, anyway. The blasted Rabbi is still runnin' around loose, as far as we know."

"So you no longer think Captain Herkimer is the Rabbi?" the Commissioner wanted to know.

"Herkimer?" Listerdale sounded surprised.

"Just an idea I had. No, Herkimer can't be. You heard the lieutenant, didn't you, sir? Herkimer was busy leadin' a raid on a bawdy house while Crandall was bein' killed. There was no way he could have done it. I just wish I'd known that before." There was silence for a while, then Muldoon said. "Commissioner, I'm sorry about what I did before. Cryin' all over your shoulder that way in front of the men."

Roosevelt's moustache fluttered. "Ha! I daresay it was a breach of decorum on my part to have embraced you. No harm done."

Listerdale smiled at the young officer. "If it's any consolation, I fear that if I learned that I had been kneeling on enough dynamite to level a forest, and it had gotten to within—what did the engineer say? Fifty seconds of going off?"

"Fif*teen* seconds," Muldoon corrected. He had to wipe his brow just thinking of it.

"Goodness. Well, as I say, if that's what I had learned, I expect I should burst into tears, too."

Muldoon laughed. "Commissioner, I want to thank you again for comin' all this way for me to tell me sisters you're puttin' me up for the night."

"Not at all, Muldoon. And this way, we are able to give Mr. Listerdale a ride home as well. By the way, Listerdale, do you happen to have a telephone in the Emporium?"

"Yes, I do. The carriage trade, you know."

"If it won't inconvenience you too much, may I use it?"

Listerdale shrugged. "No inconvenience. I have to go through the store to get to my rooms, anyway."

"Good, good. You don't mind a slight delay, do you, Muldoon?"

Muldoon did mind, but he thought it would be ungracious to say so. Roosevelt commanded the driver to go on past Mrs. Sturdevant's, and proceed to Listerdale's Literary Emporium.

Listerdale unlocked the store's back door (the one Muldoon had burst through), lit the gas, and showed the Commissioner the phone. Roosevelt soon made a connection with Police Headquarters.

"Brian? Why aren't you asleep? Is Officer Bourke there? Ha! Let me speak to him. Bourke. That matter I mentioned when I called you from the hospital?" This was news to Muldoon—he hadn't known Roosevelt had made a call from the hospital. "Have you . . . ? Good. Yes, right away." He gave Listerdale's address, then hung up.

"They have an important paper for me at Headquarters. I took the liberty of telling them to bring it here. I hope you don't mind."

"Well, I had planned to go to bed," said Listerdale, "but if it's important . . ."

"It is very important."

"Then I suggest we wait in my quarters." Listerdale led them up the stairs to his sitting room.

"Spartan quarters," Roosevelt said.

"You have been here before, Mr. Roosevelt, just last week."

"Yes, I have. We spoke about your acquaintance with Mr Crandall."

"I seem to recall our talking about the next volume of your book. We discussed that, too."

"Oh, that's right, we did. But I'm more interested in the matter of paper."

Muldoon was puzzled. "Newspapers, sir?"

"No, Muldoon, but that is an interesting point, isn't it? How important paper has been in this affair. The two newspapers Crandall was involved with; the fatal bill of sale for a poor young woman who has suffered enough; even the ballots that will be cast in November will be of paper. And here's something you haven't been told: Cleo heard the killer gain entry to Crandall's room by saying he had 'the paper.' Cleo, incidentally, also heard the so-called 'Rabbi'—which is a slur, I believe, on an honorable title and a great people—confess to Hand that he had committed the crime. Cleo distinctly heard Crandall offer to pay the visitor for the paper.

"That bothered me, you know. It didn't seem to fit. The only paper I had heard of was that bill of sale, and Crandall—as unlikely as he would be to sell the thing that kept the object of obsession close to him—was more likely to be selling it than buying it. Doesn't it seem that way to you, Muldoon?"

"Yes, sir, I said so at the time." There was a strange intensity in the Commissioner's voice. Muldoon wondered what was up. To look at Listerdale, you might have thought Mr. Roosevelt were humming "Daisy Bell."

"Baxter was an Anarchist, you know, Listerdale," Roosevelt said.

"Well, I thought he must be some kind of radical, with the bombs and all. A Red, perhaps."

"Another piece of paper we found, in Baxter's room in Hand's mansion. It was grease-stained, but readable. It was in code, but some anarchist slogans and the word 'Rabbi' were child's play to decipher.

"You know, Muldoon," Roosevelt said, "of all criminals, it strikes me that the anarchist is the worst, for besides his savagery, he must be either a fool, or a vicious hypocrite."

"Why do you say that?" Listerdale might have been questioning a student during a discussion in his class.

"I say it," Roosevelt replied, "because even a fool must realize that man cannot exist in a vacuum of power. If anarchy ever triumphs, the triumph will last only a moment; it will be immediately replaced by despotism."

"And what have we now?' Listerdale wanted to know. "Aren't the Rockefellers, the Morgans, the *Hands* despot enough for you?"

The Commissioner hissed. "I have no stomach for this. Muldoon, draw your weapon."

"Beg your pardon, sir?"

"That's an order. Muldoon, draw your weapon."

Muldoon knew he'd done it, because he saw the revolver in his hand.

"Cover him."

"Oh, no, Mr. Roosevelt, you can't be sayin' . . ."

"Yes, I can. Cover that man, I say. Yes, Muldoon. I am sorry for you, and sorrier still for your sister. Hiram Listerdale killed Crandall and Mrs. Le Clerc. Listerdale was the superior to whom Baxter reported. He was probably the brain behind the Mansion Burglars, as well. Hiram Listerdale is the Rabbi."

II.

Muldoon wanted to shoot someone, whether himself, Listerdale, or the Commissioner, he didn't know.

The two men were staring at each other. Muldoon looked from side to side.

Listerdale broke the silence. "You have no evidence, Mr. Roosevelt." Muldoon looked at him, and knew. He fought to keep his eyes clear of tears.

"Ha! I am quite aware of that, Listerdale. Is Listerdale your true name?"

"It is. I have used others."

"I'm sure I've heard of a few of them. No, I admit I have no evidence, as yet. But one of my men is coming here with a search warrant. Is that bill of sale, that piece of yellow paper Muldoon saw in your safe, still there? I suspect it is. You probably planned to destroy it after the reservoir blew up tomorrow. With Hand dead, you needed no more hold over him."

Muldoon saw Listerdale's jaw quiver. "Ha!" Roosevelt exclaimed, pressing his advantage. "It's a shame we can't have Roscoe here to crack that safe for us, isn't it, Muldoon? Well, we'll get it open just the same.

"And your make-up kit. Muldoon told me fascinating things about theatrical make-up. Was the Rabbi created each time in this room, or in your bedroom? Probably the bedroom. Have you a lighted mirror? Even if you have gotten rid of your kit—ha! See him wince, Muldoon? He still has it. But even if he hadn't, the police chemist could find traces of spirit-gum or ether somewhere in that room.

"Come, Listerdale. You are trapped. Why draw it out? I brought the subject out into the open, because I found I have been right all my life in loathing deception. *You* hate it less, but then, you've been doing it longer. Why don't you tell me what I need to know?"

"Very well." Listerdale sighed a very tired, very heavy sigh. "If I may ask you a question."

I'm going to kill him, Muldoon thought. He tightened his grip on his revolver.

"I may refuse to answer it."

Listerdale made a magnanimous gesture. It was almost as if he were *happy* he'd been found out. Or at least relieved.

"I'm sure you'll tell me. When did you know?"

"Know? Of a certainty? Just these last few seconds, with your implied confession. I ask you now formally, with Muldoon as a witness: Did you kill those people?"

"Oh, yes, I did, of course. I would like to say, sir, that if I had been the vicious monster you describe, Muldoon would be dead at this moment, as would Cleo. I expressly forbade Hand to have Muldoon killed—I couldn't help it if my orders weren't followed. How could I?" Listerdale's appeal seemed sincere, like a man arguing a summons. "This has all been very upsetting to me."

I'm going to kill him, Muldoon thought.

"But what I'd like to know is, when did you *suspect* me? Seriously."

"Just before Hand died. When Baxter looked down into the

group consisting of you, Cleo, Hand, Herkimer, and the patrolman. He yelled 'The sentence is death.' What a peculiar thing to say, I thought later. I happened to see and hear this, because I was expecting reinforcements to the Fifth Avenue side of the structure, and was looking for them around the corner.

" 'The sentence is death.' Considering he expected us *all* to die in a matter of minutes, it was incredible. But his anger, I think, pointed me in the right direction. In the ranks of Anarchism, as in the ranks of the Black Hand, or the Ku Klux Klan, or any clandestine criminal band, the sentence is death for treason, and for very little else. They may *kill* innocent victims by the score, but they only pass *sentence* on their own kind. It's a fine distinction, but an important one.

"Well, who could have betrayed him? Cleo was a victim, Herkimer a dupe, the policeman an unknown. That left Hand or you, Mr. Listerdale. That was settled when Hand picked up the dynamite and was killed, and Muldoon has told us us that Baxter, in his insanity, screamed, 'No, not you.'

"This is not evidence, of course. Not even a clue, strictly speaking. But it got me wondering about you. Ha! Day by day, since we made each other's acquaintance, I have become aware of more and more extraordinary things about you. The most extraordinary occurred tonight—you rush *to* a fire, and *to* a dangerous police operation. Why had you been there? Why did Baxter recognize you? If you were not the Rabbi, what could you have been? His schoolmaster, perhaps?"

Listerdale chuckled. "As a matter of fact I was. I was very fond of Peter, at one time."

"Why did you go to Hand's mansion, Listerdale?"

Listerdale's chuckling stopped. "I went because I was worried about Muldoon."

Muldoon's voice was filled with disgust. "You were *what?*"

Listerdale continued speaking to the Commissioner. "I have fallen in love with Kathleen Muldoon, Mr. Roosevelt. She is everything good about the common man and woman of the world— kind, loving, and strong. She—"

Muldoon stood up. "Better leave, Mr. Roosevelt. I'm goin' to kill him, and you don't want to be involved."

"Sit down, Muldoon, and don't be so melodramatic. There are procedures that must be followed. Sit!"

Muldoon sat back down on his wooden chair. His trigger finger still itched. "This afternoon—Saturday, I mean, the promises you made; the things you said about Katie—"

"All true, Muldoon. Look at me. I'm not a bad man; the system you've been deceived into protecting is far more wicked than I am. Look at the warmth your family and you showed me. That is what is real. You couldn't take into your hearts a fiend, could you? Could Kathleen consent to be the wife of a monster? *Look at me*, Dennis, and answer. I beseech you." He even had his hands folded as in prayer.

"That will be enough, thank you," Roosevelt said. Muldoon was glad he did, because if Listerdale had been allowed to say two more words, he would be crying, and Muldoon didn't want to face a crying murderer. He wouldn't be sure how to handle it.

"It didn't occur to me until much later that Baxter needn't have recognized you at all. In his mad fancy, he might have mistaken you for someone else. But by then, it made no difference, because once I had conceived of you as the Rabbi, so many other indications fell into place almost like a column of soldiers. It was amazing how many there were—none conclusive in itself, but building to a considerable, convincing weight when taken together.

"First, there was the matter of the paper. Crandall seemed to be buying paper, or a paper, the night he was killed. And that very night, *you had told us you sold him paper!* Drawing paper, for his sketch work. Crandall probably placed an order some time before; you pretended to be out of stock, so you could feign delivery and have him admit you to his flat. You probably told us so that we would be ready to accept anything we might find in Crandall's flat that could lead us to the Emporium. And there was more.

"Muldoon's seeing the yellow slip of paper in your safe, so shortly after Crandall had been killed, so shortly before the body was discovered. You were so anxious to get that bill of sale safe—and of course Baxter told you about it; Baxter told you everything that happened in Hand's house—because it would do for you what Crandall wanted it to do for him—keep Hand in line. That was the same reason you masqueraded as the Rabbi. You were so anxious to get it into your safe that you didn't even take time to lock the back door of the Emporium.

"Then there were the bruises on Crandall's neck. Cleo and Tommy Alb had similar bruises after encounters with Baxter, and we knew Baxter and the Rabbi were in cahoots, or at least Hand's behavior gave us cause to suspect it. It was a mistake to show Muldoon your skill at *jiu-jitsu judo;* if a man can pick up one strange fighting technique in the Orient, he can pick up many. I suspect there is a way to press nerves or blood vessels so as to cause unconsciousness."

"Blood vesels," Listerdale said. "I taught Peter to do it."

"Of course. You rendered Crandall unconscious, sat him in the chair, and let the gas do its work.

"Then, last night," Roosevelt went on, "and even before that, to my knowledge, you never spoke a word that Cleo might hear. Is that correct, Muldoon?"

"Absolutely, sir." Muldoon worked his jaw. "He was afraid she might recognize his voice—his real one, not the whisper he used as the Rabbi—from when she heard him killin' Crandall."

"Your aliases gave you away, too, properly understood. A Rabbi is a teacher, in the Hebrew faith; you have nerve, no one but Hand ever took you for a Jew, but . . . oh, never mind, it is no use. The word 'meister' is simply the German word for 'master,' which is an English word, meaning, among other things, a teacher. And *you* have been the only teacher in the matter.

"You are the right physical type; and if false whiskers can be used to hide a beard, they can be used to hide side-whiskers, like your own.

"But it was Muldoon who pointed out the strongest information against you, when he was building a theory against someone else. *The timing of the attacks!*

"Ha! *That* points the finger straight at you. Muldoon began his search for Cleo, and came to you for advice. Just prior to that, he met, coincidentally, Captain Herkimer, which caused a lot of confusion later. But that very day, after talking to you, and telling you *specifically* what he was about, Muldoon was attacked."

"He was supposed to be scared off the case, not thrown off a barge! Can I help it if Hand hired idiots?" Listerdale was more composed, but the pleading note remained in his voice.

"Mr. Roosevelt, somethin' else," Muldoon said, in a low, flat voice. "After Eagle Jack's boys had their first go at me, and everyone thought I was dead, that's when Listerdale came around, actin' sympathetic, and hardly able to be lookin' Katie in the face, so the girls tell me. He gave her that bottle of water from the Sea of Galilee." Muldoon looked at him. "I thought you anarchists didn't believe in God."

"That's Bolsheviks. And, please, please, *please* believe me, I wasn't acting. I *did* feel terrible. I know how much she cares for you, and I love her, and want whatever makes her happy."

"You son of a bitch!" Muldoon said. "She just got the vial back from the priest yesterday! You know what this is goin' to do to her, you murderin' scoundrel?"

"Yes," Listerdale said. "I know."

"It was the murder of Mrs. Le Clerc, Listerdale," Roosevelt went on. "The Rabbi, or Meister this time, was there waiting for us, and we had formulated the decision to ride up to the home just minutes before we left Muldoon's flat.

"But you were there when Brian O'Leary began his report, and you were in the kitchen for the rest, after 'volunteering' to leave the room—a very clever maneuver, that one. You wouldn't have had to listen very hard through the kitchen door to hear the boy speak. Or perhaps, from the first words he said, you knew you had to silence the old woman.

"That, as my friend Roscoe would say, cinched it. Only *you* could have known Mrs. Le Clerc was suddenly a danger. It is that simple. Added to the rest, it made almost a mathematical certainty that you were the Rabbi."

There was a knock on the downstairs, and Ed Bourke called to the Commissioner that they had arrived.

Roosevelt rose. "Let's go, Listerdale, it's all over for you."

"I would appreciate it greatly," Listerdale said, "if you would let me go into my bedroom. There is something I would like to do before I go to jail."

"I forbid it. Now come along."

"*No!*" Muldoon's voice came so suddenly that Roosevelt and Listerdale both jumped.

"What has possessed you now, Muldoon?"

"If we go takin' him in, there's goin' to be a trial. Katie's name'll be dragged through all the mud the reservoir would have left behind. She'll be made a *fool*. I'm not standin' by to let that happen."

"Muldoon, you're overwrought. Give me that gun!"

"No, sir! I'd spit in the devil's eye for you, but me first duty is to me family. I'm sorry, but that's the way it is. Step one step closer, and I'll shoot you in the leg."

"You'll regret this, Muldoon."

"Undoubtedly, sir, but I've got to be doin' it all the same. I hope you can understand."

Roosevelt stood still and breathed through his teeth. Muldoon turned to Listerdale. "All right, Hiram. We'll see how much you meant that vow you made to me in askin' for Katie's hand. You go on into your room. I'll count to twenty, then I'm comin' in. If you're still standin', I'll drop you in your tracks, so help me Christ, and Katie'll have a murderer for a brother, as well as for a suitor. If you've managed to slip out and get away, well, I'll hunt you down and find you if I have to skin every anarchist on two continents alive to do it. And Katie will still *most* likely die of a broken heart.

"That leaves one thing for you to be doin'. So start doin' it. I think I might be able to . . . well, never mind. Get goin' if you're goin'."

Listerdale stood, looked at Roosevelt, and whispered, "Do you see? The Common Man. Magnificent." Then he disappeared into his bedroom.

The knocking downstairs got louder, and the shouting more urgent. They started to break down the door.

Muldoon's voice was quiet and controlled as he counted off the time, but inside, his heart was in a ferment. He'd put his whole future, and Katie's too, on the word of a conspirator. Of a *murderer!*

Fourteen, fifteen . . .

The door downstairs crashed in. There had been a lot of that, too, last week. The heavy feet of the coppers pounded on the stairs.

Eighteen, nineteen, twenty.

Muldoon went to the door, holding the revolver at the ready. He threw the door open and walked carefully inside. A medicinal smell started to drift into the sitting room.

Muldoon returned a few seconds later. The coppers were in the room with the Commissioner. "It won't be hard to find the make-up kit," he told the boys. "He dug it out for you. Drank the ether. Whole bottle, eight or nine ounces. Deader than a doornail."

Muldoon walked to the Commissioner, and stood at attention before him. He presented the gun, butt first. "Your prisoner, sir," Muldoon said.

Roosevelt looked up at him. "Ha!" he said. "That is . . . hmph. Don't be so hasty, Muldoon. I think we'll let the surgeon have a look at you when he arrives. It seems to me, your behavior can be ascribed to the injuries you sustained during this investigation. So keep your . . . ah, keep your mouth closed about anything you think you may have heard or seen here.

"Justice has been done, Muldoon. Hand, Baxter, Listerdale are all dead. Sperling and his men are in custody. There is nothing more . . . ah . . . a civil servant can do. Franklyn and Libstein will stay untouched, blast them, but they always seem to. Not forever, though. Not forever. I will not use this against Bryan. This campaign has been low enough. He's not worth your sister's anguish to stop, anyway.

"Bourke, take charge here, I shall return in a few moments."

Muldoon was trembling. Roosevelt put a strong arm across his back.

"Here, let me take you to your sister, my boy. Pull yourself together. She's going to need you. She has lost someone," the Commissioner said, "very dear to her." His voice trailed away as if in memory. "Very dear," he said.

III.

So Muldoon didn't spend the night at Mr. Roosevelt's house. He spent it at Mrs. Sturdevant's, trying, along with Cleo, the landlady, Brigid, and Maureen, to console Katie.

The story was that Listerdale had had an aneurism, and the

exertion of the night had caused it to burst. The Police Surgeon would back that up.

The story appeared in all the newspapers. Practically every one called it *"CRIME OF THE CENTURY!!"* Baxter was, unanimously, *"Worst Fiend Who Ever Threatened Our City"*, Muldoon was "Heroic!" "Fearless!" "The Finest of the Finest!"

Someone at Headquarters had done a marvelous job of giving the story to the press without actually lying. Muldoon had gone undercover to track down rumors of a fiendish Anarchist plot to destroy the city's water supply.

Listerdale was not mentioned; nor was Cleo.

In the *Journal*, T. Avery Hand had died a hero's death; the story gave the impression his last words were "Vote for Bryan." In all the other papers, there was serious doubt over what role T. Avery Hand *had* played in the drama; whether he was an innocent victim, or an unlucky conspirator. This was *not* a gentlemanly Presidential campaign.

William Jennings Bryan had already gone back to the campaign trail. The bride-to-be and her father were contemplating a long cruise.

Inside pages of all the newspapers featured stories about the retirement of Police Department veteran, Captain Ozias Herkimer, because of "personal matters."

Theodore Roosevelt came to call the next morning. He expressed his condolences to Katie, who thanked him. He told her he had known she would face this bravely, and he was right.

Cleo and Muldoon said they were going to step outside for a few moments to talk to the Commissioner.

"She's going to be fine, Muldoon. Grit runs in your family."

Muldoon gave a sad little laugh. "Yes, sir. I knew she'd gotten over the worst of it when Brian O'Leary showed up with a bunch of flowers he'd been out pickin', and Katie commenced makin' cookies for him. We'll be seein' a lot of cookies baked before Mr. Hiram Listerdale is forgotten."

Cleo took Muldoon's arm. He could feel a small shudder run through her. "I'll *never* forget," she said.

"We've tracked Listerdale's past," the Commissioner said. "He has indeed been a schoolmaster—he has educated young boys into the ways of anarchism; the promising ones, he has had placed as servants in the homes of the wealthy. Blast it, this particular bunch of anarchists has been doing the Mansion Burglars thefts for *years* —they merely increased their pace to finance the purchase of the dynamite, and when Hand made himself vulnerable to Crandall, to set up the Emporium. They picked a bookstore for him, because it happened to be the subject Listerdale felt most comfortable about. He became part of the neighborhood, decided he could kill Crandall without jeopardizing the plot—the purpose of which, I infer, was to kill Bryan—and struck."

"He was . . ." Cleo couldn't think of the right word to sum up what Listerdale had been.

"I doubt there has ever been a more tangled skein of misguided passion," Roosevelt said. "Men whose lusts for power and the pleasures of the flesh, or for so-called spiritual ideals that are beyond our power to attain in this life, working at cross purposes, building crime upon crime, and evil upon evil . . ."

"The 'Lunatic Fringe,' " Muldoon said.

"Precisely," said Mr. Roosevelt.

The three of them stood silent for a while on Mrs. Sturdevant's stoop, watching the normal Sunday-morning pedestrian traffic.

"Ha!" the Commissioner said at last. "I think they mean to give you a medal, Muldoon."

"It's an honor, sir, but . . ." Muldoon was still feeling guilty about pointing a revolver at the Commissioner.

"I agreed wholeheartedly. Special session, this morning."

"But, sir," Muldoon said, "how could you go agreein' to a medal for me when you know how I acted . . . Unless . . ."

"Unless what, Dennis?" Cleo wanted to know.

"Unless you went through that whole business, the drawin' out of Listerdale just to get me to do what I did. Once you accused him, you'd committed yourself. You could've just as easily seen to takin' him to the precinct and arrestin' him along with Tommy Alb, then searchin' his place at leisure. Of course, Katie would have suffered somethin' awful, that way.

"So maybe you figured as long as you'd dipped a toe into deception, you'd might as well swim the whole river before you got out for good . . ."

"Nonsense, Muldoon. Dismiss it from your mind."

"Yes, sir. Is that an order?"

"Yes." Mr. Roosevelt wiped his glasses. "Tell me, what are your plans, Miss Cleo?"

"Oh, Dennis is going to see if he can prevail on Mr. Pulitzer to try me for a job."

Muldoon blushed. "He did take a liking to me."

"It will be a lark, in any case, to look for honest work," Cleo said.

"Yes, but have you any personal plans?"

"I'm goin' to court her," Muldoon said.

"Like a regular lady," Cleo said. "Chaperones, and everything."

"The sooner we start actin' respectable, the sooner everyone's goin' to *know* we're respectable. That's how we see it."

Mr. Roosevelt laughed. "Bully for you. Bully for both of you."

IV.

In the election of 1896, William McKinley defeated William Jennings Bryan. McKinley was assassinated during his second term in office; Bryan was twice more defeated for the Presidency. The highest government office he ever attained was that of Secretary of State in the administration of Woodrow Wilson. He died in 1925.

William Randolph Hearst and Joseph Pulitzer continued publishing their respective newspapers in some form for the rest of their lives. Pulitzer died in 1911; Hearst in 1951. Had Evan Crandall lived, Hearst would still have lost the services of E. Noon.

The Reverend Lewis Burley did not survive the cruise he took with his daughter, Essie May. Upon her return to the United States, Essie May liquidated all her father's holdings and moved to Paris, where she wrote novels of passion and was in the middle of several scandals.

Franklyn and Libstein died in London in 1904, when a dynamite blast destroyed their hotel room. Authorities guessed they had somehow set off the explosion themselves.

Captain Herkimer lived in quiet retirement.

General Theodore Roosevelt, Jr., died in France during the D-Day invasion in 1944.

Roscoe Heath spent the rest of his life working with the youth of the streets of New York City. In 1899, then-Governor Theodore Roosevelt granted him a full pardon for past offenses.

Tommy Alb died in Sing Sing Prison. Eagle Jack Sperling, confined to a wheelchair, sold pencils on the Bowery.

Brigid Muldoon parted amicably from Claude, and later became a nun of the Order of Saint Ursula.

Brian O'Leary became a cub reporter for the *Journal*, and worked his way to higher positions on the paper. As a foreign correspondent, he was gassed while covering the First World War in France, suffering lung damage. He moved to Arizona, where he commenced a correspondence with Maureen Muldoon that led to marriage.

Kathleen Muldoon never learned the truth about Hiram Listerdale. She mourned for a while, then one day in church met a man, whom she married a year later. The man patented no less than sixteen industrial cooking appliances, and became many times a millionaire. Katie bore him four happy children.

Theodore Roosevelt left the Police Department of the City of New York in 1897, and became Assistant Secretary of the Navy, bringing Muldoon to Washington with him as his aide. When war with Spain broke out, he quit that job and joined the Army, where he became a hero at the head of the "Rough Riders." Again, Muldoon accompanied him. He was elected Governor of New York, then became McKinley's Vice-President in 1900. He succeeded to the Presidency on McKinley's assassination. He was elected on his own ticket in 1904. He died, much loved and much respected, in 1919.

Dennis Muldoon didn't like Washington, D.C., liked Cuba even less, and was afraid to try Albany. Therefore, in 1898, when TR was elected Governor, Muldoon returned to New York City and opened a private enquiry agency, at which he prospered. He and Roosevelt continued to be friends, and spent much time visiting each other.

Cleo's perfect body had been marred by her ordeal on the night of August twenty-ninth, 1896. For the rest of her life, she bore two completely straight scars, one on the inside of each thigh. She minded not at all, since that was a place only her husband and her doctor would ever see. An interesting side effect of the fuse was that it had burned off the *ankh*, the birthmark that had given her her name. Cleo felt that with it, her old life had been burned away as well. The Pink Angel no longer, she was content to exercise her journalistic bent by writing an occasional humorous piece for *Collier's*, or *Harper's* magazines, raise her children, and enjoy being Mrs. Dennis Patrick Francis-Xavier Muldoon.

THE END